APPREHENSIONS

and Other Delusions

APPREHENSIONS

and Other Delusions

CHELSEA QUINN YARBRO

Five Star • Waterville, Maine

First Edition
First Printing: November 2003

Published in 2003 in conjunction with Tekno Books and Ed Gorman.

Set in 11 pt. Plantin.

Printed in the United States on permanent paper.

Library of Congress Cataloging-in-Publication Data

Yarbro, Chelsea Quinn, 1942–
    Apprehensions and other delusions / by Chelsea Quinn
      Yarbro.—1st ed.
    p. cm.
    ISBN 0-7862-5352-5 (hc : alk. paper)
    1. Horror tales, American.   I. Title.
  PS3575.A7A85 2003
  813'.54—dc22   2003049285

APPREHENSIONS

and Other Delusions

TABLE OF CONTENTS

Introduction

I first met Chelsea Quinn Yarbro back between the 8th and the 9th Punic Wars (she was a mere babe in arms at the time) in 1976, when I read her novel, *The Time of the Fourth Horseman*. I was so impressed that I called her up . . . and promptly got into an hour-long conversation that ranged over religion, politics, military history, music, and the Science Fiction community—of which we were both relatively new members. It was fascinating, wonderful and *fun* . . . and every single conversation we have had since then has been exactly the same. I'm not the only one who feels this way about conversations with this dear lady, by the way. I soon discovered that she possessed more than a few talents: composer, cartographer, playwright, student of seven different instruments, as well as voice, tarot card reader, and author of wonderful novels encompassing a number of genres—even Westerns, *The Law in Charity* and *Charity, Colorado* (believe me when I tell you this) are unlike any Westerns you have ever read; they are well worth looking up.

As you might have guessed, we've been friends for quite a while. Chelsea Quinn Yarbro is interesting, talented, good-hearted, intelligent, and has one of the greatest smiles that has ever shone anywhere. And she introduces me to wines that, when I drink them, I think the world is a pretty nice place after all.

Well, that's nice, I heard someone say. *The two of you are good friends. But what does this have to do with this collection of stories?*

Okay, I'll tell you.

All of the qualities named above go into everything she writes. And her style is measured and elegant and just plain musical. Her stories contain the most amazing historical, literary and imaginative details. Her characters are weird and multidimensional and achingly familiar. She writes about love and survival and stress and violence and the incomprehensible contrariness of the human spirit. (Therefore, we must add courageous to the list of qualities possessed by this author. Please make a note of this.) The universe and our fellow human beings and even ourselves do things—sometimes horrible things. It is a writer's duty to face them, to stand up to them and not to blink. Chelsea Quinn Yarbro *never* fails to confront each and every one.

Each of the stories in this volume, written between 1982 and 2002, whether Horror or Science Fiction or just Fiction, are lovely representatives of the above—*Do you have any favorites?* (There is that person again. Who is that? Stop interrupting when LoBrutto is composing.)

Well, yes, I do. I thoroughly enjoyed reading every story in this collection. I have truly never read anything by Chelsea Quinn Yarbro that I didn't enjoy. Some, however, do stand out in my mind: "Fugues" is just the kind of story Quinn would write, a Grand Toccata and, uh, well, Fugue on a fairly common theme in supernatural short stories (it's anything but common in the hands of this author); then there's that tasty morsel, "Renfield's Syndrome" about the joys of being carnivorous; "Become So Shining That We Cease to Be" (I do so love that title) a very neatly constructed story on the lengths some people will go to in order to be heard; "On St. Hubert's Thing" is the type of story Quinn does so well, an intricately detailed story of plots and heresy and faith.

Waste no more time, gentle reader; move on to tales of wonder by the incomparable Chelsea Quinn Yarbro.

—Patrick LoBrutto

FUGUES

Vanessa Hylas ran her fingers lightly over the curve of the forte-piano, enjoying its long, narrow shape—more like a boat than a harp—even as she pondered how she would contrive to keep the two-hundred-year-old instrument tuned through an entire recital. "We'll have to have two intermissions," she told her manager as she continued to caress the glossy wood. "And retune it both times."

"That shouldn't be a problem," said Howard Faster, making a note on his Palm Pilot. "I think people will make allowances for the instrument. This isn't just any antique. It *is* the Dziwny forte-piano—the very one he . . ."

"He killed himself playing; yes, I know," said Vanessa, more bluntly than she had intended. She coughed and spoke again, more gently. "Stasio Dziwny performed for the last time on this instrument. It was December 8th, 1803, if I recall the date, a pre-holiday private concert at his patron's most important Schloss, Schloss Lowenhoff. There were about fifty people present, not counting servants, according to what I've read." Her shiny, close-cropped, dark-blonde hair was starting to pale around her face, the fluctuating shade not unlike the beautifully grained wood of the forte-piano's case. At forty-three, she had grown into her angular features and was much more attractive than she had been in youth, something she recognized with a trace of humor. She held herself well, almost as if she were about to play for an audience rather than test an old instrument for the first time.

"Yes," said Faster, fussing with his expensive regimental

tie. Smoothing his thinning, colorless hair with one blunt-fingered hand, he looked around for the warehouse manager among the vast collection of pianos. "It amazes me that it's in such good condition, considering where it's been for the last couple of centuries, or almost a couple of centuries. It's a miracle they found it."

Vanessa nodded. "In an attic in an Austrian Schloss—not Lowenhoff; Schaumbach, or something like that—according to the documents; you saw them," she said, repeating what she had been told just four days ago. "Stored away in a sealed room on the top floor. You wouldn't think the Graf would care to keep the thing, even locked away like that, if the stories about it are true, and considering his family's role in what happened."

"Perhaps he wanted to make sure it never got used again," Faster suggested. "You know, take it out of circulation."

"If that was his intention, he did a great job with it," said Vanessa. "It makes the provenance a simple matter."

"Well, yes; the documents look to be authentic," said Faster in a resigned tone of voice. "They've been vetted legit. All the tests have come out supporting the claim. This is the Dziwny forte-piano."

The two were silent as Vanessa pointed to an irregular stain on the bass end of the keyboard. "Brown. It could be blood."

"It could," said Faster uneasily. "Or something from being stored that way, or a natural discoloration of some sort. You can bet the Graf had it cleaned."

"A man blowing his brains out all over a forte-piano must have been messy, much more than this stain's-worth—there'd be blood and skull fragments, and brain matter, according to what I've researched; those old pistols did a lot of damage," said Vanessa distantly. "I would have

14

expected . . . I don't know: something a lot worse than this." She pulled the bench out and sat down at the instrument, trying an experimental chord.

A jangle of untuned strings shuddered out of the forte-piano.

"Ye gods!" Faster exclaimed. "They said it would be tuned."

"Not yet," said Vanessa, pulling her hands back as if scalded. "There are strings to be replaced, I'd have to say. They'll need to give it a thorough going-over before it'll be ready for the public."

"No kidding," said Faster. "I'll call Shotwell right away. This is not the sound we want; I don't care how authentic it is. He's got to improve it." He pulled his cell phone out of his breast pocket and tapped in a ten-digit number, then turned away to create the illusion of privacy.

Vanessa made a point of ignoring Faster's end of the conversation, putting all her attention on the forte-piano. She played a few of the keys, her touch unusually hesitant, and winced at the sound the ancient, neglected strings made. At last she contented herself with playing one of Dziwny's own compositions half an inch above the keys, hearing the correct notes in her mind. Only when Faster was through did she relent, swinging around on the bench and looking directly at him. "Well? What did he say?"

"He said he'd arrange everything, since he knows you want to perform with it," said Faster, frowning as he spoke. "You wouldn't believe what he had the nerve to tell me."

"He said he couldn't get his usual restoration crew to work on it," she said promptly.

"You overheard," Faster accused.

"No. It's just a guess. But you've read the historical material about it, and you can bet Shotwell's crew has, too,

15

and know about the stories they've told about this instrument. It's one of the most enduring fables in the classical music world, the forte-piano that compels those who play it to commit suicide." She laughed. "Only one suicide has ever been proven in relation to this, and that was Dziwny's own; the instrument's been missing for close to two hundred years, so there's no other accounts of it doing in anyone else. The Graffin died some months later in childbirth, not at the keyboard. And it turns out now that the forte-piano was put into the attic shortly afterward, so no one else had the chance to kill themselves while playing."

"How do you account for the stories, then?" Faster asked, interested for promotional reasons.

"Because there was so much scandal around Dziwny's love affair with the Graffin, assuming the rumors about the affair were true: there's no proof that it was ever anything more than gossip. Still, it was quite an occurrence. His suicide was so dramatic. The public loved ghost stories back then, and the events were irresistible. And there was that awful book that came out in 1850, turning the whole story into a complicated Byronic romance. It's become difficult to separate fact from fiction." Vanessa laced her fingers together and looked directly at Faster. "How long is it going to take, getting this ready?"

"Shotwell said probably a month," said Faster.

"That cuts into the Canadian tour," Vanessa reminded him. "But that might be useful. We could use the tour to generate some interest in this instrument."

"Sounds good to me," said Faster, who was in favor of anything that could end up making Vanessa, his client, more money, for he would share in her good fortune.

"Then let's plan on it," she said, rising. "I want to find out everything he played that night, the night he shot himself."

"Good God, why?" Faster asked.

"Because I think it would make for a very special first concert on this instrument," she said, running her fingers lightly over the side of the forte-piano. "Think of the interest we could generate. And the myths we could put to rest."

The promotional possibilities began to percolate in Faster's agile brain. "Not a bad idea, Vanessa," he approved. "Not a bad idea at all."

Nicola van der Beck looked up from the stacks of books on her cluttered desk and managed a vulpine smile, the lines in her face punctuating her look of eager predation. She held up an old journal as if offering a jewel to Vanessa. "It took some doing," she said proudly, "but I finally found a full account in this. The Baron Gewaltheit. A dreadful name, isn't it? There were so many of those petty nobles back then, full of their own inconsequence. The Baron and his Baroness were at the concert, and he recorded the program in detail. At least, that is what he purports to do. I can't find any confirmation that he actually attended the concert. He may have been in the billiard room, and filled in the story later, from what the other guests told him. Still, he was at Lowenhoff—that much is certain." She adjusted her bifocals so that she could read the text, and began to translate.

We, along with nearly all the Graf's guests, entered the ball-room which was set for a concert with chairs in rows under the chandeliers, the elevated musicians' platform occupied by the forte-piano alone. There was much excitement, for everyone had heard the rumors about Dziwny and the Graffin, which might or might not be true. Both the composer and the Graffin behaved impeccably. You could also say *sinlessly* here. *Still, there can*

17

be no doubt that Dziwny has dedicated a number of his recent works to the Graffin, and she has been moved by them. The Graf has been losing patience with this state of affairs—the pun only works in English, of course—and he's announced that he intends to be rid of Dziwny after the first of the year. He would dismiss him sooner but it would be difficult to find other musicians of high quality to engage so near the holidays, and there are many festivities scheduled to be held here. Also, of course, with his interesting reputation, Stasio Dziwny is still a composer who attracts a great deal of attention, all of it adding to the consequence of his patron, which the Graf von Firstengipfel would be reluctant to give up.

"That's fascinating, of course," said Vanessa, not entirely candidly. "But the actual program is where my interest lies."

Nicola pretended to be slighted. "Oh, well, if that's all—" She sniffed as she scanned down the page, and turned it. "Ah. Here we go. *Six Fugues on Themes of Handel.* That's Dziwny's own composition, as you know."

"As I know," Vanessa echoed, the complex passages coming to mind. Her fingers twitched as if sketching out the cadenzas.

"Then *Nursery Songs.* That's by a student of Boccherini, according to the material here. It's a flashy piece but essentially trivial; hardly anyone plays it anymore, but it has a certain appeal, with all kinds of ornaments and runs, just the sort of thing Dziwny was said to do better than any of his contemporaries, like his knack for fugues," said Nicola.

"Knack?" Vanessa repeated.

"Oh, yes, I think so," said Nicola. "He had the mental facility for them, they were his means to an end, not the end itself, a kind of magic trick that caught the attention of the public." She looked down at the page again. "Anyway, there was an intermission; they served lemon ices and champagne. Then the *Grand Toccata and Fugue on a Polish Folk Song*, his newest work. He'd played it in public only twice before. He never finished that performance."

"Is there anything in that journal that says when he actually did it? And what he actually did?" Vanessa could not keep the eagerness out of her voice.

"Yes," said Nicola. "There is some mention of it." Her frown became a scowl as she read the journal, translating as she went.

He had reached the second full statement of the central theme, a passage with a great deal of octave work in it, and when he got to the long fermata, followed by the repeated figure in the left hand, his right went into the pocket of his coat, and he drew out a small pistol. He put it under his right ear, and before anyone could properly discern his intent or move to stop him, he fired. He fell sideways, his head striking the keyboard, then there was consternation everywhere. The Graffin fainted and had to be taken from the ballroom by the Graf, who ordered that the room be vacated at once. It was an appalling incident, no matter what the reason may actually have been; with such a tragedy, the world will assume the worst, and will no doubt fix the blame on the Graffin. The servants were charged with the task of disposing of the body. Or *reposing the body.* Some of these verbs are pretty irregular, even for early nineteenth-century German. It seems to say, *There was anxiety* or perhaps, *All felt anxiety because of this calamity.*

Nicola put the journal down. "The rest is about the inconvenience of having to leave the next morning just as it was coming on to snow."

"That's pretty dispassionate," said Vanessa.

19

"Well, the Baron was said to be a cool one. Still, watching a man blow his brains out can't have been good entertainment, can it?" Nicola closed the journal. "I think he probably heard the event described, just because of the tone of it. His wife was most certainly in attendance, and she would have told everything to her husband; we know she accompanied the Graffin to her room and stayed with her for the whole night—she wrote a letter to the Graffin's brother about the event, but put her emphasis on the Graffin, not on Dziwny."

"Have you seen that letter?" Vanessa asked.

"Yes. It's in a private collection in Salzburg. The owner allowed me to read it and copy down its text." Nicola smiled faintly. "Would you like me to read it? I'm afraid the Baroness didn't write very well, more like a third-grader than an adult—hardly surprising, given the state of women's education at the time." She reached out for the handle of the tallest file cabinet in the room.

"Never mind," said Vanessa. "I get the picture."

"It's not a very pretty one," said Nicola. "If you change your mind, I can make a translation and fax it to you while you're on the road."

"Thanks," said Vanessa. "I'd appreciate that. I'll put Howard on it, too. He's the one pushing to tie in the suicide with the concert I'm preparing."

"Are you actually going to buy the forte-piano?" Nicola asked.

"I wish. Shotwell's asking a horrendous sum for it; I can't justify spending that amount." Vanessa shook her head. "No, I'm leasing it from him, for a pretty ridiculous fee, but at least I can almost afford it."

Nicola shook her head in disapproval. "Do you really plan to perform the same program Dziwny did?"

"Yes," said Vanessa mischievously. "It's quite a hook, don't you think? I hope it makes for more money, given what I've had to lay out in leasing fees."

"It'll bring the critics out in droves," said Nicola in a disapproving way.

"That's the general idea." Vanessa came around the desk to give Nicola a peck on the cheek. "Thanks for this. You've been wonderful."

"If you say so," Nicola remarked unconcernedly.

"I'll make sure you have a ticket to the first performance," Vanessa promised as she started out the door.

"Perish the thought," said Nicola as a parting shot.

"Look at this!" Howard Faster exclaimed jubilantly as he hurried in from his lunch, the hotel door banging with the force of his entrance. "Mickey Resselot just brought them over." He thrust half-a-dozen newspaper clippings toward Vanessa. "And there's more coming."

"Fine," said Vanessa distractedly as she continued to study the score in her hands. "I'll look at them later."

"You've *never* had press like this!" he crowed, ignoring her preoccupation and putting the clippings down on the round table by the window. "Chicago! Cleveland! New York! Minneapolis! L.A.!"

"And the concert is scheduled for Seattle," said Vanessa with a slight smile. "Do you think they'll all send someone to cover the concert? I doubt it. This is just the sensation of the week, something to talk about."

"So long as they do talk about it—in advance, yet—I don't care if they cover the event or not," said Faster, adding with a smirk, "There's more: PBS may want to tape the concert if this keeps up."

"Isn't that aiming a bit high?" Vanessa asked, putting the

score aside with a suggestion of exasperation. "I can't concentrate with you bouncing off the walls."

"Of course it is! We should be aiming high, with all this lift! Besides, I've had feelers already, and that means someone there is thinking about it; I'm just following up. You know, I think I'm going to see if A&E wants to put in a competing bid. If nothing else, that should add to the excitement." He gathered up the clippings again. "You could finally get the break you've been working for!"

"On a gimmick," said Vanessa.

"Not a gimmick, on a hook. A hook, Vanessa. There's a big difference." He took one of the three chairs in the small parlor of her suite and pulled it up to the table. "You can get attention because of the history of the forte-piano, but if you can't deliver the music, it's nothing but a flash in the pan."

"Too bad Dziwny didn't have a flash in the pan, literally: if only his pistol *had* misfired," said Vanessa. "Thirty-six, and just beginning to hit his stride. He could have done some wonderful things if he'd lived. Think of the waste."

"You can say the same of Mozart, or Bellini," said Faster.

"They died of natural causes, albeit prematurely, and Mozart had a long career, longer than many others, because he started so young." Vanessa picked up the score again. "Dziwny was just finding his way, getting his composition feet under him."

"Is it true his name means strange?" Faster asked.

"Or wonderful," said Vanessa. "They made a great deal over the significance at the time."

Faster considered this. "I think I'll mention that in the next press kit. It could give us a little mileage now, too."

Vanessa shrugged. "Do we need to clutch at straws that way?"

"No, we don't, and we're not," said Faster. "But it's an interesting historical note, and that makes it worthwhile."

"If you think it's important—it doesn't seem that way to me," she told him while she made a point of giving her attention to the score. "This transition from B-flat to G-minor is sneakier than it looks. You can say it's obvious, but there's a ninth in the arpeggio that makes all the difference."

Faster gave up. "Okay, Vanessa. Okay. I won't take up any more of your time. It's about time for lunch and getting ready. You have to be ready to leave for the concert hall at seven-thirty, remember, and the *Toronto Star* is sending a reporter over at four this afternoon; you can't afford to be in the bath."

"I'll keep that in mind," said Vanessa, not entirely truthfully.

"And after the concert, we'll have a late supper and you can have a look at what they're saying about the Dziwny forte-piano, and your concert." He gathered up his material and started toward the door. "You got to make the most of this, Vanessa. You're not going to have another chance like this, and you know it. I'm your manager. I'm not steering you wrong on this. You have a real chance here, and you need to make the most of it."

"Yes. I know," she said. "That's what I'm trying to do."

"Yeah, yeah," said Faster in affectionate exasperation.

But Vanessa responded seriously. "I want to do this *right*," she said, her feelings burning like a banked furnace. "I know it's a big opportunity, and I don't want to blow it. I have to be true to Dziwny and his music. And that means preparation."

"You mean getting lost in it," Faster corrected her.

"You may think that if you like," she said with an assumed coolness that fooled neither of them.

23

"Okay," said Faster. "Have it your way."

The Dziwny forte-piano had been restrung and carefully tuned; it sat in the center of Vanessa's practice studio behind her house, smaller than her Baldwin concert grand, but more intriguing. She approached it carefully, wanting to get to know it well. Its tone was soft, almost liquid, and it responded to Vanessa's expert touch with sweetness and clarity. She practiced diligently, keeping her attention focused on the sound the instrument produced. As much as she wanted to be subsumed in Dziwny's music, she had to give more notice to the character of the forte-piano, to learn its strengths and weaknesses so that she could show off its range when she finally performed publicly on it. The bass was more vibrant than in many forte-pianos, and she began to use the low notes to support the upper melody in a more deliberately contrapuntal manner than she had done at first. Suddenly she felt the piece begin to open up to her—the instrument revealed more of the composer's intent than she had thought possible. The Handel variations went on from a playful scherzo fugue, the theme in the mid-range of the instrument, into a rocking, six/eight lullaby, left hand echoing the right in melting, lyrical phrases, each playing with the theme of the fugue until the two melody lines blended into a stirring restatement of the theme. Vanessa could almost smell the hot wax of burning candles and the heavy odor of attar of roses over sweat that must have been present when Dziwny played. Half-closing her eyes, Vanessa imagined the ballroom of Schloss Lowenhoff with its painted wall panels and the small audience in their fancy clothes. The Graffin would be sitting in the front row, the Graf next to her; she would have a shawl around her shoulders, since it was winter and Lowenhoff was draughty. The candles would waver a bit because of that, and that would add to the dramatic impact of the concert. There would be the quiet shuffling of the audience, and the occasional inevitable cough. She went on playing, finishing the last, grandiose fugue with a flourish that was unlike her usual pristine style.

"Very nice," said Faster from the door behind her.

Vanessa blinked, feeling slightly disoriented, and coughed to cover her confusion. "How does it sound?"

"It has a pretty big voice for a forte-piano," said Faster. "And a lot more complexity than I've heard before." He cocked his head speculatively. "Have you thought about where it would be best to record the CD? I think a live hall would be better than a studio. More ambient sound, don't you think?"

"It's possible," she said, suddenly as tired as if she had been playing for twice as long as she had been.

"How's the program going?" Faster asked.

"I haven't run through the whole thing yet," she said. "I need a little more time with the instrument before I can figure out how to pace myself through the pieces." It was an excuse, she realized as she said it.

"Is this going to be a problem?" asked Faster, looking a bit worried.

"Oh, no," she said, a trifle too quickly. "It just takes familiarity with the works. This isn't like programs we do now, and I have to accommodate the difference."

"How do you mean?" Faster sounded dubious.

"Well, if this program were being performed now, it would probably be the *Nursery Songs* first, then the *Grand Toccata and Fugue*, and then the *Six Fugues on Themes of Handel*, because it demands the greatest virtuosity, and the work is the most musically interesting as well as technically challenging. Fugues Five and Six in particular, are real showpieces, meant to impress the audience."

"Then why did Dziwny perform the works in the order he did? Does anyone know?"

"Well, the style of concerts was different then, and the *Grand Toccata and Fugue* was newer; most of the audience hadn't heard it before, so it made for a greater finish then than it would today," said Vanessa, adding a bit more awkwardly, "also, assuming Dziwny intended to kill himself, he wanted a work that gave him the opportunity, and it exists in the fermata, and the long thematic statement in the left hand. He had almost forty seconds to draw his pistol, aim, and shoot."

"So you think he planned the program around his suicide?" Faster looked a bit disgusted.

"It certainly seems to be the case," said Vanessa, her face showing no trace of emotion. "I don't know when he decided to kill himself, but he planned the concert at least a week before playing it."

"Ye gods," said Faster. "What a plan to carry around with you for a week. I would have thought he did it on the spur of the moment, something impetuous, but you think he could have set it up well in advance."

"It's possible," said Vanessa, getting up from the forte-piano. "I need a break. Come with me. I'll put water on."

"Or open a bottle?" Faster asked. "Some of that Pinot Grigio?"

"Sure," said Vanessa as she coded the alarm and opened the door. "Thirty seconds to get out."

"Coming," said Faster, moving past her with a wink. "You take good care of that." He waited while she locked the door; following her across the small, green yard to the rear door of her house, he pondered how to bring up the most recent request he had received about the Dziwny forte-piano.

"Well, I can't afford to have anything happen to it, can I?" she asked as she went ahead of him toward the house.

There was a mud-room that was mostly used for garden storage just inside the back door, and a good-sized pantry, then the handsomely remodeled modern kitchen with its island range on the central diagonal of the room, and double ovens against the wall. At the end of the island was a bar, three stools in place for informal dining, and Vanessa motioned to one of these. "Sit. I'll get the wine as soon as the kettle's on; I'll be right back." She grabbed the kettle and filled it at the sink, then set it on one of the six gas burners and lit it. For a long moment she stared at the yellow-tipped blue flames.

"Something wrong?" Faster inquired.

Vanessa shook her head. "No. No, I'm just tired." She bustled out of the room and returned with a bottle, two stemmed glasses, and a corkscrew, all of which she thrust at Faster. "Here."

He took them all and set about opening the bottle. "I had a call from Shotwell today."

"Not more money," Vanessa said at once. "Until I start getting receipts from concerts, I'm on a budget."

"No, not more money." He pulled out the cork and sniffed it, then poured wine into the two glasses. "Someone's approached him about the forte-piano."

"Oh, God," she exclaimed, her heart sinking, "He's had an offer to buy it."

"No," Faster assured her. "Nothing like that. A parapsychologist wants to run some tests on it."

"A what?" She stopped in the act of taking down her favorite teapot.

"Parapsychologist. He's supposed to have a pretty good reputation for psychometry." He held one of the wine

27

glasses out to her, feeling abashed.

"And Shotwell's interested?" Vanessa was incredulous. She took the glass, but paid no attention to it.

"Apparently," Faster said drily. "He's accepted a hefty fee from the guy."

"I'm surprised Shotwell didn't try to find a psychic," said Vanessa nastily.

"Now, now," Faster warned her as he lifted his glass.

"Well, it smacks of the worst kind of sleaze, if you ask me." She hurriedly turned off the flame under the shrieking kettle. "Sorry. I'm jumpy."

"Rehearsal nerves," said Faster at his most understanding.

"I guess," Vanessa said without much conviction. In order to change this uncomfortable subject, she asked, "So who is this parapsychologist and what is he looking for in the Dziwny forte-piano? If it is a he?"

"Yes, a he. Doctor Christopher Warren." He waited for her to say something, then went on. "He's actually pretty well-known, and his work is taken seriously. He's got a couple books out, and he's on the lecture circuit."

"Doing what? Psychometry?" She drank a little of the wine and then poured some of the hot water into the teapot to heat it. "I'm sorry. That was bitchy."

"No problem. You've had a hard day. You're allowed to blow off a little steam." He watched her while she got down the canister of tea. "Do you think you could use a day off?"

"No," she said. "Why?"

Faster shrugged. "I just thought it might be easier to let Warren do whatever it is he intends to do while you're out, is all."

"You might be right about that," she said after a moment. "But I think I should stay around. I'm responsible for the instrument, and who knows what Doctor Warren might do if he's left to his own devices."

"Okay. I'll let Shotwell know and we'll set the tests up," said Faster. "How soon would you like it?"

"I don't like it at all," said Vanessa. "But do as you think best." She went to empty the water from her teapot, then set the kettle boiling again as she loaded in two measures of Dragonwell leaves. "Just give me a couple days' warning."

"Will do," Faster promised, pledging with his glass to make his point as emphatically as he could.

Cummings Hall was small enough to be called "intimate" by critics, seating five hundred twenty-four, all with clear sight of the stage. The Dziwny forte-piano had been put on the broad apron, and the tuner was finishing up his work as Vanessa arrived to practice.

"Looks good," said the tuner, removing his damping felts and giving the keys a cursory run. "Sounds good, too."

"You'll be staying here, to retune?" Vanessa asked.

"That's the deal," said the tuner. "I'll be in the house-manager's office, if you need me. I want to catch the game, if I can, while I have my lunch." He strolled away, his attention no longer on the instrument.

Vanessa went over to the forte-piano and sat down, remaining still for a short while, letting the place and its ambience sink into her. She frowned as she thought about Professor Warren, who would arrive in an hour. The last thing she wanted was a publicity-seeking loony poking around the forte-piano, but Shotwell had agreed, so she had to make the best of it. Flexing her hands, she began a few Czerny exercises, her fingers moving automatically with the familiar cadences. Satisfied, she took a little time to collect her thoughts, and then began to play. The *Six Fugues on Themes of Handel* flowed more easily than she would have supposed. Fugues One and Two came and went, and Three began with a simple theme in G-minor, and Vanessa let the music carry her. The hall whispered, and the forte-piano rang, a thrilling sound that seemed to fill the space.

By the Fourth fugue, she was wonderfully lost in the music, apprehending Dziwny's vision so completely that she was no longer aware of Cummings Hall, but felt as if she were at Lowenhoff, all those decades ago, caught up in a passion that had no place to go but into the notes being played. The fugue unwound elegantly, the melody moving from bass to treble, then flitted through the mid-range only to emerge in the treble again in a dazzling display of talent and training. Starting the Fifth fugue, Vanessa was unaware that she was being watched. Her hands played as if the movements were a martial art and she their greatest exponent. The sound came out flawlessly, the repeated musical images piled one atop another into an astonishing edifice of patterned tones. Without pause, she launched into the Sixth fugue, playing brilliantly until she suddenly stopped in the middle of a thematic statement, as if she had lost track of the music.

Trembling, she moved back on the bench and sat there, dazed and breathing hard. Her face was pale. She began to rub her palms on her skirt, nervously blinking as if she had finally become aware of her surroundings. Abruptly, she stood up and walked a half-dozen steps away from the instrument.

"Why did you stop?" asked an unknown voice from the middle of the empty hall.

Surprised, Vanessa looked up. "Who's there?" she demanded sharply.

"Christopher Warren. I was told you'd be expecting me," came the answer.

"Professor Warren," she said with a hint of distaste. "I didn't expect you so early."

"It's after twelve," he said, leaving his seat and coming forward.

"I must have lost track of the time," said Vanessa, only glancing in his direction.

"The way you were playing, I'm not astounded to hear you say so." He came up to the apron and held up his hand to her. "It's very impressive."

"It's a fine instrument," said Vanessa, bending down briefly to take his hand. "I should probably get the tuner back here. The pitch is beginning to slip." She started away from him toward the prompt-side wing.

"Would you rather I go? I have some equipment to bring in, and I don't want to disturb you." Warren watched her pause. "It's no trouble."

"All right. I'll just sit down for a bit, get some water." She resumed walking.

"Why did you stop where you did?" Warren called after her.

Vanessa halted. "Did I stop?" She seemed confused. "I guess it was the pitch going. It felt like I was finished." Her frown became a glower. "I don't leave music unfinished."

"Well, if the pitch wasn't right," said Warren as he cut through a row of seats toward the side door that led to the offices of the hall, "I can see how you'd stop."

Vanessa nodded, but went back to the forte-piano, and, after a long moment, sat down and began the Sixth fugue again, concentrating on the music, doing her best to ignore the slight shift in pitch in the strings. "That's the trouble," she said. "It needs tuning." She continued on through the fugue, paying close attention to its tone and the pacing of the work. As she reached the extended passage for the left hand, she faltered. "Damn," she said aloud, and began the left-hand passage again, a bit more slowly and deliberately.

31

This time it worked, and she thundered on into the end, careening through the dizzying pyrotechnics with the verve of a race-car driver. "There," she said as if to confirm her final repeated chords. When she was finished, she was a bit shaky; the beginnings of a headache buzzed behind her eyes and she pinched the bridge of her nose to stop it.

"Brava!" called Warren from the side-door. "That was spectacular."

"Yeah. But the pitch is off," said the tuner, who stood beside him. "Still, the playing's first rate."

"Thanks," said Vanessa, moving away from the forte-piano. "The low E is really off."

"I'll take care of it," said the tuner, and brought his small case of tuning forks onto the stage. "Have to do this the old-fashioned way," he said.

"Good," said Vanessa, and sought out the soothing darkness of the backstage area. She leaned against the wall and willed herself to relax, which left her jittery. What on earth had happened to her? she asked herself.

"Ms. Hylas, are you okay?" Warren asked her as he rolled a strange-looking, metal box on wheels, ornamented with dials and gauges up next to the stage-manager's podium.

She made herself straighten up. "Just a bit tired."

"There's coffee in the house-manager's office." He studied her for a moment, then began setting up his equipment.

"And it's terrible," she said, attempting levity. "But it's hot." She started toward the door that would lead to the hall to the offices.

"You sure you're all right?" Warren called after her, his question underscored by the tuner as he started his work.

"Yes, thanks," she said automatically, and wondered if she dared to eat anything. It might help her feel better, but it could make her feel worse. She was still debating this as she reached the house-manager's office, where the odor of scorched coffee told her not to have any of it. She went to the drinking fountain and gulped down several mouthfuls, then wandered back toward the stage where the tuner was making progress on the forte-piano and Christopher Warren was busily setting up his display of machines.

"Feeling better?" Warren called out cheerfully. "You look a bit less pasty."

"Thanks," she said drily. "Rehearsing can take a lot out of me."

"If it was just the rehearsing," he said almost jauntily.

"How do you mean?" Vanessa asked.

"I'll tell you after I've finished monitoring the rest of your rehearsal," he said, merrily adjusting what appeared to be an oscilloscope.

"All right," she said, trying not to be too curt with him even though she resented his intrusion on her rehearsal time.

"Just carry on as if I weren't here," he encouraged her. "You know how to do it."

"What makes you think so?" she could not stop herself from challenging.

"Well, you certainly weren't aware of me when I arrived," he said blandly, his pleasant face showing no signs of sarcastic intent.

"No, I wasn't," she allowed, and listened while the tuner finished his work.

The *Nursery Songs* went well enough, their fancy ornaments and flourishes sounding impressive, as they were intended to be. When she was finished, she had the tuner come back again, before she started the *Grand Toccata and Fugue on a Polish Folk Song*. "If it isn't slipping now, it will be before the piece is done," she said with a wry smile. She

33

turned to Warren. "Anything so far?"

"I'm not certain," he said from his place in the first row of the audience where he was staring at the screen of his laptop.

Vanessa paced the apron, reviewing the piece she was about to rehearse in her mind. She paid little attention to her slight light-headedness, attributing it to her skipped lunch. As soon as the tuner relinquished the forte-piano to her, she sat down, ready to begin.

"This is the piece he played when he—?" Warren asked, breaking her concentration.

"Yes. He shot himself three-quarters of the way through the piece," she said testily. "Anything else, or can I . . ." She gestured to the keyboard.

"Go on," he told her, his whole attention on the screen.

The opening bars of the toccata went well, the pace a confident *andante con moto*. Vanessa let the steady four/four beat carry her along through the modulation from E-flat to G-flat, and back to E-flat again. She was part of the music now, like a raft on a river, riding the current. Gradually all sense of the hall and the strange monitors around her faded away and she seemed to be in the eerie splendor of Lowenhoff, lit by candles in chandeliers and sconces, with a select group gathered to listen to him play this newest piece he had composed, the piece that was dedicated to Maria-Antonia, Graffin von Firstengipfel, the woman to whom he was utterly devoted, and who could not express her love to him. The stage lights vanished, and the darkened concert hall was gone, and in its place was the ballroom of Lowenhoff, golden and glistening.

The Graf sat bolt upright, listening in growing fury at the scandal this man had brought upon him and his family; Dziwny could see his disapproval in every line of his body.

He knew this was the last concert he would ever give under von Firstengipfel's patronage, but he would not accept the callous dismissal he had been given—that way lay ruin for him and a tarnished reputation for the Graffin. No, he would show the Graf what he thought of his arrogant termination with one far more damaging than anything the Graf had promised. The fugue began simply enough, and he played the octaves with deceptive ease, thinking of the song he had heard so many times in his childhood: *Endless Love.* The melody, plaintive and sweet, echoed from hand to hand, growing and enlarging in long cantabile passages that led to the astonishing fermata. He laid his left hand on the keys and began to play the long restatement of the fugue's theme, while he reached for the pocket in his swallow-tail coat.

Fumbling with her skirt on the piano bench, Vanessa was transfixed by Dziwny's composition. Her face was without expression, and everything but her hands moved like a doll, stiffly and automatically. With a sudden cry of frustration, she rose from the bench, slapped the side of her head and collapsed, falling between the bench and the forte-piano as Warren sat all but mesmerized by what he saw on his screen.

Faster was on one side of her and Warren on the other when Vanessa finally walked out of Cummings Hall some three hours later. "I still want you to see the doctor tomorrow," Faster was scolding her. "I can't have you fainting during a performance."

"Not to worry," said Vanessa. She was feeling a bit embarrassed for putting these two men—and the tuner—through an hour of anxiety. "I'll be fine."

"I want to be sure of that," Faster said, then rounded on Warren as they reached the edge of the street. "What were you thinking, putting all that equipment around her? Didn't it occur to you it might hurt her?"

"How could it?" Warren asked as calmly as he was able.

"I don't know. It's your equipment. You should know better than anyone what it's apt to do." Faster signaled for his town-car, and kept his hand protectively on Vanessa's arm.

"I don't think it was his equipment," said Vanessa, startling both men. "I think it was the forte-piano."

The two men stared at her with varying expressions of disbelief. Finally Faster spoke. "You sure you're okay? That sounds a bit . . . nuts."

"To me, too," she said, watching as his Lincoln pulled up to the curb. "But it happened before Professor Warren set up his monitors, only not so intensely."

"What happened?" Faster demanded, his patience finally failing him. "What are you talking about?"

"About the fugues," she said, and laughed sadly. "It set . . . I don't know . . . something off. Something that the forte-piano is part of." Although Faster opened the door for her, she didn't get in immediately. "It's still there, you know. It's still at Lowenhoff, and it always will be."

"You mean the instrument?" Warren asked.

"If that's what it is," said Vanessa as she allowed Faster to assist her into the town car. She stared straight ahead as Faster got in and they sped away, leaving Warren alone on the sidewalk.

About *Fugues*

This title refers both to the musical and the psychological form of a fugue, both of which are present in the story.

Forty years ago, I was allowed to play a forte-piano—the immediate ancestor to the modern pianoforte—for the greater part of a month. The experience made the music of Mozart and his contemporaries much more understandable to me, including the on-going effort to keep the strings in tune.

There are many legends and stories about possessed musical instruments, and the belief that musical instruments possess magical powers is nothing new. In the 13th century, a Papal commission was appointed to determine which instruments were holy and which were damnable: those clerics decided that the rebec (ancestor of the violin) was played by the Devil, and the crum-horn (ancestor of the trombone) was holy. Assigning such virtue, or lack of it, to a musical instrument strikes me as chancy, although this forte-piano undoubtedly has an odd kick in its gallop—or perhaps Vanessa has one in hers.

CONFESSIONS OF A MADMAN

In the name of the Father, Son and Holy Spirit, Amen. I, Brother Luccio, at the behest of the Prior of this monastery, have recorded the Confession of the lunatic known as Brother Rat, though he has said he was once known as Bertoldo Cimoneisi and was an apothecary by trade—the records of the monastery show no such name or calling among the entries, but it may be that this is truly his name and his profession, for he spoke it under the Seal of Confession. Then again, it may be more of his madness.

Brother Rat has been confined here for sixteen years, during which time he has had no visitors—no inquiries have been made for his welfare and no one has attempted to seek him out. Upon his delivery here by the Secular Arm, it was stated that his family and relatives were dead of the Plague that came to Amalfi in the Kingdom of Napoli twenty years ago. He had been given to the Secular Arm before being entrusted to our care, for it was thought that he was filled with heretical notions. When he was given to our care, the Secular Arm had conducted a Process against him. It is written in the records of the monastery that all the fingers of his left hand were broken, that he was blind in his right eye, and that all the lower teeth had been taken from his head. Because of the answers he had given during this Questioning, it was decided that Brother Rat was not a heretic but a madman, and thus was sent to us.

During the last winter, which has lingered well into spring, Brother Rat developed a cough that has not lessened as the weather grows warmer but instead has grown more fierce with each passing day so that it is now acknowledged that there is no medicine but the Hand of God that can deliver him. To that end, so that he may come shriven to the Mercy Seat, I have been entrusted with the task of recording the Confession of Brother Rat for delivery to the Secular Arm and for inclusion in the records of this monastery. May God grant that I perform my mandate without error for His greater Glory.

Because Brother Rat is known to be dangerous, he has been confined to a cell alone. There is a window in the cell, set near the ceiling so that he cannot see out. His legs are shackled and a chain holds him to a cleat in the wall that allows him little more than twice his height in range. He has a pallet for sleep and the rushes are changed twice a year. A single blanket is provided him in the summer, two in the winter. He is fed twice a day, as are all the fifty-four madmen confined within our walls. There is a privy hole in the floor of his cell. He is clothed in a peasant's smock, for it is not fitting that any who are mad should be habited as monks. Brother Rat is very thin, and the cough has taken more flesh from him so that his face is gaunt as a skull. He has some hair left, most of it grey, as is his beard. The nails on his right hand are very long, but on the left they do not grow well since the fingers were broken. His speech is not easily understood because he has so few teeth, nonetheless I have striven to record every word correctly, and if I have not been accurate, I beg forgiveness and offer as my excuse the difficulty of discerning his words.

When Brother Emmerano and I entered the cell, Brother Rat was lying upon his pallet. He blinked many times at the light of the three torches we brought, and shielded his one sighted eye until he was accustomed to the brightness. As he saw who we were, he spoke.

"So I'm dying." He raised himself, spitting copiously as he did. "About time. Perhaps God is more merciful than I thought."

Brother Emmerano blessed the poor madman, and then said, "This is Brother Luccio, who will record everything we say here. He is a scribe and a true monk who will take care to be correct in what he writes. I am come to take your Confession." He spoke slowly and clearly, for he has often maintained that madmen are more sensible when they are addressed in this way. "Two of the lay Brothers wait outside the door."

Brother Rat barked; he might have meant to cough or to laugh. "I cannot attack anyone, Brothers. I am burning with fever and I'm all but starved. You'd better give me some water, out of charity, or I will not be able to speak with you for long." He folded his arms and looked from Brother Emmerano to me with the expression of a man who finds a corpse laid out at his door.

"Be calm." Brother Emmerano signaled to be brought his stool, and for my bench and table. "There is a cask of wine being brought, not sacramental wine for your absolution, which we will provide when your Confession is complete—we will use this to ease your cough. We will be prepared presently." He then nodded toward me. "Remember all of this, Brother Luccio, for you must write it down."

I bowed my head and prayed that God would not take the words from me before my vellum was spread and my ink ground. "I ask that you do not speak too much more until I am prepared," I begged, and was rewarded with silence until the lay Brothers had brought what we needed. Once I was in position, I raised my hood so that my face was shadowed, so that I would be nothing more than a cipher during the Confession. I had four nibs cut and ready in case one should fail. I nodded to Brother Emmerano and put my pen into the ink.

"It is for the salvation of your soul that we seek to hear your Confession, Brother Rat," said Brother Emmerano. "God has blighted your wits, or you were a tool of Satan. Thus you have passed your life here, where you can do no greater harm or call up the forces of Hell to aid you. Either way, you will need to have peace in your life before you depart it, for Grace to be yours."

"What does a madman know of Grace, and a drunken one at that? I haven't tasted wine for more than fifteen years—how many sips will make me senseless, do you think?" Brother Rat asked angrily. "I am addled as it is. God will have mercy on me."

Brother Emmerano nodded slowly. "It is touching to know that faith remains in your heart, Brother Rat. But if you are to be spared more suffering, you must reveal all you can recall in your Confession, and thereby find absolution and redemption."

"So you must take even this," said Brother Rat, as if he shouldered a great burden. He watched as the lay Brother poured out a cupful of wine from the small cask, a bariletto. It was the same wine the Brothers drank at supper, a thin young red that turned sour quickly.

"Do not say disrespectful things, Brother Rat," said Brother Emmerano. "It will not profit your soul to run wild this way. Your madness is beyond you, but try to govern your words." He folded his hands and murmured a prayer before he addressed Brother Rat again. "Can you tell me how you came to be here? Do you recall what is the cause of your madness, or has God hidden that from you?"

41

Brother Rat coughed and tears ran from his eyes; as soon as he could he took a long draught of the wine. He drew his smock more tightly around him. "Leave me alone."

"Were we tools of Satan, we would," said Brother Emmerano. He touched the Corpus that hung around his neck. "If we were heathen, we would not bring you this comfort. But as Christian monks, we cannot abandon you."

For a short while, Brother Rat continued to cough between sips of wine, then lay back and stared up at the window. "If I don't talk to you, you will only return, won't you?"

"We have our duty to our faith," said Brother Emmerano. He folded his hands again.

"Oh, yes," said Brother Rat, his face taking on a strange light, as if the torches had made another fever in him. He tugged his single blanket higher around his shoulders. "I wish you'd left the second blanket, but since Easter has come and gone, I suppose you . . ." He choked, and turned away.

"Let us hear your Confession, Brother Rat," said Brother Emmerano with admirable persistence. "Let us bring you the joy of Communion before you are too ill to know what is happening to you. Strive to keep God in your heart so that you will not fail."

"Ah." The madman put his taloned hand to his blind eye. "You are not content to have me die, it must be on your terms." His speech seemed to be that of an educated man when you made allowances for his teeth. He addressed Brother Emmerano with curiosity, as if his question were of nothing more than the quality of fruit grown in the orchard. "What is the reason this time?"

"You are corrupted, Brother Rat. You are the tool of Satan when you speak in that way." Brother Emmerano refilled the cup. "Here. Let this good wine calm your body and your soul." He watched while Brother Rat took the wine. "Soon you will stand before God, and the Book will be open before Him. All you have done is written there. In your madness you may forget now, but then there will be no forgetting, and without mercy you will suffer the pains of Hell for eternity." He paused. "I have heard it said that you were in Amalfi at the time of the Plague. Many who did not die of it were touched in their wits because of what God visited on that city."

"It was years and years and years and years ago," said Brother Rat, not bothering to look at Brother Emmerano. "It remains only in my dreams, and they are not sweet. What happened then is between God and me."

"You claimed that to the Secular Arm," said Brother Emmerano gently, "and they feared you were a heretic. You were examined by the Secular Arm, it is in the document that sent you here. Before they discovered your madness, they strove to cleanse you of heresy." He blessed himself, in case the dangerous word would bring contagion to him. "And though you are mad, what you say is heretical."

Brother Rat laughed and then doubled over coughing. His thin, mangled hand shot out and seized the cup. He drank quickly and deeply. "Why not, why not?" he asked of nothing and no one we could see. With that he turned toward Brother Emmerano. "My chest rattles like a tinker's pack and the fever roasts my vitals. Tonight, tomorrow, a day or two at most and I will be gone from here at last. I will escape you, and the Secular Arm." He gestured for more wine before Brother Emmerano could protest so reprehensible a statement. "Go ahead. I'll tell you what you want to know. You can't do anything to me now; you could torture me and it would mean nothing, for I would die at once." He leaned back on his pallet, looking up toward the diffuse light at the window. "Sometimes I can see shadows of things, just there on the wall. Other than that, I have seen nothing but monks and stones for sixteen years. Sixteen years." Another cough rasped out of him. There were two bright places in the hollows of his cheeks and sweat shone on his forehead.

"You know that?" Brother Emmerano asked, a bit surprised.

"I used to count the days, make months and years of them. Now I measure them by Easters." He closed his eyes.

"Resurrection," said Brother Emmerano with satisfaction.

"If you prefer," Brother Rat answered. He rolled to his side and looked directly at Brother Emmerano. "How long have you been here? Not in this cell, a monk in this monastery?"

"I came here eleven years ago, from Benevento." He waited as Brother Rat stared hard at him. He went on when Brother Rat appeared to be satisfied with his response. "It is said you came from Amalfi."

Brother Rat shrugged. "I have been here longer than you have." He regarded Brother Emmerano. "Where is this monastery? They didn't tell me when they brought me here, and"—he indicated his missing lower teeth—"I was not able to ask in any case."

"We are near Anagni, in Campagna. They brought you from Napoli." He considered pouring more wine, then did not.

"From Napoli. That was where the Secular Arm had me," said Brother Rat. "They have prisons in Napoli, such prisons. This is nothing compared to them." He moved his hand to indicate his cell.

"This is not a prison, Brother Rat." Brother Emmerano

could not keep his voice even, for it vexed him to hear such things, even from a madman.

"I am shackled and kept in a cell," said Brother Rat. "What difference to me that it is monks and not soldiers who lock the doors?"

Brother Emmerano stiffened. "This monastery cares for the mad. We have none of the Secular Arm here." He leaned forward. "You are nearing the end, but I still may have you beaten if you are taken by a demon. I do not want to bring you more suffering now, but if it is necessary I will do it."

"I am sure you will," said Brother Rat softly. He finished the wine in his cup and set the cup aside. "I would not live through the beating, not now." He made himself sit up, moving slowly as much from the wine he had drunk as from the hold of his sickness. "So I came here to Anagni from Napoli." He put his hand to his chest as if to contain his coughing in his hands. "What did the Secular Arm tell you?"

"That you claim to have been an apothecary and that you were speaking heresy, or so they feared." Brother Emmerano nodded encouragement. "Go on, Brother Rat. Let me hear this Confession. Reveal all that you have hidden for so long so that you will be absolved of your sins before you appear before God." Zeal made Brother Emmerano speak more loudly, and he paused as he realized he had raised his voice.

"It was because of the Black Plague," said Brother Rat after being silent for a time. "The Plague was enough to make heretics of saints and angels. It had more than enough martyrs." He fell silent again.

"Those are dangerous thoughts, Brother Rat," said Brother Emmerano. "It is not strange that the Secular Arm should confine you if you made these accusations when the Plague came."

"I made such statements and many others," said Brother Rat, as if he were speaking from some distance away. "So you want to know how it was. You were alive when it came—you ought to remember."

"It is not my memories that are important in this Confession," Brother Emmerano reprimanded him. "If we are to record your repentance aright, then you must tell us how it was."

"If you insist," said Brother Rat with a resignation that was touched with despair. "The Plague began as other sicknesses do, but no one feared it then, not twenty years ago in Amalfi. Today I suspect it is different. Today I would think that any minor illness is viewed with alarm, isn't it?" He did not wait for an answer. "I consulted my books, because I hoped that there would be something recorded there that would protect the people of the town. But nothing seemed to help, not the perfumes, not the tea made of rosemary and moss, none of it. So I delved further, into studies in books I was told later were forbidden though they were written by a Franciscan who had been praised for his learning, for it seemed the whole world was afflicted. As my friends and my neighbors died, with black Tokens under their arms and at the groin, I dreaded that the Plague would take my family as well." It was a strange recitation, as if he were thinking of another person, one he had never met. "I had a wife then, and her mother lived with us and our five children. Sometimes, late in the night, I think I hear them speaking again."

"With your family in such danger, did you not appeal to God?" Brother Emmerano demanded.

"Daily," said Brother Rat. "And watched as the priests died with the Host in their hands." He broke off; when he was finished coughing, he held out his cup for more wine. "Is that enough or do you want more?"

"Is that all your Confession?" asked Brother Emmerano, filling the cup with slow deliberation.

"I suppose not," said Brother Rat. He wiped his blanket over his brow. "It ought to be enough, but—" He looked at the wine in the cup. "I need what little wits I have."

"How did you come to heresy? Was it from the forbidden texts?" Brother Emmerano asked, growing intent to learn the beginning of Brother Rat's madness from whence might come his salvation.

"That is what the Secular Arm said, at first," said Brother Rat. "They were diligent in the Question. They kept me in their charge, and many times brought me to answer them. One of the Inquisitors believed that I was deep in heresy because of what I had read, but most of them were certain what I had found there had turned my wits. For I came to believe what I had read, and I believe it to this day." Until the last Brother Rat had spoken quietly, but now a passion came into his words. "The text was from that Franciscan who had gone to the land of the Great Khan, and it stated—" He stopped, his coughing renewed.

"It stated what? What is this madness you believe?" asked Brother Emmerano, his eyes bright as hot coals.

"What does it matter, after all?" He leaned back and wiped his mouth. "It is all but over. Why not? Why not?"

"Yes," said Brother Emmerano. "It is the Devil who urges you to silence, who makes you question the urgings of your soul to be purged of the evil that brought you to madness. Tell me what transpired and it will be recorded with your Confession. It will show that you have repented the pacts that made you mad. Think, Brother Rat, for the time when you will appear to answer for your sins comes quickly.

Be reconciled to God now and—"

"Yes, yes I know," said Brother Rat, waving him to silence. "I have heard it many times. But madness is obdurate, and it has held me too tightly. But now nothing but death holds me."

"The Hand of God holds you, as it holds all the world," said Brother Emmerano. He looked toward me. "Have you taken down all we have said?"

"Yes," I assured him and blessed myself as soon as I had written my response. "It is all here."

"And no matter what Brother Rat says, you are sworn to record it, is that not so?" Brother Emmerano pursued.

"That is the case," I answered, writing as I spoke.

"It will be here, Brother Rat, every word of it, and there will be no doubt of your Confession and the salvation of your soul. No one will be able to question it." He moved his stool a little closer to the pallet. "What was it that caused you to become mad? What thing did you find in those books that reduced you to this?"

It was as if Brother Rat had not heard; for some little time he stared up at the ceiling. "You know," he said after we had all been silent for as long as it would take to recite the Supplication to the Virgin, "I followed what the books suggested. I removed all the rushes from the house and set pots of burning herbs throughout the house, so every room was filled with smoke. I permitted no new rushes to be brought into the house, and I ordered that everyone bathe once a week while the Plague was in the city."

Brother Emmerano was outraged; he could not speak in the soft manner he so often employed for such Confessions. "What blasphemous book taught you that? You said it was a book where you learned this, did you not?"

"A book of things learned by the Franciscan Brother in

the great Land of Silk," said Brother Rat. "A Franciscan wrote it, good Brother. A man sworn to God and Christ. He said it was thought by certain of the subjects of the Great Khan that what brought the Plague was vermin—vermin and the vermin of vermin. This book declared that if there were no vermin there would likewise be no Plague."

"God's Wrath brings Plague: God's Wrath and the sins of man," said Brother Emmerano, his voice now very loud.

"Amen." Brother Rat blessed himself. "But the notion took hold of me, in my dread as the corpses were piled in the streets each morning and there were fewer and fewer left alive to see them buried." He had a taste of the wine and set the cup aside. "The priests were in the grave with the rest of them. And you see, only my wife's mother had taken the Plague. My wife lived, and our children were alive. So I kept to what the texts said, and made our house slaves clean each day, scrubbing the floors every morning. They all grumbled, but they lived."

"A ruse of the Devil," said Brother Emmerano.

"Very likely," said Brother Rat with a deep sigh. "It did not last. My second son began to sweat and became restless, and that was enough to panic our slaves and servants, for they deserted us." He forced himself to sit up properly and then he downed the cup of wine. "I might as well be drunk for this."

"If you can give an honest Confession," warned Brother Emmerano.

"In vino veritas," said Brother Rat. He motioned for more. "My wife nursed the boy, and though she hated all that I did, she did not stop me for she was too worried for the other children to care that I continued to scrub the floors and burn herbs once a day. She would not allow me to have the stuffing of the mattresses changed, for fear of losing the protection of the angels who guard the sick. Then she took the Plague as well." He watched the wine fill the cup. "In the book by that Franciscan there was much about the danger of rats—rats more than mice. So I killed every rat I saw, in the house and anywhere in the town. And as the people died, there were more and more rats, or so it seemed to me." He was agitated now, his cough returning as short, explosive interruptions to what he said. "I thought that the rats were bringing the Plague, because of what the book said. It spoke of the vermin of vermin, and rats, and so I—"

"It is said that you went among the dead, killing rats where you found them. According to the Secular Arm you killed every rat that entered your cell." Brother Emmerano blessed himself. "You kill rats here."

"They are the messengers of the Plague," said Brother Rat with such intense feeling that for once Brother Emmerano shrank back from him. "It is madness to think that, but I have said already I cannot make myself turn my thoughts from that conviction."

Brother Emmerano clasped his hands, but this time he was nervous, and the knuckles stood out white. "But what has brought you to this?"

"The rats," said Brother Rat. "They themselves. I have made a point to look closely at them, and they are alive with vermin of their own. And if their vermin have vermin, might not there be vermin of those, and so into the realms of angels?" He pulled at his blanket, then drank off half the wine, smacking his lips with savor. "I am now never without the conviction that there are vermin so fine and so great in number that they can penetrate anything. The rats bring them."

"But vermin are everywhere," said Brother Emmerano.

"Have you lost sight of that? There would have to be these little vermin in all things, and what would be the purpose of that? Where does it say that God brought forth vermin? We know that the Devil brings these tribulations, and it is for us to bear these things without notice so we may the sooner turn our minds from the wiles of the Devil and toward the salvation of Christ."

Brother Rat nodded several times as if his head were not tightly bound to his body. "I know. The Secular Arm reminded me. I know this is madness. But we who are mad cannot set aside our madness because it is what we wish. If it were that, we would be heretics." He finished his wine. "I wish I were a heretic, I wish I did not believe as I do, that I have been corrupted and could be saved from my error. But it is fixed, like the head of an arrow in a healed wound. Broken fingers and teeth could not budge it. This cell has not changed it." He wept suddenly, deeply.

"God will bring you to comfort, Brother Rat," said Brother Emmerano as he clutched his Corpus in a trembling hand.

When the worst of his weeping was over, Brother Rat wiped his face with his blanket once more, and spat several times, as much blood as foam. "I can see it now, or so I tell myself. They ruined this eye trying to make me tell them I could not see these vermin, but . . ."

"It is madness, and they sent you to us," said Brother Emmerano, still trying to quiet himself so that he would be able to sense God's Will.

"Apparently." He considered the cup, then signaled for more. "I suppose the fever burns the wine away. I thought I would be singing by now. There was a time when I might have sung." Now his cough shook him as if he were in the fist of a giant.

51

"Should we send for—" Brother Emmerano began but was cut off by Brother Rat.

"No. What could he do? It is ending for me." He looked away from Brother Emmerano. "And I have been thinking that one of these invisible vermin has brought this cough to me, that it has taken over my body, as the vermin of Plague took my wife and my son, and my wife's mother."

Brother Emmerano hesitated, then asked, "What of your other children? You said you had five children, did you not?"

"Oh, yes," said Brother Rat. "I did. And the neighbors thought I was possessed of a demon, for all that I did in my house. They saw the pots of smoking herbs and they said the Devil was with us. They saw that I had the floors cleaned every morning, and they whispered that I had done atrocious things in the night." He put his hand to his brow. "So the ones who were still alive decided that I had brought the Plague to Amalfi." There were tears on his wrinkled, sunken cheeks yet he made no move to wipe them away. "They gathered together and when next my children went to the church to pray for the soul of their mother, who was dead less than a week, they were met by men and boys with bricks and stones." He closed his eyes.

Brother Emmerano lifted his hand to bless Brother Rat, but faltered. "What became of them? Of your children?"

"I thought that was obvious," said Brother Rat softly, refusing to open his eyes. "They were stoned to death. I found them all broken and in a welter of blood when I came from the burial pit where I had taken flowers in memory of my wife."

As Brother Emmerano lowered his hand, he said, "What was said of that act?"

"I don't know," Brother Rat admitted as he opened his

eyes at last. "I was not told." He stared down at his hands as if he had just noticed the fingers of his left hand had been broken. "That night was when I went to the burial pit to kill rats. I had to do something."

"But such a gesture . . . surely you did not think that you could change the death of those poor people by killing rats." Brother Emmerano shifted on his stool again, glancing toward the door as if to reassure himself that the lay Brothers were within reach.

"I don't know what I thought," said Brother Rat in bitter amusement. "I was mad. I have been mad since the Plague came. Perhaps I hoped that if I killed the vermin and the vermin of vermin I might find the way to restore those who were dead." He shrugged. "I can't remember what was in my heart then." He coughed, holding his head with his hand. "I am not used to wine. Already my head is throbbing."

Brother Emmerano was not going to permit Brother Rat to turn away from the matter now. "How did you come to be in the hands of the Secular Arm? Surely you did not seek them out, did you? To hear what you say, all of Amalfi died of the Plague."

"Most of it did. Some who could afford it left the city when the disease first struck, and they returned to find a few of us picking our way among the corpses." He slid back on his pallet. "They came with priests and all of us who remained alive were taken to the church to answer the questions of the Bishop, to account for our lack of death. Anyone who gave unsatisfactory answers was sent to the Secular Arm. They burned the tailor as a heretic, and the chimney sweep. Those of us who were still in their keeping had to watch, to see what awaited us if we did not exculpate ourselves."

"A worthy lesson," said Brother Emmerano.

"Yes," Brother Rat said distantly. "Although I hoped then that they would decide I was a heretic, and burn me, for life seemed an impossible burden to me then."

"Such an assertion is close to heresy," Brother Emmerano cautioned.

"My family was dead. I had failed to save them." Brother Rat turned his face to the stones.

"It is not for you to save them, or any man. It is for God to save them, or to move you to find the means to save them. If you usurp that power, you question the divinity of God and Christ. God in His Wisdom called your family to Him, and left you to live on so that you could return again to Christ." Brother Emmerano placed his hand over his heart. "Your soul has been forfeited because you were misled by a Godless book, and for that your family was taken from you, and when that was not sufficient, so were your wits."

"It was vermin that brought Plague, Brother Emmerano. I am mad still, though I pray devoutly that God will pity me and save me from the madness that has claimed the whole of my thoughts for all these years." It was not easy to understand him with his face to the wall. "But suppose it is true? What if my madness is no madness? Suppose that there is truth in those pages, and our efforts have been spent in vain? That is what makes my days' torment: suppose the book is right, and there is vermin and vermin's vermin and vermin's vermin's vermin, and that is what causes Plague when God is displeased with mankind?"

Brother Emmerano sighed. "He should not have drunk so much. The wine has muddled his thoughts. He has had too much, and mad that he is, he is sunk into his madness." He started to rise. "I will have Brother Luccio record all you have said, Brother Rat, and in the morning it will be read to you and you will be absolved, and the priests will anoint you." His habit rustled as he rose, clapping his hands for the lay Brothers at the door.

"There could be other vermin that bring other ills," muttered Brother Rat. "There may be many others. It may not be sufficient only to kill rats." He pulled his blanket close around him and coughed, low and steady, as the writing table and two stools were removed from the cell.

As the lay Brother turned the key in the lock of the cell door, Brother Emmerano blessed him and added a blessing toward the door itself. "You will bring the Confession to me, Brother Luccio. Make sure you include my request to review it."

"As you wish," I told him, lowering my face to show him respect. "As soon as I have presented it to the Prior." I walked behind Brother Emmerano, as was proper. "They say the Plague has returned," I mentioned as we started up the stairs to the refectory.

Brother Emmerano nodded. "We have said Masses for the dead already." He paused, his face emotionless. "Poor Brother Rat, if he learns of it. But it is not likely, in God's Mercy."

I bowed my head and protected myself with the Cross. And as we resumed our climb, I could not keep from asking, "Do you suppose there is the least chance he is right? I know he is mad, but some madmen have visions, don't they?"

Brother Emmerano laughed once. "How can that be? Brother Rat has been broken by the wiles of the Devil. Madmen who have visions see angels and the hosts of Heaven and the tribulations of the Martyrs or are offered comfort by Our Lady. They glimpse the world that is beyond the earth, either Heaven or Hell. They do not see the vermin of rats, Brother Luccio."

"Amen," I replied, my faith in Brother Emmerano and God. I resolved not to be led into error, though I had received warning that my sister was ill with a cough and a fever. How simple a thing it would be to blame rats and the vermin of rats instead of God—how simple and how monstrous. I whispered a prayer for her protection as well as my forgiveness and went to my cell to prepare the record of the Confession for the Prior.

About *Confessions of a Madman*

I wrote this story for the anthology Psycho Paths *at the request of its editor, the wonderful and much-missed Robert Bloch. He asked if I could come up with something in which the supposed cause or expression of madness was not madness at all, but in which, also, the madness was genuine. This was the result.*

Renfield's Syndrome

Rats didn't taste nearly as good as he hoped they would—even spiders were tastier. He managed to choke the third one down, pulling the tail out of his mouth as if it were an unpalatable length of spaghetti. He put this in the little plastic bag where he had already stowed the heads and skins and guts and paws of his other rodent-prey, then closed the bag with a knot. That done, he sat down and waited for the energy to rev through him as he knew it must. This time it hit him hard, making his veins fizz with the force of it. This was so much better than anything he'd gotten from bugs and lizards. He got up and paced around the basement, suddenly too full of vitality to be able to remain still. It was everything that he had hoped, and that thrilled him.

When the call came for dinner, he made his way up the stairs, the bag of innards and skin at his side. After his feast he was almost convinced he could levitate, so full of life was he. Everything in him was alive, from his hair to his toes. He felt like a hero in a comic book, or maybe an action hero. His step was light and he was smiling as he emerged from his haven. In the kitchen he looked about, smelling all the odors with an intensity that made him feel dizzy. The salty aroma of Hamburger Helper seemed overwhelming and yet unsatisfying—the beef was dead, robbing it of its savor. Since eating the rats he knew it was only living meat that would satisfy him.

"Henry! Wash your hands!" His mother's voice—along with her choice of words, since she only called him Henry when she was stressed out—warned him that she had had a rough day at the clinic.

"Okay!" He stopped at the sink and rubbed his hands on the cake of glycerin soap in the dish over the faucet. It reeked of artificial flowers and he wrinkled his nose in disgust.

"And turn the heat down under the string beans!"

"Okay!" he answered; he rinsed his hands and dried them on a paper towel. He went to the stove and adjusted the gas flame under the saucepan.

"The table's set," his mother called as a kind of encouragement. "Your sister will be down in a minute. She's changing."

Henry made a face; just the idea of his sister made him want to puke, but he would not let any of it show. He licked his teeth, hoping no scraps of his meal would remain; he was not in the mood to answer questions about his basement activities. Let them think he was playing or studying or whatever they assumed he did down there.

"I could use some help with the salad."

Salad! he thought contemptuously, but spoke meekly enough, "Sure, Mom."

"There's lettuce in the fridge. I'll slice a couple tomatoes and if you'll wash and tear up the lettuce, we can use the last of the buttermilk ranch, or the creamy Italian. You can choose the one you like best." She had gone to the cupboard and taken down the bottle of vodka and was now pouring herself about three ounces into a small water-glass. "I need to relax tonight," she said, by way of explanation. She drank about a third of the vodka without ice, which wasn't like her.

"Something bad happen today, Mom?" Henry asked, knowing she wanted to talk. He retrieved the lettuce from the refrigerator and made sure it wasn't too brown.

"Things are always happening at the clinic," she said, and Henry realized whatever has taken place, it had been very bad. When she sounded like that, it meant something pretty awful.

"What about getting another job?" he suggested, knowing the answer.

"The only other jobs I could get pay less. Working with those patients—the mental ones, in the locked ward—I earn more, and we need the money." She bit her lower lip then made herself smile. "I guess I'll just have to make the best of it."

"Well, it's not fair," he said as he thrust the lettuce under the faucet and turned on the cold water, pulling the head apart. Why, he wondered, was this called butter lettuce? It wasn't anything like butter. He made a pile of the leaves and waited for his mother to say more. He began to pull the lettuce-leaves apart, remembering how sweet it had been to pull the rats to bits. He tried to imagine the soft green leaves were muscle and sinew and bone, but it didn't work and he was left to try to remember how good it had felt to kill the rats.

"Did you have a good day at school?" His mother sounded slightly distracted, but he answered her anyway.

"I guess so. I got a ninety percent in geometry and Mister Dasher said my English paper was better than the last one." He told her the good parts and left out the things Jack Parsons had called him in gym, and the bad grade he'd got in the American History quiz. There'd be time for that later. He looked around for the salad bowl and began to put the torn lettuce into it. In spite of the lowered heat, he could smell the green beans charring in the saucepan.

"Good for you," she said, going to work on the tomatoes, taking the time to make the wedges all about the same size.

"So how was the clinic?" Henry asked, trying not to be too obvious about it.

"Trouble, a lot of trouble. Old Missus Chuiso got out of the day room and into the pharmacy and started taking everything she could get her hands on. They had to pump her stomach, and there were a lot of upset people on the locked ward. The violent ones needed extra medication." She sighed. "Half of them aren't really crazy, they're senile, or they have brain damage, like Brian Bachman, who went over the handlebars of his motorcycle into a tree. He has seizures, bad ones, and he can't stand up straight." She had another drink, this one longer and deeper than the previous one. Henry knew it had been bad—she always mentioned Brian Bachman when it was bad. "I told Doctor Salazar that we ought to separate the crazy ones from the senile and damaged ones, but he says we don't have the budget for it. It would be better if we did something to make the place better for them."

"But it's county, Mom, and you say that's like charity." He scowled, thinking that it was stupid to argue with her when she was like this, but unable to stop. "The Thomas J. Doer Memorial Clinic is for people who can't afford—"

"I know, I know," said his mother, refilling her vodka glass. "But it's not doing any good, and in some cases, like poor Missus Chuiso, we're probably making things worse. Not that there is anything we can do for her." She sighed as she drank again. "It's so disheartening to try to deal with her. You should have seen her—well, maybe you shouldn't—they had to put her in restraints because she kept fighting them, even though they were trying to save her. She's miserable, and she's all alone. She needs someone with her all the time, but we don't have enough personnel to do that."

"You do a great job, Mom; the best anyone could," Henry told her as he took the buttermilk ranch dressing and held it out to her. "Do you want to toss it?"

"No; you do it." She tossed the tomato wedges into the torn lettuce and went to wash her hands. "The Hamburger Helper is almost ready."

"Great," Henry said, though the thought of something so dead left him feeling queasy. He needed something with *life* in it.

"Just put it on the table. We can toss it before we serve it." She was beginning to sound a little mellower, but not so much that Henry could refuse dinner with impunity. "I'll find a bowl for the string beans."

"Okay." He took the salad into the small dining room—it was really more of an alcove off the living room—and put it on the small round table. He thought it was disgusting, and his feeling showed.

"Why are you making such a face?" his sister asked as she came in from her room. She was extravagantly made up, with two bright colors of eyeshadow above her black-lined eyes. Her cheeks, although they had no need of augmentation, glowed with blusher and her lips were painted a brilliant crimson.

"Because you look like a clown," he answered, knowing it would silence her.

"Ha ha ha," she said sarcastically. "I suppose you know what makes a girl look good?"

"I know what doesn't," Henry said pointedly. He started back toward the kitchen, not wanting to have another fight with his sister.

"How's Mom?" his sister asked, suddenly subdued.

"Upset. Don't make it worse, okay? She'll just drink more if you do." He has kept his voice down, but he had the uneasy feeling that he had been overheard.

"So you think I'm going to cause trouble?" she challenged.

"I hope not." As he went back into the kitchen, he saw his mother top off her glass with more vodka. "Aw, Mom."

"I won't have any more after this glass," she said, sounding resentful, which Henry knew meant she was getting drunk.

"Do you have to?"

"You bet I do," she answered him sullenly. "If you knew what I go through."

Henry had heard all her complaints before, but he held his tongue. "What about the string beans?"

"In the blue bowl," she said, pointing in the general direction of the sink counter. "Put some butter on them before you take them to the table."

Henry did as he was told. The exhilaration of the rats he had eaten was beginning to fade, the strength leached out of him by the deadly sorrow and anger that filled him and his mother. He watched the butter run over the string beans and tried to conjure up an appetite for the meal without success. He pointed to the skillet of Hamburger Helper, saying, "It's starting to scorch."

"I'll take care of it." She removed the skillet from its burner, muttering as she did, "If your father would pay his child support on time, we wouldn't have to eat crap like this."

"It's okay," said Henry, knowing it wasn't.

The dining room light had only one bulb burning, but it was enough to illuminate the table. As his sister and mother took their seats, Henry did his best to look hungry. He sat down last of all. "Smells good, Mom," he said with false enthusiasm.

"It smells burnt," said his sister.

"Margaret Lynne," their mother warned her.

"Well, it does," said Margaret Lynne.

"I've had a hard day," said their mother patiently. "Can we at least eat in peace?"

"Okay," said Margaret Lynne in a tone that made it clear it wasn't. "Sure. Anything you say."

"Okay," said their mother, and put some salad on her plate, then reached for the string beans. "I hope you're not planning on going out tonight. It's a school night, and you know you need to study more than you do."

"Mo-ther," said Margaret Lynne. "I'm only going for an hour or two. And it's not like I'm doing anything wrong. I told Melanie that I'd help her with her geometry."

"Dressed like that?" Their mother was not convinced. "If your father saw you like that, he'd—"

"Well, he can't see me, can he?" Margaret Lynne asked defiantly. "He hasn't seen me for five months now. He doesn't give a shit about what I do!" She flung down her napkin as if it were a gauntlet.

"Margaret Lynne!" their mother exclaimed. "You will not use such language at the dinner table!"

"Why not?" Margaret Lynne flung back, her eyes beginning to fill with tears of rage. She pushed her chair back and rushed out of the dining room, heading for the door. "I'll be back later!"

Their mother sat still for a long while, then drank the last of the vodka in her glass. "I don't know what to do with that girl."

Henry put his fork down. "Mom. I'm not very hungry." He sounded apologetic, but he was secretly relieved: he didn't have to invent a reason for not eating. "I'll be down in the basement, if you need me." He got up slowly, not wanting to seem too eager.

"Oh, no, Henry. You don't have to run off." She reached out and took his hand. "I want you to eat. You need to eat."

"Maybe later," he said as gently as he could.

"We can't afford to waste food in this house," said his mother, spooning some of the Hamburger Helper onto her plate. "Remember that, Henry."

"I will, Mom," he assured her. "I'll nuke something a little later. Just put the leftovers in the fridge."

"Okay," she said, accepting defeat for the moment.

Henry smiled, knowing what good bait the Hamburger Helper could make. He went back into the kitchen, his plate in his hand, and put it on the edge of the sink for later. Then he headed down for the basement, planning to set some more traps.

Two weeks later, Henry caught a squirrel, and the charge he got out of eating it was way beyond what he had hoped for. It was much, much better than the rats had been! He thought it was delicious—and entirely superior to bugs and spiders. He relished every morsel of it, and vowed to catch more of them as soon as possible. But he also realized he had taken a terrible risk, hunkering down in the city park behind a thicket of rhododendron. Someone might have seen him, and that wouldn't do at all. They'd probably make him stop eating the things that gave him life. No telling what Mom would think, working with the nuts at the clinic. She might even think he was a bit crazy himself. He had to be careful: he didn't want to get caught. People wouldn't understand, he knew that. So he hid a trap deep in a clump of hawthorn bushes in the Veterans' Park, and hoped it would snare another squirrel for him; he'd check it on the way home from school.

Halfway home he came upon his sister and a group of her friends gathered around a four-year-old red Mustang convertible. Three senior boys lounged in the car, enjoying the obvious admiration Margaret Lynne was displaying as she leaned provocatively on the hood of the car, her boobs almost falling out of her skimpy tank-top.

"Hey, Margo, isn't that your creepy little brother?" the owner of the Mustang asked, grinning at the way Margaret Lynne reacted.

"Yeah," she said, sounding disgusted. "That's Henry." She made a gesture to him to go away. "He's always trying to horn in where he doesn't belong."

"Hi, Margaret Lynne," Henry said, as if he hadn't heard any of the slighting, hurtful things she said.

"Margaret Lynne?" the Mustang owner echoed in delicious ridicule. "Does he always call you Margaret Lynne?"

"Yeah," she admitted as if confessing to a major lapse. She began to pout.

"And you *let* him?" the boy hooted.

"I know, I know," Margaret Lynne said, trying to recover some of the ground she had lost. "But Mom insists."

"So, Margaret Lynne," the Mustang owner exclaimed, "you're only Margo at school."

"And other places," she said, beginning to pout.

"Hey, good for you." His false praise stung Henry as much as it chagrined his sister.

"Shut up, Craig," Margaret Lynne told him. She shoved herself off his car and stood with her back to him. "Just shut up."

Watching all this, Henry felt his new-found strength slipping away. He ducked his head in anticipation of the blow he knew would be coming, but he didn't step back—that would be too humiliating, and it would leave Margaret

Lynne without anyone to champion her. He shoved his hands deep into his pockets and stared at her, trying to keep his mouth shut without seeming to be too much of a fool.

"Hey, Margaret Lynne," Craig called out derisively. "Better keep an eye on that brother of yours. Who knows what he could say to someone who cares." He started his Mustang and drove off in triumph.

"You little bastard!" Margaret Lynne shouted, rounding on Henry. "You screwed all this up for me. I hope you die!"

"I didn't mean—" Henry said, trying to placate her.

"Sure you did!" She lifted her hand and brought it down on his shoulder with more impact than he had anticipated. It took him aback and he tried to maintain a stoic disposition while she continued to rail at him. "You wanted me to look like a slut, didn't you? You like to make me look bad. You did this on purpose!" She swatted him again.

"I don't!" Henry protested. He started walking toward home, feeling completely dispirited. He wished he had another squirrel to eat, to bring back his vigor and restore his sense of dominion in the world.

"Yes, you do. You just did. Craig will tell everyone about my name, and everyone'll laugh. This is just impossible! I can't stand it!" She had started to cry, her wrath increasing with her tears; she was working herself up to a fine tantrum. "You just couldn't shut up, could you? Oh, no! Not you. You had to keep talking. I asked you not to, but you didn't listen!" Her weeping increased. "You're turning my life to shit, and you like it!"

"No, I don't," Henry insisted, "really, I don't."

"Of course you do," scoffed Margaret Lynne. "You're a turd, Henry. Just a turd. And it's Margo! Not Margaret Lynne!" She tossed her head and hurried ahead of him, doggedly ignoring him as he tagged after her.

★ ★ ★ ★ ★

Mother took her time getting up, emerging from bed ten minutes before Henry had to leave for school. She put her hand to her head. "God. I shouldn't have drunk so much last night," she mumbled as she headed down the narrow hall to the bathroom where Henry was finishing brushing his teeth. "Can you hurry it up, Henry?" She was feeling woozy now and she didn't want to throw up on the hall carpet.

A single glance told Henry his mother was in rocky condition, so he said, "Sure. You bet." He spat into the sink and gave his mouth a quick rinse, then left the bathroom to her. "I'll be on my way to school in a couple of minutes." He went toward his room, wondering if he had time to check his traps in the basement before he had to go.

"Good. Great." She closed the bathroom door, saying, "Make sure your sister's up."

"Okay," said Henry, who knew Margaret Lynne hadn't been home all night. "See you this evening, Mom," he called out as he went to the kitchen and pretended to make himself a bag lunch. As he left the apartment he heard his mother start the shower. It was going to be a long day.

School was eleven blocks away, but he could cut that short by taking the walk through the city park; it took up two blocks and was in need of upkeep, which suited Henry just fine. He moved steadily along and was almost out of the main cluster of trees and shrubbery when he heard a little sound, hardly more than a whisper, from the bushes under the Stone pines. He stopped still, listening with all his senses, his thoughts keen as the high, tiny sounds that he struggled to identify. Succumbing to his curiosity, Henry left the walkway and ducked under the branches, hoping against hope that he would discover something worthwhile, and trying not to be seen as he sought out the source of the noise.

It was a baby jay, not much bigger than the egg it had hatched from not very long ago. It was trying to lever itself upright on its toothpick legs, but could not coordinate its effort enough to do more than flop about clumsily, its beak open in obvious hunger.

Henry knelt down beside it and gently took it into his hands, all but mesmerized by the tiny bundle of pinfeathers and need. He brought the little jay up to his face. "Can't let you lie on the ground. Something'll get you there." He smoothed the outsized head and made soft cawing noises, reassuring the baby bird before he broke its neck and reached for his pocketknife to flay and gut the tiny creature. He forgot about school, about his mom at home, about everything, as he took the new, sweet life into him.

"I want to go live with Dad," Margaret Lynne announced at dinner that evening. She and their mother had had a dreadful argument when mother got home from work, followed by sullen silences and put-upon sighs from both combatants. Henry had listened to it all from the safety of the basement, but now he could not escape the tension that filled the cramped house like summer lightning.

"If your father agrees, then you might as well. Maybe he can do something with you."

"Well, I'll call him tonight," Margaret Lynne said, a bit nonplused to have her mother concede so readily to her demands. "But I mean it, Mom—I'm going to live with him."

"If he agrees, it's fine with me," she reiterated, sounding worn out.

Margaret Lynne grinned. "Do you want to come with me, Henry?"

But Henry had no wish to get dragged into this. "Let's see what he says first," he answered cautiously.

She shot him a single vitriolic sneer, then tossed her head. "I'll talk to you in a little bit," she promised nastily.

"Just tell him hello for me," said Henry as he got to his feet and made an apologetic gesture. "Sorry, Mom. I don't have much of an appetite."

His mother studied him for about ten seconds, then said, "All right. You may be excused. Take your dishes to the kitchen and make sure you put the food into leftover containers."

"I will," he promised her. When he had finished in the kitchen, he headed down into the basement where he was hoping to find something in one of his traps. He really needed to get some life into him. To his disgust and alarm, he saw no mice, no rats, nor anything else waiting for him, so he sat down and began to work on a new trap. He had the thing half-assembled when he became aware of Margaret Lynne's voice raised in pleading indignation.

"But why not? . . . Da-*aad* . . . But you promised . . . You've got to help me! Come on, Dad . . . I know it's a long way! Sixteen hundred miles. See? I know . . . I don't *care* if it is. School'll be over in a month or so . . . It'll be like vacation . . . I can come then, and it won't matter . . . I'll take the bus or have someone drive me. You won't have to . . . It's so hard. It's like being in *prison!* You know how Mom is . . . But I've told everyone I'm going to live with you and . . . Oh, God, Dad, you don't understand!" The receiver slammed down and Henry could hear his sister crying. A few minutes later, her bedroom door thundered shut and the house fell eerily silent.

Henry knew that he had to be very careful; Mom would be upset now and that meant she would get into the vodka again; there was a full bottle in the fridge—Henry had seen it. Mom was in her room now, changing from her work clothes to the pale-blue sweats she preferred of an evening after dinner for watching TV or videos of old movies. With all this fighting with Margaret Lynne, Mom would be more depressed than ever, and Margaret Lynne—Margo—would be furious at everything for days on end.

She should have known better, Henry thought. Dad didn't want to see them, not really. He had a new wife and three new kids and he didn't want to be reminded of the hard years with Mom. Dad had left and that was all there was to it. He went into the kitchen and took a liter of soda from the fridge and got ready to go down to the basement. It was better to keep away from the conflicts between his sister and mother. He'd longed for something *good* to eat, something with life in it that would strengthen him for the next couple of days. His trap in the park had remained disappointingly empty and his appetite was sharpening with every passing hour.

"Hey, Mom!" Margaret Lynne shouted as Henry began his descent. "Mom! I'm going out!"

"Be back by nine tonight, missy. It's a school night and your grades—" Her words were cut off as the front door slammed.

The basement was cool and dark, friendly to Henry. He found a mouse in one of his traps, and after a brief hesitation, he got out his pocketknife and began his snack, finding the little life more sustaining than he had hoped at first. When his meal was done, he sat down at his old laptop—the last gift from his father, some three years ago—and began to record his meal and response. He read back through the files, finding solace in the information he had gathered about all he had eaten, and realized that it still wasn't

70

enough. Gradually he began to think about larger meals, anticipating the thrill he would have from them, and the power that would possess him. "Almost like a super-hero," he said aloud, and put his hand over his mouth, as if the sound of the words would compromise his potency. Carefully he turned off the laptop and sat in the dim basement, contemplating the problems of catching bigger prey.

The puppy had a bloody paw, and its coat was dirty—it was little more than two months old, clearly abandoned and beginning to fail. It whimpered with hunger, a mongrel with no promise of handsomeness or charm. Henry bent and picked it up, looking around to be sure no one saw him do it, and slipped the puppy into his jacket pocket. He had a half-formed plan to eat the pathetic little animal, but as he walked home, he could tell that the animal had little energy to offer him. He decided to stop and get some milk for the puppy, and something to eat, to fatten him up a bit; the way he was now, there wasn't much vitality in him. He'd have to bring down his old jacket for the animal to sleep on, too, and find some way to make sure he didn't make too much of a stink: Mom might be drunk some evenings but her nose still worked. He continued to plan as he made his way along the sidewalk, his mind only on the puppy squirming in his pocket. He wished he had more than two dollars with him, but he decided he'd manage somehow.

In the market he saw his mother—she was buying some stuff for dinner, and, of course, another bottle of vodka. He was careful to avoid her, not wanting her to find out about the puppy, so he hid out behind the onions and potatoes until he saw her leave. Then he bought a pint of milk and a small packet of dog-kibble. When he finished paying for it, he had thirty-four cents left, and he had no idea what he'd buy lunch with the next day. All the more reason to get the puppy ready to eat. It was going to be a hard few days.

When he arrived home, he headed for the basement at once, his nerves strained just the way Mom said hers were at the end of the day. He could hear Margaret Lynne's CD player blaring out an electric-guitar-and-drum with three voices wailing about disappointed desire and the general unfairness of societal pressures on young lovers. Most of the time he was pissed off at her for causing such a rumpus, but now he was glad for her defiance, for it assured him more privacy than he had expected. "Okay," he said to the puppy as he took the little mutt out of his pocket and set him down on the floor. The little dog began to sniff out his surroundings, then found an upright pillar and urinated on it.

"Hey!" Henry cried out. "Don't do that. I'll bring some papers for you. But you can't go around doing that. Mom'll notice."

The puppy looked up at him and whined.

This was going to be difficult, Henry realized, but he was determined to carry on; he had so much to gain and he'd waited for so long for such splendid opportunity. The puppy was everything he had been hoping for.

"Henry!" his mother called from upstairs. "Are you down there?"

"Yeah, Mom," Henry called back. "I'm on the computer."

"What?" She was shouting now to be heard over the clamor of the boombox. "What are you doing?"

Henry raised his voice and repeated himself, holding his breath, hoping she wouldn't try to investigate.

"Make sure you do your homework!" his mother yelled.

"Yes, Mom," Henry told her, and looked over at the puppy. "I'll do it."

"You're a good boy, Henry," she told him, her voice lowered but still loud enough to be heard.

"Thanks, Mom," he said, mistrusting her praise. He waited for the greater part of a minute, as if there was a possible hazard in her good opinion. When nothing more happened, Henry went to put out food and milk for the puppy, selecting a Styrofoam burger container from among his collection on a rough basement shelf for the kibble. "You can start out with this." He was careful to move quietly, making an effort to keep the puppy from romping around too much, and hoping he wouldn't howl or whimper or bark or anything like that. "You gotta be quiet," he admonished the little dog. "You're not supposed to be here." He wondered briefly if he had made a mistake in bringing the puppy home, then decided that he needed to learn how to catch and fatten prey. "You eat your food. I'll bring down paper for your piss and poop. Just be quiet. It's important that you—" He reached out and took the puppy's little muzzle in his hand, closing the puppy's mouth.

The puppy whimpered and gave a tentative wave of his tail.

Henry shook his head and went to get one of the old deli pint containers. He put this on the floor next to the kibble and poured half the milk into it. "You can drink this. I'll bring you more water."

The puppy began to devour the food, only interrupting himself to lap the milk. He was clearly famished and wanted to stuff himself. It was good to see him eat so eagerly—he would be fat and sassy soon, and he would be full of life. Henry patted the puppy's head, anticipating the day he would reap the harvest he was sowing now. How great he would taste! And the energy he would provide! Henry thought he might not be able to contain it all, and that made him feel sick and excited at once. He went over to his rickety old chair and sat down, already thinking about what he could eat tonight that would sustain him while the puppy improved. He was getting hungry for life and he wasn't sure he could wait for the puppy to reach a size and vigor that he longed for.

By the time Henry left the basement he had taken up the first layer of old papers. The house was silent, Margaret Lynne having gone out an hour ago. He stopped in the kitchen and took a half-finished Whopper with everything from the fridge as a stopgap meal. It wasn't enough to give him what he sought most, but it was better than nothing. He went off toward his room, pausing in the living room where his mother was asleep in front of the television, which had the late news on. He washed up in the bathroom, doing his best to keep quiet. He decided not to wake his mother, for that would mean helping her into bed, and that was more than he wanted to do. It would be at least a week before the puppy would be ready, and he would have to be very careful in the meantime. If only school weren't still in session, he could spend the time making sure the puppy wasn't discovered. He noticed that Margaret Lynne wasn't home yet. This meant trouble tomorrow, he knew, so he would have to get up early and take care of the puppy before things exploded at breakfast. All these possibilities kept him unpleasant company as he got into bed.

"Oh my God!" Henry's mother exclaimed from the top of the basement steps. She swayed a little and blinked against the darkness. "How can you? What are you doing?"

Henry looked up from his half-consumed meal. There was blood on his chin and shirt, and the skin and guts of the puppy lay at his feet on the last of the papers. He was so elated by what he had been eating that he was unable to conceal anything he had done or to comprehend what his mother was staring at. "Mom?"

"Henry. What . . . you . . . you're eating . . ." She started down the stairs, her face fixed in shock. "That looks like—"

"Just leave me alone, Mom," Henry pleaded, alarmed by the shock he saw in her face. "I'm not doing anything wrong."

"Not wrong?" Her distress was increasing as she was increasingly aware of what he was doing. "It's *raw!* And *still alive!*"

"It's good," said Henry, not even her outrage enough to stop the power from the puppy's life surging through him, making him feel strong, almost invincible. "It's not important."

"It's terrible," said his mother, coming down another two steps. "Eating raw meat!" She peered at the mess around him. "What's that at your feet?" The color drained from her face. "I thought you were doing fine, that it was Margaret Lynne who was causing all the trouble." Her indignation was marred by a slight slurring of the words.

For once Henry didn't want to be compliant. He got to his feet, spilling the sections of the butchered puppy onto the floor. "Now look what you made me do." He lowered his head, staring up at her from under his brows.

"Henry!" His mother wailed out his name, her face set into a mask of anguish. She reached out, shaking her fist at the boy.

"Leave it alone, Mom—I know what I'm doing," Henry warned her, convinced that he could persuade her to see his point of view if he only had the chance. "It's nothing to bother about."

"You're *sick!* God, you're sick!" she muttered. "You need help."

75

"I'm fine, Mom," Henry said, more sharply than before.

"And you're dangerous," she went on as if to herself. "Bachman isn't anything compared to you."

The mention of the brain-damaged patient at the clinic was too much for Henry, who stood up straight. "It's nothing like that!" The puppy's vitality made him brave, and he faced his mother without feeling the need to appease her.

"It's disgusting—*disgusting!*" She reached for the flimsy banister and almost had it when she lost her footing, tumbling down the stairs to the concrete. Henry could hear her bones break, and saw that she was still breathing though her eyes were glazed and there was blood around her head.

"Mom!" Henry shouted, and hurried toward her.

She was trying to talk, but failing. Only her hands fluttered a bit, but there was no control to the movement. Henry knelt beside her, helplessness washing through him in a debilitating tide. Her eyelids flickered but then they stopped; she was still breathing a little.

"Oh, oh, Mom!" Henry started to cry, but then he sighed as he realized what he would have to do. He went back and found his pocketknife, hoping it would be up to the task ahead of him. She still had life in her, and that life would endure in him; it would cancel her dying—for she had to be dying—if he could get some of her into him before her heart gave out. He couldn't do anything else to save her. "It's for the best, Mom. Let me take your life into me. You'll see: it'll make us both strong." He sliced at her arm; the limb flopped once, like a beached fish, and he continued to cut until he had a strip of skin and muscle. He began to chew on it, finding it salty and a bit stringy at first. The wonderful energy began to well in him, making him light-headed. There was blood everywhere, and he was afraid she would bleed to death before he could take all her life into him. "Hey, Mom. You're the best!" The puppy was nothing compared to his mother. He didn't know how much more he could eat, there was such vitality in his mother's body, and it filled him as nothing ever had before. He continued to eat as the life ran out of her, and left her an empty corpse.

By the time Henry had packed his mother's body into a large plastic trash bag, he was already making plans, anticipating the hour when Margaret Lynne would be home. She was so full of life, he thought, and it would sustain him much longer than poor, exhausted Mom would do. School was out tomorrow, and no one would miss Margaret Lynne—they'd think she was with their father. He began to hum as he neatened up the basement, contemplating the hour when Margaret Lynne would arrive and he could once again embrace life to its fullest.

About *Renfield's Syndrome*

There really is such a condition: the compulsion to eat bugs, small animals, and other creatures in the belief that their lives will strengthen the devourer. I wanted to see how far I could push it.

Become So Shining That We Cease to Be

When Eric first moved into the flat above Fanchon, she considered him nothing more than a noisy intruder. He played music every hour of the day and night, he spent the greater part of his afternoons doing something—she could only imagine what—that made her living room sound like the inside of a drum, and he was surly to her on those rare occasions when they actually met. She was too daunted to approach him.

"He's driving me crazy!" she complained to her old friend Naomi at the end of an especially loud two hours. "He's the most obnoxious creep Peterson's ever let into this building, and that includes the idiot with the saxophone. This guy's never quiet."

"Have you told Peterson?" asked Naomi in her most reasonable and irritating tone, the one she reserved for undergrads. "Haven't any of the other neighbors complained?"

"Once, I called him once, but so what? All he did was say he'd talk to him, and what good will that do?" She sighed. "Listen, I'd invite you over for a drink tonight, but I don't know what the place is going to sound like."

"I'll meet you somewhere," Naomi suggested much too promptly for Fanchon's current mood. "What about the Gryphon? Say ten, fifteen minutes?"

Fanchon knew she could not afford the time, the money, or the calories, but she liked the restaurant tucked into the side of a multishop building; she let herself be persuaded, assuaging her guilt with the promise that she would not touch the smorgasbord offered at five in the afternoon—the salmon paté on black bread had been her undoing more than once. "All right. The Gryphon. Four-thirty."

"And tell that bastard he'll have the place to himself for an hour or so, and to get it out of his system while you're gone." Naomi didn't sound as sympathetic as Fanchon would have liked, but her humor was welcome.

"I hardly ever see him, let alone speak."

"Small wonder, but . . . See you in a bit." Naomi hung up.

Since it was sunny, Fanchon decided to walk in spite of the nip in the air. She pulled on a bulky sweater over her silk shirt and changed into low-heeled shoes. She examined her grey slacks in the mirror, thinking that she really ought to take them to the cleaners. Above her, sound rained down, engulfing as a storm at sea. She made a rude gesture to the ceiling as she picked up her purse and went out the door, taking care to lock the deadbolt. It was senseless to take chances.

Naomi was waiting for her, leaning back in one of the comfortable, caterpillar-shaped love seats away from the window. "You made good time," she called out, waving so Fanchon could locate her.

"You're looking very smart," said Fanchon as she sat down opposite Naomi.

Naomi brushed the lapel of her cobalt-blue wool suit. "It's supposed to be impressive. I like it. I never used to wear blue." In her right hand she held a very small glass of something clear. "How's the noise front?"

"You heard it, didn't you?" Fanchon asked.

"Not over the phone," said Naomi. "Just a kind of rattle. It didn't seem very bad. But that's phones for you."

"That's more or less what Peterson said when I called

him." Fanchon leaned back and tucked her purse into the curve of the chair.

"You ought to talk to him again, get him to understand what's happening. You ought to insist he come over and listen for himself. He's the landlord. He's responsible for keeping the building in good order, isn't he? The Rent Board could probably make him put in better insulation or—" She made a sweeping swipe with her arm.

A waitress appeared behind the love seat. "Want another aquavit?"

"Sure," said Naomi, glancing at Fanchon. "You?"

"Coffee," said Fanchon. Then forgot her stern resolution. "And a small brandy, in a snifter."

The waitress nodded and went away.

"So how's everything with you?" Naomi asked. "Other than the neighbor, I mean? Any luck with the class load, or are you still stuck with that eight A.M. thing? I forget what it's called."

"Working Women of the Nineteenth Century," said Fanchon. "I've got it and eleven sleepy sophomores." She looked around. "When I set this up, I thought doing all my teaching in the morning would leave me lots of time for research, but it isn't working out, and not just because of the noise."

"Does it really go on all the time? Nighttime, too?" The aquavit was almost gone.

"Day, night. Afternoons are probably the worst, but it happens any time. Loud heavy metal banging and noise." She saw the waitress returning and dug out her purse.

"Three dollars for the brandy, one-fifty for the coffee. Three-fifty for the aquavit." She took the offered money and made change. "If you want refills, try to order in the next fifteen minutes, okay? We get swamped after five."

Fanchon made a point of giving the waitress a two-dollar tip. Then she looked at Naomi. "How about your schedule?"

"Busy, busy, busy. We're seeing more faculty—not the top guys, they have their own shrinks—but midlevel. I had a mathematician in the other day, in a real state. He's so worried about ozone he can't sleep."

"What do you think is causing it?" Fanchon asked, thinking she wasn't being fair to impose on her friend when so many other demands were being made of her.

"I don't know," said Naomi, taking her second glass of aquavit. "There is a hole in the ozone, and it probably will get bigger, and that will cause problems. He's right about that. I can't say anything to dismiss his fear. Some of the others are upset about the world economy, the air quality, the crowding. They're all real things." She took a long sip. "I probably shouldn't drink this stuff, but it's good."

Fanchon picked up the small brandy snifter and held it between her palms, warming it. "Is it any worse than pills?"

"Depends on whom you're talking to," said Naomi. "Well, you're the historian. What compares to our ecological worries?"

"People are always afraid of catastrophe. If it isn't the ozone layer, it's plague or famine. If it isn't that, there are barbarians or the Inquisition or Lady Wu." She lifted the snifter and let the brandy fire her tongue.

"But what in the past has had the potential to obliterate the whole planet? Aside from nuclear war. That was what I heard five years ago." She looked away toward the frosted windows and the autumn afternoon beyond. "You ever stop to think how any people in this town are in the destruction business? The guys in math and physics are calculating the end of the world every day. They come to me with horrible things on their minds, and they can't talk about them. I tell you, Fanchon, there are times I think it's easier to go crazy."

"Better than become impervious to it all, I guess," said Fanchon.

"I guess," echoed Naomi. She glanced at the door as a group of men came in. "Ah, the sociologists have arrived."

"Is that good?" asked Fanchon, noticing how animated Naomi had become.

"Well, Bill's with them." Her blush was very out of character and Fanchon could not resist mentioning it.

"What's special about Bill?" Now she felt like an intruder, a duenna at an assignation.

"I'll let you know when I'm sure." She waved. "There he is: tall, moustache, tweed jacket, jeans."

"Well, that describes most of them," said Fanchon, taking the rest of her brandy in a single gulp.

"Red-brown hair going grey. It looks a little like cinnamon and sugar on toast." Her laughter was self-conscious. She snuggled more deeply into the love seat. "He's spotted me. I'll introduce you."

"Thanks," said Fanchon, not at all certain what she meant. "I hope things work out the way you want."

"Yeah." Naomi laughed uncertainly. "It's not always easy to figure out what that is, you know?"

"Oh, yeah," said Fanchon. "If you ever learn the trick, you teach it to me."

Naomi drained her aquavit. "Well, that's my limit." She frowned. "You want another?"

Ordinarily Fanchon would have refused, but this time she decided she might as well have another. Perhaps more brandy and coffee would warm her up, for she was still very chilly. "Sure. Why not." Impulsively she reached for her purse. "I'll buy. We'll celebrate something—things working out for you, me getting some peace and quiet—something."

"You don't have to," said Naomi.

"Let me," said Fanchon.

Naomi considered it and accepted with a quick nod. "God, it is a world of despair sometimes, isn't it?"

"General malaise?" Fanchon suggested. "It comes with fall, or the new semester, or taking chances with Bill?"

"It's worse than that, I think," Naomi said, gesturing to the waitress for the same again. "It's getting so that there's very few reasons to feel good about who you are and what you do. And that's not midlife crisis talking, it's a very scared psychologist."

Fanchon sat still, staring at her empty snifter and half-full coffee cup. "I don't have any answers. It's all I can do to try to explain to my students why Victorian women were so savagely exploited by employers. The present and the future are beyond me."

The waitress brought their drinks. "The smorgasbord is out." It was part of the same pitch she delivered at this time every evening. "Five-fifty for all you want."

"Thanks," said Naomi as Fanchon handed the waitress a ten-dollar bill. "We'll get something in a couple of minutes." She straightened up. "So. What are you going to do about that neighbor of yours?"

"I suppose I'll have to talk to Peterson again. But to tell you the truth, I wish it would just go away. The noise." She sipped her coffee and found it too hot. "I don't want it to come down to one of us moving. I'm not prepared to move, and I've got a pretty good idea that the guy doesn't want to move, either. He just got here."

"Maybe if you approached the neighbor again, talked to him about the problem as a way not to go to the landlord, maybe he'd be more cooperative."

"Are you practicing shrinkery on me?" Fanchon asked, doing her best to avoid the discussion completely.

"Habit," said Naomi. She looked up as a tall, mustached man approached her. "Oh, shit. My hair's a mess."

"You look fine," said Fanchon in the same tone she used with her older sister when she claimed to be poorly groomed.

The man reached down, putting his hand on Naomi's shoulder. "I don't want to interrupt, but I've got a table reserved for us in twenty minutes." He smiled vaguely in Fanchon's direction. "Excuse the interruption."

"No problem," said Fanchon. "I'm not staying long."

Naomi beamed at him. "Twenty minutes is fine." She patted his hand before he removed it and slipped away. "Well, what do you think?"

"Seems pleasant enough. But ten seconds probably isn't long enough for good judgment."

"Thanks a bunch. You're supposed to be bolstering me up," Naomi protested.

"Hey, with my track record, I'm the last person you ought to be asking for bolstering. Two failed live-ins in eight years isn't a recommendation." Fanchon drank her coffee quickly. Then she tossed off the brandy, feeling its jolt with certain pleasure. "It's getting pretty dark. I better head for home." She picked up her purse. "I really hope it turns out okay for you, Naomi." She almost meant it.

"So do I," said Naomi. "But what about upstairs?"

"I guess I'll try your way—I'll talk to him. It can't hurt. If that doesn't work, I suppose I'll have to call Peterson." She smiled crookedly. "I'll call you."

"Good," said Naomi, her attention already on Bill. It was colder and Fanchon realized her sweater wasn't enough to keep her warm. She hugged her arms across her chest and walked faster.

Evenings were always the hardest for her, the time when the noise was more intrusive. It made her feel isolated, empty. "Maybe I should get a dog," she said aloud. She had got into the habit of talking to herself in the last two years, and occasionally it troubled her. "Peterson doesn't allow pets." Maybe she would get a tank of fish. She doubted the landlord would object to fish. The house seemed fairly silent as she approached it, but as soon as she went in through the kitchen door, the steady, thumping, screeching wail shuddered down the walls from above. Fanchon gripped the edge of the sink and gave up on eating dinner. She hated scenes. Angry voices made her stomach hurt.

She went out the rear door and climbed to the upper flat. "Hey!" she shouted, pounding on the door. There was the sound of banging pots in the kitchen. "Hey! In there!"

Loud, hurried footsteps sounded and a moment later the door was jerked open. "What is it?" her upstairs neighbor demanded.

Now that they were face-to-face, it was difficult for Fanchon to speak. "I . . . I have to talk to you. It's about the music you play."

"Again?" He folded his arms. "I had a call from the landlord about it. I said I'd turn it down and I did."

"Turned it down?" Fanchon forced herself to be calm. "Look, I'm sorry to disturb you this way, but it doesn't sound like you've turned it down to me. I can't get any work done because of the racket. I can't sleep. I don't know what kind of sound system you have, but it's—"

Her neighbor scowled at her. "What are you talking about? You're the one with the system that takes the roof off." He sizzled with resentment. "You aren't the only one with work to do."

"Mister . . ." Fanchon began, forgetting his name.

85

"Muir, Doctor, actually," he corrected her. "Like the woods. No relation."

"Okay. Dr. Muir. It might not seem like a lot of noise to you, but maybe the floor does something. In my flat, it's really awful."

Eric Muir rubbed his chin. "What about your system?"

"I hardly ever play it. Most of what I have is Mozart and Bach. I don't have any modern music. You and that heavy metal—"

"You're kidding, right?" He favored her with a tight, uncordial smile. "You don't expect me to believe all you ever listen to is *Eine Kleine Nacht Musik*, do you?"

"Well, not all. But I don't play rock, not any kind of rock." She screwed up her courage. "Maybe you ought to come down right now and listen to what it sounds like."

"Now? I don't have the system on right now." He braced one arm across the door. "But you tell me you have noise?"

Fanchon stared at him. He was either the most accomplished liar she had ever met, or he had not been paying attention.

"Come down and listen," she said at last. Then she turned on her heel and started down the wooden stairs, hoping he would be curious enough to follow her.

As they stepped into her kitchen the sound rose up around them, battering them invisibly. Fanchon winced as she held the door for Eric, then put her hands on her hips, watching him.

"This is incredible." He had to shout to be heard. "Worse than I've had it."

"My system's off. Go into the front room and look," Fanchon yelled back. She pointed down the hall, although this was necessary since the floor plan of both flats was the same.

He lifted a skeptical eyebrow, but did as she told him. When he returned a few minutes later, he was mollified. He started to speak, then motioned her to join him on the back steps. As soon as the door was closed, he said, "God, that's terrible."

"It's not quite so loud most of the time," she admitted, wanting to turn him from her side now that he appeared to be on it. "Whatever is doing it, please, you can understand why I need it stopped. I really can't ignore it."

"How long does it go on?" he asked. "A couple of hours or what?"

"That's about all it doesn't go on." She heard the exhaustion in her voice and wondered if he did, too. "Sometimes at night it's worse."

"All night?" He didn't wait for an answer. "I never play my system after ten, and I keep the TV down after then."

"The TV doesn't bother me," she said quickly. "It's just that awful music."

"Well, I don't play the music," he said firmly. "And I think if someone else in the building next door were making so much noise, I'd hear it upstairs, and so would the Dovers downstairs. Sometimes I do hear . . . but it isn't your system, and it's nothing like the noise you have." He stared hard at the back door of her flat. "This makes me very curious."

"Curious?" she repeated. "How can it?"

"You're not a theoretical physicist, are you? I am." His expression just missed being smug. "There's got to be a reason why this happens. And there's got to be a reason why it's loudest in your flat. How long has it been going on?"

"Since shortly after you moved in, maybe three weeks now. I thought you'd bought new speakers." She did her best not to sound as irritated as she felt. "I only complained when it had been over a week."

"I can't blame you, not with that going on." He opened the door and sound rushed out like a tidal bore.

"What can you do about it?" She hated asking the question, and dreaded the answer.

"I don't know. I don't know what I'm up against." He listened for a moment. "It's hard to hear if there are any words to it, or just some kind of howling. I'll want to bring a tape recorder down and hook it up, if you don't mind."

"Fine with me," she said wearily. "I tried it once, but all I got was static."

"Probably overloaded," Eric said. "I'll check this out with acoustics first, so we can make sure we get it all on tape. We'll be improvising, but there should be an answer somewhere." He smiled once. "I'm glad you told me about this."

"I wish I didn't have to," she responded at once. "I hope you do something. I can't wait around forever, waiting for a lull in the storm."

He chuckled because it was expected of him. "I'd feel the same in your position." With the suggestion of a wave he left her on the back porch and climbed up to his flat.

Fanchon had a loud evening; by ten she was seriously considering breaking her lease without notice. Sacrificing the various deposits seemed like a small price to pay for sleeping through the night. She set aside her tables of salaries of domestic servants in London in 1870–1880 and turned on her television, hoping to find a late, late movie to distract her. The pounding on her door at last broke through the relentless moaning of the walls.

"What is it?" she shouted as she fumbled her way to the back door. It was early morning, the sun not strong enough to break through the haze.

Eric Muir held out a tape recorder as she pulled the door open.

"Sorry to stop by at this hour, but I thought you'd want this set up as soon as possible." He strode into her kitchen without invitation. "Where's the noise the worst? I want to put this as near the epicenter as possible."

"In the front. The main room or the bedroom, it's all about the same." She rubbed her fingers through her hair.

"There's a sound-activated switch on it, and it's an extended reel of tape. It'll pick up sound for six hours." He went about his self-imposed task, ignoring her as he worked.

"Some coffee?" She had to bellow it twice before he refused.

"It's all ready to go," he told her a little later as she sat in the kitchen, unable to eat the light breakfast she had made for herself. "It ought to pick up all fluctuations pretty well. That thumping part must be the hardest to take."

"It's pretty bad," she agreed.

"There's half a dozen guys in the department who're interested in what's going on here. We'll probably come up with some kind of answer in a day or two."

A spattering kind of rattle joined the twanging beat. Fanchon winced. "Any idea what it is?"

"Perturbed spirits?" Eric ventured enthusiastically. "Demon CBers? Dish antenna misfocus? Underground water carrying sounds through the plumbing? A misfunction of a cable? They're all possibilities."

"How delightful." Fanchon got up from the table. "What am I supposed to do while you figure it out?"

"You might want to find somewhere to stay while I work on this," he said.

"Any recommendations?" she inquired, knowing already that her sister lived too far away and her stepfather preferred she keep her visits to a minimum.

89

"Call a friend. You must know someone who can let you have a spare room for a few days." He was unconcerned. "Leave me a number where I can reach you."

That night the noise was endless, a crooning, moaning, wordless scream over steady banging and deep sobs. Fanchon went to bed at two, trying to recall everything she had read about sleep deprivation and hallucinations. It was disappointing to see the windows lighten with approaching dawn. She dragged herself into the bathroom and dressed for running, selecting her warmest sweats against the gelid fog.

By the time she got back, the sound was less oppressive. While Fanchon showered and dressed, the noise was no more distressing than recess in a schoolyard might be. She gathered her materials and hiked to campus, doing her best to convince herself that in a day or so her ordeal would be over.

The plight of working-class women a century ago seemed as remote as the extinction of the dinosaurs. She could not concentrate on her lecture, and when she opened the class to questions, she gave arbitrary answers that left her students more puzzled than before.

When she got back to her flat she found Eric Muir waiting for her. "How was last night?"

"Terrible. What about you?"

"Bearable but not pleasant. If you don't mind, I want to change tapes." He let her open the door, then hesitated as a series of deep, clashing chords shook her entry hall. "Nothing that bad, certainly."

"Want to trade flats?" she inquired weakly.

"No," he answered. He checked the microphone to be certain it was functioning properly, then switched one cassette for another. "I'll talk to you later."

The noise was not as ferocious as it had been, but Fanchon could hardly bear it. She felt as if her skin had been made tender by the noise. When four aspirin made no dent in her headache, she picked up the phone and did what she had vowed not to do.

"Hello?" she said when Naomi answered the phone.

"What's the matter?" Naomi asked, her tone distant.

"It's Fanchon. I wondered if I could sleep on your couch a couple of nights?"

"Your neighbor's being a prick about the music?"

"It's not him. At least, it doesn't seem to be. He wants to check it out for me." She let her breath out slowly, hearing Naomi's hesitation.

"Does he have to do it now?" Naomi asked.

"Well, something has to be done, and he's the only person who's interested in finding out what it is." She wanted to bite her tongue.

"You mean you don't know if he's doing it, after all? That sounds a little ooo-eeee-ooooo-eeeee to me. Maybe we'd better send over some of those flakes from the parapsych division to have a look around." She tried to laugh. "They really like poltergeists, and this one sure has the polter part down."

"Naomi, please," said Fanchon, doing her best not to beg.

"Oh, Fanchon, I don't want to let you down. I know I'm being a pain about this but, it's just that . . . well, the way things are right now with Bill and me, it would be . . . touchy to have someone else in the house. You know how it is. Maybe Gail or Phyllis would have room if you asked them." She paused. "Any other time, I'd love to have you here. I don't like to say no, but . . . Fanchon, it's important to me not to fuck this up. I'm sorry."

Fanchon sighed. "Never mind. I'll buy some earplugs."

"Call Phyllis," Naomi urged her again.

"Phyllis doesn't like history, and we're not close enough to make up for that." What was the point in feeling sorry for herself, she wondered. It wouldn't do her any good.

"Then take a couple days off. Go somewhere. Tell Bassinton that you have a family emergency, and get away." Now that she was off the hook, Naomi was doing her best to provide an alternative. "What about your sister?"

"No chance there. She's moving to Boston next month. And I've got two papers assigned in my classes. I can't miss them. The students are depending on them for a third of their grades." She stared at the window, seeing the plants growing on the far side of it. "I'll call you later, okay?"

"Go to a hotel," said Naomi, determined to make some contribution. "There's places around here that don't cost an arm and a leg, and they aren't awful. What about that place down from campus that does bed and breakfast, the old Victorian place? This time of year they must have a lot of space. And it's a great building, all that gingerbread. And quiet room service, too, so they tell me." This last was embarrassed.

"Yeah," said Fanchon. "Well, thanks anyway." She was ready to hang up; there was nothing else to say.

"Give me a call when you decide what you're going to do, Fanchon, will you? We can get together for coffee or lunch or . . . we can talk over everything. Okay?"

"Sure," said Fanchon, hanging up. So she was trapped in the house, and there was nothing she could do to change it. No matter where she went, the road would bring her back here.

She found an excuse to go back to campus for a good part of the day and into the evening. So much research, so many appointments with students—it took time, and time was what she wanted to have away from her flat. She hated to think of Eric as an insensitive clod, but she could not avoid such conclusion, not after everything that had happened to her. He wanted more statistics and he didn't much care where they came from, except downstairs was convenient. It was easier to resent Muir than to think about what might be happening to her. There was too much mystery, too much of the unknown for her to dismiss it as a freak or an accident. Somehow that made the whole thing worse.

By the time she had been back in her flat for twenty minutes, Eric Muir was knocking on her back door. Reluctantly she let him in, not bothering to apologize for her bathrobe and ratty slippers.

"It's been worse," she said, indicating the low level of throbbing that echoed through her rooms.

"You could put it that way," said Muir, leaning back against the old-fashioned kitchen counter and crossing his arms. "We listened to the tape today."

"And?" She had started to make some soup, and offered him a bowl with a gesture instead of words. She was pretty sure she could keep soup down.

"Let's go out for some fish instead. I'll give you fifteen minutes to change. There's a lot to tell you. This whole thing is damned weird. And that's a rare admission for a theoretical physicist to make." He looked at her more closely, as if seeing her for the first time. "You're exhausted, aren't you?"

"I suppose so. I haven't been sleeping much." She might have laughed if he hadn't been so worried.

"It's more than that. You're . . . drained. Get changed. Find your coat. It's starting to rain and you shouldn't get wet." He did not wait for her to refuse but turned off the fire under her pan of soup. "You can eat that tomorrow, if you want to."

"I can't afford another dinner out," she warned him, recalling the twelve dollars in her purse that was supposed to last her until Friday. "I don't have enough for anything fancy."

"Then I'll buy. I think I owe you something. You've been through a lot, and you haven't anything but circles under your eyes to show for it." He rested his hands on the back of one of her two kitchen chairs.

"Yeah," she said, trying to remember the last time she had had dinner out with a man for any reason other than professional.

"Good."

She changed and ran a brush through her hair. As an afterthought she put a little lipstick on, then took her four-year-old trenchcoat from the closet before joining him at the front door.

They drove in silence, and when they reached the restaurant they were told that it would be a twenty-minute wait until they could be seated. Eric accepted this with a shrug and left his name with the hostess. "No smoking."

"It might be a little longer for that," the hostess warned.

Muir found a table as far from the large-screen TV as possible and held the chair for Fanchon. "I've spent the afternoon going over the tape we made in your flat. It's almost completely silent," he said as they were waiting for his name to be called. "There are sounds of you moving about the flat, talking to yourself occasionally, and muttering about the noise, but for the rest, there's a few whispers and something that could be the sound of traffic in the street. We took more than four hours to go over the tape. We can make out a little rhythmic pattern, but that's all there is."

"Oh, come off it," she said, not willing to fight about it.

He looked directly at her, as if eye contact would convince her where explanations would not. "I'm telling you the truth, Fanchon. I listened to it first, and we checked out the equipment, to make sure it was working right. It's delicate and sophisticated, and if there were any sounds there that were real sounds, that machine would pick them up. I guarantee it. No question. It didn't fail. We checked it for that."

"Then there has to be noise on the tape," Fanchon said reasonably. "Lots of noise."

"As I've already told you, only a few whispers and the hint of rhythm. Nothing else. Nothing like what I heard in your flat. I know what I heard in your flat, and it isn't on the tape."

"Oh." She realized her appetite was gone. No matter what they were serving tonight, she could not eat it.

"I don't know what's going on there yet, but I want to put my graduate students on it." He looked over at her. "I know it isn't convenient for you, but all that noise has to be less convenient than a couple of students monitoring the noise. Can't you stick out a couple days more?"

"And then it'll be over?" she said wistfully.

"I don't know. I damn well hope so. You don't want any more of the noise, and neither do I. But we'll have a better understanding about it than we have now, that much is certain." He paused as the waitress approached. "I think our table is ready."

"Fine," she said, rising and following him so automatically that she might have been mechanical instead of human. "Lead the way."

"Come on," said Eric. "Let's get some food into you."

She couldn't eat much at dinner, no matter how she tried. She was embarrassed that Eric had to pay when she wasn't able to eat anything. By the time he drove them back to the house, she was so tired that all she wanted was a chance to

95

sleep the clock around. Maybe, she thought as she opened her front door, I should give up and move out. Maybe I should call Peterson and tell him I can't deal with this any longer.

The noise pressed on her like thick blankets when she went to bed. All attempts at sleep were useless.

For three more days there was no news from Eric Muir. Fanchon saw him only once, and he had nothing to say to her then. She made herself go to her classes, did extra research to keep away from her flat, and tried to catch naps at her office when her partner was off doing other things. She wasn't certain if the noise were getting worse or if she were losing her ability to cope.

When she met Naomi for lunch, Naomi said that it was probably nerves, since she—Fanchon—had gone so long without real sleep. Going without sleep was an invitation to disaster. She wanted Fanchon to know that at any other time she would have taken her into her house. But Bill had just moved in, and there was less time for things outside their relationship.

Her own depression deepened as Fanchon once again wished Naomi the best of luck.

The next morning when she returned from running fifteen minutes early, she saw Eric Muir was waiting for her.

"We've been over the tapes and over them," he said without any greeting. "It's still a mystery, but we've been able to add a few more wrinkles to the mystery. That might or might not help you out." He indicated the stairs to his flat. "I've got some fresh coffee brewing."

"I ought to shower," said Fanchon, but followed him up the stairs.

"There really are some words in that noise, did you realize that?" he said when he offered her a white mug filled with hot coffee.

"Really?" She didn't care about the words, just the noise. She had nothing to contribute to his revelations.

"And they're recognizable with a little fiddling with the tape." He sat down opposite her. "They're from a song that was popular back in the early seventies, done by a local group called The Spectres. They never got very far, and apparently they broke up in seventy-four or -five. Their lead guitarist went to a better band, their main songwriter went to L.A. to write lyrics for commercials—they tell me he's been very successful—but the others just . . . disappeared."

"Okay." Fanchon tugged at her fleece pullover. "So they disappeared. What has that to do with the noise in my flat. If anything?" She thought about the many times she had used the present to make a bridge to the past, for she did it often in her classes. But what could a rock band have to do with a history instructor?

"I said disappeared," Eric repeated.

"College towns are like that," Fanchon reminded him. "Take any five-year period and about a third of the town will change."

Eric ignored her. "And no one knows what became of them. We called the two we could locate and they haven't heard from the other four since they broke up, and that was years and years ago. They don't know what became of the others."

"What's all this leading up to?" Fanchon asked, drinking the coffee he offered her. It was strong and bitter; she found it very satisfying.

"People disappear. They disappear all the time and no one really notices, especially in a place like this. Students move and transfer and drop out. No one expects them to stick around, so they don't pay much attention when they go." He held up his hand. "Bear with me."

"Go ahead." There was some noise in his flat, but not very much, nothing like what she endured downstairs.

He gathered his thoughts. "People disappear. We always assume they go somewhere else. And in a certain sense, they do. Everyone goes somewhere; into a grave or . . . away."

"Is this physics or mysticism?" Fanchon asked, looking past him to the window where tree branches waved.

"It's something between the two, probably," he answered without a trace of embarrassment. "Consider this: a person disappears sideways, to use a metaphor. This person goes somewhere else not spatially but dimensionally."

"More spooks," said Fanchon. "Naomi suggested poltergeists."

Eric would not be distracted. "And when there is someone who is also slipping away—"

"Now, wait a minute—"

He went on. "When someone is slipping toward the same dimension, they become sensitized, like an electric eye, and . . . and that person, it's as if they're being drawn to that sideways place. Do you follow this at all?"

"Not really, no," she lied.

"You're triggering this because—"

"You mean it's my fault? I'm going sideways and all this noise is the result?" She put down the mug. "A few unsuccessful rock musicians disappear fifteen or twenty years ago, and this noise is the result? And it's my fault?" She started to leave, but he took hold of her wrist.

"You live alone, you do most of your work alone. You have no close friends here, and your family is scattered. That makes you—"

"Makes me what, Dr. Muir?" She pulled away from him; she slammed the door as she left.

"Fanchon!"

98

Outside, she paused long enough to shout, "Just do something about the noise, that's all!"

Back in her own flat, she listened for the words that Eric claimed could be heard in the sounds, but she could make no sense of it. She went to the bathroom and filled the tub, hoping that a warm soak would help her to sleep. She felt sweaty and sticky, and solid as granite. She wanted to be free of Eric Muir's absurd notions. "He's ridiculous," she remarked to the walls as she peeled off her clothes. It would serve him right if she used all the hot water and he had to shave with cold. "He doesn't want to tell Peterson to fix the wiring, or whatever's wrong. He's making it up." She stared into the full-length mirror on the back of the bathroom door, examining herself. In the cream-colored, steamy bathroom, her pallor made her appear transparent.

She leaned back in the bath, letting the pulse of the music blend with the movement of the water and the blood in her veins. It wasn't as bad as she used to think, that music. Once you accepted it, it could be fairly pleasant. The music wasn't as disruptive as Muir's ludicrous theories. Her life, she thought, was not so empty as Muir had made it sound. It was not awful or painful or degrading; it was not pleasant or fulfilling or challenging. It was just . . . ordinary, she supposed.

Perhaps it was nothing, and she was nothing, too. She laughed, but could not hear herself laugh over the welling music.

"Do you hear something?" Sandra asked Paul as they stopped at the top of the stairs, a bookcase balanced between them.

"Just my joints cracking," said Paul. *"Where do you think this ought to go?"*

"In the living room, I guess," she said.

"It'd probably make more sense to put it in the hall," he said.

She nodded at once. "Sure. In the hall's fine." She got into position to drag the bookcase a few feet further.

"We were lucky to get this place on such short notice," he said for the third time that morning.

"Great," she said. "We didn't have a lot of time to pick and choose."

"All the more reason to be glad this place was available." He shoved at the bookcase, cursing.

"The upstairs neighbor said it was haunted." She hadn't intended to tell him that, but she was getting tired of his insistence at their luck.

"Hey, he's a theoretical physicist. Peterson told me about him. You know what those guys are like. Give me engineering any day." He stood up. "Why don't you bring up a couple of boxes? I can manage the sofa cushions on my own."

"Fine," she said, glad to escape. As she came back up the stairs, she paused once more. "He said—the man upstairs—that she just disappeared. The woman who used to live here."

"Come on, Sandra," Paul protested. "What's in the box?"

"Kitchen things," she said, squeezing by him. As she passed the bathroom door, she paused again. "Do you hear something?"

"Not again." He rounded on her. "This is an old house. It makes noise. We're not used to it. Okay?"

She continued to listen, a distant, distracted frown blighting her face. "I could swear I heard . . ."

"There's a lot to unload," he warned her.

She made herself go to the kitchen and put the box down. She stood listening a few minutes.

"Sandra!"

She shook her head. "Never mind," she said. "It's nothing."

About *Become So Shining That We Cease to Be*

This story probably developed out of visiting a flat here in Berkeley, which, owing to some engineering oddities, magnified sounds from the apartment next door. The couple living there joked about their "haunted house" and it eventually—a decade later—mutated into this flat. The characters in the story came from wherever it is characters come from.

ECHOES

"They were much wiser than we are, you know." She stood behind the gift counter at the Dry Plains International Airport, a woman with shag-cut, grey-struck hair and enormous light-blue eyes behind small wire-rimmed glasses; she looked as if she had been stuck in 1967 for the last quarter century.

"They?" said Philips absentmindedly as he paid for the two magazines of local interest; one boasted a long section on the delights of Mexico, just over the Texas border, the other had a gorgeous series of photographs of restored turn-of-the-century houses in Dallas and Houston. He wanted to keep his mind off Dry Plains—the place gave him the creeps, always had.

"The Comanches. They used to live around here, long ago. Sometimes, at night like this, I think they're still here. They were a very spiritual people." She beamed at him, handing him his change with an expression that said, "Have a nice day," though it was now twenty minutes after two on a windy autumn night.

"I don't know about Comanches," Philips said, his manner suggesting that ignorance was just fine with him.

She smiled and indicated some of the Indian necklaces in the display case—Hopi and Navajo, for the most part, and with very unspiritual price-tags—with a gentle sigh of approval. "The Native Americans understand nature so much better than we do. They're so empathetic, so much in tune with the earth. It's part of their way of life, not like us

102

at all. They respect everything in nature. You can see it in everything they do."

"Thanks," said Philips, moving a short distance from the counter so as to end her version of small-talk. He paid no attention to her, choosing to put his mind on the superior photographs of the magazines. After a little while he wandered out toward the lobby area for private and corporate airplanes, half-reading the first of the magazines and trying to decide if he ought to call the Trager International office in Dallas before they called him. Just because it was the middle of the night didn't mean that Trager wasn't barreling along. He decided that he ought to get another cup of coffee so he wouldn't be tempted to doze.

He had taken a seat on one of the high stools at the only snack counter open at that hour and had just been handed a large, biodegradable cup filled with lukewarm coffee when he heard his name on the PA system. He picked up the carry-out cup and hurried toward the nearest courtesy phone, preparing to defend his decision to land here rather than at Dallas/Fort Worth. "Galen Phillips here," he said as he lifted the receiver.

"A call for you, sir," said a woman's voice with a faint Spanish accent. "I'll put you through."

"Thanks," he told her in order to be polite. He waited, wondering who would be on the other line.

"Philips!" boomed D. A. Landis, as if in the middle of the night he was ready to participate in a jousting tournament or emcee a banquet for a thousand people. "Good to talk to you this way."

Philips sighed. He had a strong distrust of the hearty, venal Landis who ran the Trager division in Chicago. "Good morning, D.A.," he said, trying to infuse a little good fellowship into his voice.

"I had a call from the maintenance people there about half an hour ago." He made every word portentous. "They told me that you had to be one lucky son of a bitch to bring our company jet down without any harm, considering the malfunction of the instruments. We ought to listen to you veteran pilots more often. Your hunch about the plane was right. If you'd tried to push on, you might have crashed; that's what the night supervisor just told me. We can't have that."

"I guess not," said Philips, his guts feeling suddenly hot, then cold.

"You experienced flyers, you've got instincts." He coughed once. "You better lay over there until the plane is fixed. They say it shouldn't be much more than two days. They can start work on it in the morning; their night crew is just a skeleton, a shift of five guys. They can't handle the trouble, and according to them it'll take a day at least to check it out. Hell, we can spare you from the roster that long. Besides, you're due for some ground time, aren't you?"

"Pretty much," said Philips.

"Too bad we don't have a corporate apartment there you can use—there's no reason for it—but find yourself a hotel and get a good room. Not the most expensive suite in the place, but we don't want you camping in a broom closet, either. Looks bad to the stockholders." He had a plummy chuckle that sounded like ripe fruit bursting. "Put it on your corporate account. We'll cover anything reasonable like car rentals and meals, providing you don't eat steak and lobster three times a day, or drive to Nevada."

"Thanks," said Philips, feeling a bit dazed by his good fortune and suspicious of it all at the same time.

"Use this as your long rest time. You're supposed to take

three days off at the end of the month. You might as well do them now." He sounded more hail-fellow-well-met with every word, and Philips distrusted that.

"Why now? I've got other flights logged." He did his best to sound mildly curious instead of worried.

Landis did not answer him. "Oh," he said as if it had just occurred to him, "would you mind sticking around the airport until the morning maintenance crew comes on? Stay with them while they go over the report on the plane? You were there when the trouble started and you know the right things to ask. They'll be able to give you a better picture about the repairs, and you can relay that to me when you get to the hotel."

Philips swallowed hard. He knew that the morning crew at this airport arrived at six, which would mean he would have to wait another three and a half hours to talk with them. He was glad now that he had bought the magazines. "Sure. No problem."

"That's terrific," said Landis. "That's just fine."

As reckless as it was, Philips could not keep himself from asking, "What about the Amsterdam flight? Who's going to cover for that?" He was scheduled to leave late tomorrow afternoon with a group of executives bound for a crucial meeting in The Netherlands.

"We'll find someone," Landis told him confidently. "We can probably bring Chapman back from vacation a day early."

"I could take a commercial flight up in the morning, after I get the report on the plane. I could be out of here by noon," Philips suggested. He did not want to admit that he hated this place and the thought of being here for more than a couple of hours made him edgy. "I'd have enough time for sleep and sufficient hours off to make the flight."

Again that high-calorie chuckle. "I wish more of our people had your dedication, Philips."

He wanted to say it wasn't dedication, it was dread, and a sense of being drawn here, as if the very place itself were reaching out to snare him. But such an admission could earn him a psychiatric evaluation and enforced retirement; he was close enough to that already. "You know me. I like to fly, and Amsterdam is a great place. I had some plans for the trip, that's all. I was hoping to get in a little . . . play."

Now the chuckle had a licentious spice in it. "I enjoy playing in Amsterdam myself. I can't blame you for wanting to go there. Maybe we can arrange for you to have a couple of extra days there when this is over." The offer was a sop and both men recognized it for what it was. "Let me know what the maintenance people tell you, and we'll figure out what to do next. How's that?"

"Great," said Philips, who thought it sucked.

"I'm relying on you," said Landis, and went on to assure Philips that he would be sure to credit him with saving the company's second-largest jet, and planned to inform the Board of Directors that there ought to be a bonus in the deal for him.

When Landis had finished finessing Philips, he hung up abruptly, leaving Philips to stare down the long, empty corridor toward the main part of the airport. From the air, he thought it looked a little like a lopsided galaxy, with four spiral arms stretching out from the center. Now he had the disquieting impression that he was at the edge of a whirlpool, turning and pulling, turning and pulling. He wanted to avoid the center as long as possible, for once there he would not escape. It was hard for him to shake off that irrational sensation as he went back to the snack counter to buy a couple of stale doughnuts.

106

The woman from the gift shop was there, getting a cup of herbal tea. "You're still here," she said in that lilting way that brought back memories of flower children. "Are you waiting for a connecting flight?"

"No," he said. "Worse luck."

If she noticed his terseness it made no difference to her. "At night like this, there aren't many flights coming in on this arm. It stays quiet here. Over there"—she cocked her head to the south where the international flights arrived— "there's things going on all the time. People leave at one in the morning and land at three. But here, we don't see much of that. They try to keep traffic to a minimum after nine." There was a faint, romantic smile on her face. "I used to work in the international shop, but they moved me over here a couple of years ago. It was exciting, seeing all those strange things in the shop, and meeting people from all over the world. Don't you think it's exciting to meet people from other countries? Isn't it wonderful to learn about them and the places they come from?"

"I guess," said Philips, who had no desire to talk.

She beamed at him and held out her long, slim hand, nails unpainted. "I'm Senta. It's a pleasure to meet you. I don't often get to talk to people, working the night shift. But most of the staff don't like working at night, even though it pays better."

Reluctantly he took her hand. "Galen Philips."

Her eyes brightened behind the granny glasses. "You fly for Trager, don't you?"

Since the badge on his jacket was embossed with the Trager logo—a sixteenth-century merchant ship called a hulk—he only nodded.

"I like the way Trager planes look," she said. "You can always spot them, with their wings and the tail painted red and the ship in black. It's very distinctive." Her expression changed, became distant. "When I first worked here, Braniff had jets painted neon orange and shocking pink and bright lime, colors like that. They were beautiful, like huge butterflies. I loved it. No one does that anymore."

"I remember them," said Philips, drawn by the memory. "The first time I saw one I thought I was hallucinating."

She laughed, sounding much younger than she looked. "So did I. I was still doing mushrooms then, so it made sense. Still, it was a relief to know that I wasn't just seeing things. Sometimes, around here at night, I worry about that." She glanced in the direction of the gift shop, then looked back at him. "I'm sorry. This is great, talking to you, but I've got to get back to work. There's nobody here, but I have to stay in the shop. We have rules. Things could happen. You know how it is."

Now that he had the opportunity to get away from her, Philips decided he would rather talk a little longer. "I'll come with you. I haven't anything to do until six, anyway, and if I read I'll probably doze."

She looked mildly surprised. "That would be nice," she said with curious formality. "My relief comes on at eight. But things pick up before then. The first of the commuter flights arrives just before six. The first is from Atlanta, and then the one from Chicago, and then two from New England—Boston and Hartford, I think, or maybe Providence—and then L.A., St. Louis, Seattle, Omaha, Atlanta again, Salt Lake, Albuquerque, Buffalo, San Francisco, and Cleveland, and that takes us almost to seven. I guess you'll be gone by then."

"You've memorized the schedule," said Philips, wondering if there was somewhere he could sit in the gift shop.

"After all the time I've worked here, it would be hard not

to. I know some of the regular passengers now. There's a man who comes in on the seven-ten flight from Denver. I've seen him twice a month every month except December ever since I've been working here. He told me he's a courier for some international outfit. He always dresses in expensive suits; he carries a briefcase handcuffed to his wrist. He buys the local paper, a couple packages of gum because he gave up smoking, and he says something about the weather. Every time. It's unreal. And one of the men on the L.A. flight makes the trip on the first Monday of every month. He's some kind of attorney, real flashy. He always comes in, picks up magazines and the paper. Another one, on the seven-forty-nine from Dulles, stops in to ask about traffic. He talks fast, in bursts. He's a kind of a flirt. He's the assistant to the Congressman in this district." Her color was heightened, like a girl boasting about her suitors and not a middle-aged woman discussing her regular customers. "They have news, sometimes, but not like over in the international arm. It's not as exciting here. Those people were real different."

"Because they're from far away?" Philips guessed.

"Oh, yes. They're out doing all kinds of things, things you can't imagine; they're seeing things." She gave him a winsome smile, the kind of smile that usually fades by the time a woman reaches thirty. "I used to like the trans-Pacific flights, because everyone was trying to figure out what day it was. No one has that trouble over here, except sometimes when we have real bad weather." It might have been a joke because the lines around her light-blue eyes crinkled.

"I suppose not," said Philips, who decided her conversation was a welcome distraction after all; it muted the gathering sense of disquiet that Dry Plains International roused in him.

"I did a little traveling when I was younger. I wanted to go to India, but I ended up getting six weeks in Spain and Portugal, right before I dropped out of college. I did two years, and my grades were good enough, but it didn't seem relevant to what was going on in the world. You know how it was, back then?" Her hands moved quickly and delicately, reminding Philips of small, industrious birds. While she talked she rearranged the jewelry display, shifting price tags and merchandise into an arrangement that drew more attention to the case. "I had friends who were killed in the Vietnam war, and one of my cousins was shot during a riot. He wasn't even part of it, he was just watching the news people set up their cameras, and bang. I didn't think that getting a degree in English Literature and then getting my teaching credentials made much sense. There had to be another way, you know?"

"And you ended up here, instead of teaching," said Philips, being careful to make this not seem to be critical of her.

"After about four years of just checking out the country, yes. There was a *feel* to this place. I felt I could live here because of the feel. I'd be in touch with something important." Her chuckle was self-deprecatory. "I know how that must sound to you, but—"

He interrupted her. "No. I agree. Dry Plains has something about it." That was as far as he was willing to go.

She rewarded him with another winsome smile. "You're real nice," she said with earnest sincerity. "It *does* have a feel, and I couldn't get away from it, you know? I tried a couple of times—I spent a year in New Orleans when my kids were little—but I came back here."

Philips was mildly startled to learn she had children. "How many . . . kids do you have?"

"Just one now," she said, with a trace of sadness. "My daughter. My son died of AIDS three years ago. He was twenty-two. He worked here with me for two summers when he was in high school. Doing loading and unloading in the back, stock work, that kind of stuff. He got injured in one of those freak accidents that . . . The paramedics got here right away but they had trouble stopping the bleeding. It turned out the transfusion they gave him was bad. It's funny, you know? We thought at the time it was saving his life." The lightness went out of her, and she struggled to recover it. "My daughter's twenty. She's in college in Oregon, where her father lives. She says she's going to get an engineering degree." Now her smile was puzzled; as if she could not imagine any child of hers wanting to be an engineer. "I thought she'd want to be an astronomer. As a kid she liked the stars so much. She knew where all the constellations were. She would sit out at night and watch the sky, making up stories about what she saw up there. Some of them were pretty far-out. Monsters and massacres. You know how kids love gore."

"Not really." Philips, who had lost touch with his ex-wife fifteen years ago, shook his head. "I don't have any kids." He could not imagine raising children anywhere near this place. The thought of what they might see in the sky around here made him wince. "Your kids grew up . . . ?"

"Mostly around here. I settled here just before Kirsten was born. Her father got a job at the local newspaper as a photographer, but it didn't work out between us." She looked a little sad and more nostalgic. "He left the area twenty years ago. He said the place was wrong for him, that it made him want to get violent, and he was a pacifist. When we had those bomb threats five years ago, he said I should get out of here, too. He said that there were too many dangerous people using airplanes—terrorists and crazy people. He's not a very open person."

"And you raised the kids?" said Philips. "Here?"

"Sure. He helped some, taking the kids during the summer and all, and sending money when he could. He got married about four years ago." She shook her head in remembered incredulity. "I never thought Bram would get married." She left the jewelry alone and turned to the shelves where a number of hardback gift books were for sale. As she rearranged the titles so that the ones dealing with Indians and Indian lore were most prominent, she went on, "Some friends of mine and I got a place out toward Santo Muerto—it's not far from here."

The name made Philips start. "Santo Muerto?"

"It's one of those little villages that's turning into a suburb, about a mile and a half from here. It used to be off on its own ten, twelve years ago. We ran a thirty-acre farm there for a couple years about ten years back; it's the richest soil in this part of Texas, and we wanted to use it right, at least at first." She felt evident pride at this. "We studied all the old ways, the way the Indians did it, planting the right kind of crops and raising them with all-natural fertilizers and like that. But we had some hard luck. It happens to farmers when they're not in tune with the earth, you know, and Kevin lost sight of that. He began using pesticides after the first two years because we had a lot of insect damage to our plants, and it kept getting worse. And something went wrong with the stuff he used. He got sick, and some of the people who ate our produce got sick. So we had to close the farm down and sell off half the land. Kevin's got cancer now. He's been in the hospital for the last five weeks."

"That's too bad; I'm sorry," said Philips, his heart thumping. This place is rotten, he thought, rotten to the core. And it pulls on me like an unholy magnet.

Senta looked up suddenly. "I've been prattling at you. I'm sorry." She gave him a direct, uncomplicated stare. "You're a pilot. That's got to be a lot more interesting than working at a gift counter at an airport."

Philips almost said, Not *this* airport, but managed to stifle the remark. "It's a job I'm good at," he said. "I've been doing it for what feels like forever."

"Have you always worked for Trager?" she asked, concentrating on his answer.

"Pretty much. I flew for TWA when I started out, but Trager made me a better offer after my second year, and I took it." He glanced toward the waiting area, and noticed that there was an indistinct figure at the far side of the cavernous space. The sight of that lone figure made him apprehensive.

She saw where he was looking, then showed him a reassuring smile. "It's just one of the airport staff. They have to check all the stations out before the airline people arrive."

"Oh," said Philips, with the unsettling feeling that this facile explanation was not entirely accurate.

"It's funny how the eyes play tricks on you," she went on, soothingly. "I thought I saw an Indian out there, late one night about six years ago. It was probably one of the security people checking out where the 747 crashed earlier in the day. It was because of the storm, they say. A terrible thing, you know? The storm knocked out all their instruments and they never realized how *close* to the ground they were as they came in. Almost everyone in the plane was killed, and two of the fire fighters too. I wasn't here when it happened, but I saw some of the wreckage, and it was on the news." She saw the revulsion in Philips's eyes. "Oh I'm sorry. I didn't think. You pilots probably don't like to hear about crashes, I guess."

"Don't things like that ever get to you?" Philips asked, suddenly appalled by her.

"Oh yes," she said. "If I'm not careful, any sad thing makes me lose my centering, you know? And I have to work hard to restore my balance, my proportion. I have to think of all the other people who die in senseless accidents and put that behind me before I can clear the negative things from my mind." She glanced in the direction of the shadowy figure again. "Sometimes, when I'm here alone at night, I use the time to meditate, to get in touch with my higher centers."

It struck Philips that there were few places in the world he would like less to meditate in than this airport, if he were into meditation. "I hope it helps," he said to let her know he was listening.

"Sometimes," she answered, and switched her attention to him again. "So I guess you don't live around here?"

"No," he said, adding silent thanks to himself.

"Where do you live?" she persisted, her bird-like hands now picking through the gum and candy, restoring order and improving the display.

He hesitated. "Not much of anywhere, really, except on Trager planes," he said. "The corporation rents apartments for their pilots in a dozen cities. Most of the time I stay in one of them. I'm registered to vote in San Diego and I carry a California driver's license. I get most of my mail through Trager's Chicago office. I get three weeks' vacation every year; usually I go deep-sea fishing." He admitted this apologetically, as if his way of life required it.

Senta's eyes were bright again. "That sounds like a wonderful way to live, just going anywhere in the world you want to."

"Not quite that," said Philips. "I go where Trager orders

me, and I go when they tell me. It's a pretty rootless—"

"But still, they're all over the world, aren't they?" She did not wait for his answer. "I bet you've been to India."

"A few times," he said, and did not add that the poverty of the people and the unfamiliarity of the culture bothered him. "To Calcutta and New Delhi. Trager has projects in both places."

"That's wonderful." Her hands were more animated. "Have you ever been to China?"

"Yes," he said, finding her fascination flattering and amusing. He had not thought of his life as adventurous in a long time.

"And Tibet? Or Katmandu?" She leaned forward for his answer.

"Neither; sorry." He hated to disappoint her. That sudden realization shook him and he watched her more closely. "I've been to Sri Lanka once, does that help?"

"I'll bet it was beautiful." She directed her gaze at him with such intensity that he thought she was trying to absorb his memories of the place with her eyes.

"It was very hot," he said. "I didn't see much of the place; I was taking a couple of company vice presidents to a meeting there, that's all."

"I met someone from Sri Lanka once, when I was working over in the international arm. That was before they moved the customs area, so I got to see more of the foreigners. Now all you find in that part of the terminal is returning Americans and people getting things at the duty-free shop before they leave." She braced her elbows on the counter and stared at him. "You've been everywhere, haven't you?"

He shrugged. "Mostly I've been in the cockpit of a plane," he said.

She clearly did not believe this. "But you get to see things, to watch the whole world."

"Sometimes," he admitted. "When there isn't too much cloud cover, or it isn't dark." Or when he was not approaching such godforsaken places as Dry Plains International Airport with the electrical system on the fritz and the controls sluggish as they were tonight when he landed, he added to himself.

The figure at the far side of the waiting area had vanished.

"You must have a copilot," she said suddenly.

"Yeah," he said, "and a navigator."

She looked around as if she expected to find them. "Aren't they with you?"

He sighed. "My copilot went into the city to get some sleep and my navigator's down at the medical station. He's been having stomach trouble." Poor Conrad had been bent nearly double when he got out of the plane, breathing in gasps because of the pain. "He thinks it's a bad case of turista. Maybe it's a bad case of flu." As he said this, he found it harder to believe than he had when they landed: Philips had seen lots of cases of turista over the years, but none as severe as the case Conrad had. It was this place, he thought, this damned airport.

"I hope it isn't anything worse," said Senta, picking up some of his anxiety. "We had an outbreak of food poisoning here last year. There were hundreds of people getting sick."

There were so few times that he had the luxury of unscheduled rest, thought Philips. Why did he have to be here when the opportunity struck? It didn't surprise him that there had been an outbreak of food poisoning here. He would not have been amazed to hear that the airport had anthrax, or bubonic plague. "What did you do?"

"We had to quarantine part of the airport, and some of

ECHOES

the planes that had left reported that their passengers were
sick. In fact the whole flight crew of one KAL came down
with it." She heaved a gentle sigh. "There was an investigation, but nothing was ever proven. Accidents like that
happen."

And they happen here more than any place he had ever
been, thought Philips. "Doesn't that ever worry you? A
place like this is so . . . unprotected. Someone could come
through with a deadly disease and the only way you'd know
would be when people start dying."

She did her best to look philosophical. "I don't like to let
that bother me. I mean, if you think about it, anything
might happen. Last week a guy lost control of his car on the
upper deck and it smashed into the rail and crashed onto
the road below. There was a big fire when the gas tank exploded. A couple of people said that he'd swerved to avoid
a man standing on the road, but . . ." She shrugged. "It
could have been that or a flat tire or anything. It was right
during rush hour, and I was late to work because of the
traffic. I didn't know what happened until I got here and
the afternoon girl told me." She lowered her eyes. "I hate it
when bad things happen. I just hate it."

Philips wanted to know why she worked here, of all
places, if that was how she felt, but he managed not to
speak his thoughts aloud. "I know what you mean."

Suddenly she looked at him, and there was a fanaticism
blazing in her faded eyes. "I want to be more like them, you
know? Like the Indians who lived here. They were good
people, and they . . . they were *better* than we are. If you go
out in the fields at night, in Santo Muerto, you can feel
them all around you, strong and . . . real. Sometimes they
seem more real than most of the people getting off planes.
You know?"

117

He dreaded to think that he did, and yet he could feel some of her yearning in himself; he recognized it with repugnance. "I've noticed something like that around here."

She moved as near as the counter between them would allow. "It used to frighten me. When I first got here, it scared me. I felt . . . out of my depth, you know? But not any more. Now I know how wonderful it is, to be near all the knowledge and the power."

Philips shook his head. "If you like it, I guess—" He stopped abruptly.

Senta went on as if she had not noticed he had left his thoughts incomplete. "I used to worry about all kinds of things, little things. But since I've learned how it was here, how they were wise enough to have something to die for, I've been . . . oh, I don't know. Maybe eager, or envious that they were so much more true to themselves than regular people." Her gesture took in the empty waiting area. "After my son died, for a while I couldn't stand this place. I blamed it. I thought that it had caused the trouble with the blood, that there was a plot or conspiracy or something. But it wasn't that, not really. It was that none of us were worthy yet."

A few times in Philips's career he had had conversations like this one, deep discussions with near-strangers about matters he would not discuss with anyone he saw regularly. It struck him that this was one of those conversations, and that in spite of the repellant aspect of the airport, this soft-voiced woman was drawing him toward her, as the tarmac drew his plane. "How could worth have anything to do with what happened to your boy?" He did not want to reveal his thoughts for fear of what the place would do with them, but he wanted to offer her sympathy or some consolation in this terrible place.

"I know that's the trouble," she said earnestly. "Because I don't know anyone who has something they're willing to die for, not any more." Her smile was short and wistful. "I thought I had, once, but I don't know."

This confession only strengthened Philips's resolve to do what he could to show her she was wrong. "You're being too hard on yourself, and too easy on this place."

"Don't say that," she said to him, putting her hand out as if to close his mouth with it. "This is a special place, re-markable and special, and that makes ordinary things more obvious for what they are."

"No," he protested. "That's not it." He wanted to argue with her, but all the coffee he had drunk was making de-mands on his bladder he could no longer ignore. "I'll be back in a moment," he said and went out to the men's room.

Standing in the empty room, he stared at the white sur-face of the urinal, taking care not to look in any of the mir-rors in the room. He had done that once here, and the memory of the hideous thing he saw could still sicken him. He closed his fly, washed his hands with his face averted from the mirror, and reached for a paper towel. Out of the corner of his eye a reflection caught his attention, but he re-fused to look at the image in the glass, and left with only a vision of a head with eyes removed and blood running down the hollow cheeks. I've got to get out of here, Philips thought as he rushed out the men's room door. I've got to get out of here.

"You look tired," said Senta as Philips came back to the gift shop. She was aligning the paperback books now, putting the ones with the brightest covers at eye level. "I hadn't meant to keep you up."

"I have to wait, anyway," said Philips, thinking that his

expression had more to do with what he had almost seen than with the hour. "I'll get a chance to rest once I talk to the day crew about the plane."

"That'll be pretty soon, then, I guess," she said, giving him another of her smiles. "It's wonderful having someone to talk to. Most nights I'm lucky if I have a dozen customers, and most of them don't have anything much to say. The administration talked about closing this shop down, but they decided against it. They want one service and one food area open on each arm, all the time, and for this arm—this was the best offer for me." She gestured to indicate the little shop.

"I hope they pay you very well," said Philips with feeling.

"Pretty well," she said. "Better than the waitresses and like that. And I'm bonded. They pay for that, too." She came back toward him. "You know, talking to you, I can't stop thinking about traveling again, going all those places I've always wanted to go. I think you're the luckiest man in the world, flying everywhere, seeing everything."

"It's my job," said Philips, who did not think he was as lucky as she did. "It's demanding, and it's pretty solitary, when you come right down to it."

"This is solitary," she said. "You're free."

Philips did not want to dispute the matter. "I suppose it looks like that," he conceded.

Her eyes brightened again with excitement. "I wish I could go with you when you leave. Just fly wherever you're going—"

"Chicago," he said.

"Chicago, Boston, Montreal, Hawaii, Melbourne, it doesn't matter. Houston would be different." She recited the names as if they were her saints and she their acolyte.

"You can go there, Senta," he said with a sudden welling of kindness for this woman. "Take a weekend, or a vacation, and go anywhere you want to go."

She turned to him. "It wouldn't be the same, going by myself. It would be a trip, not . . . not a journey. Don't you see the difference?" She held two paperbacks in her hands, one promising the bloodiest secrets of organized crime, the other offering the thrill and titillation of the sexual peculiarities of the very rich.

He had to answer honestly. "No, not really."

She gave a short sigh. "No, you probably wouldn't, because you do it all the time. You think it's ordinary, not special. But you're wrong." She put the books into the wire racks and came up to him. "You don't go places for vacations, or to be a tourist, you go there for the going. That's what makes you special. It's what I wish I could do."

"It's not . . . the way you think," he said, looking down at the hope that still shone in her eyes.

"But it is," she said. "I wish I could prove it to you."

Impulsively she reached out and took his hand. "I wish I could go with you. I mean that." She saw his doubt and released his hand. "For years I thought I couldn't do anything, that I had to stay here, because I had so much to do here, with the kids and all. I have a home and . . . things. Just things. But if I could be really free, then I'd chuck it all for it."

Before he could stop himself he asked, "And what about being worthy?"

She beamed at him. "But I would be, don't you see? I'd show that something meant more to me than this place, than the things I have, than any of it. I would be worthy then. I'd be able to die for something."

The alarm Philips felt was so great that he had to make

himself remain where he was instead of fleeing. "I don't think," he said, each word separate and distinct, "I don't think it would be the way you imagine it would."

"I know it would," she said with serene confidence. "Five years ago I might have doubted, but since Eric died, I've known that if I could just find a way to be free . . ."

The silence between them lengthened, widening like a chasm.

"Maybe Trager'll let me take you up to Chicago," he said at last, in an effort to reach her. At the same time he called himself a fool for making such an offer. "You'll have to find your own way back, but I guess you could arrange that, couldn't you?"

Her grin was wide and delighted. "You *mean* that? Really? *Really?*"

While he was not convinced it was true, he said, "Yes. Sure."

She reached out to take his hand again, faltered, and stepped back. "That's wonderful of you. Wonderful." She looked away, speaking more softly. "If you can't do it after all, that's okay. I won't mind. It's enough that you offered, you know?"

"I'll ask when I call in my report." He did his best to sound emphatic. "It'd be nice to have company, other than the copilot and the navigator."

She clasped her hands together to avoid reaching out to him again. "That's wonderful. Just wonderful."

"I'll let you know," he promised her. He felt restless again, antsy, and he looked out through the huge shop windows to the boarding area.

Two figures waited there this time, but they were both carrying cases and had the unmistakable look of early travelers struggling to wake up.

"It's twenty to six," said Senta, observing him. "Probably time for you to go down to the repair hangars."

"Yeah," he said, aware that the sky was lightening. He turned and stared at her. "I will ask, and if they say yes, I will take you up to Chicago. I mean it."

She nodded once. "Thanks." After a moment she added, "This is a hard place to leave. You know?"

He hesitated, thinking there ought to be something more that he could say; then he strode off toward the central terminal, still feeling the airport all around him like a clammy odor. He wanted to get away from the place, and the sooner the better.

Just as sunset slipped into dusk the next evening, the Trager jet rolled out onto runway Number Four of Dry Plains International Airport. Galen Philips was at the controls; his copilot was David Reissman and his navigator was Jose Aguerrez. They flew an empty plane because D. A. Landis had refused to allow an unknown passenger on board.

As they rolled past the arm where Senta's shop was, Philips could not help glancing up, wishing he had been able to take her along. It was such a minor thing, and it would have meant a lot to her, or so she said. He thought that maybe if she had been able to leave Dry Plains for a day or two, she might have realized what a pernicious place it really was.

There was a figure in the vast window fronting the waiting area, and a single figure stood in it, a shadow of greater darkness than the shadows around it. As Philips watched, he saw the figure raise an arm and wave to him.

"Senta," he said, and against all his professional impulses, waved back. It was the least he could do, after he had failed to get approval to fly her to Chicago. It was only

Chicago, he said to himself. It's not as if I asked to bring her along on my next flight to India.

He never saw the landing 737 skid out of control just as its wheels touched down. There was a dull sound as the 737 exploded, lifting back into the air in the midst of flames, and then pinwheeled toward the Trager jet.

"What the—" the copilot began.

The explosion reached them, slamming the plane into the side of the airport arm a quarter of a second before the ball of flames engulfed them, bursting what the impact had not broken.

In the gift shop at the far side of the boarding area, Senta lifted her hands to her face and screamed as the window erupted in fire and glass.

About *Echoes*

Although I generally dislike Wagernian opera, the story of The Flying Dutchman, *the famous ghost ship, has held my interest for some time, and I decided to see what I could do with it in a modern setting. I began this story in the Dallas-Fort Worth Airport, during a long, late wait between planes.*

GIOTTO'S WINDOW

They found him locked in the bathroom of the sixteenth-century B and B, smearing the walls with what he found in the catbox. The images were hideous, disturbing; the smell was nauseating. His robe was in tatters and his nails were broken and bleeding; he kept muttering profanities in English and Italian, his face set with a rigidity born of fury.

The police came, very polite and voluble as Italians are apt to be, and two psychiatrists; they conferred while the landlady wrung her hands and said to anyone who would listen that nothing like this had ever happened in her house before, appealing to the saints and all her previous guests to verify this for her. No one paid much attention to her; the psychiatrists made a few routine inquiries when the police had collected Thomas's passport, making sure they understood how the incident came about; they drugged Thomas enough to keep him from hurting anyone; and then they drove him off to a small hospital in the hills on the south side of the Arno, to a room that overlooked the glowing beauty of Florence, where they left him while they contacted the American Embassy and began the slow process of deciding what to do with the young man. When Thomas woke, he began howling, making sounds that hardly seemed to come from a human throat. He ran himself against the walls, the sound of impact shuddering through them. He cursed. He screamed. He slammed his head into the bars over the window, which was when the four attendants came and injected him with a powerful sedative. Thomas kicked

125

and muttered while the drug took hold, then he lapsed into an enforced sleep.

"Such a pity," said the oldest nurse, a middle-aged man from Pisa with a nose like a potato and big, fleshy ears. "He looks like an angel."

Asleep, Thomas Ashen did. He had the kind of regular, well-proportioned features that would not have been out of place in a Renaissance portrait; his hair was a sunny light-brown and curled just enough to make a nice frame for his face. With his eyes closed, the wrath that smoldered within was hidden. Lying on his utilitarian bed he seemed serene, but that was the result of his stupor.

The other three men agreed, one of them reluctantly; the man from Modena said, "One of the Fallen Angels." There was a long silence while they made sure he could not lower the sides of his bed, and then they left him alone.

It took nearly a week for Thomas to be calm enough to talk. When he did, he struggled visibly to control his anger and to hide his dread; he was drugged to help him maintain command of his emotions and to keep his apprehensions at bay. He slumped in his chair, his head and shoulders rounded forward as if he were about to fall forward into an abyss; his slippered feet dangled as if he could not see the floor, or did not trust it to support him. He listened to the gentle promptings of the psychiatrist with increasing loathing on his countenance.

"*E impossibile,* Dottore," he said, slurring his words a little as the drugs did their work.

"What is impossible?" Doctor Giacomo Chiodo asked in perfect Americanized English, the legacy of two years at Stanford Medical.

"Everything. *Tutti quanti.* It's all for nothing." He held his arms crossed tightly over his chest and he glared down at the soft slippers on his feet. "You don't know what's out there. You are blinded by reason, by rationality. You think what you see is what is there." He had to stop himself from saying more, to keep to himself the tentacles he saw writhing out of the psychiatrist's shoulders, or the huge bird talons that served him as feet.

"If I don't know, will you tell me?" Doctor Chiodo appeared calm, even mildly disinterested, but beneath that facade he was paying close attention.

"That's a psychiatrist's trick, isn't it? Turning the matter back on me so you don't have to risk anything." He scowled at the floor; it was too difficult to look at the man and ignore the tentacles. "You don't want to admit it."

"Admit what?" Doctor Chiodo sounded politely interested, as if they were discussing a film at a cocktail party. He waited, seeming to be in no hurry, his ferociously beaked face as benign as something that nightmarish could be.

"That you know what I see, that you know it's real." He glared at the Italian. "You aren't as much a fool as the rest of them. You listen to so much—I can't be the only one who has seen . . . You must know more, the reality."

"What do I know is real?" Doctor Chiodo asked with the same determined courtesy.

"Well, *look!*" he burst out. "Do you mean to tell me you don't know? Don't you look in the mirror? Can't you see what's out there?" He used his chin to indicate the window. "Do you have to think I am crazy in order to be sane yourself? Can't you see?"

"I see hillsides and the western half of Firenze," said Doctor Chiodo quietly, doing hardly more than glancing toward the north-facing windows. "With the Arno cutting through the city. What do you see?"

His jaw angled defiantly. "I don't pretend. I see what's really there; I see the monsters and freaks and grotesques. You've gotten used to them, haven't you? You think you see a man's face when you shave, that the people you pass in the streets are not macabre creatures in a macabre landscape. You pretend you haven't got a beak, that no one has one." He lowered his eyes. "You're as bad as the rest of them. You don't let yourself recognize what is there," Thomas said, then added in a soft, desperate tone, "No one believes me. No one wants to believe me."

"Why do you say that?" It was a standard therapist's ploy, and it worked well enough.

"You sound as if you don't believe me, either, but I know you aren't really convinced that what you think is there is real, not doing what you do." His eyes went sly. "You want it to be like Giotto's window, where you can show the order of what you think is there. But you sense that the order is false, a trick of geometry, or you should, a man in your line of work. If you don't, then—" He made a sound of contemptuous scorn. "You're as bad as the rest of them. Admit it. You don't want to see what I see. You'd rather look for reason and beauty than for the madness that is here. You have been seduced by all those lines Giotto drew out his window, forgetting it was all just a trick." He kicked at the chair leg with his soft slippers. "This isn't Giotto's window—that's the illusion you have accepted. The world is Bosch's, with bird-headed men and flowers in walking cages. That's what surrounds us. All the rest is sleight of hand."

"If that is so, what are you?" Doctor Chiodo kept his tone level and his gaze indirect.

"Oh, I am as much a monster as any of you, but at least I know it. I have seen my beak and my leathery wings, and my talons. I know that mirrors can lie if you are afraid to look at the truth. I am not afraid to see what I am." He snatched at the air as if to gather his thoughts. "You would see, too, if you permitted yourself to see them—I do. Oh, not the same monstrousness as mine, but some things all your own. I know you for what you are." He sounded almost proud, but he would not face Doctor Chiodo as he went on. "I can see what you are. You're one of the false men, with pink skin over the scales of a lizard, and fangs like a wild beast. The streets are full of beasts like you, chimeras and gargoyles and monsters; you all go on as if you were men: you have an armored raptor's head, your arms are not arms at all, and your feet are clawed."

"Is that what you see?" the doctor asked quietly as if they were talking about the pleasant Tuscan weather. "Is everyone so hideous?"

"Yes. And you would see it if you would let yourself," Thomas insisted again. "You will not let yourself look because you know I'm right."

"If you insist," Doctor Chiodo said, maintaining his calm and prepared for more repetition. "How does it happen that you can see these things and the rest of us cannot?"

Thomas laughed. "Because I am not afraid of seeing the world as it is." He leaned farther forward in his chair. "I know that if I fall from here, I will sink into the earth for miles. Don't pretend you don't know that, too. I can see it in your face."

"Which face is that? The pink one or the lizard one with fangs?" He wished the words unspoken as soon as they were uttered. He strove to regain the removal he sought. Finally he coughed gently. "You should be able to inform me."

"You won't believe me," said Thomas, so quietly that

Doctor Chiodo had to strain to hear him. "No one believes me."

"So you keep telling me," said Doctor Chiodo. "I wish you'd tell me more."

"Why? So you can say I am hopelessly delusional, spending my time hallucinating? So you can embrace the dream of rationality and tell yourself *you* are sane? So you can proclaim the triumph of rationality?" His sarcasm sounded exhausted; his defiance was fading, giving way to increasing dejection. "Look in the mirror, Dottore. *Guard' al viso.*" He swallowed hard. "If you used your real hands, you could touch your real face. You are not as lost as most are—you still have the capacity to know yourself." The doctor's tentacles waved at him, and the large, beakish horn that went up his nose and over his eyebrows dipped as the psychiatrist nodded.

"No doubt," said Doctor Chiodo. He wanted to pursue the matter later, when Thomas had rested, for the young American was slumping in his chair, his head nodded down onto his chest. "When you are more alert we will continue this."

"You think I won't know you for what you are? Do you think anything you do to me will change that?" Thomas challenged in a whisper. "The world isn't rational, Dottore. It never was." There was nothing Doctor Chiodo could think to say; he rang for the orderlies to escort Thomas back to his room.

"I am Jane Wallace," she said as she presented her passport and her letters of authorization; Director Biancchi glanced at them and took them carefully. "You were told to expect me? I'm here to . . . to escort Thomas Ashen home." She waited while the director of the sanitarium examined her credentials. "How is he?"

The director sighed with Italian eloquence as he gave her back her passport and letters of authorization. "He is still delusional, as Doctor Chiodo says in his report. This does not seem to have changed, although it is difficult to know. He is not saying much to us, but he flinches when he is with others, and he refuses to look out the window, so we have assumed he is continuing to see something other than what the rest of us do." This was as soothing as he could make it, and he watched Jane's response; then he waved to the chair across his desk. "Sit down, sit down. We must discuss this, you and I, if you are planning to travel anywhere with him." His face was slightly pinched, as if he had smelled something not quite wholesome.

"I wonder if it will be safe to travel with him at all, given what your reports say," she said to him as she sat down. "I read them quite thoroughly on the flight over. His family wants him back as soon as possible, but I don't know if it would be wise." She tapped the folder that held the evaluations. "I appreciate your faxing them to me before I left. It was all done in such a hurry—" She broke off. "Has he been violent?"

"Only to himself. This morning he hit his head on the door two times before we stopped him; he said he was trying to leave an impression of his beak, to prove he has one. He still attempts to eat feces if we leave him alone in the toilet. He has scratched his arms, saying that the scrapes prove he has talons instead of hands." The director sighed. "I cannot emphasize this strongly enough: He has not improved in any creditable way since we undertook his care." He folded his hands. "He is filled with despair, insisting he is surrounded by monsters." He shook his head again. "Doctor Chiodo has kept him moderately sedated, and that

131

has made him easier to handle, but it does nothing to alleviate his condition."

"No," Jane said quietly. "I can see how it is advisable, however." She was just tentative enough to encourage Director Biancchi to continue.

"You would be well-advised to keep him under heavier sedation while you are traveling; I know you are not required to, but I do think it would be prudent," he told her, a slight edge in his voice. "He has not been violent, as I have told you, but if he is closely surrounded by those he sees as monsters, I cannot promise he will not lash out. If he is in a stupor, he might endure his surroundings well enough for you to get him home."

"That's not very encouraging," said Jane.

"No, it isn't," Director Biancchi agreed. "You are a psychiatric nurse and you know how easily some patients can be overcome by their delusions. I'm afraid Thomas Ashen is wholly given over to his beliefs and regards all attempts to change his mind as confirmation of his worst suspicions." He tapped the shiny top of his wide desk.

"So I gather," said Jane, her manner a bit more assertive. "That makes him doubly troublesome; we must assume he will be responding to his hallucinations at all times. It will make traveling with him more difficult." She stifled a sudden yawn. "I'm sorry. Jet lag."

The director nodded, his manner politely concerned. "*Capisco.* You have come a long way, and you must travel again in another day or two; it is very demanding." He indicated the tall windows. "There is a guest cottage on the grounds, if you would like to rest until evening. Your bags have already been taken there. We can discuss this case further when you've restored yourself." His smile was genuine and practiced at once, the smile of a man who has spent his life putting frightened people at ease. "I will have the most recent reports prepared for your review."

"Thank you," she said, rising. "I am very tired." She started for the door. "I'd appreciate as much information as you can give me on the nature of his delusions. That way I can deal with him more effectively."

"Of course, of course; I will have all the information you need made ready," said the director. "I'll arrange for you to talk with Dottore Chiodo this evening." He rose and remained standing until she left his office; then he went to the window and looked out on the vine-covered Tuscan hill, taking solace in the beauty he saw.

Doctor Chiodo and Director Biancchi had a glass of pale sherry and a small plate of cheese pastries waiting for Jane when she came into the study at the Institute; it was glowing dusk beyond the windows as the day drained away to darkness. The building itself was alive with sounds, for most of the residents were being given their dinners just now, and some were expressing themselves vociferously. Director Biancchi shut the door, muffling the loudest of the noises.

"Does Thomas eat on his own?" Jane asked when their introductions were complete. She was in no mood to dawdle over social pleasantries, and sensed that the two men would be glad to lose themselves in small talk if they had the opportunity.

"Yes, he can feed himself," said Doctor Chiodo. "He is messy—he claims his beak gets in the way, that he can't hold on to utensils with his talons—but he is capable of eating food." He sighed.

"That's something," Jane said, trying to make herself more alert, for in spite of her nap she still felt swathed in cotton wool.

"You would think that the hallucinations are the product of a fixation in childhood, but if that is the case, he has not revealed it to me directly or indirectly. He is not very forthcoming about when he began to experience these perceptual episodes." He sipped his sherry. "I have rarely encountered such consistency in a delusion as he appears to have."

"You've had him here for three weeks; given the severity of his condition, that doesn't seem a long time, if, as you suppose, the hallucinations have been building for some considerable period. Your report suggests as much." Jane did not want to be the first to sit down, but she found standing about awkward. "I spoke to his mother at length before I left St. Louis; she told me he has drawn monsters all his life, most of them similar to monsters in comic books. She supposed he would grow out of it in time. She was under the impression he had given it up before his father became ill."

"And he may have done," said Doctor Chiodo. "But if that was the case, something triggered a resurgence of those perceptions. Perhaps his father's illness contributed to the son's deterioration, assuming such predilections existed before his father became ill, as I suppose must be the case, given the comprehensive nature of his delusions." He popped one of the little pastries into his mouth, chewed it vigorously, then finished off his sherry before going on. "And given the possible connection to a family tragedy, I want to have one more hour with him before I inform him he is to be taken home."

This startled Jane a bit. "Why delay telling him?"

"I am concerned about his understanding of the reason for his return home; it would be better for him if he did not perceive it as a punishment." He poured more sherry into his glass and held out the crystal decanter to Jane and then to Director Biancchi; only the director accepted his offer. "I would like to try to discover more about his home life before I send him back into it, no matter how briefly, in order to minimize the possible distress he might suffer because of it: surely his family would prefer he not respond negatively to this transfer? He will need proper care, of course, and the sooner he is hospitalized, the better for everyone."

Jane nodded, frowning as she spoke. "I think his mother wants to have him at home, in familiar surroundings, for a few days before she arranges . . . anything. She's hired me to stay with them until—" She stopped, not knowing how to explain Catherine Ashen's hopes to the two men.

"If you will pardon me for saying so, Nurse Wallace," Director Biancchi said in the silence, "Missus Ashen is not being very wise. I know this must be very painful for her, but if her son had suffered a medical injury, she would want to speed him to the best hospital she could find as soon as he arrived. This emergency is as genuine as broken bones are, and needs as expert care as soon as possible if he is to have any hope of a good recovery." He glanced at Doctor Chiodo. "Wouldn't you agree, Giacomo?"

"Most certainly. It cannot be sufficiently elucidated." He gave Jane a long, thoughtful look. "You have experience with delusional patients. Surely you must know that what you and I see as normal and reassuring—familiar—can be terrifying to a patient in Thomas's condition?"

Jane resented his patronizing tone but kept that to herself. "I've worked in the field for seventeen years, Doctor Chiodo. I have a grasp of the problem."

Doctor Chiodo metaphorically retreated. "An excellent one, I am certain." He coughed gently. "I will be sure you have enough medication to keep him quiet for as long as necessary. I only wanted to impress upon you the volatility of his current state."

"I believe you made the problem clear in your notes, Doctor," said Jane, a bit stiffly. "Rest assured, I will not underestimate the severity of his condition." She looked from the doctor to the director and back again, hoping the intensity of her gaze would be sufficient emphasis to convince them of her conviction. "He is my responsibility now, not yours." As she said this she saw the two men exchange a glance that was clearly an indication of shared relief.

"As you say, Nurse Wallace: Thomas Ashen is your responsibility now," Director Biancchi concurred.

Thomas's head lolled as he was buckled into his first-class seat; an attractive stewardess hovered nearby, her features distorted by worry. "You're sure he won't cause any trouble?" she asked Jane uneasily; her Midwestern accent revealed her origins as much as her fresh-faced good looks.

"He'll sleep for five hours; I have a second dose to administer later," Jane replied, more efficient than cordial. "There is no reason for concern while he is dozing, and I will give him my full attention once he awakes." She had shepherded him through Rome's Leonardo da Vinci airport, maneuvering his wheelchair with the ease of long experience, making sure he was undisturbed by the press of travelers around them. Now that he was aboard the plane and in his seat, Jane knew she could relax.

"Well, at least first-class is half empty," said the stewardess, sighing as she readied herself to tend to the other passengers.

Jane made a careful check of Thomas's seat belt, then wiped his lip of the shine of drool. She hesitated in this simple act, noticing that his flesh felt unexpectedly hard.

Thomas half-opened one eye and tried to make sense of her face. "Oh," he mumbled. "You're one of the sad ones." The eye closed and his head rolled onto his shoulder. "Long beak," he added, then fell deeply asleep.

A short while later the plane lunged into the air, heading northwest for Montreal, St. Louis, and Houston. The sound of the engines penetrated Thomas's drugged slumber for a brief instant; he saw the stewardess in the crew seat beside the door, and he gave a little shriek of dismay. "Teeth, long teeth," he whispered, then looked away toward the window, and went pale as he slipped back into his stupor.

If that's the worst I have to deal with, Jane told herself, this is going to be an easy flight, and let the acceleration and climb push her back against the padded seat until the pilot announced that they had reached cruising altitude. Relaxing, Jane let herself be lulled by the loud purr of the engines as the plane continued onward.

"Something to drink, ma'am?" the stewardess asked a short time later; she studied Thomas's slack visage and adjusted her own smile. "He's really out of it, isn't he?"

"As required, for his safety and that of the rest of your passengers," said Jane, more sharply than she had intended. "Hot coffee, black, and something light to eat—a croissant, or scone."

The stewardess stared at her. "Ma'am?"

"That's what I'd like for now—coffee and breakfast pastry. I don't care what the hour is." Jane sat straighter, squinting as she saw the stewardess move back. There was the oddest look about her, thought Jane, a shininess that seemed out of place on so perfectly made-up a face. She dismissed this as the oddity of the moment, a nervousness left over from getting Thomas to the plane. When the coffee was brought, Jane noticed the shine again, but out of the corner of her eye; again she dismissed it, reminding herself that she was a jittery flier. She leaned back, sipping on her coffee, and stared past Thomas out into the cerulean expanse. When the stewardess returned with two croissants and a sticky bun to accompany her coffee, Jane saw the suggestion of a chitinous mass on the stewardess's face; she ignored it.

There were two movies to choose from for the personal screens, and Jane selected the costume drama about skullduggery at the court of Elizabeth I; it held her attention even though she found it heavy-handed and anachronistic. Only twice did she find her attention wavering: once when the stewardess brought around an elegant tray of cheeses, and once when the man in the seat across the aisle rose to go to the bathroom and revealed a long trunk dangling from the front of his face. Jane blinked and the proboscis disappeared; she reimmersed herself in the sixteenth-century drama as quickly as possible.

Over Nova Scotia Thomas became restless and struggled against his seat belt, murmuring bits of protestations that caught Jane's attention. She reached over to quiet him and found herself staring into his open eyes. "You know. You know," he said, his voice made distant by his drugs. "Don't pretend."

"Of course not," said Jane, reaching for the kit that contained the tranquilizers he would need for the rest of the journey. "Don't upset yourself." As she administered the injection, she thought she saw a gleeful grimace on the beaked face of the stewardess, but in an instant it was gone, and the young woman's smile had nothing sinister about it.

"Is he going to be okay?" the stewardess asked as Thomas nodded off into sleep once again.

"Oh, yes; I think so," said Jane, doing her best to sound optimistic.

The stewardess patted Thomas's shoulder. "Good."

Thomas shuddered and huddled back into his seat as if he were aware of the presence of the stewardess and found her frightening.

As Jane settled herself again, she noticed the long, distorted arms of the other stewardess in first-class, and she suppressed a shudder, reminding herself that delusional people could be very persuasive; no doubt Thomas had gotten to her. She closed her eyes, and kept them closed until the plane landed at Montreal. Watching some of the passengers leave the plane, she reminded herself that none of them really had such heads, or such limbs. Frightening as they were, they could not be as hideous as what she saw. It was impossible.

Thomas's mother, her carefully maintained appearance less than perfect for once, sat in the living room, her hand to her eyes. "We hoped the year in Florence would do the trick," she said wearily, turning the last word to a tasteless joke. She collected herself enough to look up at her brother as he came in from seeing Thomas off in the ambulance. "What did they say?" Her spindly arms ended in narrow paws, more like a cat's than a human hand.

"They'll call you tonight, when they have completed their evaluation." He sat down heavily in the recliner that had been Alec's special chair. He stared at his hands as he spoke to the third person in the room. He seemed wholly unaware that his vest enclosed not ribs but a birdcage in which sat a monstrous crow with a lizard's tail. "I don't know what to say. We thought he was doing so well." The last words were lost in the wail of the ambulance siren as it pulled away from the house.

Jane Wallace could think of nothing to say to either Thomas's mother or uncle. She decided to try the oblique approach. "You told me he wasn't doing anything out of the ordinary until this morning?"

"No." Catherine Ashen sighed, glancing uneasily at her brother. "Well, not for Thomas. He kept to himself when he got home. He spent most of yesterday looking out his window, making sketches. He said he was showing the lie." Her voice grew unsteady but she kept on. "They weren't of anything specific. Just the street. You know, perspective drawings, sketches of the houses along the block. They're very good," she finished desperately.

"Thomas is a talented young man," Jordon Pace announced as if saying it importantly enough would create a validity through ponderousness.

"No one who has seen his work doubts that." She tried to think of something more she could say that would help Thomas's family to deal with his obsessions, but nothing came to mind.

"He says the monsters are self-portraits," his mother whispered. "He drew a number of them yesterday, every one worse than the last. How can he think that? He's such a handsome young man. Everyone thinks so." Her cheeks colored, as if she expected to be contradicted.

Jane sighed. "That has been part of his pattern. That's what Doctor Chiodo's evaluation says."

"And it's absurd," Jordon Pace announced firmly. "It's foolishness."

"No it isn't," said Jane firmly. "It isn't foolishness." She studied the man for a long moment, trying to decide how to approach him. "If he believes his work is self-portraiture, then we have to assume that, in some sense, he is telling the truth." It was as much as she dared to say, and she kept her voice low, not wanting to give herself away to such a creature as his uncle.

Catherine put her hand to her mouth; her fingers were trembling. "I can't bear to think that," she confessed, her head lowering and her eyes averted.

"For now, you will help him the most if you do not argue with him, especially about his art." Jane gave Uncle Jordon a steady look. "This isn't something he can be coaxed or cajoled out of."

Jordon Pace pursed his lips. "I should have taken him in hand as soon as Alec became ill," he said, inclining his head toward his sister. "I should have, Caty. I'm sorry I didn't."

As gently as she could Jane said, "I don't think it would have made much difference. Thomas' drawings have been . . . unnerving for some time."

"It was Alec's illness," Jordon insisted, needing to fix blame somewhere. "To have to watch his father go through such—" He shoved his hands into his pockets and looked away. "It would give anyone nightmares, let alone a boy like Thomas."

"Don't speak against him," said Catherine faintly. "His drawings were strange long before Alec got sick."

"Of course not; of course not," Jordon soothed. "But I can't help but think that those two years took a toll on the boy." He swung around to Jane, silently challenging her.

"Oh, don't talk about it," Catherine pleaded. "Today is bad enough without bringing all that up."

"They took a toll on everyone," said Jordon. "We all know how hard it was for you."

Unlike Jane, Catherine seemed to find his condescending manner comforting. She reached out and patted her brother's hand. "You were so helpful. I couldn't have managed without you." Then she blinked and turned her attention to Jane, chagrin in her expression. "You must think very poorly of us, talking about something that happened so long ago."

"Not at all," Jane responded in an even tone. "I'm sure there were many factors leading to your son's crisis, and no doubt his father's illness was a contributing factor."

"Just what I've been telling her," Jordon declared. "It's not the kind of thing a man puts behind him easily, and a boy . . . well." He shrugged.

Knowing it was a very difficult task, Jane did what she could to turn the subject back to the present. "Has Thomas talked about his father's death?"

"Not really," said Catherine, her eyes evading Jane's gaze. "It was . . . so unpleasant."

Jane wondered if Catherine had encouraged the silence; that was for another time. "Did Thomas see most of the course of the illness?"

"Well, of course he did," said Jordon, blustering afresh. "Alec was at home for most of its duration." He indicated the recliner. "He practically lived in that chair—if you call that living."

"Jordon; please." Catherine put her hand to her eyes.

There was much more to be found out, Jane told herself, but later. Today she had to follow Thomas to the hospital and try to be sure he was properly admitted. She wanted to see what kind of beings would be caring for Thomas. "I know this has been a very trying time. I won't distress you any longer," she said to Catherine. "But in a day or two we must talk. For your son's sake."

Catherine nodded numbly, her eyes fixed on a distant place; her brother took it upon himself to escort Jane to the door.

"She is not very strong," he said in a low voice. "I'm sure you'll take that into account in your dealing with her. She has had to bear so much already." He opened his hands to show he had done all that he could.

"I understand," said Jane numbly, because she did. She turned away and walked down the steps to her car; for an instant she caught a glimpse of her reflection in the window-glass. The sight of her long beak no longer distressed her, and she got into the driver's seat with little more than a flinch; she sat there and kept her full attention on the traffic, watching the cars instead of the drivers as she signaled in preparation for leaving, her mind deliberately focused on the ordinary sights. She refused to acknowledge the monsters around her, for that way was the end of reason, the loss of perspective that she had done so much to maintain. There was nothing to be gained in seeing the hideous apparitions that filled the streets; she glared at the two young men riding skateboards; they had the heads of ibises and the wings of vultures.

"I'm glad Thomas has someone like you to help him," Jordon said as he stood back, allowing Jane to depart.

"So am I," said Jane, driving away from the house into a world of monsters.

About *Giotto's Window*

The title refers to the codification of perspective and other "realistic" devices that Giotto and a handful of Florentine artists introduced in the 15th century, bringing "rationality" and the Renaissance vision to the world of art, along with a view of the world as sensible. But not all artists embraced this adherence to realism: Hieronymous Bosch was perhaps the most prominent exponent of irrational art, whose perceptions influenced, but did not dictate, the kind of delusions encountered in this story.

In spite of the rigors of rationality, it seems to me that this world is a very irrational place, but with a thin crust of rationalism floating atop the vast irrationality, rather like the oceans and continents floating atop a vast core of molten rock. An extreme version of this conviction is found in this story.

LAPSES

Just beyond the Marysville off-ramp, the big Chevy pickup suddenly braked and something came hurtling out of the back of the truck to crash and splatter into Ruth Donahue's windshield.

As she fought for control of her Volvo station wagon, she watched her hands in horror as red seeped through the splintered glass; the steering wheel was sticky with it. Ruth pulled onto the shoulder as much by feel as anything, since her vision was completely blocked by the . . . *thing* on the hood of the car. She was going little more than fifteen miles per hour then, but it felt to her as if she were racing along at seventy.

There was a whine of tires and her ear rocked as it was struck a glancing blow. Ruth screamed as much from irritation as from fright. It was with difficulty that she forced herself to stay in the car once she had pulled on the brake. "I want out of here," she said in a soft, tense voice as she stared at the blood on her hands and arms and skirt.

The thing on the hood, she realized with revulsion, was a dog. She remembered seeing it in the back of the pickup. It was—had been—good-sized, faintly spotted, with floppy ears, and Ruth had wondered why the driver had neglected to put the tailgate up with an animal loose in the back. When the Chevy had slowed so suddenly, the dog had been thrown out of the truck bed and—

She lowered her head and vomited.

A sharp rap on the window caught her attention, and she

looked up, embarrassed to be seen. A Highway Patrol officer (where had he come from?) indicated that she should roll down the window, and reluctantly she did.

"You all right, ma'am?" the officer asked her, concern on his face.

"I don't know. I . . ." Her words faltered and she began to cry, not soft, gentle tears, but deep sobs that left her trembling and aching.

"Hey, Gary, the lady's in shock," the officer called to another, unseen person.

"She hurt?" called the other.

"Scratches and bruises, and she's a mess, but I don't think she's hurt bad. They might want to check her over at the hospital, just in case."

Ruth tried to get the man to stop talking. She waved a hand at him and saw him wince at the sight. She forgot her gruesome hands until that moment, and now she hid them self-consciously.

"Shit, the sucker really landed hard, didn't he?" The officer opened the door and peered inside.

"I'm al . . . all right, Officer, or I will be, in a moment." She was finding the air and sunlight heady as wine. "Really."

"If you're certain," he said, with doubt. "But you better let me drive you to the hospital."

What is he seeing? she asked herself, dreading to inquire for herself. "You don't have to," she began, but he interrupted her.

"Look, lady, it's gonna take a while to get the animal off your car, and your windshield is broken. You can't drive anywhere in any case. And frankly, you look pretty rocky." He braced his hands on his hips, determined.

Ruth cleared her throat. "Okay."

"Is there anyone who can pick you up?" the officer went on.

"I . . . I'm from San Luis Obispo. I'm up here for the day." Who did she know back at home who would drop everything and drive for over five hours to get her?

"Well, look, we'll take you to the emergency room in Yuba City. You can call from there." He started to move away from her, as if her shock were contagious.

She could already imagine Randy Jeffers yelling at his secretary when he learned what had happened. Randy's main response to anything he could not control was to yell about it. He would be outraged at Ruth for her accident, the more so because she was in the Sacramento Valley on business for his company.

"You want to get out of the car, lady?" the officer asked.

"Oh. Yes." She opened the door, the movement making her dizzy. "And my name is Ms. Donahue. Ruth Donahue."

"Yeah," said the officer. Then, grudgingly: "I'm Officer Fairchild. Hal Fairchild."

Ruth could think of nothing to say. None of the admonitions she had received as a child covered meetings with law officers after accidents. I'm thirty-six years old, she thought, and I don't know what to say to a cop.

"You want to get in the car, Ms. Donahue?" Officer Fairchild offered. "Hey, Gary, how's the guy in the pickup?"

"I don't think the ambulance is gonna get here in time." The answer was flat, so without inflection that he sounded more like a machine than a man.

"Hey, Gary, get away from there." It was a friendly suggestion. Fairchild made it while holding the front door of his black-and-white open for Ruth.

"Somebody's gotta stay with him. Damn-fool bastard!"

147

"Don't let Gary bother you," Fairchild said quietly to Ruth. "It's his fifth bad accident in four days and it's getting to him." He closed the door and walked away.

"And I guess the SPCA'll have something to say about the way the dog was loose in the back of the truck."

"I beg your pardon," Ruth said, startled at finding Officer Fairchild beside her again and the car in motion. When had that happened? "My mind was . . . wandering."

"That's okay," said Fairchild. "Shock'll do that to you."

"How much longer until we reach the hospital?" She noticed that the farmlands had given way to smaller holdings and the first hint of urban sprawl.

"Ten minutes at the most. You be able to hold out until then?" He glanced at her swiftly. "Your color's a little off."

"I'm . . . doing fine." She was alarmed by her wandering thoughts, but she could not tell him so.

"Well, you hold on, Ms. Donahue. We'll make sure the doctors give you a good going-over before they let you out."

"Great." Her eyes felt solid and stiff in her head, like marbles, and she did not want to move them unless she had to. "The man in the pickup?"

"I don't know. Dispatcher says he was alive when the ambulance got there, but I don't know if he'll make it. He was pretty much of a mess."

"What happened?" Ruth asked. "Why did he stop that way?"

"Hard to tell. There was nothing on the road. We haven't had time to check the truck out. Maybe a bird came at his window. That happens around here. Ever have that problem down in San Luis Obispo?"

"I guess." She watched a school bus lumber out of a wide driveway, loaded down with young children. She followed it, thankful that there had only been a pickup in front of her and not one of those buses filled with kids.

"Just a couple more minutes," said Officer Fairchild.

"Good."

The doctor was middle-aged and harried; he ran his hand through his rumpled hair and made some hasty notes. "Well, Ms. Donahue, I don't know what to tell you. You're suffering from mild shock and that's not surprising. You could do with some sleep since there's no sign of a concussion. I'd recommend you get a checkup from your regular doctor."

"I don't have one," Ruth murmured. She had been in the hospital now for more than three hours and was disoriented.

"Then call a clinic or something," he said with asperity. "You've had a rough time of it, and it isn't good to neglect any symptoms."

"All right," she said, staring at the clock. She still had not called Randy; as far as the office knew, she was off checking on the County Planning Commission and the Zoning Commission regarding the possibilities for developing the old Standish Ranch. When he learned that she had lost more than half a day, things would not be pleasant.

"There's a motel near here. They're not too unreasonable. They can help you rent a car. But I don't think you should plan on driving for at least twenty-four hours." He cleared his throat.

"I'll have to be on the road tomorrow morning," she said.

"I'd advise against it," the doctor said, with a weary sigh. "Look, isn't there someone we can call for you? You're not married, I noticed, but there must be—"

"No one," she said, cutting him off. "I'll call my boss from the motel."

149

"If that's the way you want it," the doctor said. "I'm going to give you a prescription for something to help you rest and relax. Don't mix it with alcohol or dairy products. And wait at least an hour after a meal to take one."

"I'm not hungry," Ruth said softly.

"You will be," the doctor told her. "I'll call the pharmacy for your prescription. You can pick it up in about forty minutes."

"Thank you." Her mind was drifting and she found herself not wanting to resist.

"If you get any sudden headaches or other unusual symptoms, call me." He handed her a card. "My beeper number is the second one, and the answering service is the third. If it's late at night, insist that they wake me. I'll leave your name with them, just in case."

Ruth could not imagine calling this man, now or ever, but she took the card and put it into her purse. "I'll call if anything happens." What a ludicrous thing to say, she thought. Something had already happened—that's what all of this was about.

"The pharmacy is opposite the emergency admissions office." He gave her a last quick look, and then he was on his anxious way toward another examining room.

Very slowly Ruth got back into her clothes and gathered up her things. Her hands felt as if she were wearing mittens and nothing she donned seemed to belong to her. Her eyes ached, her jaw was sore from clenching her teeth, and there was a stiffness in her movements, the legacy of strain.

At the pharmacy window they asked her to wait. She found a badly shaped plastic chair, picked up a battered magazine, and thumbed through it.

The child at her elbow was screaming, his jacket sleeve soaked in blood. The two paramedics were trying to cut the material away, but the boy avoided them, kicking and yelling.

"He's in shock," one of the paramedics panted.

"Some shock," the other scoffed. "The little bastard just bit me."

How long had they been there? Ruth wondered.

The boy gave a yowl of pain and outrage as the paramedics finally lifted him from the floor. His foot glanced off Ruth's cheek and his flailing left hand caught strands of her hair.

"Sorry, lady," said one of the paramedics as he forced the boy to open his fist.

"It's nothing," said Ruth. Her thoughts were still disordered. She could not remember the boy coming in. Certainly he must have been crying and making a fuss, and yet she could not bring this into any focus in her mind.

A thin, agitated woman with a tear-streaked face rushed out of the emergency admissions office, her eyes filled with dismay as she reached for the child. "Jerry . . ."

The boy shrieked, renewed his struggles, and succeeded in hitting one of the paramedics on the nose.

"Hey, fella," said the paramedic, doing his best to ignore the blood that had started to leak down his face.

"Let us handle this, ma'am," said the other paramedic to the woman. "We've got to get his jacket off him. We can't do much with his arm until we do."

"He wasn't this way in the car," the woman protested. "Jerry, let them help you."

Ruth moved two chairs away from the commotion, wishing she had not seen it. She was still distraught by what had happened on the highway, and to see the boy with a bloody sleeve was too much like the dog on her windshield.

"Ma'am, please tell this kid of yours we only want to

151

help him," said the older paramedic.

"Jerry, let them—" his mother began, but her boy lashed out again with his good arm.

I must get away from here, Ruth said to herself. I must. She moved over two more chairs, but it was still not enough. Her breath came raggedly and she rose, prepared to leave through the first open door.

"Ms. Donahue," called the clerk at the pharmacist's window, repeating herself twice before Ruth was able to respond.

"Thank you," Ruth whispered as she scrabbled in her purse for her wallet and her MasterCard.

"Don't let the commotion bother you," the clerk advised. "Kids get that way when they're hurt sometimes. It's not as bad as it looks."

"How much do I owe you?"

Behind her, the paramedics succeeded in bringing Jerry under control; his screams turned to miserable sobs. Ruth could not force herself to look around.

"It comes to twenty-nine eighty-six." The clerk took the plastic card and ran it through the imprinter. "Did Doctor Forbes warn you about alcohol and dairy products?"

"Yes," Ruth said. She watched her hands tremble.

"Good. Sometimes they forget. Remember that you're likely to sleep for a long time—twelve hours isn't unusual. If you can arrange not to be disturbed, so much the better." She handed back the card and offered the receipt for Ruth's signature.

As she scrawled lines that looked nothing like her name, Ruth asked for a good motel nearby, repeating the name twice when the clerk offered her suggestion. "Can I call them from here?"

"Pay phone in the lobby," said the clerk with a hitch of

her shoulders. "I'd let you use the phone here, but those are the rules."

It took almost an hour to get a taxi, for there were few of them operating in the city. After the brief drive, Ruth searched out the gifts-and-sundries shop to purchase a toothbrush and deodorant before she went to her room. The last thing she did was call San Luis Obispo to tell Randy Jeffers what had happened.

"Tough," her boss said after an initial show of concern. "Better rent a car tomorrow and head back. I'll tell Stan to take over for you. Hey, and drive carefully, won't you?"

At another time Ruth might have felt touched by this, but now it struck her badly, and she bristled. "If you didn't think I could handle this, why did you . . . ?"

"Hey, kid, easy," Randy interrupted. "I didn't mean anything like that. Jeez, you better get some rest. You sound worn out."

"I am worn out," she admitted, feeling tears start at the back of her eyes. "It wasn't very nice."

"Shit, no," Randy said with more feeling.

"I'll call you tomorrow before I leave. Tell Stan I've already got the material from Sacramento"—she realized her papers were still in her car; she would have to phone the police and find out where it had been taken— "and the man to see at County Planning is a Mister Gafrick."

"Good work." Randy was clearly trying to help her feel better. "I'll tell him. He might be able to catch a shuttle out of Fresno. It could save us a little time."

Ruth wanted to ask him why he had made her drive when he was willing to pay for a shuttle airline for Stan, but the words caught in her throat and all she could do was sigh, hoping that she could hold off her tears until she was off the phone.

153

"Well, we'll see you soon, okay? If you can rent a compact, do it. I want to keep the costs down if I can. And, Ruth, take your time getting back. You've had quite a time of it, I can tell. So I won't expect you tomorrow or Friday. Take your time and get steady. We'll arrange for this to go on your sick pay."

His tone was indulgent, but Ruth did her best to accept the offer gracefully. "Thanks a lot," she said, knowing what was expected of her. By the time she put the receiver down, she could feel wetness on her face.

She called the Highway Patrol and requested that her briefcase be brought to the motel. It was in the trunk of her car, and she said she would need it in the morning. The woman who spoke with her assured her it would be done.

Last, Ruth called the front desk and asked that she not be disturbed. Then she took one of the capsules Doctor Forbes had prescribed, and in her pea-green motel room gave herself over to oblivion.

The Ford Escort was the cheapest car available from the local rent-a-car, and as she started to drive it, she realized that it did not have the performance she was used to from her Volvo. Driving made her nervous, and she kept to the slow lane as she made her way south toward Sacramento. Her hands were sweating although the day was cool, and from time to time she had to wipe them on her skirt.

Interstate 5 was mesmerizing, stretching out across the San Joaquin Valley. Ruth had driven it before, but this time there seemed to be many extra miles added to the road. She kept her speed at fifty-five and ignored the huge trucks barreling along at higher speeds. She promised herself that she would not stop for lunch until she reached Coalinga. Then she would take the time to have a good solid meal and collect herself for the last leg of the journey across the hills to 101.

Two Highway Patrol cars shot by and Ruth flinched at the sight, hating to look at the road ahead in case there was another accident. She tried singing to herself—the Escort had no radio—but her voice sounded thin and cracked, so she fell silent again.

She could not recall the last thirty miles before Coalinga. The off-ramp came as a surprise and she nearly overshot it, blinking at the overpass as if it were a mirage. She decided that she had been driving too long, and gratefully pulled into the parking lot of Harris Ranch, resolving to dawdle over her food, giving herself enough time to calm down. She had heard of highway hypnosis, but until now had not experienced it, and it frightened her.

It was less than ten minutes after she left the restaurant that Ruth saw the animal lying beside the highway, drawn up into a protective half-ball in a last futile attempt to keep its guts in its shattered body.

Ruth was assailed by nausea, the excellent meal she had so recently eaten threatening to spill out of her. She stared ahead blindly, her face ashen, her breath fast and shallow. What was the animal? A cat? A raccoon? She had not seen it long enough to glimpse more than the destruction and dark striped fur. The headache, which had retreated to a painful itch behind her eyes, now gripped her skull in its vise.

It was all she could do to hold her car on the road. Dust was blowing from the west, reducing visibility with the tenacity of fog. The highway surface was made slippery by the sand, and she could not be certain how far she had come.

When had the wind come up? Ruth could not recall. It had to be her headache or the memory of the dead animal that had distracted her, but for how long? What had happened in the last—how many?—miles? She was not at all sure where she was. Had she taken the off-ramp to San Luis

155

Obispo? Was she still on Interstate 5? *Where was she?* The question echoed in her mind in a shriek. She looked at the clock on the dashboard and saw that it was after three. She should be almost home by now, but instead she was caught here in the blowing dust.

She saw dimly another sign, an off-ramp beyond that, and after a moment of hesitation she took it, hoping that it would bring her quickly to a town where she could make a few phone calls and find out how far she had strayed.

Immediately adjacent to the off-ramp there was a service station, but as she drove up Ruth saw that it was closed. She pulled into the dust-covered parking area, her tires slithering for purchase on the asphalt. She opened the door of the Escort and felt the bite of the storm. There was a telephone booth not more than thirty feet away. She walked toward it, her purse held to shelter her face.

The telephone was not connected, and where there had been phone books, the securing chains hung empty.

With a cry of vexation, Ruth flung herself out of the phone booth and struggled back to her car. She was moving against the wind now, and there was little protection. Dust made her blink, and when she sneezed her whole face hurt.

Back in the car, she lowered her head against the arch of the steering wheel and sobbed. Within a few minutes she was on the verge of hysteria. Everything she had endured for the last two days caught up with her at last. She was ashamed at her lack of control but powerless to remedy it. Sometime in the last forty-eight hours something crucial had deserted her and left her rudderless. The minutes and hours she could not remember, the panic that welled in her at this admission. Her body was shaking as with palsy. She looked, appalled, at her hands, which no longer seemed to be part of her.

Where am I now? Where?

As her high sobs dwindled, she tried to make a sensible decision, but was capable of little more than restarting the car. I have to get back to the freeway, she told herself, her thoughts moving as delicately as an invalid with a walker. I have to find the exit for San Luis Obispo.

Once in motion, she managed to feel her way through the blowing dust to the overpass and the on-ramp leading north. She was certain that, wherever she was, she had come too far south. But now she was determined to find her way back.

Driving was even more difficult than when she had been southbound, but she kept her hands locked on the steering wheel and her attention on the road ahead. She blinked often, as if that might clear the obscured windshield.

The street was almost empty and most of the storefronts were boarded up. Litter blew in the gutters and trash stood uncollected in overflowing bags at curbside. The stop sign canted at two o'clock, token of a mishap long past.

Ruth braked, staring around her.

It was night, late night by the look of it, and the few operating streetlights revealed that most of the block was deserted. Her dashboard clock said one twenty-seven; she stared at it for some little time, listening to her engine idle, refusing to believe what she saw. On the passenger seat there was a gasoline receipt from a Union station in Buttonwillow. She refused to touch it, fearing that it might be real. A quick look at the gas gauge showed that the tank was almost empty. Presumably she had driven more than two hundred miles since she left Buttonwillow, if the tank had been full then.

As she peered down the side street, she saw three motorcycles drawn up near a small metal-roofed building. The machines were large—Ruth did not recognize the symbols emblazoned on them—but their very strangeness added to her apprehension.

"I'd welcome a Hell's Angel," she said aloud, giggling in a way that made the fine hairs on her neck rise. "God. Oh, God."

A page of newspaper, open as a scudding sail, flew down the street, twisting and moving until it wrapped itself around a lamppost. Something metal clanged, perhaps a garbage can, perhaps a door. Its echo rattled off the buildings.

On a billboard angled precariously over the intersection ahead, Ruth saw enormous letters advertising Spring cigarettes. The whole thing was faded and there were slogans and symbols spray-painted over the face of it, but it was still possible to make out two faint figures walking in a meadow, long since turned from green to gray-brown. Ruth stared at the billboard for some time as if she hoped to learn something from it.

"I've got to find a phone. Ruthie, you've got to call someone." She said it sternly but in a girlish voice, the way she used to talk herself into doing her homework, a quarter of a century ago.

She put her car into gear once more and drove down the wider street. She looked for a lighted storefront or a business open at this time of night—a 7-Eleven or a gas station or a motel—and was dismayed when after several blocks she found nothing like that. True, the decaying brick buildings were behind her and now there were houses, vintage 1925, with faded paint and weed-grown front yards. Occasionally there were cars parked on the street, but nothing was moving. The houses were dark. She saw no one.

She did her best to ignore the wail of panic that was

forming between her mind and her throat.

When, fifteen minutes later, she reached the outlying small farms beyond the empty city, she noticed a church with a light on over a discreet and old-fashioned billboard:

Lodi Methodist Church
"Learning to See through Others' Eyes"
11-12 Sunday Morning
Wednesday 8 p.m. Discussion and Prayer

Lodi? The name came off the sign and hung in the air before her. Lodi was east of Interstate 5, and certainly north of Buttonwillow. Had she been driving in the wrong direction for most of the night? And why had it taken her so long to reach this place? Where had she been before that?

Reluctantly she pulled into the gravel-paved parking lot and stopped. She sat for some time, not thinking, not permitting herself to speculate. She decided that she needed to rest, to calm down. Obviously she was still in shock of some sort and the stress was causing her to do irrational things.

What things? demanded a treacherous voice within her. *What have you done that you can't remember?*

"I won't think about that now," Ruth said aloud in her most sensible tone, the one she usually reserved for business meetings. "The most important thing is to get back to San Luis Obispo and find a doctor. Just in case." She could not bring herself to wonder in case *what* . . .

Then, as she sought to avoid such probing, she drifted into unrestful sleep.

"Are you all right?" The knocking on her window was louder and the voice was raised almost to a shout.

Dazed, Ruth opened her eyes and tried to recall where she was. Scraps came back to her, each serving to make her more distressed. Carefully she rolled down the window. "I'm sorry," she began, not sure what she was sorry for.

The man standing by her rented Escort was over fifty and appeared to be both benign and ineffective. "Is there something wrong?"

Ruth cleared her throat. "I was driving late last night. I . . . got lost."

The man nodded. "That's the usual reason strangers show up on this road. Most travelers stick to the freeway and bypass us entirely." He stepped back and made a kindly gesture with his knobby hands. "Would you like a cup of coffee? We don't have much in the way of breakfast, but I can probably scare up a stale doughnut, if you want one." He smiled. "I'm George Howell. I'm the minister to this flock." This was said with a self-deprecating smile that was clearly designed to put her at ease.

"I'm Ruth Donahue," she told him automatically. "I'm from San Luis Obispo and I was trying to find the way home . . . yesterday." She opened the door and stepped out.

"These side roads do get confusing," he agreed as he led the way to the side door of the church. "I was here for more than two years before I really learned my way around." He slipped a key into the lock, saying as the door swung inward, "There was a time we never closed the church, but these days, what with vandals and all, well . . ."

"Is it very bad?" asked Ruth, trying to make conversation with this mild-faced man while she worked up some explanation that he might accept.

"There have been problems. The cops try to hold the worst of them down, but they can't do everything. And you know how difficult it can be to establish some kind of order in a district like this. We're on the edge of things."

To her horror, Ruth laughed.

If the minister took offense, he made no sign of it. "I've heard that there have been problems in other places, too. I guess you've had your share in San Luis Obispo." He had led her to a pantry adjoining the kitchen, a large, featureless room designed to handle the occasional church dinner or wedding reception. A huge black stove squatted on the other side of the half-open door, six burners and a grill showing on its top.

"Sometimes," Ruth said. She found that the sight of the kitchen was making her hungry. God, how many meals have I missed? she wondered, her thoughts slipping away from the question.

"The doughnuts are in here somewhere," George Howell said to her as he opened the old-fashioned cooler. "My secretary is always getting me things to eat, and I can't convince her that it isn't necessary." He found the bag and pulled it out. "Not much left, but you take all of them if you like. She'll bring me something else at ten-thirty." He gestured toward the low table under the window. "Sit down and I'll make some coffee."

"Thank you," said Ruth, beginning to hope that her life was at last returning to normal.

The minister bustled happily about, clearly delighted to be of help to someone. He chatted about the weather—how strange for this time of year—and cuts in the county budget ("They expect us to provide charity, but how can we? Who has the money to spare?") and the progress his two children were making with their music lessons. It was all so wonderfully ordinary, so very predictable and sane, that Ruth felt herself smiling at her own boredom. What could be more normal? She was reassured.

"Do you take milk in your coffee?"

"No, thank you. Just black." As she accepted the mug, Ruth asked herself if she might find the caffeine too much on so little sleep and food, but she was so eager to make herself alert that she overruled her own caution.

"I always like a little milk in mine. I guess it reminds me of being a kid, having a cup of chocolate after school." He sat down opposite her.

Ruth smiled, recalling her mother and the many stern warnings about indulging in such treats. Her mother had had a dread of fat children, especially her own, and had instilled in Ruth a level of austerity that resulted in the lean angularity she now possessed. "This tastes very good," she said, though the scalding liquid nearly burned her mouth.

"I'm glad you like it. My secretary brings the coffee, too." He sipped at his cup.

"You're lucky, I guess," said Ruth, relaxing even more into the commonplace.

"Yes, I thank God for her often." He beamed, to show that he had not intended for her to take his reference to God as introductory to any spur-of-the-moment sermon.

Ruth gazed at the blood on her skirt and blinked twice, as if she expected it to go away. The coppery smell was very strong in the room, along with other, less pleasant odors. Blood festooned the pantry walls and swagged along the floor toward the sanctuary.

The coffee in her mug was cold.

"What?" Ruth whispered, shaking her head slowly at the carnage she sensed lay beyond the sanctuary doors. Her wrists ached, and she saw with amazement the distinct, raw impression of ropes pressed into her skin.

Obscenities were scrawled in spray paint on the walls of the kitchen and pantry, and from the grill of the stove, George Howell's head, gory and canted on one side, stared out at the wreckage of his church.

In her fright she fled westward, first to Stockton, and

then along the narrow levee roads of Highway 4. She would pick up 580 or 680, whichever it was that would lead her back to Highway 101. All she would have to do then was to drive south.

At Oakley, she stopped and endured the sniggers of the high school boys pumping gas when she claimed that her period had started without warning and she had to wash her skirt. She had already got (another?) tank of gas in Stockton and hoped it would be enough to get her home. She considered calling her office again, but could not bring herself to attempt to explain what had happened. She was afraid that no matter what she said, it would mean her job.

Not that she would blame Randy if he did fire her after what had been going on. She asked herself if it might be best for everyone if she simply resigned, but that in itself seemed too trivial a response. She was missing bits and pieces of her life and had no means of finding out what those losses were. Not that she wished to, for the aftermath was so dreadful that she was certain the events themselves must be hideous beyond her imaginings.

At Pittsburg, she pulled off the road, feeling light-headed from tension and hunger. She found a burger place with a drive-through window, and was horrified to discover that she had barely enough cash to pay for a frugal meal. She could not remember what had happened to her money, or even how much she had had. She noticed that she had a Visa card in her wallet, but thought that there should be a MasterCard as well. When had she lost it, if she had had one to begin with?

The food was tasteless to her, and she thought for a while that she would not be able to keep it down, but slowly she felt herself grow more calm, more *present*, less caught in the nightmare.

"It was only a nightmare, wasn't it?" she asked the air. "I got carried away after that trouble near Marysville and I fell asleep in the car, and that disoriented me. The rest was a nightmare. That's all."

Somewhere in the treacherous alleys of her mind, the image of the blood on her skirt remained, but she refused to look at it, confident that if there was any explanation needed, it was that the blood had come from the unfortunate dog that had fallen onto her windshield and died there, impaled on shattered glass. There was no minister in Lodi, she had never been in Lodi, and the rest was only the distortion of her memories of that terrible incident. She kept repeating this to herself as she drove toward Concord and the turnoff leading south, away from those dreadful visions.

She was southbound in little more than half an hour, and that refreshed her. The simple satisfaction of going in the right direction, of being in control, once again gave her a burst of confidence. It was a pleasure that truly delighted her. It would not be long before the entire ghastly episode was safely behind her. She would never have to endure such a thing again. She felt that her ordeal was finally over.

By three-thirty, she had reached Paso Robles, and was so near home that she was willing to get off 101 long enough to have a proper meal on her Visa card. She wanted to be refreshed when she walked back into her apartment. There were so many things to attend to once she was home—the return of her rental car, the arrangement to get her own once again, the whole business of filing necessary reports with the insurance company, they all piled up oppressively in her mind—that she decided a brief respite over an early supper or late lunch would give her the steadying influence she so truly sought.

She found a nice restaurant set back from the road, a

building in a subdued Spanish style with tall willows growing around it. There were not many cars in the lot, but a discreet sign on the door assured her that the place was open.

Service was prompt and pleasant, the waitress taking her order with a smile. When she returned with the salad Ruth had ordered, she also brought a glass of wine.

"I didn't ask for this," Ruth said guardedly, afraid that she might have forgotten the request, or missed the order.

"No; it's on the house," said the waitress and set it down with the salad.

"I very much appreciate it, but since I still have a way to drive, I'd really rather have a cup of coffee, if you don't mind." Ruth said this politely, hoping her good manners would mask the fear that nearly choked her.

The waitress shrugged and took up the glass once more. "Suit yourself. Your broiled chicken will be ready in about ten minutes." She turned away and went back toward the bar.

Ruth ate the salad and, when the waitress brought the coffee, made a point of thanking her for it.

The man in bed beside her rolled over and touched her arm.

Ruth almost screamed.

"Hey, did I wake you, Enid?"

"Enid?" Ruth repeated in disbelief.

"I ought to be leaving for work pretty soon. Want me to skip breakfast with you?" He smiled at her in easy familiarity, this stranger whom Ruth had never seen before.

"You feeling okay, honey? You look a little strange." His concern was genuine, which made it worse than if he were as alien to her as she felt to him.

Ruth shook her head slowly, not daring to move too

quickly, as if that might upset the precarious balance of this place. Did she dare ask the man who he was? Or how she came to be here with him? She gathered the blankets around her, making them tight and heavy, enclosing herself.

The man braced himself on his elbow and put his free hand on her shoulder. "Enid?"

Ruth turned away, knowing that she was about to cry. She was shaking, as weak as with a sudden fever. Did she have courage enough to look in the mirror? And what would she find there if she did? What place was this? Why did he call her Enid? Why had she lost herself—or was she lost at all?

"Honey?"

She flinched as he touched her.

"What's the matter?" He sounded genuinely concerned, but then the blood had been genuine, and the dog crashing into the windshield and the empty, disorienting freeway.

"1 don't know—"

He tried to turn her toward him, but she pulled resolutely away, deep in her misery and her doubts. "You're like a stranger again."

Why did he say *again?*

"Enid?"

At last she met his eyes, finding them completely unfamiliar, their warmth and worry all the more terrible to her because he was so completely unknown to her.

The car was hurtling toward the embankment and she screamed.

About *Lapses*

When I wrote this, I made it a rule that as soon as I began to understand what was happening, I had to change it.

Inappropriate Laughter

"How grateful we are to have had Marjorie with us for so many years. That dear, good woman, with enduring faith and strength and purpose . . ." The minister faltered at the sound from the second row of folding chairs at the graveside, something precariously close to a snort. He cleared his throat and resumed his comments. "So generous, so willing to extend herself on behalf of those less fortunate than herself. She was an example to us—"

Jessie Lealand Hart had never been so embarrassed in her life; here it was—her great-aunt's funeral—and she was sniggering at the fond remarks as the family and friends gathered at the grave, carrying on as if she were nine or ten. But she couldn't help it, not with what she knew. As she attempted to apologize, another snicker burst from her and she felt abashed. She did her best to shut away the memories she had of Marjorie. "Sorry," she muttered, and ended on a cackle. Try as she would she could not stop it.

The minister made a gesture of consolation to the eighty-six people seated around the casket where it waited to be lowered into the ground. "For all her life, she was stalwart in her love of her family. She sustained the burden of sorrow more than many of us have had to, and in doing so, showed her devotion to her dear ones more truly than any more extreme demonstration would have done. Without her staunch support, what might have become of her children?" He looked at the group of middle-aged mourners nearest the coffin. "Louisa, William, Melanie,

167

Albert. You all know how much your mother did for you."

Jessie blurted out another clump of laughter, and reddened at the affronted stares she received. "I'm so sorry," she murmured, trying to look properly chastened, but not succeeding.

"So those of us who were honored to know Marjorie Bateman will miss her voice of experience, and her timely wisdom, her generosity of spirit as well as her kindly example," said Reverend Maynard, a hint of rebuke in his delivery as he stared directly at Jessie. "She was steadfast in her purpose, even in misfortune, willing to wait for God's will to be shown to her, a reminder to us all that faith can give strength and comfort even in the most trying ordeals. Surely her strength through the losses in her life can serve as a reminder to us all that we are never given more than we can carry. The burdens she bore were many, yet she did not falter in her convictions and in her dedication to her family; she put her trust in God and persevered. She endured her years of poor health with no complaint and genuine nobility of example."

Jessie giggled audibly, her cheeks flaming; her cousins seated near her turned toward her in dismay. She put her hands to her face as if to disappear.

Scowling, Reverend Maynard continued, "Yes. Her example of acceptance of trial during her long illness—"

Jessie strove not to guffaw.

"—and her dignity during her last days showed how much she had grown in trust of God and in understanding. How many adversities she had to overcome in her long life. A widow four times, and yet each time able to endure the portion God had given to her. She survived tragedy without loss of her belief, or hope, and those of her children who are still with us must be grateful for all she did for their benefit.

Ninety-six years is a long life, and through every day of it, she thought of her children. They are where they are today in large part because of their mother's selflessness. She dedicated herself utterly to her family. In spite of the deaths of six of them, she remained determined to be an example to the rest, and not to dwell on her losses but to be grateful to those who survived. Their interests were always uppermost in her mind." The Reverend once again directed a piercing glance at Jessie, as if daring her to be amused. "Let us remember her now, in our thoughts."

It was an effort for Jessie to do no more than chortle. She squirmed in her cold folding chair as if she were a child again, and not fifty-one; she had known this would be a trying day, but had not thought it would be so hard.

"Jessie, for heaven's sake," hissed Louisa, Marjorie's youngest daughter, a few years older than Jessie, who was sitting nearer to her than anyone else. "Can't you stop?"

"I think I better excuse myself," Jessie whispered, fishing for her handbag on the ground next to her chair; it was slightly damp to the touch.

"Yes," said Julie, her first cousin once removed. "I think you should."

At any other time, Jessie would have been tempted to argue, but just now all she could do was nod as she grabbed her purse and got to her feet, doing her best to move away from the grave as inconspicuously as possible. To the accompaniment of the benediction, she made her way up the path, past the small chapel with a reception hall behind it, to the rest rooms and the entry to the function rooms; the larger of the two would house the wake to follow the graveside service. Jessie ducked inside the rest room and did her best to contain her consternating amusement. She tried to bring her thoughts into order, to observe the gravity of the occasion with appropriate solemnity. She jammed her knuckles into her teeth and bit down hard enough to cause pain, hoping it would put an end to her barely subdued laughter.

It didn't work. She had to swallow hard several times to keep from being overwhelmed by whoops and chuckles. This was dreadful, she reprimanded herself inwardly even as her shoulders shook and her face colored from the effort of containing her mirth. She told herself this was a solemn occasion, one that was reserved for grief and tears. Guffaws marshaled at the back of her throat, and a few stray snickers erupted from her tightly pressed lips. Mortified, she stood still, trying to control herself. She went to the bank of sinks and wet a paper towel, thinking if she put it to her face, her laughter would stop.

"What on earth is wrong with you?" asked Jessie's niece Deborah from the door. "What made you do that?"

"I don't know," said Jessie. "Stress, I suppose." She splashed water on her face. "It's been a hard time."

"You'd think you were possessed," said Deborah, trying to make light of a difficult situation. "I don't know what the family's going to say, considering everything." She paused significantly. "The others may have forgotten, but I haven't."

Jessie looked up, meeting Deborah's eyes in the mirror. "I didn't mean anything by it."

"Well, mother's very upset. She's been beside herself today, anyway, and you only made it worse. Father said you were trying to get attention, and I think he's probably right. Not that I think you'd want any." Deborah went to the middle of three stalls, slipped inside, and closed the door.

"The last thing I want is attention," said Jessie, not quite able to stop her burst of laughter. She wished now she had done what she had originally intended to do and stayed away from the funeral. But family pressure had won, and she had agreed to attend both the church service and the graveside one, for the sake of the relatives. Now she regretted it, and understood that the regret came too late.

"Father doesn't believe you," said Deborah. She dabbed at her eyes with a small linen handkerchief.

"He doesn't have to; I'm not trying to convince him of anything," said Jessie sharply, remembering how her older brother had glared at her as she left the graveside; his eyes blamed her for being disorderly and unappreciative, just as he had said to her the day before at the funeral home. "I can't help it. I tried, but I can't." She pressed the wet paper towel to her mouth and then her cheeks. The laughter continued to percolate within her.

"Well, it isn't right," said Deborah.

"I know," said Jessie, not quite stifling her laughter. "I know."

"They're *burying* her, for God's sake," said Deborah indignantly. "This is the last thing any of us can ever do for her."

"I know," Jessie repeated, and almost choked trying not to whoop. She thought she did the last thing she would ever do for Marjorie four days ago; this was just the epilogue, tacked on to make Marjorie's life orderly.

"You should. You of all people. You lived with her," said Deborah at her most condemning. "I should think you'd be weeping."

"Yes, I did live with her," said Jessie, suddenly serious. Then a chuckle burbled out. "And I do miss her. After so many years together, I'd miss anyone. Hell, I'm going to miss her insufferable little dog." She had to clap her hands across her mouth to keep out the burst of risibility that surged through her; as soon as she dared she did her best to speak in a normal tone and almost succeeded, although she kept her hands at the ready to stop any more flare-ups. "He's going to the kids at Saint Cecilia's, just as Marjorie stipulated. They can deal with him now, and welcome." Slowly she lowered her hands and said, "I didn't mean that the way it sounded." She wished she would cry—people would understand crying.

"Jessie, stop it; stop it right now," Deborah exclaimed as she flushed the toilet. "Great-aunt Marjorie would be—"

"Shocked," Jessie finished for her. "So she would. And small wonder," she added in an eerie approximation of Marjorie's voice.

"So why don't you stop?" Deborah came out of the stall. "You're upsetting everyone." She took a comb out of her purse and flicked it through her neat helmet of shining hair.

"I can't help it," Jessie protested; she turned helpless eyes on Deborah. "I can't make it stop. I try. Really. I don't want to laugh, believe me." She took a deep breath and attempted to keep a proper demeanor. "I didn't expect to react this way. Do you think I intended to . . . to make light of her passing?" She had washed most of the make-up off in an effort to contain herself. In the mirror her face looked tired and wan, but she still had to struggle to keep from laughing. She cupped her hands and managed to drink a little water.

Deborah shook her head. "You ought to be ashamed."

"You sound like your father," said Jessie.

"Well, you *ought*," Deborah insisted.

"I am, Debbie, truly I am," Jessie promised her, adding to herself, *but not for the reasons you think.*

"How long are you going to stay in here?" There was suspicion in her eyes now, and a quiet condemnation that Jessie found dismaying.

"A while."

172

"Well, don't take too much time. People will begin to ask questions." Deborah took her lipstick out of her purse and redefined her mouth. "You ought to apologize to my father."

"I will. And the rest of them. When I'm done here," said Jessie.

"Well, if you stay in here, they'll know something's wrong," said Deborah. "That won't make things easier."

"I won't be much longer. I'll go into the reception room. I don't think I can go back to the grave without disgracing myself, or the rest of you." Jessie patted her face again with a paper towel. "In any case, I've got some repairing to do. I look a fright."

"You need to fix more than your face. Don't come out until you think you can comport yourself appropriately. This is a funeral, and a wake," said Deborah, heading toward the door in stiff abhorrence of Jessie's conduct. Her high heels rapped out her disapproval as she went, and Jessie had to stifle snickers.

"I bet your father told you to say that," Jessie remarked to the closing door; it was a cheap parting shot, and she told herself she was petty for using it. "You're a good girl, aren't you?" She wasn't certain if she was speaking to Deborah or her own reflection; now that she had been left alone, she went and sat on the settee by the bank of mirrors. She felt weak, and loose, as if she had been on a crying jag instead of laughing. Catching sight of herself, she realized her hair was disarranged and that she would have to do something with it before she left the restroom. It all seemed too much—the grief that everyone claimed to suffer, the extravagance of the funeral, the ludicrous wake—as if anyone expected Marjorie to rise from her coffin. The whole thing was an elaborate travesty, with a choir and an extended

173

service at the church before they all came out here to the cemetery, extravagances that would have brought Marjorie Batemen's stiff-rumped disapproval, and the prayerful graveside rites that would have made Marjorie aggravated to the point of anger. But for Jessie, the whole event was a sham, a fantasy invented to permit the family to ignore the truth about the dead matriarch. Whomever the mourners were remembering, it wasn't the Marjorie Mignonne Victoria Lealand Richardson Noyes Avery Bateman that Jessie had come to know so well in the nine years she had been her companion, nurse, and, ultimately, her confessor.

"Let me tell you," Marjorie would begin, and Jessie would put aside whatever she was doing and listen to her great-aunt reminisce about the four husbands and six children who had preceded her to the grave, and the five who were still alive.

"You should have seen Lysander Richardson when he was a young man," Marjorie had said. "So handsome, with mustaches waxed just so and his boater held as if it were made of porcelain, not straw. A little old-fashioned, and arrogant, but when I was young that appealed to me, and, of course, his fortune. Easily the best-looking of my husbands, and the most feckless, as it turned out. He quite doted on me, at first. He said I was his everything—sentimental and not very original, but he was eager and rich, and that was enough to make me think he was the rarest thing in nature. And I was only seventeen when we married; I had no more real experience than a bisque-china doll. You should have seen me. Straight out of finishing school and a year in Switzerland. Pretty and spoiled and eager to make my place in the world, which meant marrying the right man." She had fallen silent, then added with a sly smile, "They never found out what happened, why he bled to death in the garage."

But Jessie had, of course. Over the nine years she tended to Marjorie, she pieced together the whole story: how Lysander had begun to keep company with chorus girls, squandering his money and ignoring his infant daughter as well as his wife in order to carouse with his cronies and their doxies. "He had kept a mistress for a time, an expensive piece of fluff called Vivian; she was rapacious and mercenary but pretty in the popular, and common, style. It was no worse than what most of his contemporaries were doing, men and women, myself included, although I had demanded marriage instead of lavish gifts, because that's what girls of my class did. Lysander treated Vivian like a pet and me like a blood-stock brood-mare—which is what I was expected to be. He assumed I would stop complaining about Vivian in time, as most wives did, as soon as I had more children." But of course Marjorie hadn't been willing to accept his waywardness, and over the next year she grew increasingly vehement. All Marjorie's efforts hadn't been enough to reform him, not even her most desperate gamble: little Serena had wasted away and her father had paid no attention other than to buy her an expensive casket. He hadn't mourned the loss of his child in any way beyond what was expected of him. So there were those who thought his death, a year to the day later, was a delayed act of grief rather than an accident, the only gesture the bereft father could make. And for the sake of the widow and her second child she miscarried two months after her husband's death, they didn't speak of it aloud, although the whispers continued for years.

On the settee in the restroom, Jessie felt laughter rise in her again. She could never tell anyone that Marjorie had killed her daughter to punish her husband, and when that failed to move him, had found him alone working on his automobiles and contrived to drug his beer, and once he was semi-conscious, sliced his arm with a metal-snip, then locked him in and left him. She couldn't prove that Marjorie had killed her child, of course, it was only a guess based upon the ramblings of an old woman who was drugged and slowly dying. The family would dismiss anything Jessie reported as being the result of the painkillers and anti-spasmodics that Marjorie took. It was amazing to hear her devotion as a widow, her perseverance in the face of adversity praised so fulsomely, when she knew that Marjorie had seen herself in vastly different lights. It was like seeing a cartoon version of *Citizen Kane*, with humorous little talking animals instead of Orson Welles and Joseph Cotton. Jessie giggled, and clapped her hands over her mouth.

A noise from just beyond the door brought Jessie upright on the settee. She felt her face flush; her laughter stopped abruptly, and she turned as Evelyn Grant came in, her ancient face sorrowful in its mesh of wrinkles. Her black suit hung on her and the long rope of pearls around her neck swayed with her every movement, making it appear that she had borrowed all her clothes.

"Oh, God," she said with disgust as she saw who was in the restroom. "I thought you'd gone home. Huh! I should have known better."

Jessie regarded Marjorie's oldest friend and did her best to smile. "Sorry about what happened."

"I just bet you are," said Evelyn, her face drawing down. She was eighty-eight, and as she saw it, dressed in her best Chanel black suit with her good pearls to set it off, no matter how unflattering it now was: it was what she wore to funerals, and for Marjorie, she had donned her ugliest, most expensive, pearl earrings. "Let them say what they want about the way you took care of Marjorie—you were always one to take advantage of her, that's what you took. Huh! You and your obsequious service! I know. I saw how you encroached on her good nature."

"I lived with her a long time," said Jessie. Looking back now it seemed as if that was part of her distant past instead of something that ended four days ago. And everything that happened before Marjorie was lifetimes away.

"She paid you well enough, not that you appreciated it," said Evelyn, disapproval in every lineament of her body. "Marjorie would never have let you stay with her if she hadn't needed someone to fetch and carry."

"Thanks," said Jessie.

"You never did value her. Never," said Evelyn, as she stomped through to a stall and slammed into it.

"Perhaps not," said Jessie. "You're probably right about that. Probably no one did."

"She deserved better," said Evelyn through the stall door.

Jessie bit her lower lip. "She deserved something else," she said cautiously. She wanted to argue with Evelyn, to tell her about everything she had learned about Marjorie during her years of caring for her, but there was no point to trying, for Evelyn would not believe her, and the rancor she would create would be lasting.

"You always took advantage," Evelyn repeated as she flushed the toilet. "You should be ashamed."

"Perhaps you're right," said Jessie in the same tone she had used when she used to talk to Marjorie.

"Huh!" Evelyn scoffed as she emerged from the stall. "You're ungrateful, just ungrateful."

"I must seem that way," Jessie said quietly, and put her hands to her mouth to stop the chuckle.

"Think about it," Evelyn recommended as she slammed the stall door.

"I'll do my best," said Jessie. She looked toward the door and wondered if she dared to escape yet. The attendees were still straggling in from the graveside, the low buzz of their conversation droning on the other side of the bathroom door. In another ten minutes the mourners would begin the toasts and twenty minutes after that they would have mellowed to the point of forgetting her laughter or joining in it. By then, no one would mind if someone laughed occasionally, so long as it wasn't Jessie.

As Evelyn checked her reflection, she looked over her shoulder. "What do you plan to do now that your meal ticket is gone?"

"I don't think about that yet," said Jessie, feeling demeaned. It was the truth, and she knew that she would have to make some arrangements soon. Her years of caring for Marjorie would receive only a minor bequest from the estate and then she would be on her own in the world at an age that would make finding new employment difficult; she knew her inheritance was small because Marjorie had delighted in telling her that, usually when she was gloating over some past achievement—such as the successful doing away with her third husband, Gardner Avery. All but one of her children by him had died with their father, and the sole survivor of that group, Michael, had kept away from his mother for many years. Marjorie had all but cut Michael out of her will, leaving him only a pittance. "He got that trust from Gardner's parents. He has his own business and it's made him very comfortable. He hardly needs much from me," she had declared. "You don't need much from me, either. You've been eating my food and living under my roof for almost a decade. That's enough."

"Well, you'll have to, won't you? All that time at Marjorie's beck and call, what will you do now?" She powdered her forehead. "It is sultry."

It took a moment to recall what she had been saying. "Well, better than cold and dank," said Jessie, and sniggered. What was making this day so funny, she asked herself, and winced at the answer her mind supplied: *murder is a joke in bad taste.* But was she certain it was murder? There was absolutely no proof of any wrongdoing, and at the time they had happened, no one had so much as whispered about Marjorie. If Jessie should say something now, would anyone believe her? She did her best to think about all she knew, and the more she tried the less certain she was that she really understood what Marjorie had told her. Surely the old woman had been pushing the limits of senility, and what she had said was nothing more than the muddled maundering of a fading mind. If perhaps she felt some measure of responsibility—no matter how unfounded—she might have blamed herself, making up tales to account for her sense of guilt. At least the family might very well think so. She stared into the mirror and did her best to focus on her reflection, hoping to read her real feelings, and perceived only the ambience: there was no escaping the weather, not even in this place, for Jessie's hair had frizzed in the humidity. The heavy air and overcast skies made the August afternoon threatening, and promised the release of rain by nightfall.

"Don't come out until you can behave properly," said Evelyn as she left the restroom.

Jessie stopped the protest that mounted in her throat. It wasn't as if she was unaware of her gaffe; she felt her lapse keenly, and wished she hadn't succumbed to this most perplexing amusement. She told herself that she shouldn't be surprised that Evelyn should reprimand her like a child, for she had been childish, laughing as she did, and Evelyn must be feeling ancient, now being the last woman alive in the group that had centered around Marjorie a decade ago. By comparison, Jessie was a youngster, and at the moment, she felt juvenile; even her good dark dress seemed designed for a younger woman than she, and she had to fight down an urge to stamp her feet in aggravation with herself.

Finally she felt composed enough to go into the reception room. She smoothed the front of her clothes and patted her hair as if to assure herself she was wholly composed. It was nerve-wracking to go out into the hallway, and from there down the hall to the handsome room beyond where mourners stood around two long tables laid with breads, cheeses, cold meats, veggies, and dips. At the far end was a small portable bar where a man in a black jacket poured out drinks. Jessie lingered in the doorway, taking stock of the people who had come in for the reception: Willard Fisher was already showing the effects of three stiff bourbons, his face flushed and his voice a bit too loud; his wife Emily wasn't far behind him, smiling inanely and beginning to slur her speech. They had been Marjorie's long-time neighbors, inclined to visit when there was gossip, but otherwise confining their contact to phone calls about trash pick-up day. Next to them, Marjorie's youngest brother Desmond Lealand sipped morosely at a vodka-and-tonic. He looked fragile and faded, every one of his eighty-two years; he occasionally glanced at Annis, his second wife, who was listening attentively to his cousin George discoursing on the state of the stock market.

From her vantage-point, Jessie did her best to maintain her decorum, so that she could join the company. But the absurdity of it all got hold of her and she had to battle a renewed eruption of chuckles. She broke out in a burst of tactical coughing, and muttered, "Mis-swallowed," to the air.

Albert Noyes came up behind her and patted her on the shoulder. "I know how hard this must be for you. Don't let those vipers get you down. It's the shock and grief that makes them ungrateful. I know they're all very much obligated to you for all you did for Mother. She would have been a burden on anyone, no matter what they like to think just now. In time they'll acknowledge it." He offered Jessie an encouraging smile. "You were a real trouper, taking such good care of her, with so little support from most of the family. No matter what they say, most of them couldn't have done it if they wanted to. You know, Mother always had a soft spot for your father—he was her favorite nephew. She told me that many times."

That wasn't what Marjorie had told Jessie, but she said, "Thanks, Uncle Albert."

"I don't suppose the rest of them will say anything, but I want you to know how indebted I am to you for all you did for Mother. If it weren't for you, she'd have had to be put in a home, and that wasn't any kind of life for a woman like her. It was hard enough, being cooped up in the house for years on end." He held up his drink—brandy and soda, Jessie knew from long experience—saying, "Go along now, and get a drink. Daniel's about to offer the first toast."

"Thanks, Uncle Albert; I'll be in in a moment, just as soon as I can be sure I won't do anything—" Jessie said again, thinking how of all her relatives she liked this kindly, ineffectual man best; although he had lived off his mother's generosity for more than two decades, he had always been pleasant and concerned for her welfare. Albert had been loyal in a way his father never was, and Jessie had always suspected that some of his devotion was in compensation for his father's lack of concern. Jessie also knew that Marjorie had been most distressed about killing Albert's father, and had looked after Albert more devotedly than she had her other children because of it.

"But it had to be done," she had explained during one of her long, late-night discourses. "He was running through all Lysander's money, and the Depression was on, so what could I do? He had insurance, a lot of it, and his trust fund that would pass to Albert, so there was nothing left for me to do. I did try to make it as easy on him as I could— without making it seem I had done anything, of course." Marjorie had told Jessie how she had learned how to disable the brakes in Ernest's sedan, that she had stepped out one evening when she knew Ernest would be going to the country club and made sure he would not make it home. Ernest always drove fast, and it was only to be expected that he would do the same this night. His Cord went off the road and down the steep side of Stewart's Bluff, and the insurance money had put Marjorie and her three surviving children back on easy street: Albert, Melanie, and Edmund had been able to prosper when others were struggling to get by. It had been a pity about Edmund, the youngest of Ernest Noyes's children: Edmund had died in Korea, his plane shot down on an early morning reconnaissance run.

From the table with the cheeses came a sudden eruption of weeping, and the various people standing nearby hurried to comfort or escape the outburst of Louisa, Marjorie's youngest child, a thin woman of fifty-seven who had been born when Marjorie was thirty-nine, three years after her last marriage, to Theodore Bateman. She had given him William within a year of their nuptials and considered him a late child; but Louisa came later. Everyone in the family believed Louisa to be high-strung and usually said her long-delayed arrival in her mother's life accounted for it. Her half-brother Albert hurried over to offer his shoulder for Louisa to cry on, much to the annoyance of her husband Jim, who stared at his wife as if he couldn't bear one more outburst.

"What do you think?" asked a voice slightly behind Jessie.

"Daniel's going to make a toast," said Jessie, not looking around.

"Not yet. He's waiting for the good champagne." The voice laughed slightly. "I don't blame you for what you did, Jessie. You knew her better than anyone, I bet."

"I suppose so," said Jessie, and turned to face Christian Wilmot, Marjorie's grandson, one of only three grandchildren.

He tugged on the neck of his black turtleneck, worn under a navy blazer, his fair skin a bit flushed, by heat or drink was hard to tell. His face was handsome enough, but with a certain softness about it that showed he lacked resolution. "I bet she told you all kinds of shit. She really liked to talk, and you had to listen, I bet," he said, shaking his head slowly. "I'm sorry she's dead, but she was ninety-six. I didn't want to come, but since none of the Averys are here, I thought I might as well."

"There are only two Averys who could come," Jessie reminded him. "Michael and Charlotte. Charlotte is ill, and Michael is in Europe." Charlotte, Gardner Avery's spinster sister, had lived with Gardner and Marjorie for five years, and Marjorie had still blamed her for the troubles she had had in that marriage, decades after Gardner Avery and four of his children had died in a small-plane crash. Michael had been home with chicken pox, and lived. The rest had gone down in the mountains; it had taken almost a year to find the wreckage, and to gather up the bones that could be found in order to have something to autopsy and bury.

"Charlotte would have done more than laugh if she'd been here," said Christian. "She hates Marjorie's guts to this day. She still says Marjorie's responsible for the crash, you know."

"Why does she say that?" Jessie asked, curious about what that old-style Bohemian potter had perceived in Marjorie that roused her suspicions.

"Because she's jealous, of course. You know how possessive she's always been about her brother; she clung to him like a leech," said Christian. "She has to say Marjorie did it or she has to admit that her sainted brother fucked up. That could never happen." He shook his head. "She claims that Marjorie put something in the thermos, something that made him crash the plane." He pulled at his single ear-ring, the gesture oddly flirtatious. "Why would Marjorie do that? I can understand killing Grandfather Gardner—not that I ever met him, but still—but not her kids. Marjorie wasn't the type to do that."

Is there a type? Jessie asked herself, and felt a smile squeeze out the corners of her mouth. "Then it's probably just as well that she didn't come."

"Y'know," Christian remarked, "machines sure had it in for Marjorie."

"Machines?" Jessie repeated incredulously.

"Yeah. Her first husband got cut up working on his car, didn't he? And the brakes failed on Ernest Noyes's car, didn't they? And then Grandfather Gardner went down in his plane, and Theodore Bateman had that boating accident: who would've thought that a powerboat could catch fire and burn like that? Something wrong with the engine, isn't that what they decided? All machines, one way or another. And didn't Marjorie's oxygen machine go out on her?" He snapped his fingers. "Oh, yeah. It was the power failure during the thunderstorm. More machines. You see what I mean?" He gave Jessie his best impish grin. "Dad could've come, you know. If he really wanted to."

"He's in Europe, Christian. His business—" Jessie said, feeling she had to apologize for Michael.

"Business? In Paris? My dad? He's just farting around. He's probably just as glad he has an excuse to stay away. There's always a way to get back here in twenty-four hours from almost anywhere on earth, and Paris is easier than a lot of other places. Year before last, he made it home from Karachi in twenty hours, and that routed him through Australia and Hawaii." Christian almost smiled. "I think you've got guts, Jessie. I don't blame you for letting go that way. You might as well laugh. Half these sticks probably want to do what you did, or something like it, but they don't have the balls."

"Christian, that's a terrible thing to say," Jessie admonished him.

"Do you think so?" He kissed his fingers in her direction. "Then where's Lindsay and Gerald? Why am I the only grandchild here? Where are my half-cousins? Where're Louisa's kids? Or William's? You don't see either of them here, do you?" He stepped back with a flourish. "See what I mean?" And with that he was gone.

Jessie pressed her lips together, and wondered if Christian might be right. Could some family members have known what Marjorie had told her, or might they have heard whispers over the years? Might Marjorie have told someone else about her activities? Certainly Marjorie was proud of her accomplishments: could she have boasted of them to someone other than Jessie? She went over to the bar, longing for a cognac, but asking for mineral water.

"Quite a show you put on," said Annis Lealand, her head at an angle and her hip cocked. She was forty-nine, but admitted to forty-two, a fanatically fit and skillfully maintained woman with the kind of determination that Jessie found unnerving. "It takes the mind off all the shock."

"I'm sorry about it," said Jessie, taking her mineral water and sipping carefully. "I never meant—"

"Whatever possessed you? Did you do it deliberately?" Annis interrupted her apology. "Or did things just catch up with you?"

It was hard to tell if this was a literal or allegorical question, for Annis subscribed to any number of cosmologies that might explain her behavior. "I don't know," said Jessie, giving the safe answer.

"Well, I can tell you had a lot on your mind. It's not surprising at a time like this." She ran her finger around the rim of her glass. "You know, not every culture weeps at death." She looked at Jessie.

"How many giggle?" Jessie asked, chagrined.

Annis paid no attention to this. "You carried it all for them. Don't think I don't know it. Desmond thinks he was helpful with Marjorie, but he really wasn't. He just fussed a lot, and called it caring. It spared him having to do anything much." She gave Jessie a long, sympathetic look. "I know how hard your job has been. Most of them couldn't do it, and wouldn't do it, so they just dumped it all in your lap and tried to forget about it. And it can't have been easy, dealing with Marjorie."

Jessie would have been glad of a sympathetic ear, but she doubted that Annis was one, given the amount of family gossip that filtered through her. "It wasn't easy for Marjorie—to have her body give out before her mind went."

"The other way isn't much better. Not that any way is really good, unless you're prepared for it and your soul is ready to move on," said Annis, posing elegantly; her chocolate-colored silk pantsuit was a bit too low-cut for formal mourning, and the brilliant diamonds that dangled from her earlobes were ostentatious, but it was what everyone expected of Annis.

"No," said Jessie.

Annis sighed. "So have you made any plans yet? You do need to start thinking about what comes next, you know. Don't mind my asking, do you?"

"Well, I have to help inventory and close up the house so it can be put on the market. That will take a couple of months, according to the lawyers, and it'll take that long to get all the paperwork done. What happens after that will depend upon—" What would it depend upon? she asked herself, and giggled. "Oh, dear."

"Hey, don't worry about it." Annis held out her glass for a refill. "Barkeep. Single malt. Make it a double." She turned back to Jessie. "Might as well splurge a little. I'll do another half hour on the treadmill tomorrow."

"For a drink?" Jessie asked.

"And that yummy brie," said Annis. "I'll say this for Albert—he set up a good send-off for his mom; best of everything and plenty of it. Desmond didn't want any part of it."

It was Jessie who had made the actual arrangements: Albert had signed the checks. "Yes."

"I know Albert will give you a good letter of recommendation, Jessie. And he'll make some calls on your behalf—I promise. You did so much for Marjorie. I suppose I could get Desmond to write one for you, too. I wouldn't count on the others. William doesn't do favors, and Louisa isn't useful for that sort of thing. Melanie might." She offered a practiced, brittle smile. "Desmond was pretty fond of Marjorie, and he knows he's lucky to have had you to take care of her. I let him know she needed someone full-time a couple years before you were hired. The rest of the family couldn't see that Lorna was out of her depth. Lorna was a good maid, but she wasn't up to anything like what Marjorie needed. And she wanted to go home in the evening. Her family didn't like her being gone overnight. Marjorie needed someone with her 'round the clock. You were a godsend."

"Lorna didn't want to stay on once Marjorie had to use the wheelchair. She said Marjorie was too demanding." Jessie said this with the full intention that Annis would tell the rest of the family. "Not surprising, really. She wasn't trained for anything more than keeping house, and Marjorie needed more than that."

"At least you're a nurse. That relieved everyone, in spite of what happened before," said Annis, taking her drink from the bar and leaving a dollar coin in the tip glass.

"That was twenty-three years ago," Jessie said without a trace of hesitation or embarrassment.

"So it was," said Annis as if she had forgotten that. "And nothing was ever proven, was it?" She took a long sip. "You've always said there was nothing to prove."

"Because there wasn't." She wanted to get away from Annis but couldn't do it without fueling Annis's worst speculations. "As the investigation revealed. They proved the vials had been in the wrong place and improperly labeled." It had been a long time since anyone had brought that up— except Marjorie, who would make some reference to that incident almost every day.

"Not the kind of thing to talk about now, is it? I didn't

mean to distress you," Annis said with too much an air of satisfaction to make her contrite expression mean anything.

"No," she said.

Annis smiled. "Well, I didn't mean to touch a nerve."

"You didn't," said Jessie quickly. "I'm still edgy from Marjorie's death. We all are, don't you think?"

"I'd say so," Annis agreed, and had another sip. "This is very good."

Jessie drank more of her mineral water and wished she could come up with something to say that would send Annis away without offending her. She stared up at the ceiling, at the exposed beams with their Celtic carving. "It's a handsome building."

"So it is," said Annis, and glanced at George again, pursing her lips. "Excuse me, Jessie. I have to ask George about an IPO." She turned on her heel and went off at a rapid clip.

Jessie stood by herself, relieved and forlorn at once. She put her hand to her eyes and pinched the bridge of her nose, as if to block a sneeze. It would be so easy to laugh again, and she couldn't stand the thought of losing it again. Her face ached from her efforts to keep her expression somber.

"Want another?" William Bateman asked in a stiff tone.

"Mineral water?" Jessie asked, holding up her glass. "Not yet, thanks."

William studied her, his face expressionless. "It's been a difficult day."

"It has," she agreed. "But that's nothing new," she added.

"I wanted you to know that I'm trying to understand about what happened," William said.

"She stopped fighting. It was time. She was tired. The

power failure just gave her the opportunity to stop breathing," said Jessie, and bit the insides of her cheeks as she sensed more laughter gathering in her solar plexus.

"No. I mean about what happened with you." He folded his arms. "You, of all people."

"I'm sorry. How many times do I have to say it?" She knew she sounded testy. "It was a long, hard battle, and I suppose I'm just thankful it's over. For both of us."

"But laughing?" He shook his head.

"That . . . that was unfortunate." Jessie sighed. "I didn't intend to. And really, I don't know why I laughed. I just did." She was becoming exasperated, in large part because she couldn't shake the remnants of amusement that had not released its hold on her. Her hands began to cramp around her glass.

"Well, these things happen," said William in a pious manner, as if excusing a major disaster, like a hurricane or an earthquake. He glanced toward his sister, Louisa, who was nibbling on a small helping of pasta salad. Shaking his head, he studied her. "It always seems strange to eat at these occasions, don't you think? For Chrissake, someone's dead: I should think we ought all to fast."

"I see you aren't eating," said Jessie in what she hoped was a respectful tone.

"Of course not; nor should anyone else," said William sharply. "Oh, I know it's tradition, and most of the family wanted it. I went along, because it would have meant putting the funeral in a bad light: I wouldn't do anything so disrespectful." The implication that much worse than eating had already been done was not lost on Jessie.

"Well, Marjorie wanted food at her funeral reception; she said so. Everyone is supposed to have a good time, so that their last memory of her can be pleasant. She didn't

190

want to call it a wake, because she said once she left, she had no intention of changing her mind and coming back. Once she left, it was her intention to stay gone." She chortled and averted her face. "I'm sorry. It's just that your mother had such a decisive way about her."

"Decisive," said William. "She did it all for us, of course, making up her mind about this . . . funeral reception, and spelling out how she expected it to be. She wanted to spare us any possible disagreements. If she had bothered to ask me about it—but she never would. It's all her doing."

"Of course," said Jessie, who had often been treated to long tirades on the inadequacies of Marjorie's children: Albert was wishy-washy, Melanie was foolish, William was fussy, and Louisa was a flibbertigibbet. "I don't know why I bothered so about them," Marjorie would exclaim. "None of them is worth half the effort I put out for them. None of them appreciates me. None of them knows a hawk from a handsaw." At those times, Jessie would make commiserating noises and fluff Marjorie's pillows, trying to ease her discomfort. Now, recalling the harangues, she was hard-put not to tell this self-important man what his mother had said about him. Somehow she managed to hold her tongue.

"I know you did your best for her. I know we ought to be thankful about it, but it's never easy." He went to the bar and ordered a second glass of white wine, saying over his shoulder to Jessie, "Not very good, but adequate for this, I suppose."

"I suppose," said Jessie, who had chosen the wine as the best value for price. "I know Marjorie liked it."

"Well, toward the end, with the drugs and all, I don't suppose there was much left of her . . . discernment. And she used to be so fussy about wine and food. Still, it was right to go along with her requests, I suppose. It's our duty to fulfill her wishes." He took the glass of wine and carried it toward the table where the salads and cheeses were set out; he lurked over them, rather like a vulture on a lightpole waiting for roadkill. "It's a shame you had such an unbecoming outburst, but I don't suppose you could help it. You're probably over-tired, with all the preparations for this, and organizing all the paperwork for the estate." He didn't wait for her to speak, but turned to Nowell Harbinger, Marjorie's lawyer, and began to ask him prying questions which Harbinger dodged artfully, promising full disclosure at the formal reading of the will.

"I know it isn't done too often any more, but it was her specific wish that you should all attend the reading," said Harbinger. "It's day after tomorrow, you know. Ten-thirty. Sharp."

"Yes. In your office." William glowered at him.

Jessie laughed again, this time in response to a memory that was as sharp as anything happening around her. "They'll all be like ravens perched on rooftops, making noises like rusty gates," Marjorie had said with relish. "It's a pity I won't be there to see it. All my dear relatives." Her smile had reminded Jessie of the grin on a crocodile. "Little do they know what I've done."

"You!" said George, who had extricated himself from Annis's clutches. "What's the matter with you?"

"I don't know," said Jessie, although she had a pretty good guess now. "I don't plan it."

"Good God, I hope not," said George. "It's really disconcerting."

"At least," said Jessie. She finished her mineral water and went for a refill. "I haven't enjoyed it much, myself."

"Sure you don't want something stronger?" asked the bartender.

"Actually, I'd love something stronger, but I know I'd start guffawing again, and that would be too much, even for this lot." She shook her head once. "Thanks for asking."

"My pleasure," he said, and upended a bottle into her glass. "Let me know when you change your mind. I'll pour anything you like."

George made a grunt of disapproval. "You've been through a lot, but you still ought to be willing to behave suitably."

"And what would that be?" Jessie asked, making no apology for her exasperation. "Do you think I ought to be overcome? I might have felt that during her last couple days. They were pretty harrowing. Or the night the power went out and the thunder and lightning went on for two hours—that was excruciating—do you think I had an excuse to lose it then, even though I didn't? But now? When it's all over? And everyone is beginning to turn their memories into myths?" She gulped a generous amount of mineral water and sputtered as a new burst of laughter took hold of her.

"Can't you control yourself?" George demanded. "Given all she did for you?"

"Oh, yes. All she did for me," said Jessie, and stopped the indignation she felt; it would be less welcome than her laughter.

"She took you in," said George emphatically. "Knowing what you did, she still took you in."

Enjoying the double meaning of that remark, Jessie said, "She certainly did. She was very good at taking people in."

George understood some of her meaning, and frowned again. "What an ungrateful thing to say."

"Why should I be grateful? I never did anything wrong. I was followed by a whispering campaign that was wholly un-founded," said Jessie with as much vehemence as she could

summon, which was surprisingly little. "You know that.
Marjorie knew that. The cops know it."

"You should have been grateful for the work," said
George righteously.

"And she should have been grateful for all I did above
and beyond nursing. Her room had fresh paint on the walls
and new sheets, so she wouldn't have to look at dull walls
and sleep in a dull bed. I did that for her." Jessie giggled.
"And I arranged for the elevator to be installed on the stair-
case so she could come down for dinner. It wasn't much,
but it was all she could do those last eight years."

"She paid for it," George reminded her.

Jessie cackled. "You can't tell me any of the others
would have thought to do any of it."

"If we were there every day, we would have," George
said.

"Do you think so?" Jessie laughed again.

George scowled. "That isn't a very kind implication."

"But true, George, true," said Jessie. "I did my best for
her."

"Your best," George scoffed. "If that's what you think,
no wonder you laugh." He turned away from her in con-
spicuous disapproval.

Jessie wanted to yell at him, to pound his back, and demand to know how many times he had emptied Marjorie's
bedpans, or struggled to wash her while she lay against her
pillows, complaining about being wet. Or the constant
struggle they had had with her oxygen tank, and, toward the
end, her ventilator. But it didn't seem worth it, and after
all, she was a nurse; they had paid her reasonably well—not
as much as some, but not badly—and it was all part of her
job. She handed the glass to the bartender. "Vodka, almost
no ice," she said.

The bartender filled her order without comment, although he winked at Jessie. He gave her an encouraging smile and handed her a small napkin; it was pale peach with a black edge, just as Marjorie had specified.

"This is for Marjorie." She lifted the glass, looking over at Daniel, who was pacing back and forth at the front of the room, occasionally glancing at his watch.

"Some folks get mad when people die," said the bartender.

"I know," said Jessie.

"You laughing gives them an excuse to be mad," he went on. "If it wasn't you, it would be someone else."

"I know that, too." The vodka was beginning to seep into her, its hot little fingers loosening her tight shoulders and filtering down into her stomach almost like a sexual thrill; she swallowed more of it. "Thanks."

"No one's ever as good as people say they are at funerals," the bartender went on. "No one really expects the service to tell it like it is, but the way they can all stand it."

"Ain't that the truth," Jessie said.

"And they're never as bad as people say, either," he added.

"Do you think so?" Jessie asked.

"It's gotta be that way," said the bartender. "I do maybe fifty of these a year, and they're all pretty much the same— everyone slightly embarrassed that someone's dead and secretly relieved they're still alive. It makes them all a little crazy." He poured a second vodka and handed it to Jessie. "Go ahead. Take this. It'll make it easier. Don't worry about how much you drink. If you need a cab, I'll see you get one. By the look of it, you won't be the only person taking one. I'll bet they'll have to pour at least eight of these mourners into taxis before the night is through. I'll keep an eye on you." He winked another time and waved away the tip she proffered. "You keep it. It sounds like you deserve it more than anyone here."

"That's a sweet offer. Thanks." For the first time her smile was genuine and without tension.

"Pleasure," said the bartender. "Get the most you can out of this party. It looks like things'll turn nasty in a couple of days."

Jessie considered this as she took the second glass and sipped it. "This is really good," she said.

"Taking care of that old lady must have been a lot of work," said the bartender.

"She could be demanding," Jessie admitted, feeling a bit conspiratorial for saying so much to a stranger with the family all around them.

"And they stayed away," said the bartender. "And now they're bitching about you. Typical." He winked at her again, more broadly than before. "Just come back here when your glasses are empty and I'll take care of you again."

"Thanks," said Jessie. "Thanks a lot." She took a couple of steps away from the bar so she wouldn't be tempted to have another vodka too quickly. This was more than she had had to drink in the last six months; not since New Year when she had had two rum toddies and three glasses of champagne had she allowed herself to indulge in more than a single glass of wine at dinner. She glanced over the room, trying not to catch anyone's eye. There was a couch against the wall and she was tempted to go sit down. But if she did, she could be trapped there if anyone decided to join her, so she remained where she was, slightly in front of the alcove that concealed the entrance to the kitchen.

"You read the autopsy report, I suppose?"

The question seemed to come out of the air. "What?" Jessie nearly dropped her drinks as she swung around to face Julian Bachs, the sleek young physician who had taken care of Marjorie for the last two years; Marjorie had distrusted him and she had insisted on calling Bradley Ferguson, her former physician who had retired almost three years ago and had checked each and every recommendation, prescription, and piece of advice that Bachs gave before she was willing to do anything. Bachs was in a charcoal-grey business suit and looked as if he was about to pose for *GQ*.

"The autopsy. You should have received a copy. Marjorie stipulated that Brad Ferguson, Nowell Harbinger, and you be given copies. It was authorized." He could not conceal his disgust at this arrangement.

"Yes. I received a copy, and I read it. Death was due to the failure of the ventilator during the power outage. Everyone knows that. This was obvious from the first. No one can say I made lightning strike the substation. The power company has the whole event in their records. And the drug levels in her body were where they ought to be for the treatment she was receiving. There was nothing suspicious about her dying."

He held up his drink—gin-and-tonic—and said, "That should shut up anyone who wants to cast blame for her death."

"Do you think there could be any questions about it?" Jessie asked, a rush of queasiness coming over her.

"In this family? I'd be shocked if someone didn't accuse you or one of the others, like Albert, of trying to do away with Marjorie. William has called me twice about the autopsy." He patted Jessie on the shoulder. "If there's any question, there's the autopsy report, and it removes all doubt."

197

For the first time in almost an hour, Jessie didn't feel in danger of laughing. "I don't want to have to go through any more investigations."

"You mean the one over twenty years ago?" Julian Bachs nodded. "Oh, yes, Marjorie told me all about it. She said she was safe having you take care of her, because you would have to do everything right, just in case. She said if anything was the least bit wrong, you'd have to move heaven and earth to make it right for her." He tapped his temple. "She was a little preoccupied with the fear that someone would kill her. I can't imagine why—she had no reason that I could think of to suppose any of her relatives might kill her. Everyone knew she was in failing health. And everyone knew that she couldn't last very long. If it hadn't been the power loss, it would have been something else. As it was she survived more than three years longer than anyone expected." He offered Jessie a polished smile. "You did a superb job for her. No one can possibly doubt you took excellent care of her."

"It's good of you to say so," she managed to tell him.

He drank the rest of his gin-and-tonic and put the glass down on the occasional table near the alcove; four glasses already stood on it. "I've had two already. I should take a break. But I might not. This is a pretty dreadful affair, isn't it?" He did his best to look reassuring. "If you take any grief from the family, you let me know and I'll explain it to them."

"You sound as if you expect trouble," said Jessie, and suddenly had to press her lips together so that she would not succumb to more laughter.

"Families get strange when there's been a death, especially of someone like Marjorie." Bachs cocked his head. "You shouldn't worry about anything."

Jessie took a moment to compose herself. "Then I'll do my

best not to," and in spite of her best intentions, she giggled.

"Stress, I know." Bachs wandered away to the bar only to return a few moments later with a glass filled with gin and ice, with a little tonic to give it sparkle. The sharp juniper odor caught Jessie's attention before she heard Bachs speak. "It was a long ordeal with her."

"I don't think she wanted to die," said Jessie, and fought back another roll of chuckles. Small wonder, she thought. With all Marjorie had done in her life, from Lysander to Theodore, she had made herself a widow four times over, all without compunction, and only when death was looming did any of her actions bother her. She had told Jessie, "I don't suppose there's a halo waiting for me in heaven. Not with what I've done. Still, I had children to think of, and the men couldn't be relied upon to bother with them. I reckon I would do it all again, if I had to. I might get rid of William—he's such a fussbudget. I could leave the others better off and I could have afforded to send Albert to Stanford. He might have made something of himself if he'd gone to a really good school. I don't see how God could hold any of that against me: He helps those who help themselves." She had looked apprehensive as she had repeated the adage. "But we're not supposed to kill, even when they're feckless spendthrifts."

"You were fortunate to get to know her so well," said Bachs. "I tried, but she didn't want any part of me. She paid me well, I'll say that for her."

Jessie drank more of her vodka, sputtering a little as she stopped her laughter. "I don't know if you'd call it that—knowing her."

Bachs looked over at her as his curiosity was spurred, and was about to add something when Jessie stepped away from him, for she was certain she was about to start laughing again. "Well, call me if you need anything," he said a little vaguely.

"Sure," said Jessie, her lower lip caught in her teeth. She went toward the bar, more for the company of the bartender than another drink.

At the front of the room, Daniel cleared his throat and nervously raised his voice. "It's gonna be a couple minutes more, folks. We'll have the Cliquot in a little bit. It's coming. Just be patient, please." He looked over at Jessie as if to dare her to laugh now. "They'll bring out glasses for everyone."

"What's the hold-up?" asked one of the mourners from out of town, a man in his fifties whom Jessie didn't recognize.

"Who knows?" said Daniel. He coughed once to show he was aware of how much of an imposition this delay was.

As if on cue a deliveryman in denim coveralls swaggered in behind a hand-truck bearing four cases of premium champagne. He held out a clipboard, and, after a moment, Albert went and signed for it. There was a sudden surge in conversation, as if all the people in the reception hall had been waiting for this moment.

Jessie finished her vodka and handed the glass to the bartender. "Keep it," she said. "And don't give me any more, even if I ask for it." She glanced away from the bartender; there were half-a-dozen guests gathering around the stack of cases. "Flies around honey."

"In more ways than one," said the bartender, and when Jessie glanced his way, winked at her.

In spite of her efforts, Jessie laughed again, this time without apology. As the others scowled and stared at her, she let herself continue to laugh. Finally it began to fade without any effort on her part, and, as three waiters distributed glasses of pale, fizzy champagne to the mourners, she wiped her eyes with her handkerchief and was surprised to see tears there. Why would she weep for that wretched old harpy? she asked herself. Marjorie had killed four grown men and five children, if she had told the truth. What on earth was there to cry about?

"You all right, ma'am?" the bartender asked.

When Jessie laughed again, there was a note of despair in it, a concession she had never expected to make. "She made me miss her, goddamnit."

George swung around again. "Well, I should think so. There aren't many women like Marjorie around. They don't make them like her any more."

As Jessie's laughter welled afresh, she said, "Yes. Let's hope," and drank her champagne before Daniel could propose a toast.

About *Inappropriate Laughter*

When I first wrote this, back in 1997, I hadn't a clue where I could sell it. It falls in between so many forms that it ends up belonging in none of them. The Spook *on-line magazine finally took it—trimmed down by 2,000 words—in 2002, and it is in that form that you see it now.*

The story's experiential inception, I think, stems from a memorial service I attended when I was 18. Two of my friends got the giggles about halfway through the event, and from that point on, small explosions of not-very-well-suppressed laughter punctuated the expressions of grief. I remember wishing they could/would stop, but that seemed impossible. For the next five months, the two regularly apologized for causing such an uproar, admitting that they couldn't recall why it had seemed funny to them. Certainly their chagrin has infused the story, along with a host of implications that may or may not account for what is happening.

NOVENA

On the third day of battle, the bombing drove Sister Maggie off the roof where she had taken refuge in an abandoned dovecote; she returned to the enormous, wrecked hotel, dreading what she would find in the four floors of pillaged rooms. Since the local uprising—calling itself a revolution—destruction had escalated. In was worse than she feared: in what had been the lobby injured children were left to their own devices while their parents labored to shore up defenses or joined various ragtag resistance movements, nipping at the enemy with captured guns, with improvised weapons, with knives, with stones.

The smell was like a slaughterhouse in summer, pungent and heavy. A continual moan made up of all the cries and whimpers and grunts of the wounded ebbed and flowed through the pillared ruin. Most of the furniture had been broken up and now covered the large, gaping holes that had once been windows. Two of the long couches had been pressed into service as examining tables. The village's midwife, usually shunned, was doing this work, practicing her own sort of triage.

Sister Maggie approached the old woman. "Let me help," she pleaded. "I am a nurse." She was reasonably certain she was the only person with clinical medical training for half a day's journey in any direction. It wrung her soul that no one in the village would accept her assistance: she was here to give it, yet remained ostracized.

The midwife pretended she did not understand, although

Sister Maggie spoke her language expertly. The peasant-woman continued to pour vodka looted from the hotel stores over the jagged, puffy flesh of a shrapnel wound.

"You've got to take the fragments out first," said Sister Maggie desperately, wishing the clinic still existed. She could use the equipment there, and the antibiotics. "If you don't clean it, it will fester and he'll lose the whole leg. Or his life." She crossed herself and noticed two of the children waiting for help make a sign to ward off the Evil Eye as she did so.

Finally the midwife looked at her, deep-probing eyes lost in furrowed wrinkles. "You have no right here. Leave us."

"But I can help," Sister Maggie protested.

"You have helped enough," said one of the wounded children, a girl of fourteen who had lost an eye and whose body was starting to swell with her first pregnancy. Her resentment drove Sister Maggie away from her as a fire or a stench would have done.

Still caught in the intensity of the girl's stare, Sister Maggie almost tripped over a three-year-old with a savage scalp wound. The child, pathetically thin and breathing in fast, shallow gasps, was already sinking into coma; as Sister Maggie watched, his breathing became more irregular. He would be dead in less than an hour without concerted treatment for shock. Without such intervention, he would die quickly, if God was kind. Sister Maggie paid no attention to the angry faces around her as she knelt to cross herself, and traced the sign of the cross on the boy's forehead, saying her prayers for him silently so that she would not be ordered to stop.

"Leave him alone!" shouted one of the old men guarding the place. In his arthritic hands he carried a rifle that was more than fifty years old.

"But I can help," Sister Maggie protested.

"No one can help him," the old man declared with the authority of age.

Sister Maggie moved away at once, leaving the dying child. She hoped God would understand and show His forgiveness, not only to her but to these people as well. There was so much she had asked Him to understand over the past five years, and always with the conviction that she would eventually be given the opportunity to make amends.

There was another boy, nine or ten, although he looked younger; everyone called him the Rat because he was the most adept thief and scavenger in the hotel, possibly in the entire village. He was especially good at raiding opposition materiel, but for this prized skill he was distrusted, too, and avoided. He was off in a corner of the lobby by himself, ignored and neglected. His right sleeve was stiff with dried blood. His huge eyes, a deep, soft brown, showed a cynicism that would have been troubling in a grown man; in this boy it was appalling. He watched the nun in the patched jumpsuit come toward him, saving nothing, his face expressionless, even of pain.

"Hello, Rat," said Sister Maggie, speaking his language with the ease of practice.

"Hello," he answered without emotion.

This would be difficult; she had been afraid he might not be willing to speak with her at all. She decided to behave as if the calamity around them were usual. "Has anyone had a chance to look at you yet? That arm could use—"

He regarded her with scorn. "Why would they look? What will they do?" He attempted to wave it, to show how minor a matter it was. His mangled hand flapped uselessly; unshed tears brightened his eyes, though he steadfastly refused to cry.

"Because they want you to keep stealing ammunition from the revolutionaries, and you need both hands working to do that," said Sister Maggie in her most reasonable voice. "Do you mind if I look at it?" She prepared herself for a rebuff and offered a short, inward prayer to the Virgin, hoping she could offer up the shame as well as her lost opportunity to serve.

"They don't care who steals the ammunition as long as someone does," the Rat said, but let Sister Maggie come over to him and cut away the lower part of his sleeve with the scissors of her Swiss Army knife. The only indication of his concern for his injury was in his reluctance to look at it. "There have been worse."

But not where a hand could be saved, thought Sister Maggie as she looked at what had happened to bone and muscle and flesh: an explosive had shattered half his hand and the lower end of the ulna. Fragile tendons showed above shattered bone. The Rat would be fortunate if he could salvage a thumb and the first two fingers, and that would require expert medical treatment. It was a grim prospect for the boy. What would he do with his life after such a loss? The possibilities were unbearably grim. "You should go to a hospital. You need help. You could lose . . ."

The Rat laughed.

"I mean it, Rat. You need a doctor, with drugs and medicines and machines to help him. That hand should be . . ." She made herself look away from the terrible damage. There had to be a way to save him. She had to do something. She wished she were not the only one left from the clinic—that the clinic was not a burn-scarred ruin. "A surgeon could save your hand, or some of it, and it would work right afterward. There is a hospital at the army depot, isn't there? It's only two days from here."

"Two days if there's no fighting and the roads are open. But if I go to the army, they will not help me, they will arrest me. They will put me in a cell with other boys, or keep me to amuse an officer. The army is like that. The soldiers are given their choice of men or women, for rewards. You have light hair. You are a Sister. A lot of them will want you." His smile showed how completely he understood his predicament, and hers, and what little patience he had for her suggestion. "I won't go to the army."

"Where else can you find a doctor?" Sister Maggie asked helplessly. "There must be a doctor who is not part of the army, or who does not answer to the army. Not all the doctors live in fear of the soldiers, do they?" Since Father Kenster died two years ago, she had not been able to find anyone willing to take his place—the village was too remote and in a district where rebel and counterinsurgent bands roamed at will, taking what they could carry and burning the rest in the name of reform and revenge. "What about the . . . the town where they have the sheep market?" She could not remember the name, if she had ever known it.

"The sheep market?" The Rat made a contemptuous motion with his good hand, smiling without mirth. "Everyone thinks there are doctors at the sheep market. There are. For the sheep. None of them would touch me, or anyone like me."

"Then where?" Sister Maggie demanded.

"Nowhere, you idiotic woman." He let his voice drop, his face haggard. "There are no doctors for us. Doctors do not come here. It is only a lie to tell people when they get sick, so that they may be taken away when they are dying, and no one will make trouble about it. 'We are going to the doctor,' they tell the dying ones, and everyone is satisfied." At last the Rat looked at the destruction of his hand. Aside from turning white around the mouth, his face might have been set in cement for all it revealed.

"You need medical treatment." She said it more forcefully, watching the boy, wishing she still had even a few basic supplies. She wanted to know his blood pressure, body temperature, pulse rate; she wanted to monitor him for shock. But the last of the supplies had been lost when Father Kenster died defending the clinic.

"Your medicine is wrong. It would kill me." He stared at her. "I don't want it."

"But—" Sister Maggie squatted down beside the Rat. "You can't ask me to ignore you. I can't forget what's been—" She gestured toward his sleeve.

He swung away from her. "I will forget. I am forgetting already. You will forget. The others"—he jutted his chin toward the children lying in the refuse of the lobby—"will forget. It means nothing."

"I can't do that," she insisted. "I'm a nun. I took vows, Rat. I made promises to God and the Church, before you were born. I promised to help people." It was sixteen years ago, she realized distantly. The idealistic young nurse in her habit and veil and wimple was a third of the world and a third of her life away. It had seemed so wonderful, being a medical missionary, someone who could actually make a difference in the world, someone would could heal the body as well as the soul. Sixteen years ago, in Boston, it had all seemed so possible.

"God will not mind if you stop being a nun after so long," the Rat said with something like kindness, all he was capable of offering her. "Forget your vows. You cannot keep them here, and your Church has already forgotten you."

"You don't understand," said Sister Maggie, grateful for

his attempts at softening the blow; steady, seductive despair tugged at her, tantalizing her with the balm of helplessness. "It would make me a . . . a fraud." The word was softer than the one she had chosen at first, but she doubted the Rat know who Judas was, or cared.

On the north side of the village the bombing steadily increased.

At dusk the next evening the Rat found Sister Maggie back on the roof in the remnants of her dovecote. He was looking pasty but for his wounded hand, which was ruddy and swollen, shiny of skin and hot to the touch; corruption had set in. "Not even the birds want to live here anymore. Why do you?"

"For peace," she said, refusing to be distracted by the tracer bullets against the northern sky. "It was this or the streets."

"But the bombs will ruin it. If not now, soon. At first it was just pistols, then rifles, but now they are serious. You could die." He was feverish, his eyes brilliant as broken glass. "It was stupid, getting hurt. I picked up a bomb. I couldn't throw it away fast enough." He laughed angrily, rocking with pain.

"Come out of the sun," said Sister Maggie, trying to lead the boy to what shelter remained of her dovecote.

"No." He lunged away from her. "Keep back."

She reached out to the boy. "Don't do this, Rat. Please don't do this."

"Why?" His voice broke. "Because it makes you unhappy? Because you don't have a way to stop it?" He could not swagger the way he liked but he was able to get an arrogant lift to his chin. "You came here! We didn't ask you, you came! None of us wanted you. We wanted help to kill our enemies. We didn't want a clinic, we wanted guns."

Hearing this from the infection-dazed boy, she had to struggle to maintain a little composure. "If you outlive your enemies, if you can live better than they do, then you triumph over them," she said patiently.

He spat. "They will come and take everything." He moved his good hand in an encompassing gesture. "The village will be gone before the year is out. Now that they have noticed us, there is nothing we can do to save it."

"They killed Father Kenster, and the other Sisters," said Sister Maggie, crossing herself as much out of habit as conviction. "May God forgive them for their sins."

"May God fill them with the plague that kills and kills and kills, and rots their bodies to nothing for ten generations!" He stumbled and would have fallen if Sister Maggie had not caught him. She settled him back gently onto the sheet metal and planking that made up most of the roof. "Get away from me," he muttered. "I do not want your help."

"You will have to endure it, anyway," she said, almost grateful to the boy for collapsing. At last there was a chance—a slim one but a chance—to do something for him, to expiate the many times she had not been able to help. She did not want this boy to be like the others, turning away from her. She might not have all the tools she wanted, but she was a good nurse as well as a nun, and neither of those callings had changed because her circumstances had. As long as she had her skill, her training, and her faith, there was hope. The lessons learned long ago were still with her. She went about her tasks with the automatic ease of long practice. First she felt the pulse in his throat, finding his heartbeat fast, not quite regular; his forehead and palms were hot, dry; his body had a meaty odor about it. She would get one of her blankets to put over him, that was a start. When night fell, she would give him her own blanket as well, so that he would not be chilled. His feet ought to be raised above the level of his head, to lessen the work his heart had to do, but she had no means to accomplish this, and abandoned the effort.

"I do not want your help," the Rat said again a little later. He was distracted and remote. When he moved his good arm it was in an aimless, swimming gesture.

Sister Maggie improvised a stethoscope made of a small metal cone from a spent shell casing. She did what she could to determine how ill the boy was, and was left with only a few incomplete impressions that were more distressing than helpful. She rocked back on her heels and crossed herself, starting to pray for the Rat, and herself. For the time being it was the most she could do. He needed to have his fever reduced, she was certain of that, but there was no ice in the village, no aspirin, no cold cellar or underground bunker where she could tend him. There was no place to bathe him, for the water here was rationed and guarded; none of it would be wasted on a boy filled with infection.

Gunfire rattled in the street below, and occasionally a heavier report thudded on the air. Once there was a display of tracer bullets and the distant pounding of an antiaircraft gun poking holes in the dark. Sometime after the middle of the night a mine went off, and an instant later the vehicle that triggered it exploded in a gasoline inferno. Random shots from sniper rifles cracked in irregular observance of the passing hours.

By morning the Rat's arm was hard, more than twice its normal girth, the lacerated flesh mounding out of the wound, bright with red starburst patterns around it, radiating toward his shoulder. The smell of infection was stronger and his mouth was dry, lips chapped and bleeding.

Now he could not move his damaged hand at all.

Knowing it was a useless gesture, Sister Maggie began to cut up her last set of sheets; she had salvaged them along with two crates of bedding from the bombed-out clinic. Now all that was left was this one pair of sheets and three pillowcases. She began to roll pressure bandages, and methodically tied them in place above the ominous red streaks. If she could do nothing else, she might be able to hold the infection at bay for a little while. "I should have done this last night," she muttered as she bound the bandage in place with long strips of sheeting. "I ought to have done this when I first saw him, I should have insisted." She whispered a prayer for mercy as she knotted the strips on the boy's chest, taking care to be certain that the bandage would stay in place no matter now much the Rat tossed and strained.

At midday the desultory firing stopped and the streets grew still in the oppressive heat. There was no place on the roof where Sister Maggie could find shelter.

The Rat had begun to howl softly every time he breathed, plucking at the single blanket with the fingers of his good hand. There was no strength left in him.

Desperately, Sister Maggie took the second blanket she had wrapped around the Rat during the night and now spread it over the shattered frame of the dovecote. The tent that resulted was clumsy and inadequate, but it kept the sun off the child, and for that Sister Maggie thanked God in the prayers she offered for the boy, the village, herself.

By sundown there were three bullet holes in the blanket.

A sullen-faced young woman, no more than sixteen but with her face already marked by harsh lines, climbed onto the roof in the dusk, approaching Sister Maggie with an assault rifle in her hands. She had given up the traditional women's dress of the region for a soldier's fatigues; her manner was deliberately unfeminine. "You have to take that blanket down," she said without any greeting. "They're going to use it for a target. They know someone's up here. You can see that for yourself." She used the barrel of the rifle to point to the dry undergrowth at the end of the bomb-pocked road. "They're coming."

"Which group is it this time?" asked Sister Maggie, distressed that she should feel such animosity to the young woman for speaking to her. "Or do you know?"

"We think it's DRUY," she answered with a gesture of disgust. "We want no part of them. They're turds. But they're after us. They're coming here to find us. They'd been through the hills around here for the last six days, looking for us."

"DRUY," repeated Sister Maggie. "Whose side are they on?" She wanted to show the young woman she was interested, though she was unable to keep the various factions straight in her mind.

"Their own," said the young woman. "They're led by one of the generals, who was chucked out of the army, five years back. He thought they owed him something for all he was doing, so he took his best troops with him when he left, to get even. Supplies for them, too. They're better fighters than most of the others. They have better equipment, too." She patted her assault rifle. "We've been told they're getting money and supplies from outside."

"Who?" asked Sister Maggie, dreading the answer.

"Who knows?" The young woman shrugged. "The U.S. China. France. Tripoli. Venezuela. India. The Crimea. Ireland. Zambia. Who can tell? Saudi Arabia. Argentina. Korea. Brazil. What difference does it make? Their weapons are German and Japanese, but that means nothing. Who paid for them and brought them here? No one knows." She walked to the edge of the roof. "There are only three other safe buildings left in the village. Just three; that's all. If this battle lasts much longer, there won't be any."

Sister Maggie was busy holding the Rat down while he thrashed in pain and delirium. It was a demanding task, for in these outbursts the weak child had the strength of a large grown man and fought without quarter. There was a bruise on the side of her face to attest to his demented fury. She hardly noticed when the young woman came over to look at the boy.

"He's dying," the young woman announced impersonally. "You might as well let him go. You can't save him. Don't make it any harder on him than it is."

"I have to try," said Sister Maggie.

"Why?" The young woman looked at the Rat with flat, pitiless eyes. "It only means that he suffers longer. Leave him at the other end of town."

"No!" Sister Maggie declared. "I will not leave a human being—let alone a child—on a refuse heap. Not this boy, not anyone. I told him I would do everything I can to save him." She put her hand to the Rat's forehead, knowing his temperature was much too high.

"You can't expect anyone to bury him, not with the DRUY coming. It wouldn't be safe. Anyone who can get out will be gone before midnight." She hunkered down beside Sister Maggie. "I'll help you get him off the roof. I'll try to get a place you can take him, somewhere you won't get shot, somewhere the pigs won't eat him. But don't try to hang on to him. He's lost already. All he has left is pain." She pulled out a brown cigarette and lit it with a wooden match. "Come on. Let's get to it."

"I can't abandon him to death," Sister Maggie persisted,

reaching for new rolls of torn sheet in order to change his bandages. "I must do what I can to help him, as long as there is life in his body. And mine."

The young woman chuckled once, a sound like a pistol shot. "There isn't life in him anymore. There's infection, that's all." She stared at the Rat's sunken features. "He's gone, you foolish cunt. He's just breathing meat."

It was all Sister Maggie could do to keep from screaming. "He is not dead. Until he is dead, he is in my hands and I have an obligation to do everything I can to keep him alive. I took an oath, one that most of you prevent me from keeping. I promised to heal the sick, for the honor of Christ. It is my sworn duty as a nurse." She hated the way she sounded, more pompous than devoted, but it was all she could do to keep her rage under control.

"Well, if you have to torture him—" The young woman shook her head once and stood up. "I'll help you get him off the roof. He won't broil down in the hotel."

This time the offer felt more like a threat, and after a brief hesitation Sister Maggie rocked back on her heels. "All right, but I need a protected place. I don't want you—any of you—near him."

"If we get to fighting at close range, you'll have more to take care of than the Rat. It won't matter where you're hiding then. They want the village, the group out there, DRUY. We don't know why. This place isn't important now that the clinic's gone." With that she ambled a short distance away, showing her indifference to danger. She took up a guard stance on the corner of the roof. She finished her cigarette while Sister Maggie pulled down the tented blanket and rolled it so that it could be turned into a sling-stretcher for the Rat.

When Sister Maggie had shifted the moaning boy onto

the blanket, she signaled to the young woman. "He's ready. We can carry him down now."

"Fine," said the young woman. She took one last look around the roof, then came back to where Sister Maggie waited for her help. "You're a fool," she told Sister Maggie dispassionately as she knelt down to pick up one side of the blanket.

The shot tore through her shoulder and neck, spraying blood and tissue in sudden eruption. The young woman lurched, her arms suddenly swinging spasmodically. She half-staggered a few steps, then collapsed, twitching, blood surging out of her destruction. Her assault rifle, flung away at the bullet's impact, clattered down the side of the hotel to the street below.

Sister Maggie made herself go to the young woman's side, though she knew there was no help left to her, not in the world. She knelt beside her, trying to block out the continuing violent trembles and shudders of the young woman's body while she made the sign of the cross on her broken forehead, uttering the prayers of redemption and salvation; there was nothing else to do.

She knew the Rat was dead, but would not permit herself to admit it, not until she had reached safety for him, where he could lie in peace. The body in the improvised sling tied around her shoulders and across her chest was limp, flopping against her back as she made her way through the street in the first light of day. He would not be flexible much longer; he would become as rigid as carved wood. His shattered arm was bloated with the infection that had killed him; the stench of decay riddled his flesh.

A blackened bus lay twisted on its side, and Sister Maggie decided to avoid it—the wreckage had been there long enough to provide cover for one side or the other. It would give them no protection.

A helicopter fluttered overhead, searchlight probing the long shadows as it hovered near the tallest rooftops in the village. From time to time its machinegun beat out a tattoo in counterpoint to the chatter of its blades. The morning light struck its side with glare; there were no identifying marks painted on it, no way to know whose it was or what it presaged. Once someone hidden in the old tannery took a shot at the helicopter, but the bullet missed and fire from the helicopter blasted the south face off the old building, setting the rest in flame.

As she walked Sister Maggie made herself pray, reciting the rosary although she had not held one in her hands for more than three years; people here regarded rosaries as bad magic, the tools of witchcraft rather than religion, and so she had not been surprised when hers—a gift from her grandmother—disappeared. She was on her ninth *Hail, Mary* when she heard the sounds of voices up ahead. As quickly as she could with her burden, Sister Maggie found a doorway and stumbled through it, seeking the dark corners where she could wait until the voices were gone. As she drew away from the light her lips continued to move in prayer, but now she made no sound at all.

More voices came, men's voices, and the sound of marching feet. This was more than a few resistance fighters returning from raids. Sister Maggie wished now that she had given more attention to the young woman who had been killed the evening before, to what she said about the DRUY, if that was who these men actually were. She felt the stiffening weight of the Rat's corpse drag at her shoulders, but she would not put him down, not here.

After an hour or so there was a flurry of gunfire from inside one of the buildings—the hotel? the school?—and some sort of heavy vehicle—more than Jeeps and less than tanks—roared and lumbered down the streets, lurching through the blasted pavement to whoops of approval. There was one large explosion, and the impact of one of the vehicles hurtling into the side of the building where Sister Maggie hid, followed by several minutes of intense firing that left her with ringing ears. And then the remaining troop carriers were bouncing down the street again, and the men in them laughed and shouted their victory. Two of the officers posted men at the door to the old hotel, where the injured lay in the lobby, joking about the makeshift first aid station and the suffering children.

Sister Maggie shut out the coarse yells and bursts of laughter. She was fiercely thirsty, and she could feel the relentless heat growing as the sun climbed higher in the sky. The body she carried made breathing nearly unbearable, but she realized it provided her a curious protection, for the stench might keep the invaders away from this building.

"Later," Sister Maggie whispered, a promise to the Rat. "Later we'll make sure you have a proper grave, and a cross with your name on it. It'll take a while. I'm sorry. I'm sorry." She knew no name but the Rat, and she hoped he would understand when she wrote it. Perhaps, she thought, during the afternoon while everyone else was napping, then she might be able to sneak out of the village and find a place where the Rat could be laid to rest. She tried to think of an apology to offer the boy, to make amends for what he had endured. "It has to be done, for the sake of your soul, and mine. God is merciful, Rat. He understands," she said in an undertone. "God will welcome you, for your courage and your youth."

A ragged cheer rose up outside; she flinched at the sound. She inched closer to the door, crouching down as far as the body on her back would allow. The posture was uncomfortable and precarious, for if the corpse shifted Sister Maggie would be pulled off her feet. But it was most important to know what was going on. It was too risky to peek around the door, so she contented herself with listening. Soon she wished she had plugged her ears.

"What about this place?" one soldier called to another. "Worth holding?"

"No," the other answered from further away. "We'll mine it later. Don't leave anything for the terrorists to use. They've probably been given refuge here, anyway. Villages like this one—what can you expect?"

"Tonight?" His question was laconic, utilitarian.

"No rush. Not for a shithole like this. Tomorrow's soon enough." The indifference in his voice made Sister Maggie want to vomit.

Four villagers had been found and driven out of their shelters to provide the invaders with amusement. One was an elderly man, whose high, piping voice screeched with fear and wrath; one was a woman who wept constantly, begging for her life; one was a blind boy who used to play a hammered zither for coins but was now a beggar; the last was the retarded daughter of the last village leader, a sweet child who had no more reason than a puppy, and no recognition of danger.

"Make them run," suggested one of the invaders who stood not far from Sister Maggie's hiding place.

"Too easy," said his companion. "Look at them. No sport in running these beasts." He clapped his hands several times for attention. "Is this the best the village has to offer? Those wounded are useless to us."

The old man hurled insults at the newcomers.

There was a short burst of automatic fire, and the unmistakable sound of a body falling. And then there was silence.

The retarded girl began to whimper.

"Think of something you can do to amuse us," said the second man, and his boredom made this a fatal pronouncement.

It was all Sister Maggie could do not to scream, to run from her protected spot and flail at these proud men. It was too much to bear. She felt it shiver through her, the enormity of her burden. She folded her hands and pressed her forehead against her fingers, as if faith could blot out what was happening just four strides away from her. She made herself remain still, thinking of the work she had yet to do for the Rat. If she were discovered she would not be able to help any of the villagers, she would only be able to join them in suffering and the Rat would be cast onto the refuse heap; she had vows and promises to honor, a purpose beyond the momentary and futile satisfaction of naming these DRUY soldiers as the murderous outlaws they were.

By midafternoon the soldiers had almost exhausted their three victims; they had tormented and tortured the villagers through the heat of the day and were beginning to run out of ideas. The woman had stopped crying some time before and now did little more than scream softly when a soldier threw himself on her. The blind boy no longer struggled but knelt passively, lost in a darkness greater than his eyes.

"Too bad the girl's dead," Sister Maggie heard one of the soldiers say; he was close enough that she could have stretched out her arm and grabbed his ankle. "But that's war, I guess."

What his answer might have been was lost in a sudden eruption of gunfire from the east side of the village.

The blind boy, his face streaked with blood and semen, stared up blankly at the sound. Then an antitank shell struck next to him and he vanished in a ruddy haze.

The DRUY troops bolted for cover, most of them swearing as they searched for shelter that provided a place to shoot from. One of the troop carriers went out of control and slammed into the entrance of the battered building where Sister Maggie crouched with the Rat, dead, locked in rigor mortis on her back.

For an instant Sister Maggie feared the troop carrier would explode, and then that fear was replaced by a more insidious one as she realized that she was now trapped inside the building. The thirst she had been able to hold at bay flared afresh, and hunger, which she had denied, sank into her body like a burn.

There were three helicopters overhead now, and the firing was constant, a rage of noise like the overwhelming shriek of a hurricane. Bits of stucco and metal and masonry flew into the street. The remaining shards of glass splintered in windows, crumbling sharp as diamonds. The wreckage of the clinic was broken again as mortar fire struck the one remaining section of roof.

The old hotel where Sister Maggie had lived in her dovecote took four direct hits and broke apart.

Sister Maggie was weeping, but she did not know it. She tried to pray for the children buried in the lobby, but the words stuck in her throat. If she were not so thirsty, she thought, then she could pray. If the guns were quiet. If she were not alone. She coughed in the acrid fumes of battle and tried again to find the words to heal the souls of that human annihilation, but could not utter them. Her eyes stung, her skin prickled, and she realized how cramped her muscles were. "It's too loud," she shouted and could not hear herself against the clamor of battle. The helicopters swung over the village, circled twice in their task of demolition. The remaining two sound buildings were their most obvious victims, one sundered from its metal skeleton, the other burning, toxic smoke blackening the remaining walls like a body in the sun.

The DRUY soldiers were cut down, their troop carriers shot and shelled.

Very deliberately Sister Maggie began to repeat the prayers for grace with which she had accompanied Father Kenster when he administered extreme unction, begrudging the few tears she shed, for she was so thirsty that even tears seemed too much precious moisture to lose. Her hands shook as she crossed herself.

And then it was quiet again, the helicopters slipping away to the east, following the rutted road that led to the next village.

"Spirit of Christ, give me life. Body of Christ, be my salvation. Blood of Christ, quench my thirst—" Sister Maggie gagged, then made herself continue. "Water . . . water from Christ's side, cleanse me. Suffering of Christ, enable me to suffer courageously. Merciful Jesus, hear me. Keep me always close to You. From Satan's wiles defend me. In death's hour, call me. Summon me to Your presence, that forever with Your saints I may praise You. Amen. Spirit of Christ, give me life. Body of Christ, be my salvation . . ." She did not know how many times she repeated the prayer; finally she realized it was nearly dark in the village, where the only brightness was the dying fire in the bombed buildings.

Insects had found the Rat's body; several long lines of them made their way across the ruptured floor slab to the now-flaccid figure that no longer seemed quite human— bloated and sunken at once. The endless, relentless minuscule armies moved industriously over the swollen corpse, searching out his wounds, his nostrils, his eyes.

Sister Maggie wrestled the blanket knots loose and flung herself away from the body, brushing her clothes to rid them of the multi-legged vermin that bit and stung and wriggled on her flesh. As she clawed off her worn, filthy jacket she stared in horror at the ants and beetles and things she did not recognize making their way along the curve of her ribs, as if they did not know the difference between the living and the dead. She felt the raw and painful tokens the insects left for her; disgust, abhorrence went through her, leaving her retching and dizzy.

Thirst was the most overwhelming of her desires, a greed so pure that it filled her soul like prayer.

She dared not look back at the Rat, for fear of what she might do. The stench was thick in the air, and if she saw what she knew he had become she would be unable to pray for him, now or ever.

Water. Without that, she was no different from the Rat, just a little less ripe. Her body shuddered, in hurt or laughter she could not tell. There were no prayers left in her, no sworn duty to discharge. There was only water. Nothing else was real.

She approached the troop carrier blocking the entrance; it filled the doorway almost entirely, and what small areas it did not block could not provide sufficient room for escape. Sister Maggie shoved at it, trembling with the effort though it produced little force and no effect. Her vision muddied and blurred and she clung to the grille to remain upright. She had to find another way out, but she knew she would not be able to move much longer, and night was closing in.

There were stairs, but after the fifth one the treads were gone; Sister Maggie moaned with despair and felt her way along the hall, listening to the cluttering and scuffling in the dark, her need for water making them unimportant. She was too consumed by thirst to be frightened. What was the more dangerous to her than her thirst? She was haunted by the sound of water falling—a faucet? rain? a river?—and it impelled her as nothing before had ever done. Water. Deep pools shimmered at the edge of her sight, brimming cups sloshed and squandered the precious stuff just out of reach. It was sacred. Her search went on though she was not able to think about what she was doing anymore.

The broken glass cut her hand, but she paid slight attention as she dragged herself out of the collapsed sliding door at the rear of the building. The ceiling showed gaping holes from the floor above, and occasionally there were bright eyes flickering in the darkness.

The storm was driven by high winds; lightning tore through the sky and thunder battered at it. Sister Maggie stumbled into the deluge, afraid that it was a continuation of her hallucinations. After her first shambling steps she fell, and the rain ran into her hair and ears. With the last of her strength she rolled onto her back and parted her cracked lips to the tumultuous sky.

By morning the rain was nothing more than a steady, pattering drizzle, likely to pass shortly as the day heated.

There were no more fires in the village. Nothing stirred. No voices called in greeting or warning or anguish. No screams or groans, no crying alarmed Sister Maggie. She sat on a fallen section of wall at what had been the jail when she had first arrived here to take up work at the new clinic, the hope of the region. Then the village was nothing more than the support to an old hotel where few tourists came. Her skin hurt, her eyes were hot in her head, her guts felt raw. The prospect of walking was hideous.

She made herself rise, then stood, wondering which way she ought to go. Which direction offered a haven? Where would she be safe? The sound she made was not laughter, though she had thought it would be.

Then she heard the crack of a rifle. She dropped into the mud and lay still, trusting she would be mistaken for dead.

The Jeep that lurched into the village was ancient, its engine grating. The three men clinging to it were scruffy, the guns they carried old-fashioned.

"They said there was a clinic here!" one of them protested as the Jeep wallowed down the main street.

"Where?" another asked in abiding cynicism.

"Shit," said the first. "What good's this place without a clinic?"

"Doesn't look like it's a place anymore," said the third voice.

"We need a clinic!" the first insisted.

"Well, there isn't one here," said the third. "We might as well leave it alone."

"God, look at it," said the second.

"It happens," said the third.

Then they were too far off and their faltering engine too loud for Sister Maggie to hear more. Within five minutes she heard the Jeep labor out of the village, leaving it to the dying rain.

Were they right? she wondered as she got unsteadily to her feet. Had the medical team brought disaster to the village? The clinic did give the village a prize, something others might want, but it had been there to help them, all of them. If the clinic had not come, the village would have sunk into decay unnoticed. And no one, she told herself inwardly, would have bothered the village. They would have been free of war but the prey of disease. Many of the villagers had resented the clinic, and Father Kenster. And her. And when Father Kenster and the other Sisters had been killed, the villagers had not mourned them. Had they been right all along? Had she come here as an act of sacrifice or suicide?

She found a canteen and filled it with water. That was a beginning. She would have to eat soon or there would truly be another corpse in the village, one last—She pushed the thought out of her mind. Later, she told herself. Later.

In case there was someone listening—if only the Rat—she whispered, "Lord have mercy on us. Lord have mercy on us. Lord have mercy on us. Christ have mercy on us," as she walked away.

About *Novena*

No one in this story has a name except Sister Maggie. And it takes place some place jungular. Other than that, everything is undefined, with the intention that it could apply to many times and places. It was written for an anthology edited by Dennis Etchison; he had asked for something that was clearly horror but without any touch of the supernatural; I did my best to comply.

TRADITIONAL VALUES

"I don't know what to do about Denny," said his mother as she adjusted the angle of the ambience control so that the cool, scented air did not blow directly in her guest's face.

"What is it, this time?" Ashe asked, accepting the tray of hybrid fruits Marris offered her. It was mid-morning and both women were taking time to relax before getting into the more arduous part of the day's work. Neither was young but had that unstudied attractiveness that comes with, and from, experience.

"He isn't listening to us anymore. You'd think he didn't have any comprehension of the past, or our values. He's got us worried, really worried. I don't know what to do about it." Marris sat down opposite her friend. "We've tried everything we can think of."

"Parents have been saying that for ages and ages," said Ashe, still awkward with her body modifications, and her maternity clothes; she did not really need them yet, but took great satisfaction in wearing them. "What makes you think you have to do anything? When he thinks about it, he'll come around."

"He's . . . he's been saying he isn't going to transfer when he and Londyl get married." She could not keep the disapproval out of her voice, though she spoke of her own son.

"Then he and Londyl will have a hard time of it, if they want children," said Ashe, not quite laughing. Everyone knew the reason to marry was for children—all the rest had domestic associate contracts. "Is Denny aware of that? Is Londyl?"

"They say they're getting married," Marris told Ashe, her mouth a narrow, disapproving line. "They're both going to stay the way they are. No changes for either of them. Honestly, you'd think they were animals." Now that this confession was out, Marris was eager to confide the rest, relieved to have the chance to have a little sympathy. "I've told him he'll never bear his own child. I've told him he will never comprehend female nature; and Londyl won't know what it is to be male. Their children will be biased, and they will all be out of place in the world—throwbacks to barbarism. I've told him, and *told* him, and . . . it doesn't do any good."

"Denny's young; he's looking for something new in his life." Ashe tried to keep herself from becoming distressed; that happened so easily now. She took the required deep breaths and steadied herself, focusing all her attention on her long-time friend. "Does he know that if you felt the way he does, he would never have been born?"

"Yes. I've told him and so has Brier, but no luck so far. He's said to Brier he doesn't think we should transfer when he marries, either. He says that we should remain as we are, too. It's lunacy." She drank some of her tisane, hoping this ordinary act would conceal her embarrassment. "Brier wants to have a second child. I think that's a reasonable desire; we've almost finished taking care of Denny. I'm willing to transfer. In fact, I want to, for Brier as much as for me, not just because it's traditional. But you should hear Denny." She set her mug down.

"Why does Denny care what you do? He won't be in the home with you. It's not as if *you'd* be doing anything *wrong*. If you want another child . . . Sounds to me as if Denny is trying to make sure you don't have any more children. He may be jealous." The more she thought about that, the more likely it seemed. "But you've provided for him as the law requires. Your second child will have the same protections. Not that that's any of his concern. Now that he's getting married, he will have his own affairs to occupy him, so even if he is jealous, he—" She cocked her head to the side. "Or is there more to it than that?" This shrewd question took Marris by surprise. She coughed.

"What makes you ask?" Marris replied evasively.

"I've known you—how many years? I think I can tell when you're not saying everything that's on your mind." Ashe selected a golden-amber fruit with leathery skin concealing a delicious, custard-like interior.

There was a long pause. "You've heard about Hirra Almeini?" Marris asked with her voice lowered; she glanced over her shoulder toward the high, narrow window as if she supposed they might be overheard.

"Him? That crazy old man! No wonder you say it's lunacy. Are you saying that Denny is listening to *him?*" Ashe was shocked. She could not conceal it as much as she wanted to. "That man is a menace. The graffiters make fun of him and his followers."

"Denny says the graffiters are paid to do that," Marris said, sounding a bit embarrassed.

"I think the graffiters go too easy on him," Ashe said indignantly. "They can claim he's harmless with only—well— lunatics for followers, but he frightens me." She put the fruit down as if the succulent pulp had lost its flavor and texture.

"Yes." Marris stared into her empty mug. "Yes. Denny has decided he wants to live the way Almeini is saying we all should." She coughed again, and Ashe realized how tense her friend was.

"Well, no *wonder* he's opposing another child for you and Brier." She was upset on her friend's behalf. "Would he object if you stayed female and carried the child?"

"I guess not," said Marris unhappily. "Almeini would approve, so I suppose Denny would, as well."

Ashe felt a rush of sympathy for her friend. "This must be just awful for you, Marris."

Marris nodded numbly. "I can't help thinking about what happened in Contanzbul last year. All those people killed, and the hospital in ruins."

"Almeini praised the people who did it," said Ashe, as if saying it aloud made it less dreadful. "I remember how shocked everyone was when he spoke out in support of the killing. How many died?"

"Four hundred twenty-seven," said Marris dully. "I looked it up. Denny was talking about it last night, saying that it was too bad there were so many dead, but it was their own fault for being in such a place." She blinked to keep from weeping.

"But doesn't he *understand?*" Ashe demanded. "Doesn't he know how important it is?"

"According to Almeini, it is unnatural," said Marris, reciting what her son had told her. "Almeini preaches that changing is perverse, against natural law."

"Nobody takes him seriously. Not the graffiters, not anyone." Ashe flung out her hands as a sign of impatience. "Everyone starts out female, we know that. Embryonic development changes females to males. Transferring is the most natural thing about us; going from female to male and back again is built into our genes. Walking upright is unnatural," scoffed Ashe. "Having artificial light is unnatural. Eating constructed hybrid food is unnatural. But we all do it. Including Denny. And Almeini."

"Almeini says he won't transfer again, and Denny is proud of Almeini's position, holding him up as an example to his other followers. He says that we shouldn't interfere with our genetic make-up. He says that once we're out of the womb, we should stay as we emerged; it's more of Almeini's doctrine." She sighed. "Denny ranted about it for more than an hour."

"We've been interfering with our genetic make-up for centuries—for eons, in fact," said Ashe, putting one hand on the slight swell in her abdomen. "Where would we be if we hadn't?"

"Almeini says we would be in a better balance with nature than we are now, according to Denny," said Marris, and broke out in tears. "I'm so ashamed of Denny. I don't know what to do."

"Nature!" Ashe scoffed. "Nature would have us digging for clams with a sharp stick. Nature would have us breed ourselves to extinction. Does Denny have anything to say about that?"

"Only what he hears Almeini say," was Marris's dispirited answer as she wiped her eyes and blew her nose.

"What does Brier think?" Ashe asked cautiously. She leaned over the table and put her hand on Marris's arm. "This is probably as hard on him as it is on you."

Marris took a deep, irregular breath. "Possibly harder; he is so proud of Denny, and to have everything we've hoped for held up to derision. Denny told him it was wrong of him to have a child. That he should father one on me again or have no more. Brier was furious; he said he was entitled to have a child just as I had. They both said some hurtful thing to one another. I . . . I hope they didn't go too far."

"What does Londyl think about all this? Have you talked

to her?" Ashe hoped that she could find a way to ease Marris's distress. "Londyl *must* have some thoughts about all this if she's going to go along with it."

"Oh, yes. She's the one who got Denny into it in the first place." She shook her head. "Why she would, I can't think. She kept going on about the essential female."

"But we're *all* essential females . . ." Ashe drank her tisane. "Doesn't she want that for Denny, too, if she thinks it is so unique?"

"She says that Almeini has declared that transference is wrong, that the fundamental human experience is destroyed when we have our three traditional transferences." She looked up at the ceiling as if hoping to find the answers she sought there.

For a short time both women were silent. Then Marris said, "I've tried to get Denny to read about how things were before transference. It hasn't done any good. According to him, all the records have been purged. The statistics on abuse and murder of spouses is nothing more than hearsay, a scare tactic to keep us from returning to the way we were. He says that making transferring possible ruined the way humans deal with one another. I asked him if he remembers anything from his domestic history class. He says it's all propaganda. I can't find a single argument he is willing to listen to about how things were. He says there would never be that kind of discrimination or oppression. I know he is only spouting what he hears Almeini say, but I—Almeini has explained that when we all remained the same sex all our life long, each sex respected the other and protected one another because anything else would have led to mistreatment of children, and no species is foolish enough to neglect its young. He says that by altering sex, the differences between the sexes becomes blurred. He says that

231

fixed sexuality ends that." The rote quality of this recitation made her sound more condemning than overt emotion would have done.

"I've heard about that; it's one of the things everyone's debating; the graffiters are making the most of it," said Ashe. "And he isn't the only one who thinks that sexual identity ought to be fixed. Have you looked over the graffiti recently? Not just the usual services?" She pointed to the huge, flat screen on the far wall.

Marris nodded, as if suddenly too tired to speak. She put her mug into the table aperture for a refill of tisane.

"I hate to think of nice kids like Denny being lured into Almeini's clutches. And Denny, of all people. He's always been so sensible. He'd be the last person I'd expect to get caught up in Almeini's rhetoric. And if Londyl is already hooked, you might have a real situation on your hands." She finished her tisane and held out her mug for a refill. "I was so happy when I transferred year before last. It isn't as if I didn't like being Wynen's father. She's a wonderful young woman, and when she transfers, she'll be as fine a young man as anyone. I'm proud to be her father. I wouldn't trade that for anything. But I don't want to lose this chance to be a mother. I'm looking forward to giving birth. And you have a right to be a father, Marris."

She nodded again, in the same automatic acceptance that so concerned Ashe. "I've told that to Denny. I've warned him that the time will come when he will want to have his own child, not just father one. He thinks it won't happen, that he will be more like human beings are supposed to be, staying male all his life."

"Just like any cow or rat or seahorse on the planet," said Ashe with grim humor. "In your position, I'd be worried, too." She had not wanted to admit so much, but she could not think of easy answers for her friend. "Can you imagine how difficult things would be with Yuki if we had not transferred when we separated? It is hard enough being former spouses, but if we had stayed in the sexes of our marriage, we would not have had such a clean break. Everyone knows how important it is to make clean breaks. Without transferring, that wouldn't have been possible." She glanced aside. "You and Brier are so lucky, remaining together as long as you have."

"If this doesn't cause so much disruption that we are shaken by it," said Marris as she dabbed at her eyes. "Brier is scheduled to transfer in three weeks. I'll have mine a week after, while she gets used to her body." She bit her lower lip. "Unless Denny makes it impossible."

"Could he do that?" Ashe asked, astonished at the defeatist attitude Marris showed.

"I don't know. If enough of Almeini's followers helped him, he might be able to make things . . . difficult." She rose and paced down her entertaining room. "I'm searching out as much information as I can on how things were, four hundred years ago. It's not easy. There's so much more recent material, and many of the old records are suspect— Almeini may be right about that."

"Have you tried legal records?" Ashe recommended, liking her sudden inspiration. "They're not easy to find, but they should help you make your point. One of the data services has a whole legal history section that goes back a long way."

"More than four hundred years?" Marris asked without much hope.

"Oh, yes. Some are well over a thousand years old. They might have some older than that," said Ashe with forced optimism. She hated to see her friend in such distress.

233

"Since Almeini is always talking about the laws of nature we're breaking, it might impress Denny to hear about the old laws. If they help." Marris turned gloomy eyes to Ashe. "It's a good idea. I'll try."

Ashe patted Marris's arm and did her best to smile encouragement. "It's just worry about transference. A lot of kids go through it before the first transfer, and getting married makes it more . . . oh, I don't know. More upsetting for some of them. It's such a big admission, the intention to have a child. Denny'll change his mind when he gets near the wedding; he isn't so radical that he'll forget everything you have taught him to respect. In a year or two, you'll all laugh about this." She chuckled. "I remember I was as scared as I was excited when I transferred the first time."

Marris achieved a wan smile. "So was I."

"Denny'll be fine." As Ashe said it, she began to wonder if he would. To make her point, she added, "It's not as if he's refused to have his voter's implant."

"No," agreed his mother. "Not yet."

Denny was dressed outlandishly: all the fabrics were natural, and of virgin production, not made from reclaimed resources; the colors, too, were unreclaimed. It was all suggestive of the fashions of two or three centuries ago, and self-consciously so. Denny wore these garments with an air of satisfaction that was the most annoying thing about him. He looked at Brier, who was recovering from transferring. "You're a freak, Father, whether you admit it or not."

"A freak because you don't approve?" Brier sighed; she was in no mood for another altercation. "I transferred when I married Marris, so we could have you. You ought to think I've stopped being a freak now, since I have become female once again, as I was born. Those years as your father should

234

be the perversity," she answered. "According to you, transferring from the sex you were born to is the wrong thing to do. You should be delighted that I've transferred back and Marris is going to: we'll both be the sexes we were born to. You can relax, son." The last was an attempt to lighten the mood; it was unsuccessful. Denny scowled at Brier without a hint of levity.

"Don't you see that's what's wrong? You transfer when you marry, which is unnatural. You get to know each other as one sex and then turn into the opposite when it is most important you don't. You transfer when you want a second child. And you transfer when you establish your maturity. Tradition! It is nothing more than the destruction of our species." He flung his head like an angry animal. "It's madness. The only reason you can't see it is because it's tradition."

"And why do you think that is? How do you think it became a tradition? I know how tempting it is to try to change the world, but do you really want to upset a system that works as well as ours does?" Brier asked. Her position on the lounge was not quite natural yet; not all the scars had healed, though the transference had been four days ago. "Why would we have such a tradition if it hadn't been good for us?"

"Because you were misled, lied to. You believe the graffiters, not yourself." He paced down the entertainment room, ignoring everything but his father reclining on the lounge, getting used to her female body. "You let yourself be taken in by all the pressure and—and the outmoded fears of long ago."

"You don't know that. You're parroting the words of Almeini. If I thought you had decided this for yourself, I might not be so concerned, but to give Almeini such . . ."

She frowned at her son. "You make me feel that I failed *you* as your father."

Denny rounded on her, his eyes bright with anger. "Do you have any idea how perverse, how obscene that sounds coming out of your mouth?"

Brier made an effort to get to her feet. "Now you listen to me, Denny," she warned. "You're not going to throw your mother and me into a crisis no matter how hard you try. If you have some grievance against me, then you and I will deal with it. I expect you to behave as if you are a part of this family."

"How can I?" Denny demanded, color mounting in his neck and cheeks, turning the skin from caramel to ruddy. "Don't you see how absurd this is? You call yourself my father, and you're waiting to get pregnant by my mother." He made a gesture that was insulting and explicit.

At that Brier laughed aloud. "What did you expect? What made you think that we'd do anything different? Transferring isn't new, after all. You're acting as if it were something radical and dangerous—that you were being put at risk. Why do you stop only with transferring? Why not refuse Cellular Integrity Therapy as well? Or your voter's implant? Why not join those Reversionists out in Manchuria, or wherever they are? With one child allowed per female, they might not want another male, but you can't be certain. Their numbers get smaller every year." She sat down again. "All right. If you don't want to honor the tradition, I can't stop you from it. That's your decision. But I think you'll be making a big mistake. You're too taken in by Almeini and his promise of species correctness. He's wrong. I know he's wrong. And if you weren't so caught up in what he says, you'd know it, too. Think about what it would be like to get to my age and never give birth—never have the chance to give birth."

"Men aren't supposed to give birth; it's unnatural," said Denny defensively. "It isn't possible, and it shouldn't happen. I'd die before I let it happen to me."

His father ignored the last impassioned remark. "That's why we transfer to women," Brier said patiently, her voice level and steady.

"You're talking to me like a school child," Denny complained.

"That's because you're behaving like one." Brier folded her arms. "Very well. You say your mind is made up. So I know you have decisions to make. I can't pretend to approve of what you're supporting, but I respect your convictions, if they are your convictions. I am not convinced they're anything more than what Almeini wants them to be, but—" She rubbed her upper lip, a gesture left over from when she had had a moustache. "You do what you need to do. But remember that your mother and I will do what we need to do, no matter what your opinion may be."

"That's obvious," said Denny, trying for contempt and achieving sourness.

"One more thing," said Brier, knowing that she should stop now, but unable to contain the impulse to make a last attempt to protect his son. "Almeini is a dangerous man, a radical demagogue, for all most of the world thinks he is a fool. I know you think he's an idealist with an urge to help the world. But what he is proposing could ruin centuries of social evolution, and that would be catastrophic. Before you embrace his movement, keep in mind that he isn't doing it for you."

"He's doing it for humanity," said Denny heatedly.

"And that makes his bigotry all right," Brier said, her voice and eyes cool.

"Of course," said Denny, unable to come up with a stronger rejoinder.

★ ★ ★ ★ ★

Ashe and Marris had spent the afternoon at the clinic, Ashe for her pregnancy, Marris for his transference. They both noticed the protest graffiti on the civic screens around the building, and after they were some distance from the clinic, Ashe said, "Do you think they're really going to burn it down?"

"I think they'd be foolish to do it; that doesn't mean they don't intend to try," Marris declared. "The public isn't as taken in by Almeini as his followers want us to think. He may have more support than we thought at first, but it can't last. With such inflammatory slogans being displayed, I think we're all aware of the potential for disaster. Catering to Almeini's demands only serves to make him more outrageous. People will understand that, in time, and all this will calm down." He cocked his head in the direction of the clinic. "Those signs are the work of his followers. They don't represent anything but the most extreme elements, and everyone knows it. The graffiters make sure of that. You've seen the graffiti."

"Is Denny still . . . ?" Ashe asked, putting her hand to her abdomen, proud of her pregnancy. "Five months. Four to go."

Marris chuckled. "I remember that part. In a month or so, you'll wish it was almost over. Be sure you take care of your back—that's what gets the most sore, and you're going to need it for delivery. And you're going to have to start getting ready for your delivery. You'll probably have to get together with your midwife in another six weeks. Don't put it off too long. The midwife will want to follow the last of the pregnancy. But you know all that."

"Not from this end. You're going to keep an eye on me, aren't you?" Ashe asked. "I haven't been through this before,

238

remember. I'm going to need your guidance."

"If you want it, it's yours," said Marris, watching the display set a course for Ashe's home. Then he frowned. "And to answer your question, yes, Denny still says he's going to get married without transferring. And some of his friends are supporting his decision, not just Londyl. He spouts Almeini's theories every chance he gets. He says he is determined. I can't believe he will not change his mind. And he says that Londyl is having her fertility inhibitor removed. Denny thinks it's a good idea." The amusement which had briefly lit his eyes was completely gone at this admission.

"Isn't there a law against that?" Ashe wondered aloud; such an action was staggering in its impact.

"There is," said Marris. "But there are enough meditechs in Almeini's movement that it isn't hard to get it done. Denny is proud of what they're planning." He rubbed his eyes. "Brier is beside herself with worry. She thinks there may be a crackdown on them, and Denny is likely to end up in real trouble. We've tried to warn him, but he fancies himself a martyr."

"And you? Are you worried?" Ashe studied her friend, concern and impatience making her question sharper than she had intended.

"Of course I'm worried. But my worry isn't going to change anything but my own resilience, and I know I'm going to need that for dealing with Denny. The trouble is, with Almeini's popularity increasing, Denny thinks he is being proven right." He patted Ashe's arm. "Can you imagine what it might be like? I don't like to think of myself as a slave to tradition, but I don't want to think about what would happen if we all did what Almeini wants."

"But you *do* think about it, don't you?" Ashe guessed shrewdly.

"I don't know how not to think about it," Marris confessed. "I don't like to trouble Brier about it, with everything she's enduring just now; you know how difficult those first few months can be." He rubbed his chin, and realized he needed to shave; he had not fallen into the routine of it yet.

"Trouble?" Ashe asked, more apprehensive than she thought was necessary.

"I hope not. Her first fertility index was low." He did his best to dismiss his anxiety. "But so soon after transfer, it happens."

"And Brier is certainly healthy and strong. If anyone is able to produce a child quickly, it would be Brier." Ashe paused, thinking that she ought to say something else, something that would show she understood the problems they were having with Denny. "You shouldn't borrow trouble, as my grandmother used to warn me." She shifted in her seat, trying to make herself a bit more comfortable.

"What makes her most upset is that Denny is determined to convince her to remain female all the rest of her life. She was born female and Denny says she ought to die that way." Marris paused as a robot announcer came down the walkway.

"Please detour to Lui Street. Please detour to Lui Street. Please detour to Lui Street." The repetition was oddly soothing.

Ashe shrugged and turned at the next corner, Marris walking slightly behind her. They had gone about half a block in silence when Ashe said, "I wonder what the trouble is?"

"You can't find out from a 'bot." He glanced back over his shoulder in the hope of discovering the reason for their detour. He saw nothing unusual.

"Marris," Ashe ventured. "Now that you're male again

. . . do you resent having been female?"

"No. No, of course not," said Marris, then realized Ashe needed more than a simple reassurance. "I know what Almeini has said about female embryos, but that's just his intolerance speaking. I can't imagine what must have happened to him to set him off this way. But he has found a real source of discontent. Transferring is harder on some than on others, and Almeini has used that to his advantage. He has to have something concrete to say in order to make his followers agree with him. Talking about the nature of the species is a hard message to convey, particularly since we know so much about gender determination in embryos."

"But don't you think there's more to it than that? Isn't he trying to create resentment among his followers?" Ashe laughed unhappily. "Resentment leads to hostility. That is another very human response."

Marris tried not to shudder. "He's had to take something specific to base his opinions on, and he's chosen to make it a disgust of transferring, as if women were not also men. I've been over this with Denny—more than once. It's all we ever seem to talk about now. You should hear him— or perhaps you shouldn't. He says very offensive things. And now everyone is getting caught up. Everywhere you go, you hear people talking about Almeini's views. Like it or not, we'll have to weather his onslaught. He's mad. That's all."

Ashe's face lost all expression. "Yes. He is mad. But if he isn't the only one, what then?" She held up her hand so that he would not answer. "I'm worried about what will happen to my baby. Typical female."

"I know how you feel. No matter how upset I am with Denny, I can't forget he's my child, I bore him, and I want to protect him, even from himself." Marris pointed at the intersection ahead of them. "We can stop at The Meerkat before we go home. You have time, don't you?"

"Yes. I'd like a chance to get off my feet." She made an apologetic hitch of her shoulder. "It's not easy, walking long distances. Waddling long distances."

"How well I remember," said Marris, putting one hand into the small of his back to demonstrate his recollection.

"Exactly," said Ashe. "I like The Meerkat."

"So do I," said Marris, and turned toward the capacious entrance.

An announcement on the graffiti board indicated a fire was raging on the east side of the city. The blaze was isolated and emergency services were on the scene.

"I hope the clinic wasn't . . ." said Ashe as she read the headlines. "It's the east side, but if the fire were so close, we'd know about it, wouldn't we?"

"If the fire's controlled, maybe not," said Marris, frowning at the implications. "They don't want to panic anyone."

"Good," Ashe approved, then added, "They'll let us know if there's any danger, won't they? I think they'd let us know if we had anything to worry about."

"So do I." He thought about the headline a moment. "Still, the fire's a bad thing, controlled or not. If the clinic's been damaged, Almeini would crow over it if he could. It makes them look powerful and dangerous, to have the rest of us worried. He's already on record saying that all such clinics ought to be destroyed. He'd encourage his followers to burn away."

"Oh, don't say that," Ashe protested. "You don't think he's that irresponsible, do you?"

"If the clinic has been damaged I certainly do, and I wish I didn't." Marris was not embarrassed to say this, but he could not keep from feeling he had spoken against her son. "Not that Denny has said anything that would make me think this. Denny has always been very respectful of the law—except this silliness about transferring. It's the way Almeini carries on that bothers me. I wish the graffiters took him more seriously. They make jokes about him, and they ignore what he advocates, which makes it easy for Almeini to seem harmless. I know Denny wouldn't get tangled up in anything illegal."

"How can he help it?" Ashe asked, doing her best to make the question light enough not to be a challenge. "Isn't refusing transference illegal?"

"Yes; of course it is. But there's a difference between defying tradition and taking violent action against it. Denny isn't going to advocate hurting people." Marris held his shoulder-pouch more tightly, protectively. "He's caught up in something he doesn't fully understand; if he did, he wouldn't continue to endorse Almeini's goals. Denny isn't the kind of young man who would deliberately harm others, no matter what his convictions might be, and no matter what Almeini advocated. Denny doesn't have that kind of anger in him." His voice was so sincere that Ashe knew Marris was trying to convince himself.

They had reached the dining patio, a wide, pleasant expanse surrounded by small shops providing more than eighty kinds of food. Ordinarily it was busy at this time of day, when the people of the city were still on their afternoon shifts or getting ready for an active evening, but now only half the tables were occupied, and most of the people were watching the graffiti screen with barely concealed anxiety.

"I want the mung bean pastries," said Ashe, thinking about the health of her unborn child, and unwilling to go into Denny's motivations; she was aware that mothers tended to defend their children against all criticism. "I think it would be good at this time of day."

"Typical pregnant fussy eater," said Marris with a reminiscent chuckle. "I got hungry for the strangest things. So will you." He indicated a table somewhat away from most of the other diners. "We won't be disturbed over here." They would also not be able to see the graffiti screen easily.

"Good. I get nervous when I think about who could be listening." As she sat down she straightened her clothes, smoothing the long tunic that was standard day-time wear for most of the population of the temperate zones. "If you're getting beer, I'll take cider." She sighed. "Giving up beer is about the hardest part of this pregnancy."

"You won't think so a month from now," said Marris. "Stay where you are. I'll get the food for us both. Cider for you." He walked toward the booth advertising mung beans, and placed an order for Ashe, then went to the sausage booth and chose some for himself. Returning for the pastry, he picked up their drinks, and carried the lot back to the table where Ashe was waiting. He saw she was scowling, and knew it was not because of discomfort.

"Thanks," said Ashe as Marris proffered the requested drink. "I was watching the graffiti screen, over there," she said, leaning back and angling her chin to indicate where it was.

"Bad news?" asked Marris, deliberately ignoring it.

"Almeini is trying to get a hearing in the Central Courts. He wants to have official recognition of his views, and the hearing would force it on us, make it seem legitimate by getting more attention. He wants to take the debate to the government." She took hold of her napkin and worked it between her fingers until it was fluted. "Do you think they'll let him plead his case?"

"Of course not," said Marris. "Why should he be permitted when the law is clear and the tradition is so old? It isn't as if we've only been transferring sexes for a generation or two. No matter what Almeini says, transference is natural to all of us; that was demonstrated hundreds of years ago. And it isn't as if the few groups who still practice ancient religion have shown that remaining the same sex makes for better societies. Their children are no better and no worse than any others, when they have children. They do not claim anything so absurd." He reached for his beer. "I know this is hard on Brier. I wish I could spare her, but Denny . . ." The rest was left unspoken.

"How long will this go on? It's not going to last," said Ashe in a forlorn voice. "You'd think he'd have more consideration for his father than to put Brier through this right now when she's—"

"He's convinced he's right," said Marris, more saddened than disgusted. "He's right and everyone but Almeini is wrong." He began to eat his sausages. "I hope that no one takes him seriously enough to dignify his stance. It's so close to religion, I doubt he will be allowed a hearing."

"Um," said Ashe, putting her attention on her mung bean pastry.

Ashe apologized for weeping. "He was your child," she said to Marris. "How do you manage to keep a dry eye?"

"I don't; I just don't have any tears left," said Marris stonily as he held the door open for his friend. "There are Guards everywhere, and graffiters. Come in, hurry."

Ashe did not argue. "I saw many streets blocked when I came; the Guards are out in force all over, not just here," she said, going to sit down on the wide couch. She did not look at the window. "I never thought it would come to this, not for Denny, and not for Almeini."

"The riot," said Marris. "It was just what Almeini wanted." His hands clenched. "He used my son to get it."

"Surely you don't think this was deliberate?" Ashe asked, sitting up as abruptly as her pregnancy would allow.

"Of course it was deliberate. Almeini wanted a martyr to his cause, and Denny was willing to oblige. He said he would rather die than have to transfer, and he proved it, with Almeini's blessing. And now Londyl is saying she'll remain female the rest of her life to honor Denny's memory, and Almeini is praising her for her decision, just as he is praising Denny's death as heroic." Marris was staring at the graffiti screen, seeing nothing. "I have to bury my son because of Almeini's inhuman, inhumane theories."

Ashe swallowed hard against the constriction in her throat. "You can bring an action against him," she suggested tentatively.

Marris shook his head. "That would only add to the attention he commands. I can't do that. It would make all this worse. Brier is . . . angry. She says something should have been done to stop him when he first began to agitate."

"But what?" Ashe wondered aloud. "No one thought his crazy ideas would be taken seriously, any more than that fellow in the Balkans who advocates ending weather manipulation is."

"But look what's happened," said Marris in a flat tone. "The lunatic no one took seriously has more than a million followers and is about to gain more because my son poisoned himself in protest to transferring. We all thought our traditional values would protect us from monsters like Almeini."

Ashe tried to find a more comfortable position, one that would ease her back and let her raise her feet. "He won't get away with it. The public won't stand for it."

"Maybe," said Marris, his eyes desolate. "But no one thought Almeini would get this far, did they?"

For once, Ashe could think of nothing to say.

About *Traditional Values*

Sometimes when I work late with my radio on to a station that usually carries classical music, I run into a half-hour program devoted to "explaining" what the preacher calls Natural Law as revealed in the Bible. Most of the time, it is a pseudo-religious justification for sexism and bigotry, although occasionally it attempts to address international politics. One of the most exasperating of all the broadcasts I heard was one that attempted to say that only heterosexuality was natural, and any other behavior was unnatural and therefore reprehensible at best, and heretical at worst, which leaves geese in a lot of trouble.

That got me to thinking—in the slightly out-of-kilter way one does at three a.m.—of how one could get around this biology-is-destiny stricture without actually going against it. This story was the result.

DAY 17

That last explosion is too big for any doubt: you are the only one left that's functional. The rest are gone.

Speed is the one thing that can save you now. If you can get out of the field and out of the range of Their artillery, then you can fight Them on your own terms, at least for a while. A solitary A.F. model-4 soldier in the open hasn't a chance against Them, so find some cover. Then you might be able to hunt Them. You might have a chance.

You are running clear now, the air too cold, your body too hot. You can hear the rough sounds of your running, the steady pounding of your legs. Grain stacks glass-brittle with frost crystals break against your legs and crunch under your feet making too much noise, too much; They'll hear you. How can you run through a winter field steaming like a volcano, your bones molten with the heat of battle, your joints hissing, and be quiet? How can you get away if you do not conceal yourself?

You trip; stumble.

You're falling. Catch yourself! If you're down, you're out.

Your ankle twists and your sinews wrench all the way up to your hip. You nearly drop your beamer, and you clutch at it.

Hang on. Hang on. You're going to need it and the rest of your weapons when you find Them. Never mind limping—run! Run for cover.

There are trees—or whatever the plants are in this

248

anemic place that look like trees—over there on the left. Up on a little rise and you're safe. There are trees, not Capuchin trees, the safe kind. You'll be out of range once you reach the trees. You'll be safe. Go on. Go on.

You scramble, slip up the rise, your ankle functioning badly, your foot unsteady, the boot-straps loosened from the fall. You cradle your beamer and run.

Top of the rise.

Duck your head so that the sharp spines scratch only your shoulders and your pack. Decaying pods mash, stinking, beneath each faltering step. You blunder against a branch and fall back on a trunk, your ankle all but giving away. Steady. Steady. Slow there. Stop.

Wait. Watch. Don't assume anything.

All right; They haven't followed you. It's going to be your turn now. Slow down the violent jerking in your chest. Assess the damage done to your leg. Restore a little order. Lean on the body of the tree-thing, press against the rough scalings and rest. Listen to your chest over the respiration of the trees, feel the cold, cold air on your face. There is damage. All over, there is damage; damage to your legs, to your shoulders and back. You have a burn on the side of your face that has left a raw patch. You want to take off your boot and realign your foot, but without the right equipment, you could make it worse, so that your foot will not function at all. Never mind. Let it go. Don't touch it. You probably couldn't get the boot back on right in any case. Lean on the tree. Try to relax.

You're safe; for the moment They can't find you—because They don't want to.

For the first time you think about why. Why wouldn't They want to find you? Why would They let you escape? What happened to your squad? Why don't They have to bother with you at all? Well, where are your lines, your guns, your forces now? What direction is safe for you? Why should They search for you? What can one A.F. model-4 soldier do? What happened to your squad?

You're lost. You're just as lost as the other.

Don't think about that. Try not to think about that.

But they were your squad, weren't they? You were cut from the same piece of cloth, all A.F. model-4 soldiers. They were just the same as you. You are just the same as them.

Forget it.

You're functioning better now, everything still a little too fast, but better. Your thoughts are more ordered. Your chest no longer feels as if it contained a caged animal. You feel your heat turn cold.

There is a smell to you now. You know that smell, inescapable. You know it from other battles. All A.F. model-4 soldiers have it when they fight, as if they carry the stench of death before it claims them.

"Forget it," you tell yourself. Put it aside. There are other things to do. There is no point in worrying about smell. It's time to look around, to find out where you are, if you can, and where They are. With any luck, you can ambush some of Them, beat Them at Their own game. Time to check your weapons. Look at the distant sun, that star with the old, old name.

The sun is behind a sheet of grey clouds and too near setting. It will be night soon, and A.F. model-4 soldiers do not see that well in the dark.

You'll have to forget about Them for now. It's time to find shelter; it's getting late and it will freeze tonight. It always freezes. The freezing here is something brand new and too grim to risk. You can go after Them later—right now, you have to protect yourself.

Rest a minute longer. Give yourself a break. No, don't move yet. Stay another minute.

But you force yourself to move on, to go cautiously through the quietly breathing forest, stepping carefully, watching where you step because of your damaged ankle, and because you want to make as little sound as possible. The dead pods are wet and make a soft, flatulent whistle when you step on them, eerie instead of funny in the on-coming dark.

Careful; keep your eyes open. Sure, They can't see you now, but you can't see Them, and there are more of Them than you. And you're the one that's lost. So watch. Listen. Ignore the ankle. You will fix that later, when there's time and equipment. The leg isn't so badly damaged that you can't go on. Keep moving. Easy. Keep the feet going and the beamer ready. Move.

Remember that you can't refuel your weapons until you get back to your lines; don't waste shots on shadows. Better to keep out of sight. You be the hunter, you wait Them out. Count your steps as you go. Anything to keep you walking.

The tree growth is different here, thinner and newer, by the look of the scales on the trunks. There's a sort of clearing ahead and on your right, down the hill from where you are. Stop. Look at it. Make sure you know what you're getting into.

There's some sort of pioneer building in the clearing. At least it looks like a pioneer building, but it might be some-thing else, something They've built to trap you. Is the building what it appears to be? Is it safe? Be very careful. You cannot afford to make a mistake, not out here by your-self. The light isn't strong and it's colder. Look around for signs of Them: tread marks, skimmer slicks, anything.

Drop onto your belly and slide forward. Easy. Get in close, but keep in the cover of the branches as long as possible. Your hands are stiffening with cold. If you could put down your beamer you could get your hands going again, but that wouldn't be safe, and so you don't do it. Look at the ground, look at the walls of the building. Look for some kind of clue.

And there are tread marks. Theirs, probably. The pioneers don't use tread machinery. But if there are tread tracks and no machines, it means They've gone, doesn't it? And the pioneer building—you think it might be a thawing shed—could be empty, could be shelter. And it could be a trap. You know They are clever and ruthless. You've fought them in six different wars. They might have the shed set to blow up, or filled with deadly gas, or set to signal if anything—anyone—gets into it.

The freshest tread marks are only about forty meters away. Inch over there, inspect them; they might be a deception. If you are convinced they're all right, then slide up to the side of the shed. There is a low-lying mist in the clearing; keep inside it and use it as you near the shed. Make no sound, disturb nothing. If anyone or anything is watching from inside, make sure They won't see you. Not first.

Keep the beamer ready. Move quickly. The ankle can wait. Run!

And you do run, skidding a little on the ice already forming in the deeper ruts. The mud is hard and cakes to your boots, sucking. You hope your ankle holds up for three more steps as you run.

You slide, your shoulder slams against the shed.

You wait. If They are in there, They will have heard you. Wait and listen. Wait.

Wait.

252

Okay. So far you're probably safe. No noise. No sound. Nothing to make you think They are aware of you.

Wish yourself invisible and start around the shed toward the door. Careful. Watch your feet. That ankle is not functioning at all well. Watch for signs. In case. Not that it would matter if you stepped on anything They've buried. You'll be blown to bits before you know or care.

Pleasant thought. Maybe it was like that for your squad, poor dumb soldiers. You know better if you let yourself think about the ambush, about the pellets with the bone-burning stuff in them. A.F. model-4 soldiers burn easily. You warned them about that. They didn't understand enough to be afraid. All they knew was that the enemy was ahead. Your fear kept you alive, keeps you alive. You are afraid now.

Move easy, you say to yourself. Move easy. Slow and easy. Your squad doesn't matter any more—it's gone. This is what matters: that you have rounded the corner and the door to the shed is about twelve meters away. It is almost closed. Almost.

What if They're in there? What if They know you're here? What if They've been watching you from the start and are waiting until you're a nice dark figure in the lighted door-frame. They see well at night. You'd be a good target. They would not miss.

The wind picks up; the heavy door groans on its hinges but nothing more.

Either They're very cool in there or They aren't in there at all.

This is the hard part. Keep the beamer ready, up where you can use it, but not so high that you can't use your arms if you have to. Move with ease. Up next to the door.

Wait now. Listen, for something, anything that might

253

tell you if someone is inside. Try hard. Listen with all the fear gnawing at you.

Be sure you're ready. All ready.

Go!

You scrape your sleeve on the weathered frame as you pull round the door to land crouched out of the light. Your ankle almost collapses. You keep ready.

It's all black. Then there are shapes becoming more solid in the dark.

"Drop everything. Weapons down and hands up."

One shape is in Their uniform, sprawled on the floor.

One of Them. It makes a sound like a sick animal. A young animal dying, and dying without reason or comfort.

The other shape moves. It is supporting the head of the dying one. It makes a sound.

You're ready. "Weapons down and—"

"Don't bother," is the reply and the voice is a woman's.

The dying soldier moves, aware of a stranger, the stranger you are. He tries to focus his eyes. He mutters something to the woman in Their tongue. She answers him gently, with reassurance, in that language you don't know. You watch, listen. This must be her lover, her brother, someone.

There is a quick movement. The soldier has an automatic aimed at you.

"Stand back!" you yell to the woman, aiming your beamer, your hand stretching for the trigger.

"Why waste the fuel? He's got two 90s in him already. He can't hurt you." As she speaks, she removes the automatic from his hand, wiping his forehead almost as a benediction.

"How can you be certain they're enough?" you ask, keeping the beamer trained.

"Because I shot him," she answers with no particular emotion; she throws the automatic into the loft.

"Hey—"

"It was empty and jammed. It wouldn't fire. Do you think I'd let this boy die this way if there were a better alternative? God, look at him."

You have seen that look before. "Let me," you offer.

"No." That's all she says: just "no."

For some reason you ask her why not.

"Because this is between him and me. I suppose I could use this if I have to"—she touches something strapped to her boot. You know she has a knife—"or my automatic, but it isn't right, not after what he did."

The soldier moves. He is young, his face almost smooth. Funny, dying all blond and young makes him a boy instead of a soldier. He stopped being a soldier when he started dying. You watch him as you lower your beamer. How could you consider him one of Them now? You're safe now. They're far away. You're in a pioneer thawing shed, the cold is outside, and you are safe. That boy is dying and you're going to live. Sit down and rest. Everything is going to be all right. For the time being, everything is all right.

"Tired?"

You say something: you are.

"Allied Federation soldier?"

"Yeah," you say. "A.F. model-4 foot soldier. Cyborg group 722." You watch her. "You?"

She shakes her head. "You don't need to know that."

You stare at her. "Why?"

"You don't need to know that," she repeats with more determination, her eyes on the dying boy.

"Why?" you repeat suspiciously.

"Because, friend, I am a spy. A saboteur."

You think a moment, evaluating what she has said. But you know that women don't go around hiding in thawing sheds in freezing weather because they are spies. That isn't reasonable, not in any way you've learned. This is a soldier's war—an infantry affair, like all wars worth the name.

"You doubt me?"

"When my company gets here"—and you hope that eventually your company will arrive—"we'll take this up with the Commander. In the meantime hand over—"

But she is holding up her hand to silence you. "If They catch me again, They will try to kill me. But first They will try to find out what I know. And They will find out, no matter what I try to hold back. They will find out. So it is best that I know as little as possible. I wish I could know nothing."

Does it add up? You wonder. Does it? Or is this some subtle trick, some devious way to catch you off guard for a moment, vulnerable for just long enough for her to use that knife she has in her boot? It's cold and you want to relax, but what if that's what she's waiting for, a moment when—

The boy is breathing stridently now, sounding as if there is something clogging his throat. You know what it is. You've heard it before now.

So has she, you think, because she moves a little, shields his eyes from the dark as he struggles against his failing body, trying to make it not die. He gasps, one hand flailing, his face changing colors.

Then she closes those blond staring eyes, moves the dead boy off her lap, stands and stares at the body at her feet as if he were an unfamiliar and faintly puzzling part of the landscape. She cocks her head to the side and looks away from the boy, looking almost-but-not-quite at you.

"And being pioneers was the way to have things even

256

again. We were going to find a real equalizer. Pioneering was going to make us all brothers. No more war, because we could all be pioneers instead. People were going to pool their talents and strengths and virtues and courages to launch a united assault on all the empty places. We had it all figured out. We would restore the world, restore all the worlds, make them bloom." She rubbed the back of her hand across her mouth as if there was something foul on her lips. "Ask this boy what the equalizer is. He knows all about it."

She is about a head shorter than you are, built strong, wire-lithe, taut. You find you're staring at her hands. They are large, would be large if she were a man; large and long-fingered with knots at the knuckles. No, you decide, she's not pretty, not by any standards you've seen. She's not much of anything. In a crowd no one would notice her unless they were looking for her.

She tilts her head, watching the door or the light, you aren't sure which, and you see that she has high cheekbones and a wide brow, what some people might call good bones. She is a human, just a human, with nothing added or taken away, so far as you can tell. There are dark circles around her eyes and the look of fatigue and hunger draws the lines in her face with shadows. In this light it is impossible to see what color her eyes or her hair are.

You realize you are staring: you look away.

"They're trying to take over here, you know," she says, her voice as remote as if she were discussing the weather or the fate of another place. "They came two years ago."

"Yes." You have heard the story. "We'll keep Them out," you assure her, knowing that you can promise her nothing.

"So what?" She looks up at you again. "What's the difference if you or They wreck our fields? Why should it make it better that you burned down our houses than if They did?"

You scowl. "It isn't the same."

"No?" She gets onto her feet slowly. "I suppose he'd say the same thing, if he could speak."

"But he's one of Them," you remind her.

"Oh, yes: one of Them." She squints into the darkness. "It makes his dying all right."

You frown. You find yourself thinking of the soldiers who were with you this morning. They were all right, this morning. Now they're—Stop it. It's night now and there's no point in remembering the men who died. "But he was one of Them."

She looks up, startled. Almost as if she'd forgotten you're here. She tries to smile, to ease up a little or to misdirect you into feeling comfortable. She's not successful, but that's all right. She tried, and you appreciate that.

"Yes, that's right," she says. But she is on her feet, pacing, and nothing is right. That reminds you that your ankle needs attention. You bend down and loosen your boot. Your foot is numb to your touch and it fits the boot badly.

She catches your movement. "What is it? Capuchin burn?" The question comes too quickly, but you try to ignore that.

"Twisted my ankle," you say.

"Where?"

"Back there. The other side of the ridge. There was a cross-fire." You talk in grunts as you pull at the bindings, the whole damned boot.

"So that's what I heard," she says.

"Our squad was caught in the open. That's what you heard." You tug at the straps, grimacing.

"Move." She's down at your feet, her attention on you as it was on the dead soldier. "Let me take care of that. You'll only make it worse."

"I don't have any replacements." You pat the kit strapped to your back. "We aren't given replacements for a short campaign, this is only Day 16. A.F. model-4s won't get anything new until day 30."

"What do you mean, replacements?" She bats your hands out of the way and works with the thongs as you lie back and allow yourself the luxury of groaning while she gently, gently, pulls the boot off your very painful foot. You feel how cold the air has become, even in the thawing shed. As she peels off your sock, you take a deep breath.

Then she touches your ankle with those long fingers of hers.

You hiss and pull back.

"Hurt?"

You say some obscenity and regret it all in the same instant. "I'm a cyborg; it's not pain," you remind her.

"You look pretty human to me. Your ankle is sprained and swollen and—"

"I'm a cyborg. I need a replacement."

"You're a human. You need a splint." She rocks back on her heels. "You've sprained the ankle. I don't think you've broken it, that's something. I can probably make some kind of brace for you. Can you wiggle your toes?"

You demonstrate, trying not to notice how painful that movement is, since there cannot be pain. A.F. model-4 soldiers are not capable of hurting.

"Can you feel your toes? Are they numb?"

Yes, you tell her, you can feel your toes. They're fine, thanks. The toes aren't the matter; it's your ankle that's bothering you.

"Good. I'll do what I can to fix you up. You can come with me when I leave here. I was afraid you wouldn't be able to travel." You know from her tone that she is capable of leaving you behind without a trace of guilt.

Just where is she going, you want to know.

"Craoi-Venduru. It's a pioneer settlement south of here. They've been there about fifteen days. They came with Their new replacements, but not a strong force."

"They? They've got replacements?" you ask, your eyes narrowed. You were not told They had landed replacements for more than two months.

"Yes. Who do you think I meant?"

You shrug.

"The pioneers were killed, oh, a long time ago, and there was almost no one left when They moved in. That's why we'll be safe there: They'll never think of looking for us there, right under Their noses. We'll be safe." Her smile lacks warmth or confidence, but it does not tremble. "The other reason to go there is that Craoi is the closest settlement to the A.F. lines, unless there have been changes since early this morning. If we can get through anywhere, it'll be there. The river runs within three kilometers of the town, and if we can get across it we'll be safe. You want to get back to the A.F. lines, don't you?"

You look at her.

She makes no apology for her implication. "There was the chance that you'd deserted under fire—"

"Cyborgs don't do that."

"—and in that case, you'd want to find Them first."

"And if I were a deserter?" It is fascinating to watch how flat her expression can become.

"Oh," she sighs and her shoulders sag. "I would have to kill you, soldier. And I am very tired of killing."

You look away abruptly, not knowing where to direct your eyes. You stare at your bootless foot—did she help you with it, or has her assistance been nothing more than a ploy to make you helpless?—and then at the dead boy on the other side of the shed, his uniform no longer recognizable in the darkness. The doorframe is now just a denser black against the night. "Why would you help me? Why should I trust you?"

"Because you're lost and I know the way back. Because I need help, and you can help me." She picks up your boot and looks at it, then puts it down again.

You laugh, once, with contempt.

"You'd better rest, soldier. We have to travel before first light. It's safest then. *No* one is out at that time of night." She takes a deep breath and looks up toward the loft.

"At night? We will move at night?" The day is more convenient if you have to fight. The day is warmer.

"Yes. Because They won't, not if They can help it. They stay out of the cold when They can. And They don't see in the dark much better than you do." She has gone back to pacing. Then she stops and bends down.

When she stands up she has something very ugly in her hands: an automatic laser.

You grab for your beamer, hoping to get a shot off before she can aim and fire. You twist you ankle again and wince. All you can get your hands on is old, damp grain.

"It's almost out of fuel," she remarks casually, lowering it and looking around at the dead man. "Do you know how to use one of these things?"

You stare in disbelief. She wasn't after you. She wasn't going to shoot you. You're not going to end here, smeared on the wall of a thawing shed, weaponless and with one boot gone.

"What are you looking for?"

"I was hoping he'd have some fuel for this." She lifts the laser. She asks nothing. You guess she knows what you almost did. She goes on searching, saying nothing about what you were going to do, would have done. Then: "I guess not. I can't find anything. Too bad. We could have used the laser."

You nod, but it means nothing. The laser means nothing. If you have to use weapons at all, you'll need more than one hand-held laser.

"You have any incendiary grenades?"

"No. Do you?"

"Two. They're Theirs, of course. But they'll blow a nice, hot hole as well as A.F. design, I guess. Grenades don't care who uses them."

Your foot is getting stiff, either from the cold or from its malfunction. "Hey," you tell her. "Hey, about—"

She looks toward you, all but invisible in the night-covered shed. "What?"

"D'you mind if I put my boot back on? I'll need your help. It's cold."

"Here." She takes off the dark jacket of pioneer-made cloth and tosses it to you. You've seen this material before, but its lightness still surprises you. "There's plenty of time to wrap it up, later. Why not get some rest? You won't freeze if you use that."

"Why don't you get some rest?" You did not mean to challenge her, but now that the words are out, you hope that she will have an answer for you.

"I will, in Craoi-Venduru. You need sleep more than I do." She starts away from you.

"Cyborgs don't sleep," you tell her.

"That's fine for cyborgs," she says, then looks at you,

"but you are not a cyborg, no matter what you think. You're just a soldier, as much a person as any other soldier."

"Crap," you answer, as you have heard others answer countless times before now. "A.F. model-4, cyborg group 722 are made to look human. Most of our armor is under our skin, so we don't look too much like machines."

"To use your word: crap."

You can think of nothing to say, not with your ankle the way it is. "I'm a cyborg," you repeat.

"Human. Truth," she counters. "You need rest because of what you've done to your ankle. Go on. Lie down."

You regard her suspiciously, standing like a ghost, a dark brown ghost in the grey gloom, pale hands, pale face, dark, hidden eyes. Luminous hands and face hung on tenuous, invisible body. You fold your arms.

She says a second time, "Go on."

You feel the desire for sleep clutch at your bones with an ache like grief. The jacket she has given you is warm on your cold legs, the grain is musty-damp but cozy. The shed is friendly if you ignore the dead soldier; it smells of grain and old dung and people. You try not to feel tired. "I can stay up," you say, though you know you need rest if you're going to fight Them again. You need rest, want it, crave it. "What will happen while I'm asleep, if I sleep?" You have to know, seeing the heap that was one of Their soldiers, remembering the knife strapped to her boot.

"I'll be up there."

You look up, to where she points.

"Up in the loft, watching."

"Why?" you ask.

"In case we have visitors. Poor boy there was left to watch this ridge. The flank of his platoon went off toward

263

the river and he was supposed to stay back, in case of counter-attack. He was under orders to report an hour after sunrise in the morning, but who knows what They might do if A.F. troops get any closer? I don't want to be surprised, do you?"

"Surprised? No." Sleep, sleep is all you can think of. They are only an idea that is keeping you from sleep. They are nothing more than the products of a nightmare, if cyborgs could have nightmares. If cyborgs could have dreams. You are a soldier. They are less than nothing. And her? What about her? What about her knife? How can you trust her? "How do I know you'll keep watch? How do I know I won't end up like that dead soldier?"

"You don't," she says flatly. "And I don't know what you'll do, either. I'm willing to take a chance." She looks around the shed. "Might as well take advantage and get some rest; there's no place we can go for a couple of hours, anyway."

"But you—" you begin.

"You, too," she answers. "But what's the point?"

You nod, hating your own weakness and the sleepiness that is seeping into your bones with the cold. You adjust yourself against the wall of the thawing shed, trying to forget the cold, the night, the dead man on the floor, the dead men of your squad lying in pieces amid frost shriveled crops. "What did you say to him, when you were talking to him?"

"I told him not to be afraid."

You hear the squeak of the ladder as she climbs to the loft, a sound like heavy wind, and you tell yourself you will remain vigilant. You don't require sleep. You require a med who can fix your ankle. That's all.

And then someone has taken you by the shoulder. Firmly.

You're awake, reaching for your beamer.

"Shush," she says. "Easy soldier. I'm here." She puts her hand into yours, gripping. "It's me."

You nod in the dark, trying to remember your day, why she'd wake you now. When is now? "What time is it?"

"About two hours before dawn. We have to get out of here now, before it starts to get light. They'll find us if we don't leave." She squats down beside you. "Look, I'm going to put your boot on. It's going to hurt. Okay?"

"It won't hurt," you say, but then you add, "But sure, okay. Go ahead."

She moves down your leg, taking the jacket off as she goes. You feel how cold it is now, much colder than it was.

"It's not too bad," she says as she touches you gently. Her hands are cold.

You pull away.

"I'm going to have to bind your ankle very tight. As tight as I can get the bandages. You'll be able to walk more easily, as soon as you're used to it."

"I'm ready." You aren't, but since you'll never be, she might as well do it now and get it over with.

First on goes the sock, which is surprisingly warm. "How?"

"I've had it in my pocket," she says.

A warm sock isn't too bad. You know better than to hope that the boot will go on as well.

It doesn't.

If she were using a vice to mash your bones it couldn't be worse, or so you tell yourself as you try to think of anything but the agony she has caused. You push back against the wall, eyes shut and smarting, sucking short gulps of air through your clenched teeth. As she tugs at the bindings to tighten them, you hear her say, "I'm sorry, I'm very sorry."

It's nothing, you say inside. It's the malfunction. It isn't pain. Cyborgs don't feel pain. It isn't possible for you to hurt. It's the malfunction, the malfunction, the malfunction. You don't know what you say to her, if anything.

"That's about all I can do without meds. I don't have one. Wait a bit and then try standing on it. We've got to be out of here, in case they check on that boy." She nods toward the corpse, as anonymous as a sack in the dark. She takes her jacket from you and for the first time you wonder how she kept warm; it was freezing in the loft.

"There's a warming sheet up there, part of the thawing," she answers. "Some pioneer farmer used it to protect his crop. Not that it's done him any good." She goes into one of the storage troughs and comes back with something strange in her hands.

"What?—" Too late you realize it's a weapon.

"Another piece of pioneer equipment." She raises the thing, resting barrels against her shoulder.

You laugh, a braying sound in the cold, as you fight against the fear and your ankle. "It looks like a beamer, a little," you tell her, because in this light even a broom would look like a beamer.

"It's a 20-gauge shotgun," she says.

Immediately you are filled with questions: what is such an archaic gun doing here? Does it even work, after all this time? You keep from asking them. She answers anyway. "There's a big pioneer center about fifty kilometers back. It belonged to one of the big combines, so there's lots of buildings with shipping centers and all the rest. They were using it for supplies. I found this in the pioneer stuff They discarded. I took it and all the shells I could find, and five incendiary grenades. When I got out of there, I used three of the grenades to blow up the bridges on the estate."

"What about the rest of it, the pioneer stuff?"

"Pioneers got them. Better than letting them go to waste."

"What pioneers?" you ask. "There aren't any left."

"Yes, there are." She looks directly at you. "I'm a pioneer, third generation. We lived at Brent's Tract until you outsiders came."

There have been rumors, of course. In war there are always rumors. You have heard about the pioneers that are left, supposed to be hiding in the forests and the hills and what's left of their towns. The rumor is that they are infiltrators, demolitionists, terrorists. Until now, it was only another rumor, what you'd expect to hear; you didn't believe any of it.

"Who's side are you on?" you ask her, throat and eyes suddenly very dry.

"My own side. If it were up to me, you and They would leave here tomorrow." She folds her arm under the stock of the shotgun.

You feel the dark thick as ink around you, matting the air inside, hovering outside. "How are . . . we going to get out of here?" What you want to know most is if you are going to get out of here at all.

"I've got a light and I know where I am."

That bothers you. In the dark the light makes you a target. "Won't They see it?"

"Maybe, if They look for it. But at this hour, They won't be, or I don't think They will. If it gets too dangerous, or there's any sign of Them, I'll turn it off and we can go to ground until it's light enough to move. I'm a pioneer—we have pretty good night vision. By the way—" She tosses something to you: there are two of them, metallic and cold. "Spare fuel for the beamer. I tried them in the laser but they're the wrong stuff. Anyway, it gives you a little more firepower. Do you want to practice walking before we go?"

You flounder, trying for traction on the stalks of rotted grain and at last, more for luck than anything else, you're up and moving. You are not functioning as well as you want, but that will improve.

"Here. Steady there." She is beside you, her arm around your back, propping up the weight your ankle won't hold. "Try again. You've got to be able to move out there, once we get started."

So you try some more, and the function improves as sensation fades. You walk better—not well, but well enough to cover ground. She moves away from you to leave you to lurch around the shed on your own.

"Here." She hands you a broken section of board, a little longer than your leg. "You can use it as a cane for a while."

"I don't want it," you say, disgusted with the thing.

"It beats falling," she points out, then she shifts her old-fashioned shotgun and goes to open the door.

The darkness is enormous, impending as doom, the cold wind slices through you as cleanly as a laser, the crunchy frost creaks when you step on it, and leaves grey tracks behind you.

In the dark there is a slash of white—she has turned on her light—and then it is gone again and she is next to you, talking in a fierce whisper, as if afraid of being overheard. "If I don't get out of this, here's how to get back to your lines, if they haven't changed much since yesterday: the village of Craoi-Venduru is about ten kilometers ahead on the road that starts on the other side of the ridge. It's very small, maybe twenty-five buildings for pioneers, and a central hall. The western end of the village is where They were yesterday, or so I was told. They killed the pioneers . . . a long time ago. No one's done any farming there since then.

Don't worry about the pioneers. There's a weather and watch station in the central hall. You've seen them?"

"Some," you say, remembering most were in ruins. "And it was part of the training for the campaign. We're shown what we can expect to find."

She looks at him, curiosity and anger in her face. "When did you get here? Are you part of the A.F. forces? Or have you been here a while?"

"I haven't been here very long. Today makes seventeen days. None of A.F. model-4 cyborg group 722s have been here very long."

She shakes her head. "Cyborg," she says, as if she still refuses to believe that's what you are. She resumes her instructions after a single, short sigh. "We'll figure you can recognize the central hall. As you enter the town, just outside it, there is a shrine, one of the very old pioneer kind, and the road forks there. One branch goes off to the left, running beside a stone wall. It's high enough to conceal you. The other branch goes off to the right, toward the river."

"So I go to the right," you say, remembering that A.F. forces are on the far side of the river.

"No; you go to the left. You don't know what's out there, and you'd better find out before you try anything." She hesitates, then resumes her instructions. "At the end of the wall, there is an old pioneer farmhouse, then—doubling back—an inn of some kind, though it's wrecked, two more pioneer houses, a graveyard, and then the central hall. Four days ago the tower was intact. And if it's still there, that's where you go, into the tower. There's an observation station in the tower. It has a good view of the countryside and it might still be safe. They've been in the town, but They've set up Their own platform, nearer the river. So far as I know, They haven't used the tower for anything."

"How do I . . . do we get into the tower?" You hope you can remember everything she is telling you, just in case.

"There is a side door, leading into the cellar. They hadn't used it at all, at least last week They hadn't. Go in there and take the stairs you find there. They aren't the main stairs—they're narrow and steep. All the access doors on the floor above the cellar are locked."

"Were locked," you correct her.

"Yeah: they were locked. The inner stairs go behind the walls and the access doors are at the backs of rooms, not very noticeable. Unless They have had to pull back into the town, They won't bother with the tower, not with Their platform set up." She stares hard at you. "Think you can find your way?"

"Sure," you say, since your life might depend on it.

"One more thing, a favor." The word hangs between you colder than the air.

"What? I owe you." And you are not sure why she has bothered to keep you alive, except for this favor, whatever it may be.

"If I should be captured and you are alive to do it, kill me."

You know you've heard right: you can guess why she asked you. "Kill you?"

"If it happens, do it, soldier."

"If I can't help any other way, I'll kill you." You sound as calm as you'd be if you were arranging to meet for a drink when it's over. You would say the same thing to any A.F. soldier who asked, no matter what model. But this is a living human, and you are a soldier so that humans will not have to be. You are not supposed to kill them. But you have made your promise.

She nods, satisfied. "Come on." With that she starts into

the ice-glittered night, away from the safety of the thawing shed. Her light makes a pitiful pool of white and the dark is vaster by comparison.

So forget your ankle. It will be fixed later. Hit the road at a jog, at a steady, distance-eating trot. Into the plants that line the road, so that you will leave no footprints to guide Them to you, if They start searching. You steady yourself from time to time with the board. Think of it as another weapon, that will make it less shameful. Keep going. Don't let yourself slow or you will have to stop.

Your beamer is heavy. Too bad the laser had to be left in the old grain tank, unusable and unnecessary. The beamer is better. And she has her shotgun. A blast from that makes as real a hole as the beamer does. Or so you hope.

Dog-trot silently, breathe as regularly as you can. Be grateful that you cannot feel fatigue, hunger, hurt. Remind yourself that your guide is a spy, or says she is a spy, and is a pioneer, or says she is a pioneer. Remind yourself that you know nothing about her, not really. Remind yourself what you've promised to do if she gets caught.

Run. Just run.

Run and forget. Not too fast—you might get careless—not too slow. Don't talk, it makes you tired and gives Them something to hear. Don't think. Just run. Keep your mind on what you're doing now. That. Only that.

Wish your ankle, will it, to keep strong and steady. It will be repaired later. The malfunction is like a danger. Use it. Make it part of the running. Somewhere up ahead is a village, a ruin. After that village, there is a river. Once over that river, you'll be safe. You'll be fixed. Other A.F. forces will take over the job you've been doing. If you make it, the cost is six lives. If you don't, the cost is eight and one of them is human.

But according to her, you're human, as human as she is.

Watch her in the dark ahead of you, running silent, swift, steady. There's a light in her right hand, shotgun in the left, a knife in her boot. She carries more than that, you know. She carries your promise. That's part of her armor, the promise you gave her, to go with her archaic shotgun, just in case.

Count your steps for seconds, watch the sky for day; beat the sun. It's the only thing to think of now. Nothing else matters. Nothing else should matter. Beat the sun to a pioneer town called Craoi-Venduru. Be there before They know it, before They can find you, before They can turn on you. The slow wind bites your face and makes your skin feel tight and raw where you feel anything at all. In the dank cold the wind eats into you, sapping your strength, leaching the warmth from you. Count your steps and forget it. You have to get there. Until you do, the rest means nothing.

It all blurs! You've been running since dawn yesterday. Running through the lines, running past the forward troop They sent to intercept your squad. Running to the brush near a loading depot. Running to the place they had stored fuel for Their weapons. Running away when They discovered you. Running for safety, though there is no safety. No stopping for heroics. Or for the dead. Or for the wounded, daubed with spots that look like rust, their bodies loaded with 90-pellets, lethal, decaying the flesh of your squad as they fall. Running as They come after you. Running.

You've got information, so now you run for your lines. Run from Them in Their skimmers when they cut you off: run! Even though the men with you drop away behind you as the 90-pellets spew, run! Run through the trees to a clearing, to a shed. Run from that shed to an unknown town.

"Wait," she pants, and you stop.

"What?" you breathe.

She switches off the light and stands utterly still. The sky is leaden grey, slate, steel at the eastern horizon where the first light shows. You can see a little.

"That's the shrine," she says, pointing through the brush to something that might be a statue.

"I remember," you tell her. Go to the left at the shrine and double back. Go to the central hall. You remember about the cellar entrance.

"No one's moving yet," she says when she is satisfied with the silence around them.

Up through the brush at the side of the road, then a dash for the shrine.

There is a luminous globe in front of a statue of what might be an enormous child with a scythe in his hand. The place is neglected, the blade of the scythe broken and jagged. The features of the figure are all but obliterated with frost.

No time now. Off down the road by the wall and around the end of it. Safe so far.

Stop.

There is a sentry patrolling up and down and up and down in front of the wreckage of the inn. Unconsciously you lock the hilt of the beamer against your shoulder, in case.

She pulls you into the shadows and gestures. You are both to go through the farmhouse.

"But—" you protest, aware of how risky that can be. The place may be booby-trapped, or so unsafe that it will collapse if you try to get into it.

She puts her hand to your mouth, shaking her head. She mouths some words: you recognize "careful," "cover," and

273

"hide," but the rest is lost to you. She points to a few of the braces that have been shifted recently.

So you angle your shoulder against the wall and slide the covering slats aside. When the opening is large enough, she slips past you, into the farmhouse. You wait until she touches your arm, and then you follow her into the gloom, taking care to close the slats behind you as best you can.

The room is wrecked, the articles in the old chest have been used for target practice, by the look of them. The furniture is broken up, possibly used for firewood. Part of the roof has fallen in. Your footsteps, no matter how cautiously you walk, seem absurdly loud and you feel the fear on your neck that suggests that there are listening devices in the room.

She beckons and you follow.

The kitchen is worse than the rest you have seen. The storage racks are gone, the furnace and oven both pulled apart, disemboweled machinery.

Out the back door—there is only a scrap of lumber now, but there was a door once—and into the shadow of the ruined inn. You crouch lower, to keep in the shadow of the place. You watch here as she moves from darkness to darkness, and you take care to do the same.

It is becoming day. Shapes are becoming objects in the advancing light. You have passed the two houses and you can see the tower of the central hall ahead. The graveyard is between you and it.

She flattens and inches forward on her stomach, snaking through the monuments for cover. You follow her, hoping that you do not leave too much of a swath through the graveyard that They can find. You are inured to the cold, or so you tell yourself, no matter how much you fear you will tremble if you stop moving.

Another one of their soldiers comes from the far end of the town. He talks to the sentry on duty. They are too far away for you to hear Them.

You pull yourself even with her behind a carved boulder and whisper: "What now?"

She holds up her hand for silence.

"What?" you ask with your mouth but not with your voice.

"I'm listening." She keeps her hand raised while They speak, her face blank with concentration. Then the second one turns and walks away toward the river, leaving the sentry to resume his patrol.

"They're going back to the shed," she says, so quietly that the sound of the slow wind is louder. Her face is very close to yours. "They want to bring in that soldier. They're shifting Their lines. They're going to mine the bridge and fall back so that the A. F. forces will get themselves blown to dust."

"How long?" you ask, as softly as she.

"Long time. Not until afternoon."

"Then we still have time to get into the spire. We can see what They're doing."

She nods, but glances once in the direction of the sentry.

"No problem," you say—and hope that it isn't.

Her face shows more doubt than suspicion.

"I'll go first. I can cover you once I make it to the door. You come after me."

"But—" She cocks her head toward the sentry again.

"Watch him."

The sentry starts his walk away from you. Watch him, so you can make a dash for the wall of the central hall while he has his back to you. As he comes forward, watch him. Count.

275

Turn. One. Two. Three. Four. Five. Six. Seven. Eight. Nine. Ten. Eleven. Twelve. Thirteen. Fourteen. Fifteen. Sixteen. Seventeen. Eighteen. Nineteen. Twenty. Twenty-one. Twenty-two. Twenty-three. Twenty-four. Twenty-five. Turn.

Twenty-five steps. Twenty-four.

Watch him mark off the same pattern again, and trust that it is a pattern. And then, as he turns away, run.

You race around the corner of the central hall (Fourteen. Thirteen. Twelve.) into the cellar door and against the wall (Six. Five. Four. Three.)

Safe—two. One.

Count the twenty-five again, and backwards.

"Fifteen, fourteen, thirteen," you say to yourself, barely moving your lips. There is a noise just beyond your hiding place. Not the sentry, you say to yourself, It's her, not the sentry. "Nine, eight, seven, six, five, four, three—"

"Two, one." She is beside you. Presses into the shadows. Presses close to you. You put your arm around her and try to make both of you blend with the wall. You see that her hair is short and shaggy and the color of dark ale. You feel it on your face, cold in a way the air is not cold.

"The door?"

"Just behind us," she tells you.

"Can we open it without making too much noise?"

"We're making too much noise now," she says. "It's supposed to open silently. I'm not the only pioneer who uses it."

You hesitate. What if there are others? What if her forces are waiting inside? Or what if They have found out about it, and are ready to take you prisoner? What if you have to fulfill your promise to her in the next few minutes? "Try it," you say before there are too many questions in your mind.

Keeping low, you work your way over to the door. Holding your breath, the beamer raised, you watch as she presses the hidden latches.

The door swings open with nothing more than a hiss.

She goes inside, and you follow.

There are papers strewn over the floor of the cellar, most of them old, by the look of them, crumbling to dust. Your feet leave indecipherable tracks as you cross them, going toward the stairs. It is a hard job to climb them, for they are metal, clanging from time to time without warning, and so steep and narrow that you have to go up with your feet turned; your ankle weakens quickly.

At the top of the stairs there is a door, and she has sagged against it.

"Locked?" you ask, afraid of being trapped here in the walls of the central hall.

"No."

"Then what?" You have your beamer ready.

"Can you lift it? It's heavy; I didn't realize I was so tired." She turns her wan face to you. "I don't want it to scrape. Too much noise."

"I'll give it a try." It is against your training to put the beamer aside, but she's right—the door is heavy and you need both arms to lift it. You struggle with it, and then there is space enough for you to squeeze through.

There are bits of weather-monitoring equipment still in the tower, most of it useless due to age and neglect. The slitted windows have glass in them still so the tower isn't too cold. With care, you can watch Them and the road to the river and not be seen yourselves.

That bothers you: if you are seen, it's all over. All They need to do is swing Their artillery around and that's the end of you. You have no place to hide other than this one hiding place, and once it is discovered, there is nothing to fall back on. You frown at the thought, and hope that you are lucky enough to last a little longer.

"They don't check this place often," she says, knowing what troubles you. "Why should They? It's secure, isn't it?" She sets her shotgun and light aside, then opens up a cabinet. There are blankets in the cabinet, and a large-scale torn map.

"How did they get here?" you ask her, suspicions flaring again.

"Pioneers, of course." She keeps her voice low. "We must talk softly. Sound carries too well. We can take turns watching so that we can both get some sleep."

"I slept in the night," you say, regarding her closely.

"That ankle needs rest even if you don't," she says.

"I'll keep it propped up," you decide. "That'll rest it until I can get it repaired."

"You mean set," she corrects you.

"Repaired," you insist.

She shrugs and sets about unfolding two of the blankets. They are quite large and heavy, having a strange, mushroomy smell that disturbs you. "If anything happens while I'm asleep—and I need to sleep—wake me. I know the area and . . ."

"And what?" you want to know when she does not finish.

"And I know where the pioneers are," she tells you defiantly. "My forces."

"They're near?" you ask, not knowing what to make of it if they are.

"I don't think I'll tell you that," she says after a short silence. "There's no reason for you to know the answer."

"But they've been here," you say, indicating the blankets.

"Not recently. It is getting too dangerous and there are better things to do than hide in towers."

"You've been here before," you say, certain that she has.

"I lived in this little room for forty-two days once. I know it well." She sits on one of the opened blankets, the dawn making a riot of color around her through the slits of the windows. "I came after I . . ." Again, she does not finish.

"Get some sleep," you say, seeing her face. "I'll take the first watch. You've got until mid-day."

"Thank you," she says, sounding more weary than you would have thought possible. She lies back, pulling the heavy, scented blanket around her like a cocoon.

You nod once, though she cannot see you nod. You look out the narrow windows and see Them below, moving like insects, busy being soldiers, busy waking up. A skimmer pulls up, leaving a slick like the wake of a slug. Four of Them get into it; they roar off in the direction you came an hour ago. You wish now you had taken the time to bury the dead boy back there. But in such hard ground, in the pernicious cold, it was out of the question.

You turn to tell her, but she is lying wrapped, her eyes closed, her hands limp. She is pale and her eyes are framed in darkness.

So you watch Them and long for warmth and listen to the voices of Their men beneath your hiding place rise on the morning air, pure and distant as the cries of children at play. You watch and rest and you think about the campaign, about the war. This is your fifth campaign, a remarkable accomplishment for an A.F. model-4 cyborg group 722. Few of you have lasted more than two campaigns. But the wars have taken their toll: once you could remember the number of Them you'd killed. Now, you can't remember the number of A.F. model-4 cyborg group 722s They've killed. And you wish it would end. It has ended for so many others; you wish it would end for you.

But you don't want to be killed. It is not part of your programming to be killed, only part of the reality of what you are. You are supposed to fight until you die. There is nothing else for A.F. model-4s.

You move your foot when your ankle starts to disturb you again. Maybe it has been irritated all the time, but you notice it now, and hate the weakness it reveals.

The sun is a shiny spot in the heavy sky, sliding over the horizon into morning. You watch the shadows move slowly along the ground, sorry now that you were not issued a timer for this campaign. Everything would be easier with a timer.

She has moved in her sleep, making a low sound at the back of her throat; in her sleep she is pushing away some horror, writhing at the dream, struggling with a phantom.

Then you throw yourself at her, reaching for her, your hand pressed over her open mouth to stop the scream.

She strains against you, eyes suddenly wide, thrashing desperately, pinned by your body to the floor, her back arched, her arms seeking purchase on your gear.

"It's me," you say as you fight to hold her, hoping to wake her before she breaks free. "It's me. We're in the tower. Remember? It's me."

She sheds the last vestige of sleep and her tension eases.

You feel her resistance fade. "I'm going to take my hand away: Will you scream?"

She shakes her head no twice, emphatically.

"Are you okay now?"

She nods yes.

Slowly you take your hand from her mouth, rolling onto

your side as you do. Then you turn her to you and wrap your arms around her shoulders. "It's okay," you say, knowing it for a lie. You feel her arms go around your waist, her head pushed into your shoulder. "It's okay. Whatever it was, it's over. I'm here now. It's over. No matter what They did, it's over, it's over. You're safe. I won't let Them hurt you again."

And under your arms her whole body shakes; no tears, no sobs, no sound, just that awful trembling. You want her to speak so that you will know how risky it is, but she remains locked in her suffering. Finally she whispers. "When They had me . . ." It takes her a little time to go on. "They wanted to wipe out the pioneers. But They wanted information, so it wasn't going to be just an execution. They knew I was a spy, after a while. They do things to spies, to get information. They did things to me."

You say nothing. All you've heard have been rumors, and you know how rumors are. But those rumors are enough to make you stop before you ask, before your curiosity wins. You know what happens to Their spies when your forces interrogate Them. Any of that happening to her sickens you.

"I got away," she says a bit later. "It was a freak chance, an accident. I escaped during on one of the A.F. raids. I hardly knew what I was doing, only that I had to get away. They were holding me at Their field headquarters. The A.F. came in with a two-prong attack—"

"That would be A.F. model-11 cavalry," you tell her, recalling the lectures you were given before arriving here.

"I ran," she goes on, paying no attention to what you've said. "Everyone was running, no one paid any attention to me. I finally found my way out of the place. I stole a skimmer I guess a day or so later. I don't know. Between the drugs and other things, I couldn't tell. But the fires were dying, so it had to be at least a day. I got away. I went back to the pioneers, but most of them were dead. The survivors found me. I was going to quit, but . . ."

Your face is colder. You bring up your hand and find wetness.

She looks at you, her expression gentle and ironic. "I told you you're not a cyborg."

"A.F. model-4 cyborg group 722," you say, as you have said for as long as you can remember.

"You're a human being, as human as I am," she says with an emotion you do not recognize. "They've done it to you, too, haven't they? Probably the same way they get spies to confess and change sides. Sides! A. F., Them, it doesn't matter." She tightens her hold on you. "I am sick of it all."

You feel too much to feel anything as you hold her. How can she be right? How is it possible that you are human and not a cyborg? It would make the A.F. as despicable as They are, and that would mean that you have been fighting for leaders as reprehensible as those They follow. "A.F. model-4 cyborg group 722," you say as if the words will make it so, will bring back that sense of order you believed in.

"Human," she insists. "Human, about twenty-five, with a sprained or broken ankle swelling in your boot. I don't know how you endure the pain." The last is embarrassed.

"It's not pain; it's the malfunction." But as you say it, there is a sensation you have refused to acknowledge, as if fangs were digging into your leg. If you let yourself know what is there, you will have to accept the hurt.

"Pain," she says. "How could they do this to you? How do they justify what they're doing?"

"They don't need justification," you say, repeating what

you have been told for so long.

"No, not Them, the A.F. forces—how can they condone what they've done to you?" She leans back but does not release you. "How do they explain what they've done?"

You start to speak and discover that you can say nothing. At last you tell her, "I can't be human."

"Yes," she says. "There is solace in it, when the world isn't too insane."

"In what?" you ask her, another fear starting deep inside you, a growing dread at the massive lie you have believed.

"Being human," she says. She kisses your cheek where the tears are, and it seems to you that there is sorrow and tenderness and that unknown emotion in the touch of her lips.

You tell yourself that you are numb, that there is no pain, not from your ankle, not from that deeper, festering hurt that she has caused. How you want to be angry with her, to accuse her of distortion and deception; you cannot. Your ankle aches. Your body aches. Your . . . soul? aches. You roll onto your back and stare at the ceiling; your vision blurs.

She rests her head in the curve of your shoulder and chest. Her heartbeat is steadier than your own. She apologizes to you, but you are not able to listen. She falls silent, discouraged by your lack of response.

It is unendurable, the things you know. You will not let yourself know them. You close your eyes against the knowing, allowing nothing into your mind. In all the world, there is nothing and no one but the two of you. Then the world goes away.

You must have fallen asleep, because the sun has moved and is coloring the windows on the other side of the tower. You are alert suddenly, attentive to everything. You listen for the sounds outside. If there has been a change, you are not aware of it. You turn your head to study her sleeping face on your shoulder. The blanket is rough where it touches your face, but you decide the sensation is a friendly one.

She moves a little, still solidly asleep, the deep lines at last less incised on her features. You touch her face, memorizing it with your fingers.

"Um," she murmurs.

"You awake?"

"No."

Gently you ruffle her hair, gently, gently.

She opens her eyes. "What time is it?"

"Afternoon. I don't know how late." You wish again for a timer, knowing it harmless to make such a wish.

"We must have slept for hours," she says. Slowly she sits up, stretching, her joints popping.

"Yes," you say, not knowing how to tell her you feel restored by the sleep, by her company.

"I'm hungry," she says to you. "But there's no food up here."

"Sorry," you say, indicating you have nothing with you. "They don't give field rations to—"

"Human beings," she says.

There's no point in debating that now. It is afternoon and the river is near and on the other side of that river are your lines. The A.F. forces are waiting. "We'd better get up," you tell her, moving away from her, from the warmth of the blankets out into the chill of the afternoon.

She goes to the window, watching what They are doing in silence. She listens to the scraps of conversation that drift up to you. "We'd better plan to leave pretty soon. An hour before dusk, they'll be starting their feint. They've trapped

the bridge, mines and trips. We can disarm it and be free."
She looks at you, with an unspoken question in her eyes.

You look out into the white sunlight, thinking.

"There's the pioneers."

You nod. You wonder again, remembering, forgetting.
You could reach out your hand to her. But They are out
there. If you listen you can hear Them. Who is this person,
this woman beside you who talks of the pioneers, as if you
could walk away from what is left of your squad. So you
stare out the window, watching Them, hearing the sounds
of mechanical thunder that announces the nearness of your
forces, of battle, of safety, of death.

"It's the noise," she says after a while, her hands pressed
over her ears. "They do it deliberately, make all that noise.
It wears you down, disrupts your thoughts."

"I don't hear it any more," you say, and know it for the
lie it is.

"You've stopped listening is all," she says, no more
fooled than you are. Her voice is rueful; you turn to her.

"Let's get out of here. While we can."

She looks at you for a long moment. "I hate Them; I
hate the A. F., I wish I didn't, but I pity you." She changes
her manner abruptly. "Let's go disarm that bridge."

This time you hesitate. In light of what she has said, you
don't understand. "Why?"

"It's a game, a game for idiots. But if we disarm the
bridge, they'll be live idiots. Live human idiots." This last is
intended to demand your attention: it does.

"Suppose that's not possible?" you ask.

"I'll find a way to set it off before the A.F. get here."

"If you set it off, you'll die," you say, and have to stop
yourself from adding that as a cyborg, you are the one who
should take that risk, not her, since she's human.

"That may be the price," she says.

"But—" You do not know what else to say.

"Human life is cheap, as cheap as real cyborgs. Maybe cheaper, or why are they telling you and other men that you are modified machines?" She turns toward the door, not permitting you a chance to argue.

"If we stay here, I can use the beamer, aim right into the heart of the camp." You offer this as a compromise, so that you can share her risk.

"How long does it take to fire one of those laser cannons? They have three within range," she says. "And it won't save anyone getting on to that bridge."

"Point made," you concede.

She laughs. "What point?"

You want to ask why she is willing to do this, since she is contemptuous of the war and the two sides fighting it. You wish you could find the right phrases to use to learn the truth about her. "Are you doing this because of me?"

For an answer she comes and stands in front of you. "It has nothing to do with you, or very little. The pioneers want that bridge saved, for our own purposes. After what was done to me, I knew that I had to do something to get back at Them, to have a little vengeance for what They did." She opens her jacket, then takes your hand and guides it with her own until you touch raised, gnarled flesh that makes you recoil inside, that makes her cringe at your touch. "That's part of it. I owe Them for that."

"You were comforting one of Them when I found you," you remind her.

"I shot him; why shouldn't I comfort him?" She shakes her head and closes her jacket, turning toward the door.

Before there is a chance for you to say anything—if there were anything you could say—she is gone down the narrow stairway to the cellar. There is nothing to do but go down the stairs after her.

As she works the concealed cellar door, she says, not looking at you, "That promise—if I get caught."

"Yes."

"I still want you to keep it." She is out the door, ducked, running to the long shadows at the end of the central hall.

You follow her, your beamer a suddenly unfamiliar weight in your arms.

Together you make a wide loop of the end of the town where They are. When you reach the fork in the road that takes you to the river, she gives you a positive sign with her hand. It is darkening, the clouds lower, heavier, oily-looking. There are about two hours of light left.

"How's your ankle doing?" she asks when she has signaled you to stop so she can watch the road.

"It's sore," you say, finding the word strange.

"Go easy with it."

"Sure," you say, having no idea what she wants to hear from you.

She pats your arm once before she veers off through the brush, moving parallel to the road. You can hear the river now, and the advancing of men and equipment. Very soon you reach the bank of the river.

It is steep where you are, the bridge at a wider but more placid bend about forty meters away. Upstream.

You're closer than you would like to be. You can see the guards patrolling the end of the bridge, near enough that if you spoke up, they would hear you.

She has taken a monocular out of her pocket and is scanning the bridge. "Clever," she breathes as she studies something.

"How?" You are afraid to raise your voice above the

287

lowest whisper, afraid that you will be heard by Their guards.

"Look." She hands you the monocular. "There's a dummy mine in the middle of the bridge, clinging to the side. It's hidden, but you can find it if you're looking for it."

You look, and you do see it. "So?"

"Two things: it isn't a real mine. It's a trigger for a couple of traps—there's light readers installed in its side and if you set them off, you probably bring half the artillery on this side of the river into play. The mines are probably directly under the roadway, and I won't find them until I get there, if none of the light readers pick up on my movement. They may even have the foundations of the supports set to go up."

"Like you said: clever." There is a tightening coil inside you, colder than the day.

"I've set smaller devices myself," she says, unaware of your reaction. "Sometimes they've worked—most people wouldn't bother looking for the light readers." She takes a deep breath. "I hate cold water."

"Isn't there some way—" you begin.

"Where?" she asks sensibly. She is pulling off her jacket, handing it to you, along with her shotgun. "Now, if you can, cross the river here, staying as far down the bend as you can. That will lessen the risk of you being seen. The guards will be looking across the river or upstream. When you get across, go find the A.F. lines. If that bridge goes, there's going to be a lot of rock falling."

"I'll wait for you on the other side," you tell her.

"Don't be foolish."

"I'll be on the other side. In case I have to keep my promise," you say, letting the harsh words settle the matter.

Her expression is puzzled; then she slides down the bank to disappear into the water. She is only a dark speck in the sinuous river. You watch the sentries on the bridge, but, as she indicated, they are looking upstream and toward the opposite bank.

In a while, you can see her hanging onto the foundation support.

It's time for you to cross now.

There are colds that are colder than freezing. The river is that kind of cold. You ease down the bank and into the water, and the breath is forced out of you. It's too deep and too fast to keep the beamer and the shotgun dry. You let the shotgun go. The cold gnaws at your bones, and for once your ankle does not hurt you. You do not want to give into the lure of the cold, and so you use more strength than you want to keep moving across, so that you will not succumb to the lassitude of the cold.

Eventually you make it to the other bank, to pull yourself dripping onto the shore. And the icy wind takes up where the water leaves off. You huddle in the bushes, your teeth clattering, uncertain that you can pull the trigger on the beamer if you have to.

The guns at your back are louder now, and closer. The sound of an army moving is stronger. Where are they? Two kilometers? Three? More?

You can't see her, she's hidden by the dark under the bridge. You aren't even sure she is there still; she might have fallen into the water and been swept downstream. You do not let yourself dwell on that.

Off to the right there is a flash and a thud and three of Their sentries collapse on the other side of the bridge. Two of Their lasers sprout from the trees near the road to Craoi-Venduru, hissing defiance at whatever is coming down the road. And all you can do is huddle in the cover of the bushes, colder than death, and watch.

There is more and heavier firing from the A.F. troops on this side.

Where is she? What's happened to her?

One of Their lasers is silent. A fine spray of 90-pellets bites into the bank about two meters away. You jump, then retreat into the brush. Then you realize, as the 90-pellets spatter again, that they were not aimed at you.

You look: she's in the river about four, five meters away, coming toward the bank. You move down as close as the cover will allow, calling "Pioneer!"

She hears you over the increasing racket; a hail of 90-pellets comes much too close. You leave the brush, coming as far down the bank as you dare, your hand stretched out to her. You almost reach her when a 90-pellet shatters your hand.

Blood, bone, flesh shatter. Your arm goes heavy, and you stare at what is left, seeing nothing of the internal armor you had been assured you possess. Blood, bone, flesh.

You feel her hands close around your leg. Automatically you start back toward the brush, dragging her behind you, over the trail of blood from the destruction of your hand.

You pause in the brush, your body slicked with cold sweat, nausea sinking into your vitals. You pull her toward you as you press your arm to your side.

She is white to the point of being blue.

You are struggling with the bindings on your jacket, trying to pull something free that will let you bind your arm.

"It's safe," she whispers. "They can cross now. The bridge won't blow." Her veins stand out, her eyes are distant.

You stare as your blood pumps out of you. You were hit with 90-pellets, you think in a calm eddy of your mind. You can bind it up, but it won't make any difference. 90-pellets are lethal. You are a dead man.

But she is still alive. You shake yourself, struggle once more to pull the binding free. You have some time left before the 90-pellets do their work. You can get her out of danger. You can do that much.

You drag yourself to your feet and, using your teeth and one hand, you manage to tighten a thong around your arm so that the bleeding lessens. You are dizzy when you move, but you force yourself to bring her to her feet. "Over that rise. That's all we have to do."

"I'm too cold," she murmurs, then sees what is left of your hand for the first time. Her eyes grow enormous. "How?"

"They were trying for you," you say before you can think of something better. "It's fair."

Her laughter is desolate.

"Get moving," you tell her, shoving her ahead of you, knowing that if she falls again, you might not have the strength to get her to her feet. You know that if she does not move, she will freeze to death. "Move," you urge her.

She's over the ridge; you start down after her, your vision swimming at the sides.

A snap from the trees ahead, and a thud. Another snap and thud.

She wavers on her feet, turns toward you, amazed, bewildered.

You lurch, stumble down to her, to have her fall against you, looking into your face, astonished.

"I've been shot."

No, you say. No, no, no. You hold her, arms across her

291

back to protect her. And all the time there is something warm and faintly sticky seeping through your sleeves, something that isn't yours. You can't stop that. Or the thread of blood at the corner of her mouth. Or the moment when she becomes heavier and her lungs are still, when her arms no longer hold you and you know you hold nothing at all.

There is a time when you drag her—you don't have enough strength left to carry her—away from the noise, to a place where she will be safe, where it won't matter if you're gone. You don't know how long it takes, because it doesn't matter.

A young cadet finds you, all questions, to apologize for firing on you because the A.F. forces mistook you for Them.

There is a time, a little later, when you lie in a darkened shelter while a physician looks at your hand and refuses to meet your eyes.

And there is a time when you ride in a skimmer to a Commander waiting for a report while you can still give it.

All you remember, see, feel, is her body; how you left her in a stand of scavenger Capuchin trees, under the carnivorous branches. Her image brands you, hot against the shock of your loss and your oncoming death.

The Commander looks you over, and whatever is in his thoughts he conceals from you.

You salute with the wreck of your hand. "Malfunction," you tell him, holding out the bits of blood and bone, now sealed in a flexible, see-through, completely useless bandage. "Cyborg malfunction."

"I'm sorry," says the Commander, and it is almost possible to believe he means it.

"Fortunes of war?" you suggest, somewhere between fury and darkest amusement.

"I am sorry," the Commander repeats.

You close your eyes against him, against the noise, against the rusty smear on your sleeve and the horror at the end of your arm, against the destruction working its way into you.

The Commander shifts. "I know how you must feel: cheated, perhaps even betrayed."

"That's human."

"Yes." The Commander is careful about his next words. "If it weren't absolutely necessary, we wouldn't do it. But They make it necessary. There isn't . . . time to explain why."

"No; I suppose not."

Once more he says, "I'm sorry."

You speak, not to the Commander, but to those things you see with your eyes closed. "So am I."

About *Day 17*

This odd tale has a past as quirky as its style: it was sold three times before it actually saw print—once to a science fiction anthology that was cancelled when its in-house editor was fired, and once when a magazine changed hands and policies. It finally made its first appearance in a small-press magazine. I was almost beginning to think that the story had a curse on it.

The second-person present-tense narration proved very obdurate—I tried to do the story in both third and first person, present and past tenses, and nothing worked except this somewhat peculiar style. I figure the story understands itself better than I do, so I stopped trying to make it fit my expectations and let it run the way it wanted to. I still find it disconcerting, but I know it's what it ought to be.

FRUITS OF LOVE

As soon as he had slammed the door in the lackeys' faces, the Baron was on her, fumbling greedily at Desiree's stays, his big, lean hands dry as reptiles as he dragged her breasts out of her corsage.

She had feared it would be bad with him, but nothing had prepared her for his rapacity, and she retreated, her voice high and shaking. "You are too eager, *mon Baron.*" She struggled to break away from him, her delicate fingers closing to fists which she did not dare to use.

Le Baron Clotaire Odon Jules Valince Pieux de Saint Sebastien laughed unpleasantly, contemptuously, as he reached for the ties of her panniers. "How can I not be eager when you are so charming?" he taunted her in a travesty of the grand manner he had learned as a young man. He was the last of a bad lot: dissipated, corrupt, some said blasphemous, and long since out of favor at court. He was also very rich and, in certain circles, powerful. Now he watched while Desiree struggled with her trailing skirts and undone corset, no sympathy in his hooded green eyes. "What is this, *ma belle?* Why do you hesitate? Surely you are not going to pretend virgin shyness?"

Desiree smiled desperately. "No," she said, more wistfully than she knew. "But perhaps . . . first . . . something."

"Courtship?" He sneered. "But to what purpose? Why should I court you when I own you?"

Her body went cold at his implacable words. "Perhaps we could talk?"

He regarded her narrowly. "Are you going to be tiresome? What prattle of yours could possibly interest me? You have one use for me, and if that is denied me, then I have made a poor bargain and I will have to recoup my losses however I may." His stare grew harder and more calculating. "There is a brothel I know; the madame takes girls like you, she prefers them, in fact, so that they can be chastised."

Desiree would not let herself scream, though she felt the sound and outrage building in her. "Tell me of yourself, then? Your lackeys said nothing in the coach. I . . . I have seen you only once before." She was inching away from him as she tried to gather enough of her bodice and corset to cover herself. While his hands had been on her she had been contaminated, debased; even his cynical gaze had a filth about it. "I know little of you, *mon Baron.*"

"Have you considered I might prefer that?" He was almost certain that her silly young lover, de Vandonne, had told her tales, undoubtedly going back to his grandfather, who had been part of de Montespan's set. "What do you need to know but that I want you and will keep you so long as you please me?" He strolled over to the trestle table and started to pinch out the candles of the nearer candelabrum.

She was still retreating from him. "But I know so little . . . I have had just one lover, and he . . . he—"

"Was a foolish, handsome young man and you think you love him, and that he adores you," Saint Sebastien finished for her. "You will come to learn otherwise."

"There has only been Michon," she pleaded, wishing that Michon were here to save her, to see what his stupid, reckless, unforgivable wager had wrought.

"I assure you, *ma belle,* I am experienced enough for both of us." There was no humor in his voice. "I pay well for my pleasures, do not doubt." He paused. "And do not doubt *you* will pay dearly for my disappointment, Desiree."

Her panic was rising, but she fought it down. She had to get out of this salon, she had to find the servants and enlist their help, or run away. If only she knew where she was, what estate this was. "I do not want to disappoint you, *mon Baron,* but . . . but I have not learned much . . ."

Saint Sebastien was tiring of their game. "I do not wish to have to hurt you, child. But I am not a patient man and your loveliness and your reluctance may drive me to it." He had taken off his heavy silk coat with the wide whale-boned skirts, and was starting to unfasten the thirty pearl buttons that closed his gold-brocaded waistcoat.

Now the door was only a few steps behind her. Once through it, Desiree thought desperately, and she would have a chance to save herself. She pretended to trip on her ripped petticoat, and flung out an arm to break her fall, her fingers closing on the scroll-handled latch. She put her weight against it, but to no avail.

"Ah, yes," said Saint Sebastien as he snuffed out three more candles. "It is locked, I am sorry to say. And I have the key. Though if you did get out of the room, the lackeys would bring you back." He tossed his waistcoat aside. "Little as you may like it, I won you in fair play, Desiree." He recalled the shock in Michon de Vandonne's turquoise-colored eyes when he realized he had gambled away his mistress, and lost her to Clotaire de Saint Sebastien, of all men. "You are mine now. I won you and have the deed to prove it. Accept that. You are mine, to do with as I wish. I could have you deported to the American colonies, with a load of whores. I could give you to my servants to use. I could blind you and leave you somewhere on the high road. I have done these things before to others, and I may do them again. So be grateful that for the moment I desire you for myself." He looked dreamily into the fire, and his expression was not a good one. "I do not want to continue your game: do not make me go to the trouble of fetching you."

The last of the candles was out; the salon was ruddy in the glow from the hearth. To Desiree, it was a vision of Hell. She stared, her courage deserting her, as Saint Sebastien dropped into a leather chair and began to unfasten his jabot.

Desiree leaned on the locked door and wept silently. She was just seventeen years old, and for one happy year she had been the mistress of Michon de Vandonne. For the second daughter of an Anjou carriage-maker, she had done well, and though her family did not wholly approve, they did not object—for they were realistic enough to know that de Vandonne could offer her more than any suitor they might secure for her—or they would not object until now. Now she knew they could cast her off. She had to force herself to look at the man who waited for her on the other side of the room. Her body was clay-cold and as awkward as a puppet with tangled strings; it seemed to her that her fine violet silk dress—quite ruined—was a shroud.

As the clock on the mantel chimed the hour, Saint Sebastien rose with a sigh and walked to the door. There was deliberation in the sound of his high-heeled shoes. "I asked you not to make me come to you." His mouth smiled, but his eyes never lost their stoniness; when she winced at his touch his lips stretched wider.

"Ah, no, *mon Baron*," she whispered as he took her chin in his hand, pressing hard.

He pulled the last of the silk out of her hands and away from her body. He flung her panniers aside. The laces of her corset were already torn and it came away quickly; in his haste, he left bruises as testament to his anger. When at last she was naked and weeping with dread, he pinned her to the floor and fastened on the secret places of her body.

When Desiree tried to escape the first time, he beat her into unconsciousness and let it go at that: his estate was an isolated one, and he was aware she had no real chance to get free. Had the game been more equal, he might have let her continue the farce, but it did not amuse him enough for that. It had taken his gamekeepers less than two hours to find her and to drag her back to his chateau. His thoughts, too, had been on other matters; there was news from Austria of the new Empress, and Saint Sebastien wanted an ear in Maria Theresa's court. He had other arrangements that demanded his attention and he did not want to lose precious time disciplining his reluctant mistress. But the second time she ran away was another matter. "Well?" he, demanded when his warden finally brought her back to him, more than a day after she had fled. A night in the open had taken its toll: her clothes were disheveled, her shoes muddied, one of them lacking a heel. Her face and arms were scratched and smirched, and she limped painfully on a swollen ankle. Her jaw was raised and her eyes hard and bright. As he surveyed her, Saint Sebastien took snuff from a gold-and-enamel box and dusted his satin coat with a lace handkerchief. From his brocaded shoes and silk stockings to his pigeon's-wing bagwig, he was the picture of the perfect gentleman. Only the lines scored into his face marred him. "I am waiting for your answer."

"I don't have one." Hatred burned at the back of her eyes, hatred for Baron Clotaire de Saint Sebastien, who had brought her to this, and for Michon de Vandonne, who had lost her with the same concern he had lost a *rouleau* of *ange d'or*. What had she meant to him, if he could let her go so easily, for nothing more than the turn of a card?

Saint Sebastien regarded her evenly, his hooded green eyes unfathomable. "I thought you understood, Desiree. I thought I had made matters clear to you. But I see I will have to demonstrate once again, this time more forcefully." He smoothed the broad cuff of his salmon-colored silk coat, a frown puckering his brow.

This was a familiar expression to Desiree and though it frightened her, she was not overwhelmed by her fear. "You will beat me, I suppose."

The defiance in her words made him look up. "So. You are growing strong in your anger." The polite bow he favored her with terrified her. "I see I will have to use other tactics. It would not do for you to learn to resist me. It would not be acceptable." He rose, taking his silver-and-ebony cane from beside his chair. He paused, then said at his most urbane, "Oh, you need not fear I will use this on you. I would do that only if I intended to kill you."

She loathed herself for revealing her terror, but she could not make herself keep silent. "Then what will you do to me?"

He pursed his lips, taking time to relish her fright. "I assumed I had made that clear, *ma belle*. I am going to make sure you learn your lesson this time." He picked up a silver bell and rang it, pleased to see her bewilderment. "I have decided to delegate my punishment to another."

She stood as if impaled. "Who?"

"You remember Tite?" It was an unnecessary question, for she had never disguised her dislike for Saint Sebastien's large, saturnine manservant who was virtually her jailer. "He was distressed when you disappeared, and requested that when you came back he might have the schooling of you." He tapped his cane lightly on the marble floor. "He is a strange man, Tite, a very strange man. Tite lusts the most where he is most angry. Your foolish rebellion has infuriated him, and therefore he is enflamed as well. He has no regard for affection, I ought to mention; he finds his greatest satisfaction in resistance and the submission of his . . . victim."

"And I am his victim?" she asked in spite of her resolution to be silent.

"Why, of course. You have shown that my chastisement means nothing, so you must have a more obdurate tutor." His glance raked over her, taking in all the dirt and tatters. He flicked his handkerchief toward her, suddenly fastidious. "Certainly you are more fitting for him, or a stablehand, or a pig farmer, than for me in your present state."

The trembling that seized her almost made Desiree fall. She steadied herself against his writing table. Her mouth was too dry for speech. Dumbly she shook her head, her body filled with protest. She wanted to take the standish and throw it at him, hoping the ink would mar his beautiful clothes and reveal him for what he was. Her hand would not move.

Saint Sebastien enjoyed her distress as he went on smoothly, "You should be grateful, *ma belle*. You have made it plain enough that my embraces disgust you, that you would prefer another; I am offering you the variety you crave."

At that she blurted out one name: "Michon!" though Saint Sebastien did not understand it for the curse it was.

"Oh, no, I am afraid there is no hope for you from that quarter, not now. That puppy de Vandonne would not take you back now, Desiree; he is too nice for that. He would never touch what I have had. Ah." He looked up as the door opened.

Tall, raw-boned, more a bodyguard than a valet, Tite came forward, his eyes on Desiree. He bowed.

Saint Sebastien looked directly at Desiree as he spoke to his servant. "I promised her to you, didn't I?"

"Yes, master," said Tite, his face avid.

"Then, naturally, she is yours." He gave Desiree a slight, contemptuous nod before he left her alone with Tite.

After the agony and humiliation, Desiree shut most of herself away, to be infected with her shame, her fear, and to fester. Outwardly she was no more than a sleepwalker, seemingly immune to Saint Sebastien's cruel amusements and taunts. Even when she discovered the profane altar in the cellar, she did nothing more than shrug, as if the inverted crucifix with its aroused Christ was little more than another tasteless decoration. She spoke rarely and, when she did, the words were gentle, emotionless, as her eyes were strangely vacant and unresponsive.

At first Saint Sebastien was pleased with this change in her, and invented new torments to provoke her into another burst of rebellion. Only occasionally was he able to abuse her enough for her to resist or object, and eventually he grew bored. Only her pregnancy kept him from turning her out.

"I do not know why I continue with you," he said to her one evening as they sat alone in the cavernous dining room. The food on her plate was largely untasted. "There are others who can conceive."

"Nor do I know," muttered Desiree. She pushed a dollop of veal around her plate with her fork.

"I do want your babe," he said, with extravagant unconcern. "I have a use for a newborn, if not for you."

She swallowed hard, but said nothing, keeping her eyes on the smear of sauce at the rim of her plate. In four more months she would deliver, and then God alone—or perhaps only the Devil—knew what would become of her. Desiree had reached a state where she was not able to imagine any life other than this one. She would not permit herself to speculate on what awaited her child when it came.

"He will be offered on the altar, before I return to Paris." He wiped his mouth with his lace-edged napkin. "Would you like to participate? It helps to have a woman on the altar, to use as a woman, and to hold the basin for the blood."

She kept silent.

"Well, in four months you may make up your mind." He patted her arm in a deceptively avuncular way. "In the meantime, Tite and I will find new ways to amuse you. As long as Tite continues to be so inventive, my interest will not slacken. Once it does, I will need to find other sport."

Three weeks later, Desiree miscarried. She lay in her room, her teeth clamped shut so that she would not scream, would not gratify her captors with her suffering. When it was over, when the blood had dried and she had come to her senses again, Tite found her.

"You brought this on! Out of spite!" he thundered at her.

"I didn't have to, not with what you have done to me," she said, weary and desolate.

Tite suddenly laughed. "It might be worth the entertainment we had, but it's a pity we lost the sacrifice." His nose wrinkled at the coppery scent of blood. "You've ruined the bed."

"Do you care the baby was yours?" she asked harshly. She looked at the incomplete lump, no larger than a clenched fist, with little of humanity to identify it. It was Tite's, and that made it despicable. But also it was hers, she

realized. It had lived in her, and now it was dead, because
of the man who fathered it. Like everything else in her life,
it had been contaminated by Clotaire de Saint Sebastien.
As she fought down her sudden rush of tears, she promised
herself and her dead child vengeance.

That night the herb woman came to treat Desiree and to
take away the thing she had lost, promising that she would
find a way to bury it in sacred ground. "For it wasn't its
fault that it had no proper birth," she said. Marta was not
as old as she looked: an ugly facial birthmark and prematurely gray hair made her appear ancient, but her walk and
the firm tone of her skin betrayed her youth. Traces of native Italy clung to her in her accented French and her lam-
bent dark eyes. She realized Desiree's predicament before
the desperate young woman could speak. "There," she said
reassuringly when she had finished bathing Desiree and assured herself that there was no infection from the miscarriage. "The men know nothing, not the worst or the best of
them. You do not need to tell me how it was."

"I could not," whispered Desiree, all her anguish wakened afresh at her loss.

"Do not worry; the infant is out of reach of that satin-
clothed pig. The child is gone to Heaven where Mere Marie
will treasure it until you come."

"I, come to Heaven?" she started to laugh, but that gave
way to weeping she could not stop. She attempted to apologize, to stem the tide of her sorrow, but for once she was
not able to control her emotions, or to disguise them.

"A mother's tears are holy. There is nothing disgraceful
in shedding them." Marta put her hands over Desiree's as if
to reinforce her prayers. "God knows what beasts like this
Saint Sebastien do, and He will judge them. It will be the
worse for Saint Sebastien, I think, because he came by his

title through the Church; Saint Sebastian is a benefice and a Vidamie. His grandfather was made a Baron, or so they say, but the estate came from the Church, for service to God."

"How do you come to know this?" Desiree was able to ask the question as if it had nothing to do with her or anyone she knew.

Marta had been searching her bag for the herbs that would lessen the bleeding and ease the hurt. "I know because I live here, for everyone near this place knows about the Baron."

"This has happened before?" Desiree told herself that she was not shocked, but new pain wrenched inside her.

"Let us say that there have been women here before, sometimes more than one, and what has happened to them has not often been good." She pulled out a cloth bag of tansy. "*Le Baron* prefers it if we all pretend not to notice."

"And you?" Desiree asked, turning even more pale. "Oh, God, what will happen to me?"

"No, no, little one. You are not to be afraid. I will stay with you," she said as she sorted out her supplies, "until you no longer need me."

It had been so long since Desiree had known kindness that she had no response to offer Marta but puzzlement. "Why would you do that?"

"For love of God, and to shame the Devil," said Marta.

"Thank you," Desiree murmured, beginning to feel for the first time since she arrived at Saint Sebastien's estate that she had an ally, and some comfort in her plight.

Marta was building up the fire in the grate. "You must lie back and pray for the soul of your lost little one. Pray God will send peace to your heart." She was heating water now, and the steam from the pot smelled of winter savory and tansy.

Desiree doubted that was possible, but did as she was told. Her body ached as it never had from a beating; she was dizzy when she moved. "My head is sore," she said, wondering why she should notice that, with so many other hurts clamoring for attention.

"I know. It will pass. I am here. We will deal with everything." Crooning other words, she lulled Desiree into a light sleep. As she looked down at her, Marta knew what it was that Saint Sebastien wanted in the girl—she was lovely, even now when her face was haggard with suffering and she was thin from her ordeal. What a pity that she should be the prey of such a man as Saint Sebastien. Marta shook her head in resignation. She had not been brought here to mend the morals of Clotaire de Saint Sebastien, but to heal his mistress. She uttered a prayer and a curse as she set to work.

Sometime that night, while her body struggled to throw off the last effects of her miscarriage, Desiree cried out, tossing in delirium and pain. From pieces of what she mumbled, Marta pieced together her story; Marta's heart grew bitter as she listened.

"There, there," she said as she wiped the sweat from Desiree's brow. "Marta is here now. Marta will not fail you. You will have your revenge. I will help you gain your revenge." Her hands were strong and sure as she lifted the young woman and bathed her in water of motherwort and rosemary. She did not let her outrage enter into the tone of her voice, which remained low and soothing. "You will have vengeance for your pains, for that is the way of justice."

Once Desiree called for Michon, and when he did not come, fell to weeping and cursing. "No, no. You do not come. You let me go for a card, a card. It is because the Baron has me. I am lost for a card. The Baron . . . I am not for you, Michon. You would not know me now. You would not know me. Or want me. I am lost. How could you gamble me away? You let me go. I could kill you. Both of you; both of you."

"Hush, poor one," Marta whispered. "Hush. There is justice in Heaven and we will have justice on earth."

The sound of Marta's voice at last pulled Desiree awake, and she opened clear, intelligent eyes. "Yes," she said faintly, but with purpose, "there is justice. I will avenge my dishonor and the death of my babe. You will help me, oh promise me your help."

"I will help you," Marta vowed as she lifted Desiree back into her bed and pulled the sheets around her. Then she took up her position on the pallet as if guarding Desiree while she slept.

Three days later Desiree had improved and Saint Sebastien stopped in her room to see her.

"Not dead yet, *ma belle?*" he asked, pinching her cheek enough to leave a red mark where his fingers had been. He was elegant and languorous in saffron satin with gold-and-topaz buttons and gold lacing. "Somehow that disappoints me."

"I am sorry to have done so, Baron," she replied with extreme courtesy, her breathing rapid. "I did all that I could to oblige you, but it was not to be."

"And yet, I would not want to raise a brat of Tite's get. Perhaps the next one will be mine. Or my groom's." He twirled his quizzing glass at the end of a long silk ribbon. "You are getting too thin; that does not please me," he observed critically. "When you leave your bed, see that you put on flesh before you come to me again. I do not want to be poked with hips and ribs."

Desiree turned her head away on the pillow, which made Saint Sebastien laugh.

306

"She is tired, Baron," Marta said as she brewed another special tea from a pot on the hob.

"Women are always tired, or so they claim. It is usually an escape so that they will not have to lie with men. Fatigue is supposed to explain their lacks. When she has come to my bed, she has been worse than a doll, lying without moving or making a sound. She has no passion."

Desiree began to weep again. She thought she would never stop, and she was disgusted with herself for showing such weakness to her enemy.

Marta was about to dismiss the remark when a thought occurred to her. She put the kettle near the ashes and said, "I venture to guess, Baron, that she longs for a more stalwart lover." Marta knew that such bold words could mean a beating and her dismissal without pay. She waited while Saint Sebastien considered what she had said.

"Go on," he said, a strange light in his narrowed eyes.

"There is a remedy, perhaps; one that I have learned. I know of a plant that can be mixed with meat, red meat . . ." She hesitated as if embarrassed to continue. "It is a remedy for the weakening of the virile parts. If I could supply you with this plant—the fruit is eaten, not the leaves—in a few months it might answer your needs. By that time your mistress should be anxious for your touch." Looking toward the bed he saw the horror and betrayal in Desiree's face, undisguised and open. "It renders the man like Priapus."

"You interest me," Saint Sebastien said with a nod as he looked toward Desiree. "In a few months, then, *ma belle*, we shall try again. If you please me, perhaps I will not give you to Tite for some time." He minced toward the bed. "Your breasts are larger now. That is satisfactory." He said over his shoulder to Marta, "In July, then, I will want that fruit. If you do not have it for me, perhaps I will give you to Tite

for amusement because you have not fulfilled your pledge."
He gave the two women the tiniest of bows and left.

When he was safely out of earshot, Desiree let her wrath
pour down on Marta's head. "How could you betray me!
How could you promise your help and then do this! Is there
a place in Hell for those who destroy the trust of those who
are in need?"

Marta came to Desiree's side. "No, no, do not say this,
my little dove. Hush," she said softly, "do not fear. No, do
not. Marta would not give you again to that monster. Never
would I do that. Before God, I would die before I would do
that. Listen to me, *poverina*."

"For more lies," Desiree said, averting her face.

"You must listen to me," Marta insisted, and in a moment, Desiree sighed and looked at her. "There have been
lies told here, but not to you—to him. I would rather open
my veins than lie to you, and I sing with the angels when I
lie to him. This fruit I told him of, it is real, but it is not for
the virile parts. It is the deadliest poison." She saw the beginning of hope in Desiree's eyes. "Now, hear me out, for
you will have your vengeance. This fruit will give you vengeance."

"What fruit is it?" Desiree asked, not quite curious but
anxious to know what Marta could offer her.

"Some have called this the fruit of love, for the shape is
like the fruits of men, the sacks that are so precious to
them. The shape is something like a pear. There are fools
who will eat it because they have heard that the shape lends
passion and lust to their parts, and for this vanity they die
hideously."

Now Desiree's face was bright and her smile held an
echo of the ferocity of Saint Sebastien's smile. "Tell me,
Marta. I want to know about this fruit."

Marta nodded, bending closer to Desiree in case someone at the door might be listening. "The fruit is mashed—it is not so firm as an apple but not so soft as a ripe melon—and mixed with meat for a pie, so that the poison will penetrate all that the man eats. It has a taste that is not unpleasant, or so they say, but that is part of the deception of the plant. Like the love of madmen, the fruit does its work. Because of how it looks it is named for love, but it gives death."

"He will not eat it. He will suspect," said Desiree, her fear returning with full power.

"He will suspect nothing," said Marta, tossing her head to show her disdain. "He wishes to believe that he will be as potent as a young goat, and he would eat a hedgehog if he thought it would add to his lust."

A second doubt came over Desiree. "This is murder. You and I will kill him, and it will be on our souls."

"It will not, not for the death of Baron Clotaire de Saint Sebastien." She considered the problem. "He has degraded you and killed your child before it was born. Those are his sins, not yours, and you are not held accountable in Heaven. Therefore you must seek the aid of Holy Church. You must confess. Can you write?"

"A little. Enough," said Desiree, listening with real attention.

"Good. Then you will write a confession to the priest at Sainte-Genevieve's, and say that you were maddened by the death of your child and the indifference and humiliations of your protector. Beg that Holy Church receive you as a penitent. Say that the loss of your babe so preyed on your mind that you wanted death for yourself and for Saint Sebastien. Say that you resign yourself to prayer and the Mercy of God, and that you seek peace not in this world but the next.

309

No magistrate can strike that down if the priest has it before the crime is revealed. We must prepare the confession before I bring the fruits, so that it will be in the hands of the priest as soon as Saint Sebastien is dead. That way no one here can hurt you, for you will be in the care of the Church on the strength of your confession. After a time you will be able to leave your penitent's cell, and you and your child will be avenged. I will carry your confession myself, and see that it is placed in the hands of the priest."

Desiree lay back, assessing what Marta has said to her. At last she let her breath out slowly and nodded. "It is good. I will need paper and ink." Once again that disquieting smile settled on her face.

It was a warm afternoon when Marta brought the poison, showing the red and yellow fruits to Saint Sebastien before taking them to Desiree and receiving her written confession.

"Now you must have care," Marta said as she prepared to leave for Sainte-Genevieve's. "Mash the fruits well and see that they are thoroughly mixed with the meat for the pies. I will be back by the time you are ready to serve him, and I will help you then, you have my word on it."

Desiree followed the simple instructions, mashing the fruit so that skin and pulp and seeds were little more than a paste in the bottom of a big crockery bowl. She was elated at Marta's plan, at her foresight in arranging for the confession to be in the hands of the priest before any magistrate or courtier could attempt to detain her for questioning and torture. With her confession in the hands of the Church there was not a court in the land that would be able to hold her. She knew she could endure the seven years of penance that would be required of her for the joy of killing Clotaire de Saint Sebastien.

At supper that night Desiree found she was almost happy as she watched Saint Sebastien eating his pie with such gusto.

"The taste is not bad," he said. "I was afraid that you would want to make it horrible, because of how little you want to come to my bed again." He sipped a little of the white wine he favored. "I might come to like these fruits in my food; do you think you would enjoy me then, with my lust enhanced?"

"How can I know?" It was not difficult to answer him, realizing how soon it would be over. She waited for him to die, and wondered how long it would take. It could not possibly be long, she knew: for in 1741 everyone in the world knew that love apples—sometimes called tomatoes—were virulent poison.

About *Fruits of Love*

I wrote this story in 1975, as a tangential tale to Hotel Transylvania, *the first of the Saint-Germain novels. At the time, I couldn't sell it because the book wasn't out yet. After the book was published I couldn't sell it because the story wouldn't be out until the novel was more than a year old. So I hung onto it, and sold it years later, when the series had developed a following. Which just goes to show that nothing is wasted.*

311

On Saint Hubert's Thing

So we rode out for Holy Lodz on the ebb of night while the clouds rolled their ominous portents above us. We were both in unadorned armor, no more obvious than any men-at-arms: the Metropolitan carried only the secret dispatches and his episcopal ring; I had just the patent of my sword. We took the more remote roads that avoided the larger towns and villages with their gates and guards where our passing would be marked, and we pressed the horses to the limits, changing mounts but once before dawn, at the Nevsky Monastery on the old Pilgrim's Road.

"Who comes at this hour?" the gatekeeper demanded in response to the Metropolitan's sharp rapping.

"Emissaries from the Cantonment of Praha," was the reply the Metropolitan was authorized to give. He was still erect in the saddle, but I had been with him on the road and I knew how near he was to the end of his strength.

"Your destination is the Thing?" the gatekeeper asked in less churlish accents.

"It is. Open to us. We need fresh horses and I must speak to your Superior."

The gatekeeper hesitated. "Pope Honorios is advanced in years . . ." he protested even as he moved at last to open the door. "In a few hours, perhaps, it would be better."

"I am aware of the man's age," the Metropolitan said as if he wore his vestments and held the censer in his outstretched hands. "This is urgent. I would not ask if it were not."

The gate groaned and rattled upward and we dismounted to lead our blowing destriers through it. As soon as the gate was lowered again, the gatekeeper came bustling around to us, his arms folded into his sleeves and his face set into a mask of condemnation.

"I'll summon the Warder Brother," he announced as if he were making a great concession.

The Metropolitan began automatically to give his blessing, then stopped as he saw the amazement on the gatekeeper's face. "Tell the Warder Brother that the second son of the Margrave Pavel of Jutland wishes a word with him."

"The Margrave of Jutland is Adam," the gatekeeper informed the Metropolitan with a gesture of defiance.

"Tell him," the Metropolitan ordered quietly, and looked around the courtyard. "Where is your stable? These horses need feed and care. We will require two fresh horses within the hour. Have our saddles used and tend to it promptly. When we have finished our business, we will have to leave at once."

The gatekeeper broadened his stance mulishly. "On what authority do I do this?"

"On mine," the Metropolitan said coldly. "We have no time to waste."

I stepped nearer, my hand on my sword, resting my fingers around the quillons. I did not have to speak.

"It is an offence against heaven to assault its servants," the gatekeeper said, piously crossing himself. "The second son of the Margrave Pavel of Jutland, is it? I will tell the Warder Brother, and if he throws you out, it is no matter to me." He stalked away, his hands thrust into his hempen belt.

"I trust that there will not be many such to hamper us. If this is aid, what is hindrance?" The Metropolitan was not

313

speaking to me as much as giving his thoughts voice. I had known him to do this when he was immersed in a problem, but it still troubled me to witness his distress. "What do you think, Euchari?" he said suddenly, turning to me.

"That we are not followed?" It would be his most pressing worry now, and one I shared, not entirely because we rode together.

"In part. Do you think they have discovered that we have got away ahead of their spies?" He had always had a martial air and it was never more apparent than when he wore mail. He pulled off his helm and tucked it under his arm. "I pray that gatekeeper will not be too long. The Patriarch ordered all haste without compromising secrecy." He began to pace, a steady, long-legged stride that quickly covered the court-yard. "Come on, come on," he muttered to the cobbles under his feet.

As if in response, the gatekeeper came back and bowed grudgingly. "The Warder Brother will receive you in the Visitors' Hall," he said, indicating a passageway not at first apparent.

"What of the horses?" the Metropolitan asked before motioning me to accompany him.

"They will be attended to," the gatekeeper said, and again indicated the arched door. "That way, and to the left before the chapel."

"God will reward you for your services, Brother," the Metropolitan said with darkest irony as he started toward the passage.

I saw the flicker of anger in the gatekeeper's eyes before I went after the retreating figure of the Metropolitan.

At the sight of the episcopal ring, the Warder Brother made a proper reverence and asked from his knees, "What do you require of me, Eminence?"

"Your aid and your silence," he answered. "Pope Honorios must hear what I have to say, and I rely on you to bring him to me at once. It is not to be announced that I and . . . my companion have come, for idle talk might undo us." There was a plain chair and he dropped heavily into it; he was thirty-nine, no longer young.

"Our monks are discreet," the Warder Brother insisted.

"Possibly, but we will not tempt them with so juicy a tidbit of gossip." He folded his hands over the buckle of his belt. "Send for Pope Honorios, Brother. Speed is essential."

"At once, Eminence," he said, rising from his knees and leaving the room without ceremony.

"Protocol, protocol," the Metropolitan, who had been Protocol Secretary to Archpatriarch Ivor IX, said under his breath. "Monks are as bad as any of them. Worse."

I knew that I was supposed to smile, and did what I could, but I sensed that it was not convincing. My hopes had sunk with every league we covered, now my helm was heavy in my hand and my limbs were leaden with the need for sleep. What the Metropolitan must be feeling, I did not wish to consider. "Will he be long?" I could not admit that I wanted time to rest for fear that it would appear I had failed him.

"I hope not," the Metropolitan answered. "We are exposing ourselves to discovery every moment we remain here." He said it calmly, but I saw that he was becoming restless and somewhat ill-at-ease.

"Surely the Alexandrians won't attempt to reach us here. The arm of the Northern Church is around us by now." I was not as convinced of this as I made it appear, but I did not think the danger was as great as the Metropolitan feared it was.

"There are those in the Northern Church who are in

sympathy with the Southern. Loyalty is not so certain a thing as we would wish it to be. Many Alexandrians have come this far and seduced the faithful from our stewardship with their hedonism and mysteries. Local churches attempt to placate the Alexandrians by pandering to them, adapting the rites and liturgy to Southern practices." He shook his head in disgust.

"But the Archpatriarch has forbidden that," I objected, recalling the day that my father had taken me to hear Kazamir teach. At that time, he had outlined the ways that the Alexandrian threat could be ended. That had been more than seven years ago, but I still remembered the ringing tones of the saintly man as he stood before the High Altar of the Cathedral of the Most Holy Dormition in full regalia, inspiring all who heard him with his devotion and piety.

"Because the Archpatriarch says that a thing is so does not always make it so," the Metropolitan said with a trace of bitterness. "In Lodz we did not speak of such things except behind properly closed doors, where our realism would not offend the faithful. Also, it was thought that this precaution would keep our worries from giving comfort to our enemies. Yet the Alexandrians have always learned of our difficulties, and boasted of them."

"Haven't we done much the same thing?" I asked, pleased that the Metropolitan was confiding in me. "Haven't we sent our monks and popes into Greece and Italy and the Frankish Provinces?" I knew that we had, for my father had spoken of it often, but not when there were members of the clergy present.

"Of course it has happened," the Metropolitan admitted. "But we are not so well-received as our Southern Brethren. They praise ecstasy and we preach discipline. The former is so much more attractive to the undiscriminating."

I did not want to challenge him, but it troubled me that he spoke so. "Did not the Christ and the Saints have such experiences?" I had made similar inquiries of him before, and had yet to be satisfied with his answers.

"Of course, but that was not for most men. The Christ and the Saints are anointed of God and their rapture is not of this world. It is not for any churchman to provide this, but the Holy Spirit. It is blasphemy to offer indulgences and hallucinations in place of transcendent faith." He scowled down at his feet and sighed. "How does one explain this to a poor peasant whose crops have done inadequately and who wants an excuse to forget his troubles? A night of frenzy and feasting is the answer the Southern Church provides, but it is empty." He looked at the torches in the wall brackets. "The old man should be awake by now. I wish we did not have to do this, but the Patriarch has given his mandate, and I am bound . . ."

I had overheard a little of the instructions the Metropolitan had received from Patriarch Roedrich's herald, and recalled that the Metropolitan had expressed his lack of satisfaction with the orders he had been given. "You gave your vow of obedience."

"I am true to my Church and my calling," he said unhappily. "I vowed obedience and I am faithful to that vow, but I would be inexcusably stupid if I permitted my vow to blind me to the risks we take. I am troubled. It worries me that this Nevsky Monastery, of all we might have used, was chosen. Pope Honorios is righteous and will defend us, but if there are those who wish to press the other Brothers—and it would be folly to suppose they will not know we have been here—they will be easily able to identify us, and, Heaven forgive them, they will, so that they will have a moment's excitement." He stopped before one of the ancient

Cimric ikons near the door and examined it with a knowledgeable eye. "Yes, very old no doubt, and with great merit accredited to it. Adam would find it delightful." He crossed himself and folded his hands for a little peace.

He had just raised his head when there came the uncertain slappings of sandaled feet in the hall beyond. "Metropolitan . . ." I ventured but he waved me to silence and put his hand to the hilt of his sword.

The door opened slowly and an old man, very straight and thinner than my poignard, stepped cautiously into the light. He looked first at me and then at the Metropolitan. An odd smile came over his composed features. "Jirus!" he said quietly, but with great feeling. It startled me to hear the Metropolitan addressed by a nick-name, and some of this must have showed in my manner, for the old man nodded toward me. "A tutor has privileges over his student, no matter what heights the student attains." Then he turned again to the Metropolitan for his blessing.

This was hastily given, and then the Metropolitan began once again to pace. "We are changing horses here, did they tell you?"

"Yes, Jirus, they did," Pope Honorios answered. "What can you tell me of this mission of yours?"

"Not a great deal, I fear. The Patriarch at Graz—you know him—sent a herald to me, and my vows bind me to . . ." He paused by the chair he had occupied and set his helm down on it. "We are for Lodz, and need your prayers that we may be in time. The Thing begins in two days and there is great danger."

"Do you have leave to tell me what it is?" Pope Honorios asked, showing some curiosity but not so much that the Metropolitan would feel he had disappointed his old tutor if nothing was told him.

"In part. But it concerns me that . . ." He broke off again and rubbed at his beard, which was trimmed short as any captain's. "This monastery has not always been faithful to the Northern Church. That was one of the many reasons it was entrusted to you. No one in Lodz has doubted your zeal or the commitment you have made to the Brothers in your care, but there are still those who do not . . . Letters have been sent to Alexandria, many of which have come along the old Pilgrim's Road, a few of which were thought to have originated here." It was difficult for the Metropolitan to say this, and his voice, which was musical and resonant on most occasions, now dropped to a rough whisper.

"I have done all that I may without making unwilling anchorites of the Brothers," Pope Honorios said, stooping under the burden of this accusation. "I have addressed the Archpatriarch on this subject before, but he has not extended my power. It is not that I seek to punish my Brothers, but I fear for their souls and the Northern Church when they err. Alexander Nevsky is a militant saint, and in his monastery, we should all be vigilant in his name."

"Ivor might have granted your request," the Metropolitan said with the compassion of his high office, "but I fear that Archpatriarch Kazamir is not the one to press such positions now. He encouraged the Alexandrians to attend the Thing, saying that we must make common cause with them against the Islamic heresy. The Archbishop in Rome has acted as intermediary in this, and he is a most subtle man, one of the old Roman families who were noble long before the coming of the Christ. I have warned Kazamir that the Romans are scheming to bring the center of the Southern Church to Rome, but he will not listen to me." He shrugged. "Why should he? I have no place in Lodz now. It has been the Archpatriarch's decision to move me away from Holy Lodz, and I am submissive to his will."

"You have been in Brno?" Pope Honorios inquired, knowing that news did not often reach his monastery quickly or accurately.

"Yes; and before that, Praha. My disgrace is not marked, but it is often wise to remove the officers of former Archpatriarchs from Lodz when the new Archpatriarch is elevated." He touched his helm again, rubbing the blackened arms he had carried when he had been the Knight Jeronim of Jutland and not Metropolitan of the Northern Church. "Patriarch Roedrich has learned of a plot—he does not say how, but those in Graz and Trieste have means and contacts the rest of us do not—to assassinate the Archpatriarch and the Patriarchal Archmandrites while they are all accessible. It has been suspected that the Alexandrians have infiltrated the ranks of the Northern Church and have promised to put those they have suborned in the places of those they kill."

"Eminence," Pope Honorios said with a sad expression, "this is madness. How could such a plan hope to succeed? While it is true that the Archpatriarch and the Patriarchal Archmandrites will be present for the Thing, so will tens of thousands of those faithful to the Northern Church. It would be more than suicide to venture to harm Kazamir and the rest in such a gathering."

"They have been assured of their place with the martyrs. Those who gave this information in Graz died joyously. So will those sent to do the murders." The Metropolitan stood still. "We believe we will be followed. We believe that there are those who will ask questions of you and the rest. It is essential that they be misled for as long as possible. Should anyone stop here, delay them. Give them our spent horses to ride, direct them to the wrong roads, describe us incorrectly."

Pope Honorios bowed his head. "The young man with you?"

"Euchari," the Metropolitan said to me, summoning me forward. "As you were my tutor, so I am his," he said to the old man as I showed my respect. "This is Marek Euchari, Crown Prince of Poland."

"Highness," Pope Honorios said, with some surprise.

"For the moment, he is the Knight Euchari and nothing more. It is dangerous enough that we are carrying our messages; if our identities were known, it would be much more risky than it is now. Those who wish to murder the Archpatriarch and the Archmandrites would not balk at adding a Metropolitan and a Prince to their victims." He rubbed at his eyes. "If you must say someone has been here, then two knights, Euchari and Jeronim, have. You will not pollute your soul with lies and you will not expose us to more hazards than we face already."

Pope Honorios had observed the Metropolitan closely, and said now, "Would you not like to rest for even an hour, my son?"

The Metropolitan smiled briefly at this old address. "Of course I would like it; but we must not linger. We are far from Lodz and the Thing begins soon. Pray that we have a speedy and uneventful journey, old friend, and keep our secret as you keep the sanctity of your worship." He lifted his helm and nodded to me. "Prepare, Euchari. Dawn is not far off." As he secured the shoulder buckles, he said to Pope Honorios, "I am sorry that you were not better treated by Ivor and Kazamir. Don't think badly of them; they were influenced by the Patriarchs in Brittany and Friesland, who had candidates of their own to promote. I tried to get you posted to Praha, but it was not possible."

"God rewards His servants," Pope Honorios said mildly.

"There was a time when I fostered envy and anger in my heart, but no more. I will pray for you, my son, and for the Thing."

"My thanks, Pope," the Metropolitan said humbly, and motioned to me to follow him.

As I did this, I saw that Pope Honorios was watching us closely, a tranquil, regretful smile on his austere features.

We were away on fresh horses before the Brothers had risen for morning prayers, and the gatekeeper bid us a churlish farewell as the gates slammed down behind us. The road was empty, but we had been warned that it was market day in Saint Vincenty and the peasants would be bringing animals and produce to sell. With the summer fading, the bounty of the harvest made such occasions more boisterous than usual, and in many villages, Things were kept in the churches for those who could not make the trek to Holy Lodz.

At the first crossroad, the Metropolitan drew up his gelding and gestured to me to do the same. "We will not stop but to rest the animals until after the mid-day meal, when many are sleeping. There is a hostelry on the other side of the Vien Road which caters to men-at-arms. We will change horses there and go."

This was contrary to what the Metropolitan had told me at the Nevsky Monastery, and I was taken aback. "You were planning to stop in . . ."

"We were overheard. It is important that we take as few chances as possible." He pulled in the reins more firmly and peered down the dark road. Now that the moon was down and the sky just on the turn to dawn, we took more care of how we went. The Metropolitan regarded me with bleary eyes. "How long can you stay in the saddle, Euchari?"

"As long as you can, Eminence," I answered, seeing how exhausted he was.

"Longer, probably," he murmured. "There is a stream a little distance onward, and there we will water the horses." He tested his sword to be sure it was loose in the scabbard, then added, "When we are among others, address me as Jirus or Knight, not Eminence. That would bring us the very attention we seek to avoid." Before I could respond, he clapped his heels to his mount's sides and was away at a steady trot. I followed him in silence until we reached the stream, and then, as we dismounted and pulled the horses to the edge of the stream where ferns and mosses grew in the shadow of pines and spangle-leaved birches, I voiced a number of my fears.

"Is the main road faster, Met . . . Jirus?"

He gave me a look of approval. "Yes, it is faster, but it is being watched and, with the pilgrims making their way to Lodz for the Thing, we would not be sure of where we could change mounts or where we would be safe. This way we are able to travel largely unobserved. It may be that we will make better time this way than the other because of that, if no other reason." His horse was pulling at the grasses by the stream between long draughts, and the Metropolitan pulled at the bridle to stop this. "I do not need you logy with food and drink," he admonished the animal as he moved aside to give my mount room.

"Yet you fear we are being followed in spite of our precautions," I said, hoping to appear more sensible than alarmed.

"Yes," he said heavily. "I pray that it is not so, but I have not forgotten what I learned as a knight, and all that warns me of treachery." He made a single, puzzled sound that was not the laugh he had intended it to be. "They are subtle, the

Alexandrians, and determined to have the ascendancy over the Northern Church. It is their concern for the Islam heretics, since that threat presses closer to them than us."

"Is there someone at the Nevsky Monastery you suspect?" I asked him, thinking of how very few Brothers had seen us.

"Not specifically, no, but I am worried. We do know that there have been renegades there in the past, and Pope Honorios is not bastion enough against such infiltration." He pulled his horse back and swung up into the saddle. "Come, Euchari. With luck we can sleep a few hours tonight."

I wondered what he meant when he said "with luck" but I did not pursue it. I mounted and came up beside him.

"We can walk for the next several leagues. That will give the horses some respite. It would be senseless to ride them into the ground." His saddle creaked as he swung around in it to look down the dark road at our backs. "We will be into the hills tomorrow, and the day after we will be in Lodz, if we can find fresh mounts tonight. If necessary, I will speak to the elders of the churches we pass, but that would mean I must reveal myself, and that is what we wish most to avoid." He was looking ahead now, glaring into the night with eyes like granite.

"Do we go to my father when we arrive, or to the Cathedral?" It would be easier for the Metropolitan to gain access to the Archpatriarch than it would be for me, but either of us would find my father more accessible than Kazamir.

"You to your father and I to the Cathedral. One way or the other, they will be warned." He brought his gauntleted hand up in frustration. "Kazamir has little use for me. I was one of Ivor's men, and those around Kazamir do not trust the old patriarchal court."

"Then why take the risk? Why not send your own messenger?" It was my exhaustion speaking, and my indignation on behalf of my tutor.

"The Patriarch of Graz entrusted this mission to me, not to my messenger. And I am faithful to my office and my oaths, no matter who wears the tiara. It is the Northern Church that matters, not you, not I, and not the Archpatriarch and the Patriarchal Archmandrites, for all their holiness. We are all transitory, but the Church endures. I will not stand by in pettiness and spite to watch the Alexandrians bring us to our knees." He sat more erect now, and the horse, responding to the sharpness of his voice, bounded ahead for several paces until the Metropolitan brought him back under control. "Euchari, how would I answer to God if I permitted this to happen? How could I abhor Judas and then commit the same monstrous crime he did?"

We had argued such questions before, but in the comfort of the Metropolitan's study with servants around us and fires rattling on the hearth. The issues then were little more than theories, pleasant exercises that permitted us to explore the nature of our beliefs. I had not understood how profound his devotion was until this seemingly endless ride. I was humbled by what I saw in him, and wondered if I was as devout. I rode beside him in silence, examining my soul and recalling that one Alexandrian service I had attended in Trieste. Had that made me a heretic? The ritual, with its long periods of chanting which culminated in rapturous frenzy, had shocked me and I had not gone again, but I feared now that the taint was on me. I knew I should confess this lapse, but I dared not hope for absolution. Yet I rode with my tutor to defend all that was most holy in Lodz. Might not that exonerate me? "Did you never have doubts?"

325

"There is no faith where doubt has not been present. When I was much younger, I was more interested in glory in battle than glory in Heaven. Seeing my father die of his grievous wounds opened my eyes to the horror of fighting, and his unswerving trust in God banished my doubts." He had put his hand on the hilt of his sword, riding now as he had done as a young knight. "When Adam became Grave of Jutland, I told him of my vocation and he released me from my knightly oaths."

I had heard something of this before, but was still puzzled by his brother's willingness to permit the Metropolitan to enter the Church. There was only one other brother, and he had been sent by the King of Denmark to Britain as ambassador. Questioning him about this was awkward, but we had many hours ahead of us, and this was not the formal setting of instruction. "Did your brother try to dissuade you?"

The Metropolitan took a moment to answer, and when he did, I knew he was troubled. "No. It is not Adam's way to . . ." He turned his head. "Horses."

I heard them, too, and reached for the sword at my side just as an abrupt motion from the Metropolitan stayed my hand. "Shouldn't we . . ."

"Not yet. They may be nothing more than local peasants coming early to market. The horses are only trotting." He sat forward. "If they are after us, we must not battle them unless there are few. Otherwise, galling as it is, we must outrun them. Our messages are more important than the pleasure of a few blows."

"I am not so callow that I must turn aside from combat," I protested, chagrined at the thought of even so minor a disgrace.

"It has nothing to do with turning aside from combat.

We fight a greater foe than a few mounted men; we are at war with the Alexandrians, and it would be reprehensible to lose sight of the greater goal for a . . ." He lifted his head, falling silent. The trotting horses were coming up behind us and would be passing us by the time we reached the next bend in the road. I could not help but notice that this might well be a good place for an ambush.

"Very well, we will run if we must," I said with some annoyance. It appalled me to think that there were those who would be able to boast of rousting me from the field. No doubt the Metropolitan was right; nevertheless, my pride smarted at the thought of what I must do.

"Keep close, and if we must fight, let it be back to back," the Metropolitan said in a low voice. "If they pass us, note how they are dressed and what they carry."

I nodded while my pulse hammered its anticipation. The horses behind us—there were no more than four—broke into a canter, and a groom came up to us astride a strapping chestnut with a common head and deep chest. He waved in greeting. "Good knights, make way," he shouted to us, then waved to those behind him.

The Metropolitan nodded to me and we moved to the side of the road, on guard against what might next occur.

A sorrel mare came up with a laughing young woman in the saddle. Her skirts were caught up and the tops of her boots were plainly visible. She was laughing and fresh-faced, no older than sixteen. Her tabard showed the arms of Nizety. She acknowledged us with a nod, and then a young man-at-arms came abreast of her, crying out to us, "Valeska, daughter of Lukash Nizety goes fairing!" He was well-armed and regarded his charge with possessive, protective eyes, permitting no one to rob her of her delight.

"Good fortune," the Metropolitan called to them easily,

though his hand still rested on the hilt of his sword.

The three horses cantered on ahead of us and were soon lost to sight around the next bend.

"Lukash Nizety is a peculiar man," the Metropolitan said a bit later to break the silence.

"I have never met him," I said, but, like everyone else, I had heard rumors.

"And his daughter is going fairing," he mused, his mail turning ruddy with the rosy light of dawn on it, as if he were a furnace and his armor hot coals. "Where is her father, I wonder?"

"In Lodz," I answered, since my father had informed me of the great banquet he planned to mark the occasion of Saint Hubert's Thing. Odd though he might be, Nizety was high enough in rank to be included in all court functions.

The Metropolitan shook his head. "How many men do you think he has brought with him? A dozen?"

"At least," I said, thinking it was like Nizety to take his train of soldiers to Lodz and leave a pretty creature like— what was her name? Valeska?—his daughter behind, contenting her with a fair instead of the Thing.

"And the others are similarly protected," the Metropolitan said to himself. "Where does one begin, with so many possibilities?"

"We begin by arriving," I said lightly, giving his lesson back to him.

There was another bark of angry laughter from the Metropolitan as we rode into the brazen dawn.

The innkeeper grumbled, but he provided a change of horses for an outrageous amount of money. When the Metropolitan commented on the price, he opened his hands and with an expression guileless as a baby, protested that the demand for mounts was overwhelming with the Thing at Holy Lodz, and were it not that we were bound for it, he would not have been able to give us anything to ride, not even a mule.

The Metropolitan swore his annoyance, as any fighting man would, and inspected the animals brought out for us. "They are not bad," he conceded.

"Superb," the innkeeper corrected him. "And newly-shod. They won't go lame or cast a shoe on you, be assured of that."

"For your sake, I hope that's true," the Metropolitan said, then handed over the final gold coins. "There. If I have any cause for complaint, I will let it be known among other men-at-arms and your business will suffer."

We were favored with a smile that was ingratiating and sour. "Of course, good knights. A man in my position cannot afford to offer poor horseflesh."

"It is good you're aware of that," the Metropolitan growled. "Have these nags saddled and we'll be off."

The innkeeper was taken aback. "At this hour?" Most of those at his inn were like the villagers—they slept after the noon meal.

"We are under orders," the Metropolitan said, as if he, too, were displeased with the idea of riding out now. "Get them ready. We will buy wine, water, bread, and sausage from you, and bags of barley for the horses."

"Of course," the innkeeper said at this familiar request. "Do you have a set of food satchels?"

The Metropolitan handed them over without comment, then lifted on his helm. "We wish to leave at once, inn-keeper," he warned as the innkeeper toddled over toward his scullery.

"Yes, yes, yes," he called over his shoulder, moving a little faster. "Shortly, good knights."

The Metropolitan stared around the courtyard at the inn as he buckled the helm into place once more. "I have been wondering," he said conversationally but with an underlying lack of ease that alerted me to his distress, "if we are the only messengers sent by the Patriarch to Lodz. I was told there were no others, but it might have been a prudent lie, in case we should fall into the hands of those who wish to prevent our warning from arriving. If we know of no others, then we cannot speak of them. It is not impossible," he said thoughtfully, "that there are other messengers on the road to Lodz. Some may ride with the pilgrims, and some may go by the Royal High Road." He crossed his arms over the mail on his chest and I could see that the camise beneath was already darkened with sweat.

"Do you think this has happened?" I asked as the ostlers brought the tack for the horses.

"I don't know. But were I the one sending the message, I might have done it." He turned to watch the girths being buckled and paid little attention to the sound of an approaching wagon.

There were shouts behind us, and the riotous good-humor of the harvest fair as the passengers on the heavily-laden wagon tumbled out into the courtyard, many of them shouting for wine and beer in drink-sodden voices. One of the men reeled toward us, singing bits of lewd songs, and brandishing a wineskin over his head.

"Sots," the Metropolitan said softly. "It's as well we're leaving now."

I could not argue with him, but my condemnation was not as severe. "It is as bad for most attending the Thing."

"True," the Metropolitan said. "It does not please me to think so, but I have seen the streets of Lodz at each of the Four Yearly Things and always I marvel at the debauchery that is excused as zeal." He turned to the ostler. "Our food should be ready. Get the satchels for us." To sweeten the order, he tossed a brass coin to the man, who caught it and bowed as he scurried off toward the kitchen.

The man who was loudest of the lot came toward us again, subjected us to a bleary-eyed scrutiny as he swayed in an effort to keep upright. "Have a drink!" he insisted, holding out a freshly-broached wineskin. "Haven't tasted it myself yet. Two men like you need the drink more than I do." He laughed loudly and the wine dribbled out onto his leggings, staining them as if with blood.

"We would, soldier, if we did not have to leave. We're under orders. You know how that is." The Metropolitan was good-humored still, but firm in his resolve.

"Damn the orders. It's almost Saint Hubert's Thing and we're keeping harvest fair. What orders supercede that?" He belched heartily.

The Metropolitan's eyes narrowed behind the visor of his helm. "Then drink for us, soldier, and we'll thank you for the sympathy."

The other man shoved me away as he leaned forward to glare into the Metropolitan's face. "Take off the helm and drink. You think to insult me!"

"Another time," was the short answer, and the drunken soldier swore and fumbled for the dagger in his belt just as the innkeeper came puffing across the courtyard with our satchels in his hands.

"Here, good men-at-arms," he said with rancor. "Take them and be gone." He gave a disgusted glance to the third man and shook his head. "You'll have to sleep it off. Get along with you."

The drunkard raised his arms pugnaciously, then tottered away, muttering threats as he spilled more wine on his leggings. The innkeeper flapped his apron at the man's back as if shooing away flies.

"It's the fair," he said to us. "They all drink and roister, all through Saint Hubert's Thing. They may sing hymns in Lodz, but here it's bawdy songs and tippling."

"Pray for deliverance," the Metropolitan advised as he took our satchels and handed one to me. "Where are the waterskins?"

"The groom has them at the well," the innkeeper said, and accepted the silver coin the Metropolitan held out with a practiced, swinish deference.

"It's madness to ride in the heat of the day," he said by way of farewell. "But the roads will be clearer."

The Metropolitan was into the saddle before the innkeeper was back in the kitchen door. I mounted and followed him out into the hazy warmth of the afternoon. As we passed through the town gates, the Metropolitan pointed out the tawdry sprawl of the tents and stalls of the fair.

"They'll be idle for another hour or so, and then they will rise to their revels again. Tomorrow there will be Masses, and they will attend, heads aching and limbs stiff, to be assured of their salvation." He shook his head ponderously as much as the helm would permit. "What can we do for them, but pray? If God sends them brutish lives, will not the glory of Paradise be all the greater? The Alexandrians promise them delirium and call it joy, and it is wrong to blame them if they are seduced by it, but they defile their souls with hedonism and heresy." Again he was speaking to himself much more than to me, and I said nothing as the Metropolitan took the road leading north and east away from the fair.

By sunset we had changed horses once more, this time

obtaining the animals from an ancient and eccentric Grave who kept a round-towered fortress over a deep gorge. He knew the Metropolitan from his soldiering days and was delighted to aid us. He cackled in anticipation of the lies he would tell any who asked of us, but I heard the somber note in the Metropolitan's warning that it might be too dangerous to dissemble. What the old Grave would do, neither of us knew. We had the best horses in his stable and his blessing, and fresh water to still our thirst as we left the massive, elongated shadow of the towers for the steep, rutted road that followed the river.

As we came to a sharp turn in the road, the Metropolitan held up his hand to stop us. "It's too late now," he told me, cocking his head toward the setting sun. "We will not reach Erl Dru by nightfall."

I had not known our next goal was Erl Dru, and was not wholly pleased to discover that we would be at the mercy of a family who had been for so long the most bitter rivals of our House. "Erl Dru," I heard myself say.

"I know, Euchari," the Metropolitan said quietly. "But they are faithful to the Northern Church and the Patriarch of Graz has used them before as way-stations for his personal messengers. I told him once that the Moricin are not as politically safe as they are religiously, but my cautions were dismissed."

"It's just as well that we have not reached Erl Dru. I could not think myself, or you, protected there." I could not shake off the cold dread that clutched at me, holding me in icy bands.

"I share your concern," the Metropolitan said, putting his hand up to shade his eyes from the reddened glare of sunset. "There are clouds building up in the east. We may have rain soon. It is best that we find shelter to rest these

333

horses as well as ourselves, so that we can be away before first light. I have two sausages left, and a little wine."

There was roughly the same amount in my satchel and I had learned, as had the Metropolitan, to travel on light food so that my horse would not be more burdened than was absolutely necessary. "If there is firewood, and water, we will have enough," I ventured in the hope that there would be no need to forgo the fire.

"There is a copse of brambles and larches ahead, and a stream near it, clear enough in the spring. I doubt it's too brackish to drink." He set his gelding in motion and gestured to me to follow.

As we rode, I could not keep from worry. Why had the Patriarch wanted us to stay at Erl Dru? Even the Metropolitan traveling alone would not be welcome there, so closely was he allied with our House. The Moricin had once held the throne of Bohemia and had been brought down in an attempt to seize Poland as well. They had fled to the Prince of Saxony and had only recently been permitted to return to their holdings at Erl Dru. The Patriarch was from Kiev and might not know how long the fury had burned between our families, or how deeply. Perhaps in his quest for secrecy he played into the hands of the enemies of our House, who wanted only the opportunity to do us harm.

Once in the shadows and concealing bulk of the copse, we both dismounted and made our way along the shepherd's track that branched away from the road. It would not be too intolerable to sleep here in the open, if it did not rain and there were not too many insects and vermin to contend with. I took the bag of grain from behind the cantel of my saddle.

"Good. Barley now and then we can hobble them for the night so that they can graze." The Metropolitan pointed ahead in the gloom to the stream and then reached to remove his helm.

"Do we keep watch?" I asked as I took my helm off.

"For the first half of the night. I waken early." He was loosening the girths of his saddle and preparing to lead the gelding to drink.

"Then perhaps you should take the first watch," I suggested. "There is less chance of over-sleeping."

By the time we had boiled the sausages in the tin forage pot, it was dark night. The glow of the fire was carefully banked so that what little light it provided did not penetrate the dense foliage around us. We huddled near the low flames so that we would stay warm a while longer. Now that the sun had faded, the heat of the day drained away into the dark. The Metropolitan blessed the sausages as if they had been royal fare, and we ate them as contentedly as our mounts munched the grain in their nosebags.

"Riders passed in the night," the Metropolitan said as he wakened me to a dead fire and clammy morning mists.

"While you were on watch?" I could hardly see him.

"No, much later. There were more than six of them and they were heavily armed; I heard the jingle of them quite plainly." He had brought up his gelding and was rebuckling the cheekstrap of the bridle as he spoke. "We will have to go carefully, for we do not know what visitors arrived at Erl Dru last night."

"We know of two that didn't," I remarked acidly as I got up. My shoulders were stiff and creaky as unoiled leather.

"For which we may both thank God for His protection." He pulled the girths tighter and then jabbed the gelding's belly sharply with his knee. As the horse snorted indignantly, he secured the buckles.

I stumbled to my feet and stepped into the bushes to re-lieve myself, trusting that if we were still followed, they would not use dogs to track us. When I had returned, the Metropolitan offered me half of what was left of the rind of cheese. It was little enough to break our fast with, but we both ate gratefully before we set out once more.

When the sun was half way to the meridian, the Metro-politan reined in and pointed to a dark plume of smoke rising over the brow of the hill we were ascending. "There is a monastery in that defile," he said as the cloud became denser.

"The riders, do you think?" It did not seem possible that armed men would attack a holy place, and I wondered if there had been a mistake, and there was another explana-tion for the coiling smoke.

"I don't know. I don't know." He hesitated, holding his restive gelding with calm authority. "We dare not stop now. The Thing is tomorrow and with the greatest aid from God, we will not reach Lodz until late tonight."

"Do you wish to stop?" I asked without considering it.

"How can you doubt it?" he demanded of me. "There are good and blessed men there who have given their lives and fortunes into the keeping of God and His Saints. Were there nothing more than a blaze in a hayrick, it would still be an obligation of my rank and office to give them any help I could. If I stop, I disobey the Patriarch and endanger the Archpatriarch and the Patriarchal Archmandrites in Holy Lodz. God will weigh my sins and judge me for my neglect now." He spurred his horse so suddenly that it reared, al-most throwing him from the saddle.

There had been times before when I had seen the Metro-politan wrestle with his conscience, but never was it more apparent how demanding he was on himself. "Can't we send aid, or ask for help in the next village?"

"It is not what the Patriarch wanted, but . . ." He made an impatient motion with his arm. "The smoke may be seen in the next valley, but many villagers will not rush to where there is smoke. It bodes ill for them, and they will retreat to their houses and their churches to keep safe. How many times since the Church was sundered have wars been fought for monasteries and churches as much as for fields, crops, and wealth?" He wheeled his horse once. "It is unpardonable that I should leave them, but there is the threat to the Archpatriarch." His words were rough with the force of his emotions.

"How long would it take, to . . ." Even as I said it, I knew it would be too long, that we could not linger, though the monastery and its monks burned to ashes before noon for our neglect.

"We must go on, but it is a dire thing we do, and it will not be forgotten in Heaven, I fear." The last was little more than a mutter made nearly indistinct by the rattle of our horses' hooves on the pebbles of the road. As he drew ahead of me, the Metropolitan called back over his shoulder, "Be careful. It would be easy to lame the geldings."

I had been riding with more attention on our goal than on the way itself and I felt abashed as the Metropolitan reminded me of this simple precaution. I waved to acknowledge his warning and determined to be careful as we rode.

It was more than an hour later that we entered the little hamlet that straddled the old Pilgrims' Road. Most of the men were in the fields, but a few of the women waited in the doors of earthen huts, children clinging to their shapeless skirts, the stench of the open ditch at the side of the road attesting to the degraded lives of the inhabitants. One of the women flung a handful of refuse at us as we passed and the children copied her, so that we were pelted with offal and rocks.

One rock struck the Metropolitan's horse on the rump and it bucked, kicking out with its back legs, narrowly missing my mount's chest. The children scattered, screaming like frightened fowl, and at the sound a man in long robes emerged from the best of these miserable hovels.

The Metropolitan could not hold his horse, nor did he try. He let the animal run as he crouched over the neck as if riding into battle, and for that reason he did not see the robed figure who watched us ride out. I had but a moment to watch the stranger, but I knew he was an Alexandrian priest, and was much too far into the territories of the Northern Church for an accident. I whipped the reins and raced after the Metropolitan as he sped away. I was resolved to tell him what I had discovered, and dreaded what his response would be.

We were six leagues from the hamlet when the Metropolitan drew rein again and waited as I rode up beside him. He dismounted and began to rub the chest and flanks of the gelding with expert fingers. "He is failing. The stone that hit him must have done more than irritate him."

"Is it bad?" I asked, knowing there was no way it could be otherwise.

"It slows us down," he said. "I wish there were a place we could safely change mounts again, but there is nothing between here and the crest, and we are not there yet. We must go at a walk; I doubt if this horse can sustain a trot much longer." Reluctantly he got back into the saddle. "If he fails, you must ride on ahead and do all that you may to warn the Archpatriarch. Go to your father. Explain to him . . ." He said no more. He let the gelding choose his own

338

pace and I rode beside him in silence.

Thunder was rumbling beyond the distant mountain peaks by the middle of the afternoon, and the road had grown steeper. The Metropolitan's horse had been laboring visibly for the last two leagues and as the upward turns became increasingly severe, the gelding turned shiny with sweat and his flanks heaved.

"There is a lake not much further on, and a bridge. Once we are over it, it can be destroyed so that we will delay any behind us. If we can reach the Monastery of the Visitation, we can change horses." The Metropolitan was almost as exhausted as the horse he rode.

"How far is the monastery?" I had heard of it, but did not know precisely where it was in these remote hills. Most of the valleys were high and narrow, more canyons than not. It was a wild region, where brigands lived and preyed upon unwary travelers, where bridges and fordings were critically few. There were ruined forts, little more than heaps of tumbled stones left over from the Lombard Wars, three centuries ago. These were places of ill-omen and few but the most desperate ventured near them, for they were known to be cursed and haunted.

Just as we came to the lake, the first rain began to spatter down on us and the lightning quivered behind us. The willows that stood in the marshy ground between the road and the shore bent hissing leaves to the water that now boiled with rain. Our horses were too tired to shy as the storm worsened, but nonetheless we kept firm hands on the reins, knowing it would take little for them to bolt.

We came to the bridge at the far end of the lake, where the water dropped away in a torrent down a narrow, rocky channel. The bridge spanned the water at its narrowest point, but still was a goodly length. The planks were thick and echoed with the plodding steps of our mounts as we went onto it, accompanied by the thunder. That may have been the reason we did not hear the other riders until that moment. At another time we would have been warned of their approach, but with the storm, the falling water, and our horses' hooves, we noticed nothing.

They came toward us down the avenue of pines flanking the road on the far side of the bridge. There were seven of them, riding fresh horses, armed with swords and maces, all carrying blank shield. Lightning winked; thunder shattered the air, and the men bore down on us, drawing their swords as they neared the bridge.

"Brigands!" I shouted to the Metropolitan as I drew my sword and brought my shield up from where it hung on the saddle.

"Traitors!" he cried out, already prepared to meet the first rush. "Forward!" He spurred his faltering horse to an uneven canter. "Don't let them get on the bridge!"

I followed him, hefting my sword to strike. A little way beyond the bridge we closed with them. I heard the crooning rush as a mace swung by my head, barely missing me, as I brought my sword up from my side. I took the jarring impact with satisfaction as the man flailed at the deep wound in his thigh. Pressing the advantage, I spurred my mount against my opponent's, and the animal toppled, kicking and neighing in terror. There was not time enough to determine if the wounded man would fight again: I saw three of the men converged on the Metropolitan, driving him back to the bridge.

As I turned toward him, I was almost knocked out of the saddle by a glancing blow from a mace which had caught the edge of my shield. My horse stumbled, but I held him together as I turned to face the other riders. In the wavering glare of the lightning, I thought I saw wine-stained leggings on the nearest man, and I remembered the drunken soldier in the innyard. Then the light was gone and the thunder burst over us and we closed for the fight.

There was a madness on me, as if the demons of the Wild Hunt were in me, as I thought it must be in the skies for Saint Hubert's Thing. I fought without thinking, without fear or anger, for the unholy joy of killing. I heard the shrill scream of a wounded horse once, and the cursing shouts of the men under the clamor of the storm. The ring and thud of blows were music to me, sweet and good to hear. My arm grew heavy and my hand was hot and slippery with blood, but whether it was mine or my enemies', I did not know. It was enough to battle them and trust to the Mercy of God if I fell.

At a signal I never saw, the attackers turned and galloped away in the direction they had come, through the avenue of pines. Two of the men were barely able to stay in the saddle and one of the others had lost his helm. I started after them, then drew in as my mind came back to me. I could not battle five men alone, though two were wounded. I pulled in my panting horse and turned back toward the bridge. Now it was painful to move and I heard the rasp of the breath in my throat. I felt for the first time the raw agony of the wounds I had sustained and felt my own blood soaking my leggings under the mail, and filling my boot. There was a gash over my knee and a swelling bruise on my back where a mace had struck over the cover of my shield. I had been lucky; without the shield to break it, such a blow was fatal.

One of the attackers lay dead, propped up against a tree where he must have crawled to be away from the hooves of the horses. I saw that he held an Alexandrian talisman in his ruined hands, and I damned him for such blasphemy. The man whose leg I had opened was moaning, and his horse stood not far from him, cropping grass at the side of the road.

The Metropolitan was off the bridge, near his dying horse. His helm was off and I could see the red froth on his lips; his face was gray.

I dismounted and limped toward him, filled with despair. When I was close to him, I heard the wheeze and rustle of his breath. In anguish I crouched over him, letting my sword fall at last.

He had taken a mace blow directly on the ribs, and they had splintered. Blood foamed on his side, running with the mail he wore. The steel links were broken where the bones poked out. He tried to speak, but the blood choked him and the agony of coughing was hideous. With tremendous effort he beckoned to me. "Boot." He gasped and the breath whistled through the wound. "Boot."

"This one?" I touched him, my hands wooden.

"Dis . . . patch."

It was not possible to remove the boot without adding to his pain, and so I did it as quickly as I could and tried not to listen to the sounds he made.

"Ring." One hand moved weakly. I nodded.

"Yes. I will take it."

Two of his fingers trembled as he made the blessing. He fixed me with his eyes. "Strike deep."

With no feeling at all I drew my sleeve dagger, and drove it hard and true under his ribs to the heart.

The man I had wounded said little, though I worked on him for a short while. He admitted that he had come from

Lukash Nizety and that he was to prevent us from reaching Lodz for the Thing. The rest was babbling and heretical Alexandrian prayers, and I left him by the road, took his horse, the dispatch and the Metropolitan's episcopal ring, and rode to the treason at Lodz.

That is my testimony, and it will not change, no matter how long you keep me in a penitent's cell. I say that Archpatriarch Honorios rules in Lodz by treachery and that the lords of Erl Dru who have claimed the throne of Poland are murderers and heretics. It makes no difference that the Alexandrians have come to Rome; they are still officers of the Southern Church and my foes for as long as there is breath in my body. I saw the Standard of Christ raised by bloody hands on Saint Hubert's Thing, and no prayers of yours will erase that defilement. Nothing you do to me, though you kill me, will change my mind: I am by Holy Right King of Poland and you will die with my curse upon you.

About *On Saint Hubert's Thing*

While researching the background for an historical horror novel set in the 5th century that I was never able to sell, I began to wonder what would happen if Christianity had split north/south instead of east/west. This puzzling eventually led to imagining a mystery-religion Christianity centered in Alexandria, and a Russo-Teutonic hierarchical religion centered in Kiev. Then the characters introduced themselves and we were off.

This was originally published as a chapbook, handsomely produced by Cheap Street Press and beautifully illustrated by Alicia Austin.